FRIENDLY NEIGHBORHOOD WIZARD

FRIENDLY NEIGHBORHOOD WIZARD

BOOK 1

SmilingSatyr

Podium

For Jess and Kittra, without whom there'd be no book.

Cover design by KittraMcBriar

ISBN: 978-1-0394-5412-5

Published in 2024 by Podium Publishing, ULC
www.podiumaudio.com

FRIENDLY NEIGHBORHOOD WIZARD

CHAPTER 1

First Train Home

Six years was a long time to be away from home. Wilbur McKenzie felt the weight of all of those years easing up as the train chugged along and the miles vanished. The two weeks after graduation had dragged on forever. Now that he was on his way, it all passed in a blink, like a rubber band stretching and then snapping forward.

One second he was walking onto the stage to accept his diploma and award, the next he was sitting with his head pressed up against the window watching the countryside roll by. In truth, the three-day-long train ride had passed by in a fog. Now with only an hour to go, Wil found himself just staring outward, thinking about the family and town he hadn't seen in over half a decade.

Harper Valley was a small city or a large town; Wil couldn't tell the difference. Maybe it would be different now. Maybe a drought had blown in and everyone had moved away and they no longer had use for a resident wizard. Maybe it had grown and his work would overwhelm and consume him and he'd have a nervous breakdown at the ripe old age of twenty-three. Wil closed his eyes, sighing.

The job scared him, but not half as much as facing down his friends and family. Would they even remember him at this point, or were they going to be strangers and have to get used to each other again? Did they hate him for leaving and staying away longer than he'd planned? What had changed since he left?

As much as he yearned to be home after all of this time, things were complicated. It warmed Wil's heart to see the familiar sights of Appleton and the orchards whizzing by. It tormented him to know time would keep ticking away until he got off the train and had to face his family. There was only one thing to do about it.

The dining car remained open most of the day, and a good snack would take his mind off the terror of homecoming. Inside sat a little old lady at a table, and the young woman running the place stood behind the bar. Smiling at the old lady, Wilbur quietly bought a coffee and slice of pie from the bartender, taking a seat at the counter. The rich smell of the roasted beans instantly soothed him.

"You wouldn't happen to be the VIP passenger, would you?" the bartender asked, sliding his coffee and slice of pie over to him.

Wil snorted. "VIP? I don't think so. I'm just going home." He added just a tiny bit of sugar and took a sip of his coffee.

"No, I'm pretty sure they told us you were a VIP. Are you really a wizard?"

Oh, so it *was* him. Wil smiled awkwardly. "Oh. Yeah, that's me, then. Not that I'd call myself a VIP, mind you."

Her bright blue eyes glittered with interest. "What kind of things can you do? Can you throw big fireballs?"

"Well, sure," he said, "but I—"

"Can you fly?" Her eyes widened.

"Sort of. It's very difficult, but I guess I—"

"Oooh!" The pitch of her squeal pierced Wil's brain. "Show me something, show me something!"

It always came down to this. At school, he rose above about two-thirds of the class. Above average, but nothing he'd consider special or notable. Outside, though, everyone had questions and everyone wanted a demonstration. Most of them would be bored if they knew he focused on magic dedicated to farming and taking care of the land. But that didn't mean Wil neglected his personal passions or that he was opposed to giving them a show.

"Alright," he said, smiling and setting his coffee and pie to the side. "Watch this—it's one of my favorite things to do when I'm bored."

The server clapped her hands and watched intently.

Taking a deep breath, Wil pictured in his head what he wanted. Images, sounds, textures, behaviors. Something half between imagination and memory, letting his instincts guide him. At the same time, he opened himself up to the ambient power of the world, becoming a channel for power and intent to flow through and become reality. That sense of wonder and euphoria came, as it did with every spell.

The train shook violently. Wil grabbed hold of the counter and caught the server before her head could hit it. He released her at once and looked around. The trees and fields passing by through the windows slowed as the train ground to a halt.

"Was that you?" the server asked, wide-eyed.

"No," said Wil, frowning at his spilled coffee, "definitely not." His stomach did a little flip. Something was wrong. Ever since he'd opened himself up to arcane power, his gut had been telling him many things that ended up being true. Every wizard eventually developed a danger sense. Wil thought he didn't have it, until now, when it screamed for the first time.

"Excuse me," he said, leaving her behind. He helped the old lady up off the ground and back into her seat and then went to the next car over. People stood out in the hallway, staring out the window with a mixture of boredom and anxiety. No one knew what had caused the train to stop, and either it was nothing and a waste of time, or there really was something he needed to handle. Wil pushed his way through, apologizing every three seconds until he got to the driver's compartment.

"What's the trouble?" Wil asked, peeking over the heavyset driver's shoulder.

The driver turned around and glared at him. "None of your concern, sir. Return to your compartment. We'll have this dealt with in no time."

Wil ignored him and twisted, finally getting a good peek. "Oh, a tree on the tracks? That's no problem. I can take care of that if you'd like, and we can be off."

The driver considered him, and then considered the way he looked. The academy uniform favored formal suits and looking like dignified gentlemen, no matter how low a status you came from. Here, only a few miles out from Harper Valley, Wil was overdressed. "You? You know what? Sure. I'd love to see you take care of this." The driver pulled on a lever and the door on the side opened up. He gestured for Wil to go first.

The first step into early summer warmth felt like waking up. Wil took a long, deep breath. They were miles out still, but it smelled like home. Smiling, he stepped up to the tree. Trees. There were three in a row that had very clearly been cut down intentionally. Probably recently. The driver seemed to realize it right as Wil did because he let out a gasp.

Then out of the trees came a dozen men, armed with pitchforks and clubs. "Afternoon," called out a particularly husky man Wil pegged as their leader. "Sorry for the inconvenience, but this is a robbery. If you'll kindly empty your pockets and sit on the ground, we can get this out of the way with minimal violence. Cross us, though…" He slapped his club down in his other hand.

Wil looked behind him. All along the train, heads were peeking out of windows to get a better look at the problem. There were kids there. Violence toward them wasn't acceptable, no matter how minor. He pasted a smile on his face and held his hands up, pretending to be harmless.

"Yeah, sure, no problem. I don't carry much money on me, though. Mind if I get my friend? He's way richer than me."

All around, the bandits waited for the signal to strike. The leader held up a hand. "Sure. Whatever makes this smoother. We'd rather not have any trouble if we can avoid it, you know?"

"Of course," said Wil. Still holding up his hands, he breathed in and opened himself up. The power he'd already gathered flickered back to life and greedily sucked in more mana from the surroundings. He knew this land, even before he knew his powers. The same image he'd obsessively created in his mind remained fresh. All he had to do was make it bigger. Much bigger.

First came the wind, summoned with practiced ease, kicking up bits of dirt and buffeting the bandits. When Wil opened his eyes again, he saw the first signs of realization on the bandits' faces. Too late to stop him now! A loud, thunderous crack knocked several of them on their asses as a rift appeared in the ground. Massive red arms topped with horrible black claws burst upward in a mess of dirt and flames as an archdemon ripped itself from the earth.

As it stood on two cloven hooves, it opened its beaklike mouth. A jet of flames shot out and the few bandits still on their feet took off running, while those on the ground scrambled to get away. The demon screeched, letting loose a deep, ugly piercing noise. Within seconds, all the bandits were gone, their screams tapering off as they fled for safety.

He waited as long as he could to make sure they weren't coming back. Then he cracked.

Wil threw his head back and laughed, perhaps a little too maniacally. A gasp behind him made him whirl around. The driver and the other passengers were looking on with horror, jaws dropped. Children were crying. Well, that just wouldn't do.

Wil made a show of snapping his fingers. The illusion wavered, becoming a giant unicorn with a glowing white body and shimmering rainbow mane. It whinnied and reared up, kicking its hooves up at the treetops. He must have chosen the right animal because the fear quickly turned to understanding and then delight. Families stepped off the train to get a better look.

"I think he wants to help out," Wil said in an over-the-top stage voice. Once created, the illusion wasn't too hard to maintain. Seeing it himself helped feed into itself becoming borderline self-sustaining. He directed the unicorn to the trees along the tracks. Another deep breath and he harnessed raw magic, letting it out in one of its purest forms.

To his audience, it looked as though the unicorn threw the trees with its horn, when in reality Wil pushed out with force and threw the trees as if they were twigs, hiding the strain. He snapped his fingers again and the unicorn turned to bow to the people before disappearing in a rainbow flash.

Wil turned from the cleared tracks to the driver. "I think we can get moving again now," he said with a smile.

For the most part, he tried not to make it a bigger deal, graciously thanking people for their applause and even feeling a little embarrassed about it. He didn't regret solving the problem and keeping them from being robbed, but maybe he didn't have to be flashy about it. On the other hand, what good was his education if he didn't get to have fun with it?

He returned to the dining cart and got another coffee and slice of pie. This time, on the house. With a rolling lurch, the train got moving once more.

CHAPTER 2

Welcome Home, Wilbur!

When the train pulled into Harper Valley Station, Wil breathed a sigh of relief. Things were getting embarrassing.

"I've always wanted to be a wizard too! Can you tell me how to be one?" one young kid asked, getting entirely too close and making Wil back up against the window.

"I'm afraid it's something you're born with," said Wil. "But that doesn't mean you don't have a bit of magic in you. I believe everyone's got something special they can do, something magical."

The boy nodded slowly, in awe of the very idea. The last half hour of the train ride had been an exercise in patience and graciousness. Wil almost immediately regretted being splashy when everyone tried to talk to him as he ate his snack, and several came up to shake his hand and thank him for averting the train robbery. At a certain point, it stopped feeling good and started being weird.

"Look, I've got to go," he said, standing up. "You might have magic, so don't be afraid to test it out. You'll be able to feel if you do. But be careful, okay?"

"Okay!"

Wil smiled and went back to his compartment to get his luggage. The four suitcases were linked together by a length of rope. He tugged on the length of rope and focused. His luggage floated into the air like a half-deflated balloon, rising a couple of feet off the floor and staying there. He pulled it behind him as he left the train and met with the ultimate embarrassment of all.

Some of the passengers were already waiting for him on the polished wooden platform and, when they saw him, broke out into applause. Wil froze mid-step, eyes darting around wildly. His cheeks burned. He raised one hand and gave a half wave, turning away from them with a stricken look. To make it even worse, it all happened in front of his family.

His little sister, Sarah, wasn't little anymore. She'd been just a preteen gremlin; now she was a mischievous-looking woman with her blond hair pulled back in a loose braid. She carried a sign that said "Welcome Home Butthead" along with a fairly decent hand-drawn picture of what he used to look like.

Behind her was his brother, Jeb, looking at him and the other passengers incredulously. Seeing him was like looking into a funhouse mirror. Jeb had the same messy brown hair, horse face, and green eyes. Jeb was just bigger and had a scowl on his face. Maybe that was new.

Just to the side stood their father, Bob McKenzie. He was a strong-looking man in his mid-forties, tanned from extensive work in the sun, and had more lines around his face than Wil remembered. Still very much the same burly farmer who had seemed like a giant to Wil at sixteen. He remained bigger than him now, but his shadow was bigger still.

"Well, look who it is," Bob said, stepping forward and holding his arms out.

Six years later, and his father had tears in his eyes. Wil was still welcomed home. He threw himself into his father's arms and squeezed him as tight as he could, and Bob did the same until it felt like his bones creaked. Almost as one, they slapped the other on the back and parted. "Welcome home, Wilbur!"

Wil winced. "Actually, nobody calls me Wilbur anymore. I'm just Wil now."

"Two syllables too much for you, college kid?" Jeb said, scoffing.

"I don't need a reason to change my name, *Jebediah*," said Wil, grinning so hard it hurt. He had his family again, and nothing important had changed. "You got old," he said to Sarah. "You're older than I was when I left home. Isn't that weird to think about?"

"I guess," said Sarah, shrugging. She gave him a hug that ended as soon as it began.

"Would've been less weird if you'd come home to visit," Jeb said, smile dropping from his face.

It was a punch to the gut. Judging from the expressions on their faces, they'd talked about it before and probably warned Jeb not to bring it up. That wouldn't stop him. Wil lost count of how many arguments he and Jeb had before he left for school. This was exactly what he'd been afraid of. Luckily, Bob came to the rescue.

"So, what's all this about?" he asked, gesturing to the passengers who were still waiting on the platform, watching him.

"Oh," said Wil. "It's not a big deal. Some bandits tried to ambush the train and I drove them off."

"Right," said Sarah. "No big deal. Happens all the time. I beat off a bunch of bandits last week." She laughed, and Wil joined her.

Bob, on the other hand, looked impressed. "How on earth did you manage that?"

Wil tried to fight the dumb grin on his face. He raised his hands and wiggled his fingers. "With magic!"

"You're still such a dork," said Sarah, rolling her eyes. "That much hasn't changed."

"So what did you do, fight off an entire gang by yourself?" Jeb said.

Wil shook his head. "No, what happened was…"

On the way to the cart, Wil went over the brief stop and the illusion he had summoned to scare them off. It really hadn't seemed like such a big deal to him, just the easiest way of avoiding a fight. Some wizards lived for battle and showing off their capabilities. Wil would never be one of them. They loaded up his four suitcases after Wil released the spell keeping them afloat.

"Jeez," Jeb grunted, shoving one suitcase into place. "I don't remember you leaving home with this much stuff. Nice to see you spent the money we sent you well."

Bob shot him a warning look, but Jeb stared Wil down. Clearly he wanted a fight, but Wil didn't. This stung, but he expected it. Maybe he even deserved it. Still, he wasn't going to rise to the bait. "Books, mostly. And some tools I'll need for the job. I bought most of it with money I made working between classes, actually."

"I can't wait to hear all about it," said Bob. "You've probably got a million stories about the academy, but you should save those for dinner. Your ma's been cooking up a storm all day to celebrate. She's missed you so much. We all have."

"I haven't!" Sarah sang.

"Even Sarah has," Bob insisted, grinning at his kids. "Let's get a move on. I know you've been traveling for a bit and are probably eager to get home and rest up."

"Yeah," said Wil, "I really am. But I've had nothing to do for three days. Walking home will be nice. I missed everything about the place."

That hit him hard as they walked down the road. Their ancient horse, Percival, pulled his luggage and several crates full of supplies. It felt right being home again. A full quarter of his life had passed before he'd made it home again, and it made him want to cry. It was hard not to fall into memories as they passed by old haunts and landmarks. The town hall still had that goofy statue of a man on a rearing horse, but no one had put underwear on its head. Surely they had to still be doing that.

"And the Joneses' oldest got involved with Mitch's boy, and you know how Mitch can be," Bob said, pointing at a house. Wil listened as closely as he could, but couldn't follow gossip while drowning in memories.

There was the shop where Bob would take his family to get ice cream whenever they went into town. Here was the wall Sarah fell off of and lost a tooth. Memory after memory after memory. The academy had been his life for the last six years, but this was *home*. On a hunch, Wil opened himself up to the feeling of the land.

Harper Valley thrummed peacefully all around him, like a song he could feel but not hear. He felt the richness of the soil, and the sweet summer breeze keeping it from being too hot and sticky. Miles and miles around him, the sense of the land washed over him as it had when he was a kid, but now it was at least ten times more potent. It struck him then that home would never have felt this way if he hadn't left. That alone made it all worth it.

"You alright?" Sarah asked, screwing up her face. "You've got this weird look like you're about to cry or something. You gonna cry, Wilbur?"

"Shut up," said Wil good-naturedly. "I'm doing fine. Just tired and glad to be home."

"And we're so glad to have you back," said Bob, throwing an arm around his shoulders and giving him an affectionate shake.

The rest of the walk home was uneventful, but nevertheless impactful. Wil kept his senses open the entire time, drinking in the land of Harper Valley as he walked it. All of this effort, all of this loneliness, had been to make him worthy enough to serve the valley and its residents, and to be a custodian of the land. It was nice to walk through, like it belonged to him in a way no one else in the valley could ever truly understand.

Finally, their home came into view. Well, the fences did, starting at the road and stretching on as far as the eye could see. Their farm, far from the largest in the valley, was enough for their needs. They weren't rich, but they were comfortable and loved what they had. Wil's heart rose the moment the sprawling, ramshackle house came into sight. They didn't have a mansion, but as the family grew, Bob built onto it, resulting in an uneven house as ugly as it was wonderful.

Wil opened his senses wider. Home. He sighed, breathing it all in.

"You're acting funny," Sarah said, poking him in the side.

"She's right, it's getting weird," Jeb said.

Bob put his arms around both of them and got them in a playful headlock. "Hush, you two. It's a big moment. Welcome home, Wilbur! I mean, Wil."

Home.

"Let's go. I'm starving," said Wil. Together, they made their way up the lane.

CHAPTER 3

Dinner Table Troubles

I f seeing his home wasn't enough to bring a tear to Wil's eye, then the smell of dinner cooking certainly did. His mom had made his favorite dish, jambalaya, and the pungent smell of spices in the air would've made his eyes water no matter what. One by one they crammed into the entryway. With his luggage floating behind him, he looked at his father.

Bob motioned for him to leave his luggage in the den. Wil stowed it away, looking around. They had rearranged it in the last few years. Nothing major—the chairs were in different positions and they had gotten a new table, but the layout rotated. He expected things to change, though the den hadn't been touched for about ten years before he left. It threw him off more than he wanted to admit.

"Wiiilll!" his mother shouted from the other room. Wil jumped out of his skin and then laughed and turned the corner. His mother, Sharon, waited for him in the kitchen doorway, arms spread wide. She grunted as he collided with her and hugged him tight enough to make his ribs creak.

"You're back. My baby's back!" Sharon said, sniffling. And then the water-works came. Wil patted her back awkwardly, fighting back tears of his own. Behind Sharon, Sarah gagged theatrically and Bob shook his head, laughing. Jeb was nowhere to be seen, so he must've already been in the kitchen.

"Yeah, I'm back," said Wil, squeezing her one last time before pulling away. "I'm sorry it took so long. But I learned a lot!"

Sharon looked him up and down, really drinking in the changes. "You got so tall!" she said. Jeb still had a couple of inches on him, but they both broke six feet, like their dad. "Are you hungry? You have to tell us everything about the academy! Your letters were great, but it's nothing like having you home and hearing from you directly."

"Starving," said Wil, with a smile. "I'll tell you anything you want to know."

They all went to the kitchen, where Jeb finished setting the table. On the stove sat a ludicrously large pot, steam rising off the top. They all had their biggest bowls on the table. Being the man of the hour, Wil got his food first for a change, scooping a heaping portion of jambalaya into his bowl and getting a bottle of beer from the fridge. His father raised an eyebrow but smiled and got one of his own.

There's nothing in the world like coming home and tasting some of your mom's cooking, and for that alone, Wil could've cried. The first bite of spicy rice, meat, and peppers made him sigh in contentment. Luckily, his family understood, and he demolished the first bowl and his beer in just a couple of minutes. He got another helping of each and took his time.

"I missed this so much," Wil moaned.

"At least you missed something," Jeb muttered. He made a face as though someone had kicked him in the leg, and a warning look from Bob kept him quiet.

"Did they not feed you at that school?" Sharon exclaimed as she ate her portion much more slowly.

"Oh no, the food was great," Wil said between shoveling bites into his mouth. "Would've been worth going just for the food alone, but they've got nothing on you, Ma."

Sharon beamed. Sarah rolled her eyes. "Kiss ass!" she declared.

"Mama's boy," Jeb added, a little less playfully.

"Damned straight," said Wil proudly.

"Tell us about some of your classes," said Bob, getting up to get another beer for himself and Wil. "Your letters were kinda hard to follow there. What's it like, learning magic?"

Finally, something Wil could talk about for hours in front of a new crowd. He took another bite and pushed his half-full bowl to the side for the moment.

"Hard," he said. "Mind-numbingly hard. You don't just have to be born with the capacity for magic, you have to learn to make it happen at your command. Which means opening yourself up to magic power, letting it become part of you, and then focusing and channeling it out as a spell. Like this."

He opened himself up just a little. There was no need to do something especially impressive or dangerous at the dinner table. The magic flowed into him, the mana around his house tasting sweet and familiar. Wil pointed his finger at the saltshaker. It was one of the simplest spells they had learned and been drilled on. Mild telekinesis could be fun and useful. A second later, the saltshaker spun around in circles while Wil twirled a finger.

"Yeah, but can you do anything *impressive?*" Sarah said with a mischievous grin.

"That *is* impressive," Sharon said. "Can *you* do that?"

"Sure." Sarah grabbed the pepper shaker and held it up with a flourish. "Ta-da!" Jeb clapped for her.

Wil grinned. "Yeah, okay. Hold on tight, then." The salt fell back to the table with a clatter. Wil held up his entire hand this time, drawing in more power. Sarah shrieked in surprise as her entire chair lifted three feet into the air.

"Okay, put me down," she said. "I'm impressed." From across the table, Bob burst into laughter, coming right from the belly in big guffaws.

"You sure?" Wil asked. He twirled his finger again and the chair rotated. Slowly at first, then faster and faster. Sarah clung on tight, screaming more but in delight rather than fear of what her brother would do.

Eventually, a look from Sharon made him put her back down again. But because he was her older brother, the chair faced the wrong way. "Ta-daaa!" Wil said, taking a gulp of beer.

Jeb shook his head, frowning. Sharon, however, clapped enthusiastically. "That's fantastic, Wilbur! I'm a little surprised. I thought you had to say magic words or have a wand or something to do proper magic."

Wil chuckled. "I do have a wand upstairs in the den, but I don't need it. Plenty of other wizards need to say words of power, but I'm something of a specialist. I'm what's called a spellshaper. I do things by feeling it out and making it happen. But there's a trade-off. If something doesn't come naturally to me, I have a hard time learning it. But the things I can learn I'm really good at now. I learned a lot while I was there."

"Is that why you stayed two extra years and never came home?" Jeb asked. His tone was neutral, but there was something in the way he looked at him that Wil didn't like.

"We've talked about this," Bob warned him.

"He's not wrong, Dad," Sarah said, crossing her arms over her chest and mimicking Jeb's expression.

"No, it's okay," said Wil. This was inevitable, and as much as it hurt to see Jeb resent him, he kept a cool head. "You're right. I should've visited. But I had good reasons. Things I didn't want to say in a letter because I knew you wouldn't understand."

"Wouldn't understand?" Jeb scoffed. "What's there to understand?"

"Jeb," Bob growled.

"No, we're doing this." Jeb jabbed a finger in Wil's direction. "What's there to understand, Wilbur? You got to go to a big, expensive school that everyone in town paid for. A four-year course, that's what we were told, right? What, did you like it so much you wanted to stay there as long as you could? Embarrassed about your farmer family, wanted to stay in the city? I'm surprised you even came home at all."

Silence, save for Bob's resigned sigh. Sharon looked too upset to speak, but Sarah looked excited that Jeb couldn't hold himself back. As for Wil, it hurt. A lot. Jeb wasn't wrong.

"Forget this," Jeb said, pushing his bowl away. Wil looked down. He heard the scrape of the chair against tile and then the thunder of Jeb storming off and down the far hall, where he had a room separate from his siblings. Wil always envied that, but Jeb deserved something good. This fight didn't change that.

"We don't really believe that," Sharon said, reaching over and taking his hand. She had tears in her eyes but looked calm. "You have to understand, it was really hard on him and Sarah."

"Naw, I'm fine," said Sarah brightly. "I mean, it's not like I didn't miss you. If I could've gone there and stayed longer, I probably would too. But I would've visited," she added.

"I'm sure you had your reasons," said Bob, finishing his beer. "I wouldn't mind hearing them, but I'm not gonna push you, son."

"It's okay," Wil said again. He took a deep breath and forced a smile. "He has every right to be mad. I didn't visit. I made excuses every time because I didn't want you to worry. But I didn't visit because it was too expensive."

"Oh, hogwash!" Bob shook his head. "I don't care how much it would've cost, I would've found the money."

"I didn't *want* you to find the money," said Wil. "I know how expensive it was to send me there. It took so much just for the first four years. But the thing is, I had to work harder than everyone else there to get where I am. That meant staying longer and working harder. And for those last two years, I got a job to help pay the tuition increase. I scrimped and saved everything I could to try to make it easier for you guys.

"And those extra two years were critical." The guilt was still there, maybe would always be there, but Wil appreciated getting it out early. "I graduated with the rank of master. It opens a lot of doors for me, and I think also might affect how much I get paid. I had the opportunity and I had to make the most of it while I could. I wanted to be able to come home and make you all proud."

"Aw, hell, Wil." Bob sighed. He leaned sideways in his chair and clasped Wil's shoulder. "We're already proud of you, obviously. But you shouldn't have to worry about the money. That's my job."

"We would've been okay," Sharon said.

Sarah made a face. "I mean, if you wanted to pay for it yourself, it means I got to get spoiled while you were gone. And if it makes things better for you, then good for you. Jeb'll come around. Unless you start acting like a know-it-all."

"You think I'm going to be able to avoid that?" Wil scoffed. "I'll be a know-it-all until the day I die, and proud of it. Here, Ma, let me clear the table."

"You don't have to do that!" Sharon swatted his hand.

"I want to, though. I'm glad to be home, and I've got a lot to make up for." Wil collected his and her bowls and took them to the sink. From behind, he heard Sarah mutter something about one less chore for her. While the water heated up, Wil took some time to be grateful things had gone as well as they had.

As much as the guilt and Jeb's words stung, he found himself mostly content with his decision. It may not have been a popular one, but it had been his to make. Things were going to be good, he decided. He smiled and did the dishes.

CHAPTER 4

Smoking with Dad

After dinner and dishes, Wil tugged his floating luggage up the stairs, glad he didn't have to carry his things to his room. The familiar creak of the stairs sounded like a song to him, and he instinctively dodged the loose step. Such a stupid, simple thing to make him happy, but after six years away, Wil found himself just relieved his life could finally really begin.

His room hadn't changed a bit. A nice bed, a sturdy desk, and a couple of bookshelves full of adventure books and scientific guides. He pulled his bags into the center of the room and let the spell go. They dropped half a foot with a dull thud.

"This room used to be so much bigger," he said, chuckling. Opening the desk drawer, he retrieved a battered old journal. Back before school, Wil had journaled almost every day. He didn't have time for writing at school outside of his notes, and part of him mourned the loss of the habit. Smiling, he opened the book to the last entry, the attached ribbon still keeping his place years later.

This is my last entry for a while. At least, until I come back next summer. I'll have so much to talk about then! But for now, all I can really think about is, I'm kind of scared. What if I fail or wash out? Everyone's pooled so much money to send me to Saint Balthazar's Academy of Magic, and I'm terrified I'm going to let everyone down. I know I have the gift, but what if I'm the worst wizard ever? I'd have to spend the rest of my life paying everyone back while they hated me forever!

I'm worried about leaving Jeb and Sarah and Mom and Dad behind. Sarah doesn't care, she's a menace like usual, but Jeb seems mad at me for going. I don't know why. He's going to inherit the farm when it's time, and this could be a great chance for me to find something I'm good at and make everyone proud. Mom and Dad are sad to see me go, but no one's been more supportive than them. They seem to think I can do it, so maybe I can.

Anyway, I leave in, like, four hours. I'm so nervous I haven't been able to sleep! I can probably sleep on the train, and I might do that. I might stay up all night, might go for a walk and see this place for the last time. I'm going to miss it. Yeah, I think I'll do that.

Wil hadn't signed or dated it. He just left off there, and if memory served, he did go for a walk, got back home before dawn, and got two hours of sleep before breakfast and the long train ride toward his future. Funny enough, he'd been wrong about two things in that entry. The first was that he very much did *not* fail. And he could attribute that to not coming home that summer.

It was odd, being able to see the last traces of himself as a child, a completely different person at that point, and still feel as if that kid's ghost haunted the room. Then he was gone, and Wil stood there alone. He closed the journal and put it away. Maybe he'd start entries back up once he got settled in. Maybe it would be better to start a new book entirely, a new chapter in his life. Yeah, he'd start tomorrow. Tonight, he was too tired.

Wil opened his suitcases and changed into loose sleepwear. Climbing into bed, he imagined he'd fall asleep the instant his head touched the pillow.

He didn't.

Wil closed his eyes and snuggled into the bed, noting every lump and bad spring. The beds at the academy had been like being swallowed by big, fluffy clouds. He rolled over and tried to relax. Three days of traveling after six years of hard schooling. He was back in his room, back in his home, and it was time to sleep.

No go.

Groaning, Wil sat up. He lay in the sweet spot of being brutally exhausted without feeling sleepy. Or maybe he was overtired. Either way, Wil was no stranger to insomnia and figured there was nothing to do about it just then. He fished out his slippers from his luggage and headed downstairs, creeping carefully to keep the stairs from groaning too loudly.

The lights were still on, which didn't surprise him. It was still fairly early, but his parents tended to be early to bed and early to rise. All the better to get the hardest work done before the hot summer sun made the task unbearable. Both Sarah and Jeb were probably up for a while longer, but Wil didn't think he'd bother either of them with his problems. Especially not Jeb.

"Come on out," his father's voice came, hushed but clear. Wil went outside to find his father on the porch, sitting in one of the five rocking chairs with his pipe and a jar next to him. "Having trouble sleeping?"

"Yeah," Wil admitted, taking the rocker next to him.

"You've never been an easy sleeper," said Bob, taking a puff of his pipe. The smell of the smoke prickled Wil's nose, but he liked it. It was another familiar smell. "You've always been a night owl. Not a great quality in a farmer, eh?"

Wil shook his head with a smile. "No, but a great one for a wizard, as it turns out. There's plenty of rituals and rites you can perform during a full moon, or with certain stars overhead."

"Is that so? Huh." Bob took another puff and offered the pipe to Wil.

"You sure?" Wil asked, taking it. "You've never let me before. You and Jeb used to smoke without me." He brought the pipe up to his lips and inhaled. It didn't taste like much of anything until he exhaled and a puffy cloud of white smoke rose into the night sky. Then there came an earthy, pine flavor. Wil didn't know a single farmer who didn't wind down at night with some staggerleaf.

"Yeah, well, you were a kid. And it's not like it stopped you from getting into my stash from time to time." Bob took the pipe back and puffed, laughing at the look on Wil's face. "You really think I didn't know?"

Wil shrugged. "If you knew, then why didn't you say something about it? Every single time, I thought you were going to catch me and whip my ass!"

Bob chortled again, his big belly jiggling. "When you have kids of your own you'll understand. We knew what you got up to, and we let you because it was important for a young man to explore and push boundaries. I did the same when I was your age." He paused. "And as you showed more and more signs of having magic, I knew how stressed you were getting. Remember those headaches you'd get when you pushed yourself too hard? You'd be doing some basic magic, like making things move or setting a fire, and then it was like, 'Oops, out of magic,' and your brain would come out your nose."

Wil nodded.

"Well." Bob dumped the pipe out into an old coffee can, scraped the bowl, and then refilled it with some fresh staggerleaf. He handed it over to Wil. "I know you first tried it on your own to deal with those headaches. I saw how much it meant to you, and I just didn't have the heart to stop you from getting some relief. Besides," Bob said, chuckling again, "it clearly didn't make you stupid."

"Hah, thanks. For all of it, I mean." Wil held the pipe up to his lips. Bob offered the matchbook, but Wil waved him off. It took just a small amount of power—all wizards learned to do this first at the academy. Just a tiny spark of power and the air ignited, a small flame coming out the tip of his finger. Wil ignited the staggerleaf, puffed a couple of times, and exhaled. His head swam pleasantly and he passed back the pipe. Not all but some of his stress melted away, along with parts of his body.

"You excited about starting work as the region's wizard?" Bob asked. "You worried? Yeah, I know you. You're a worrier."

"Well, how could I not be?" Wil said, staring off into space. The night was beautiful. A sea of stars twinkled down on him. He smiled, melting into the chair. "Everyone pooled together so much money to send me to school. There's a lot of expectations on me. I'm worried I won't live up to them."

"Well, you won't," said Bob. He puffed away, smiling at the stricken look on Wil's face. "No one ever does, least of all smart young men with ridiculously high standards. You're not gonna be able to live up to what you hope to be. Not at first. The best thing you can do is give yourself permission to be new for a while. Let yourself learn on the job and get better." Bob puffed and then blew out a perfect ring of smoke.

"Show-off," Wil said. He thought about what his father said. He was probably right, in all honesty, but that didn't mean Wil's worries weren't still there. Though now he easily dismissed them as unimportant. His dad had some good staggerleaf.

"I learned everything I can. I…I know I'm good at what I do. There were only a handful of us that made master."

"Is that the best rank there is?"

Wil shook his head. "After that is grandmaster, mage, and archmage. I'm halfway up the list. But you don't get to be a mage or archmage without serving in the military, typically. That's not for me. I took the bare minimum of combat classes. I focused on utility and everything I could to serve the community. That's why it took so long."

"Don't worry about Jeb," said Bob. "He's been grumpy about you for a while, and it was bound to come out sooner or later. He'll come around."

"I'm not sure about that," Wil said, taking the pipe again. "He seems to be really pissed at me, and I don't blame him. But I don't regret staying the entire time. Without it, I never would've learned my limits and how powerful I can be." He opened himself up to the land and took one big puff of the pipe. When he exhaled, he twirled the pipe's stem in tight circles. The smoke stopped in front of him and swirled together in a tightly packed, wispy tornado.

"Ha! Show-off." Bob clapped him on the shoulder.

And then for a couple of minutes, neither of them said anything. They didn't need to. Wil and his father had always been able to do this—just enjoy each other's company without needing to talk endlessly. It was enough to soak in the night and feel the staggerleaf turning his legs and will to jelly. Wil started to doze and nearly jumped when Bob finally spoke.

"You got anyone in town you're particularly happy about seeing again?" He grinned and waggled his bushy eyebrows. "Darlene's still in town."

"Dad," Wil groaned, covering his face with his hands. "That was a silly crush and that was six years ago. We're entirely different people."

"Yeah," said Bob. "You're single and a wizard. You might find yourself beating 'em off with a stick."

"Goodnight, Dad," Wil said, standing up and wobbling in place for a moment. He went back inside to the sound of his father's hearty chortles. He climbed the stairs and fell into bed.

This time, he did fall asleep, the second his head touched the pillow.

CHAPTER 5

A Meeting with the Mayor

For the first time in his life, Wil fretted over what to wear. Fashion had never mattered to him, or to much of anyone in Harper Valley outside of the bigger farmers who fancied themselves proper businessmen. But this was a meeting with the mayor. His new boss! If he didn't make a good first impression, then he was doomed.

Maybe it wasn't *that* bad, but Wil couldn't help his anxiety. His casual clothes were probably fine for working out in the fields with people, but they wouldn't do for a formal meeting. Neither would his school uniform. Wil imagined showing up fresh out of school with his uniform still on, looking like a damned child. His graduation outfit was an even worse idea. He pulled at his hair, glaring balefully at the clock above his bed.

In the end, he decided on most of his school uniform, just not the jacket with the patch that said, "Saint Balthazar's." It left him looking fairly nice, if not quite complete. Wil thought he looked good in just a vest and an undershirt, but was it professional enough? His eyes drifted over to the clock. It would have to do; he had to be there in ten minutes.

He ran down the stairs, each step like rolling thunder. Bob and Jeb were already working the fields, and Sarah and Sharon were at the kitchen table, eating. Sharon looked up at Wil and smiled. "I made pancakes!"

"Sorry, Mom, I'm running behind," he said, grabbing a piece of already buttered toast and cramming it into his mouth. "I'll be home for lunch, though!" he said, or at least tried to. It came out more like, "Ah be hmrf unsh" but it had to be good enough. A few seconds later, he dashed out the door.

Harper Valley was the largest town in the region, settled down in a natural valley between peaks. It put them in a special position to be a trade leader between the north and south of the continent, and you couldn't find a more fertile or varied part of the land.

Running through it in the morning was nice, if hot. He got to see the other farms he knew already up for the day and hard at work. Wil passed by fields of wheat and corn on either side of him as the road led to the center of the town itself, down in the southeast pocket.

Wil might've considered the town hall impressive when he was a child, but now that he'd grown up and seen the world a bit, it was just a slightly bigger and prettier building than those around it. Nothing special, just big enough to house the mayor and the valley's small police force and jail, the courthouse on the other side, and, of course, the goofy statue. Big enough for a decent-sized town, but nothing much after he'd been at the academy. That comforted him some. He stepped inside and was only five minutes late.

"Mayor Sinclair is waiting for you," an overly made-up woman in her early thirties told him. The name in front of her desk read, "Mary Stamos," but Wil didn't recognize her. She looked down her nose and through her glasses at him like he was an inconvenience. "He's been waiting."

"Yeah, sorry," Wil said, raising a hand and smiling as he went to the mayor's door. Just to be certain, he knocked before the voice inside told him to enter.

Mayor Bartholomew Sinclair was sitting behind his desk, and he stood when he saw Wil. He had an overly large smile on his face as he grasped Wil's hand and shook it enthusiastically. "There he is, our new resident wizard. A couple years later than expected, but I'm sure you've got your reasons!"

Wil felt like his hand was being shaken off. He pulled it back and smiled sheepishly. "I wanted to make sure I was good enough to represent the people who made it happen," he said, hoping it sounded smooth rather than nervous. "I felt that reaching the rank of master would reflect well on the town. I paid for the difference in tuition myself."

The mayor was a man in his mid-fifties, balding with brown hair turning gray at the temples, but his eyes were lively and his lined face lit up. "That's some good thinking, Wilbur! That's good dedication to the town and public service. You oughta be proud of yourself." He ushered Wil over to his desk. Wil took a seat, and then Mayor Sinclair sat in his plush chair.

"Not much to be proud of yet, sir," Wil answered, looking around the office. It was busy, with tons of pictures of Mayor Sinclair meeting with high-profile citizens of the town as well as several from festivals and fairs. A giant map of Harper Valley hung on the wall to Wil's right. "But I hope to make everyone proud very soon. I studied hard, and I think I'm ready for the job."

"Fantastic, that's just fantastic. Well, I have some good news and bad news,

Wilbur." Mayor Sinclair steepled his fingers together. "The good news is we got a whole pile of work orders ready for you. Once people heard you were finally coming home, they lined up with problems for you to solve." Out of his desk, he pulled a medium-sized box filled with form papers.

Wil leaned forward and peeked in. Filled to the brim. Dozens and dozens of multi-page packets of work orders, filled out thoroughly. He lifted one and gave it a brief scan. Mr. Anderson had an issue with his fences rotting or breaking. Well, that was easy enough. The hardest part would be Mr. Anderson talking his ear off. Another had a rat problem. No problem at all. He looked through a few more.

"I'm happy to get started soon," said Wil, taking the box and setting it in his lap. "I'm going to need to make a plan for the order I tackle these in, and make a list of which of my tools I'll need for each job. Do I have an office or something here at town hall?"

Mayor Sinclair grimaced. "Welll," he drawled, "that's the bad news, and something I hoped to clear up before you got here. Your house isn't ready and won't be for a week or two. We're working on it now."

Wil blinked. "My house?"

"Yes, your house!" Mayor Sinclair laughed. "Don't tell me you forgot about it. As Harper Valley's resident wizard, there is a property assigned to you for as long as you hold the job. It's a modest estate that'll make a nice home. Your office will be there. For now, you could use the jail as a temporary office or…I understand you're currently staying with your parents?"

It took a while for the mayor's words to penetrate. Wil was stuck on having his own house. And of course everyone knew the old wizard's residence—the huge place was nothing more than a ruin. Huge, but in terrible disrepair. It had been the previous wizard's home more than half a century earlier.

"Yes," said Wil. "I'm staying at home for now, but…my own house? I don't even really have any furniture or anything to bring to it. If that place is as big as I remember, it's going to be one empty house," he said, chuckling.

The mayor leaned forward, grinning mischievously. "Then I guess it's good that you're receiving a damned fine salary. As a master wizard, you'll get an annual salary of a hundred and fifty thousand zynce. Or just over twelve thousand a month. Paid directly by the state, so it doesn't even come out of our budget!" Mayor Sinclair laughed, clearly pleased. "And after paying your way through school, I gotta say, we're relieved. You're the second-highest paid civil servant in town, after me!"

Again, Wil wasn't quite sure he'd heard things correctly. He was not only getting a large house for his personal use, but also being paid a salary that would technically make him rich in a town like this. His father made more than that, but he also had an entire farm and family to look after. The shock on Wil's face must've been apparent, because the mayor laughed even harder.

"I'm not doing it for the money," Wil said, his face heating up. "Honest. I really do want to serve the community and give back to people who've given me so much."

"Sure," said the mayor, "but getting paid well for it isn't too bad, now, is it? I've got high hopes for you, Wilbur. I nearly lost reelection when you didn't come home on time, but I managed to buy some time. With you showing that our taxpayers' money wasn't misspent, I'll be a shoo-in to keep my seat! You and me, Wil, we're going to do good things for this town, and we're going to prosper." He stood and extended his hand.

Wil stood too, awkwardly shifting the box of work orders to his left hand to shake the mayor's hand again. His grip was tighter this time, not threatening but pointed. Wil squeezed back just as hard. They broke apart and the mayor motioned with his head toward the door. "If you want to use the jail for an office, Sheriff Frederick said he's got a spare desk you can use."

"I'm good for now, thanks," said Wil, keeping the grimace from reaching his face. Sheriff Frederick made him nervous; the man seemed to suspect everyone of doing something wrong or hiding things at all times. "I'll go back home and get working on these. I might be able to do a couple today, but I'll be through the box by the end of the week!"

"That's the spirit," said Mayor Sinclair, opening his door and ushering him out. "You and me, Wilbur!"

Wil had one stop to make before he went home. Not far from the town hall was the house the mayor had mentioned. Wil's new house. The very idea made his heart pound. He walked down the road, past Angus's butcher shop and Angela's bakery. He wondered if those two ever had stopped dancing around each other. On to a spot right next to a creek, spillover from the nearby river.

His house sat on a hill overlooking a decent chunk of the town and the forest to the east. "Big" was a good way to describe it, as it topped three stories and had a basement. The outside looked like crap, but even now a crew worked at repairing a hole in the roof and were in the process of replacing the windows of a rounded room on the side of the house near the front door. It would make a perfect office when it was fixed up.

His very own house, as long as he had the job. Which meant he had to be worthy of the job to be worthy of this house. Wil didn't expect it to be easy. He expected hard work and was more than prepared to meet the challenge. With one last lingering look at the place, a thought entered his mind. Jeb was *really* going to hate him now.

CHAPTER 6

Magical Handyman

Honestly, the paperwork wasn't so bad. Wil found a sense of order in reading through the work slips and then separating them based on the severity of the problem and how complicated it would be to fix. He gave priority to the people who had donated the most to send him to school. Wil wasn't proud of that, but he figured it was the least he could do for them giving him the opportunity in the first place. From there, Wil laid out a schedule for the week and went to bed, confident he'd rise to the challenge.

The next day found him bright and early at the Johnson residence dressed in sensible overalls and boots and, with a big bag of tools, looking more like a handyman than a powerful wizard. The Johnsons' home was one of the bigger ones in the valley, originally a small two-bedroom that had eventually become a six-bedroom sprawl on a few acres of decent land. Jonathan Johnson had a laundry list of things he wanted done.

It was just Wil's luck that Darlene Johnson answered the door that morning. His crush was about his age, with short, spiky black hair and vibrant blue eyes. She had a million freckles and was just about the coolest girl he'd ever met.

"Oh, hi there," said Darlene, smiling and opening the door wider. "Didn't expect you so soon. It's been a while, Wilbur. How was wizard school?"

Wil stared before realizing he should say something. "Uh, hi, yeah. School was…school." He offered a weak smile.

Darlene nodded, chuckling. "Yeah, I guess even learning magic's gotta still be just as boring at times as learning anything else." She motioned for him to follow her in. "What's Dad got you doing for us today? I lost track a while ago."

The inside of the Johnsons' residence screamed new money. Jonathan had done well for himself running the general store, expanding several times until he got to the point where a lot of the farmers sold directly to him, and so did some of the farmers from the surrounding towns. Wil looked around at the many paintings and a few sculptures of things he couldn't quite make out.

"Well, he wants me to make sure there's no mold in any of the bathrooms, that your chicken coops are protected from predators, and your kitchen is free from pests. I'm supposed to reinforce some windows and also set up an alarm system for him. He, uh…he's definitely the kind of man who knows what he wants." Wil shrugged.

Darlene rolled her eyes. "He knows what he wants and he thinks he knows what everyone else wants too."

Wil blinked at the bitterness in her voice. Well, not like it was any of his business. "I should probably start with the nastiest part of the list. Do you happen to have any mousetraps that are, uh, occupied?"

She looked at him funny, realized what he meant and grimaced. "Probably at least one. What are you going to do with it?" She got a lantern and turned up the flame. They headed down to the basement.

"That depends," said Wil. "You squeamish at all?"

"Me? Squeamish?" Darlene let out an unhinged cackle. "I seem to remember you having trouble dissecting your pig. You looked pretty green around the gills there, Wilbur. Meanwhile, I was making the little hooves do a little dead piggy dance."

His face heated up. "You remember that? I thought you never noticed me."

Darlene paused partway down the stairs. Looking over her shoulder, she asked, "Did you want me to notice you?" She raised an eyebrow.

"Um."

She burst out laughing. "You should see the look on your face right now, Wilbur."

"Wil."

"Oh, okay," she said, as they reached the bottom. "Wil, then. Of course I noticed you. You were a damned know-it-all and teacher's pet. And then after you went to school, Dad talked about you plenty. Especially when you didn't come home. Guess he's got you working extra hard to make up for it."

"Guess so." Wil chuckled. The rest, he put out of his mind. If he thought about Darlene Johnson, of all people, noticing him or thinking about him, he wasn't going to be useful to anyone. A line of mousetraps sat in view within the flickering lantern light. One of them was indeed occupied. Wil set the bag down and went through it. He retrieved a pair of gloves he put on, as well as a piece of cloth and a meat cleaver.

"The hell are you going to do with *that*?" Darlene demanded, taking a step away from him.

"You might want to look away," said Wil, smiling. "Well, maybe not. Since you're not squeamish or anything." He lifted the meat cleaver. Darlene had just enough time to register what he was talking about when the cleaver came down, separating the dead mouse's head from the rest of its body. Wil wiped the blade down with the cloth, then ran a jet of flame from his finger over the edge.

"That's pretty gnarly," Darlene admitted. "But why did you behead that poor dead mouse? Did you come back from school with your head cracked? Should I be worried?"

"I needed it, yes, and possibly—in that order." Next from the bag came a stick of chalk and a book. Wil flipped it over to a marked page containing elaborate sigils he'd never remember on his own. They were easily one of his weakest areas, but he didn't need to be good to make a simple ward. Darlene left him alone as he scratched out the appropriate markings and placed the mouse's head in the center.

"This is where you keep your main storage for food and stuff, right?" Wil asked, kicking himself for not asking sooner.

"Yeah. Why? What are you doing?" Darlene crossed her arms over her chest.

"This is called a ward," said Wil, standing. "It's kind of like a mix between a shield and, like, citronella oil. With the ward up and powered, it'll drive all mice away by making this place feel dangerous and unwelcome."

Darlene snickered. "Yeah, I guess if I saw a human skull in the middle of a weird circle, I'd be pretty damned scared too."

Grinning at her, Wil folded his hands together and channeled some power. The actual spell didn't matter because that was what the markings on the ground were. Wards and enchanting could be easier than normal spellcasting if one prepared enough. All Wil had to do was breathe a little of his power into the circle until it came to life. The lines glowed pure white before fading out.

Darlene cocked her head to the side. "Huh. Neat. Is that all?"

Wil opened his mouth to answer but was interrupted by a squeak. First one, then another squeak, even louder than the first. And then more and more. Darlene screwed up her face in confusion, but Wil understood his mistake immediately. Before he could warn her, a mouse ran by, followed by more.

"Oh gods, what did you do?" Darlene gasped, laughing incredulously. The mice came by the dozens, from the walls and some of the big, tightly packed barrels. The squeaks picked up in volume and intensity as the mass of rodents tripped over each other to get away from the newly powered ward.

Wil shrugged, trying not to scream or move or start kicking things. The mice ran over his feet and kept going up the stairs, not lingering long on him. He turned to Darlene, shooting her a sheepish smile. "So, I may need to place a couple of other wards to keep them out of your house entirely, but this is totally fixable!"

"Oh, I'm sure. Great going, wizard boy," she said, but she said it through a big smile.

Luckily for both of them, some mice ran over traps on their way out. It was unfortunate because it meant those mice died when most others survived, but it also meant fresh mouse skulls for the wards. This time, with fresher mice, Darlene looked away and Wil himself had to swallow back a gag at the bodies mangled by the traps.

"I'm not sure my family's going to want mouse heads hanging around the house everywhere," said Darlene. "As much as I think your decorating choices are bold and unique."

"Well, the good thing is you don't need to leave the skull," said Wil as they headed to the kitchen. "It needs to be there for the activation of the ward, as the ward is keyed into it as a focal point. It 'sees' the mouse skull and then it affects other, similar creatures. After about an hour or so, you can toss the mouse parts and be fine. You're going to want to leave the chalk drawings for a little longer, though."

"No problem," she said. Darlene grabbed the lantern and motioned for him to lead the way. "We're lucky Mom's out of town for the moment. If she had to deal with this many mice, she'd lose it and the screams would pierce your skull."

"Lucky us," said Wil.

It took three other ward locations to make sure the mice all vacated the premises and wouldn't be back for at least a few months. Darlene's cats, on the other hand, were some mixture of horrified and ecstatic at the flood of panicked mice running out of the house as fast as their little legs could carry them. The two cats picked out a couple of mice each to play with and eat later.

Clearing out the pests was honestly the hardest part of the visit. Darlene stayed by his side the entire time, watching him as he worked. Next came the bathroom, where Wil cleared out mold in the shower and under the sink by heating the air around the mold until it died and could be easily wiped away. He did that out of courtesy. The windows were nice and easy but required something that made Darlene blanch.

"You're going to etch something into the window?" Darlene said, making a face. The two massive windows in the front of the house had received a rock or two through them in the past. You didn't end up one of the leading barons of business in the area without making a few enemies. "Mom's not going to be happy about that."

"It'll be really small, and it beats having to replace the window every time someone gets angry at you," said Wil. From his bag, he got out a special chisel that could cut glass. Very carefully, he etched out a single rune on each window. Then all it took was another flex of power and the rune did the rest of the work.

"That's it?" Darlene asked.

"That's it. Watch this." Wil retrieved a hammer from his bag. He held it up for Darlene, giving her just enough time for her to register it before he brought it crashing against the bay window. The hammer bounced off with an incredible *thunk* that made her flinch, but the glass held. "Ta-daaa!"

"Don't scare me like that!" Darlene swatted his arm. "You get some kind of sick thrill out of that?" she demanded.

"Yes," said Wil.

Darlene snickered. Wil grinned. Soon they were laughing together, and it was enough to make Wil grateful he chose to start his workday there, as tedious as it was.

Once they recovered from laughing, Darlene said, "Was all of that school worth it?"

"Hrm?" Wil met her eyes and tried not to focus too hard on them.

"Was it worth it?" Darlene repeated. "Going to school for six years only to come back and have my jackass father make you do menial odd jobs around the house like some kind of magical handyman?"

"I don't think of it that way," Wil said. "I got to learn how to bend the world to my will, and I get to help people out. What's not to love about that? What do you plan on doing? You going to take over the general store from your dad?"

Darlene shook her head fiercely. "No. That's his business, and I may have to work there right now, but I'm not going to be there forever. I've been saving up and I'm going to start my own business, without any help from him. And it's going to be better than his."

Wil couldn't say that he understood, but he respected it, at least. "That's what's important right? Doing it yourself and in your own way? That's kind of what being the resident wizard is for me. I've got a long list of various jobs to do, but it beats just carrying on the family farm or trying to do something else. Besides, this way I get to have nice chats with the good people of Harper Valley."

"Uh-huh," said Darlene, unconvinced.

Wil grinned and shrugged. "Today was nice, at least. I should probably get moving and clear out some more work orders. You know, make sure my first day gets as much done as possible. Can I come back and see you sometime?"

Darlene raised an eyebrow. Her short, dark, spiky hair did a lot for making her look sassy and sharp, even when she wasn't trying. "And why would you want to come see me?" she asked. She waited just long enough to make Wil nervous before she laughed again. "You're not really subtle, are you?"

"Never been good at it," Wil admitted.

Darlene shrugged and opened the front door for him. "Yeah, you can come see me sometime. Visit me at the shop when you're not busy. You can help me blow off work."

Grabbing his bag, Wil gave her a mock salute. "Until next time." He left her behind, trying to ignore how his stomach jumped and kicked. There was still plenty to do today, but this was a decent start. Maybe he was a sap, but the mental image of Darlene's sardonic smile made the rest of the day so much better.

CHAPTER 7

Leylines and Leisure

There was nothing like the feeling of a hot sun beating down on you in a lush field. Wil drank it in, enjoying the summer and the setting. An airy breeze, and a nice earthy scent in the air. After a few demanding days on the job, the current one gave him a much-needed breather he used to appreciate nature and his sense of the land. It was hard not to feel euphoric around a leyline.

All over the world, leylines intersected with this reality at points that produced strong currents of magical power. The power hung there in the air, inches from his fingertips, begging to be used. There was so much that could be done with a leyline, and some people were lucky enough to own land with one or even multiple leylines crossing through it. Like Mr. Carrey, who owned some of the best land in the valley for both crops and animals.

"So, is it doable?" Mr. Carrey asked, chewing some tobacco and spitting to the side. Wil fought the urge to gag.

"It's doable," he said, rubbing his hands together. "And it's not just doable, but it's going to work really well. You have some really great land here, and it's going to do almost all the work for me."

"Oh," Mr. Carrey said, sounding unsure, "that's good, then. What do you mean?"

Wil thought about how to word it. He turned and pointed to the gentle swell of the farmland. "I want you to imagine that there's an invisible river going through your land, okay? It doesn't flood and it doesn't spill, it just flows constantly and is right there to be used. I can use that river to make your crops healthier and keep your goats from wandering too far from your land. If I do it right, you're going to have the best harvest of your life!"

To his surprise, Mr. Carrey scowled. "And if you do it wrong, what's it gonna cost me?" he demanded.

"N-nothing," said Wil. "There's pretty much no way for me to screw it up. I'm good at this."

"You sure about that, boy?" Mr. Carrey narrowed his eyes. "I don't know nothing about magic 'cept what my pappy told me as a kid. How do I know whatever it is you're doing ain't gonna give my goats two heads, or make my crops come to life and try to eat me?"

Wil had to resist covering his face with his hand. While it wasn't the most common reaction, some farmers had an iffy reaction to the idea of using magic to solve their problems. Everyone wanted help from Harper Valley's newest civil servant, but a few people had their suspicions. Well, that was just part of the job now. Wil forced a smile he hoped looked honest and not impatient.

"Wasn't there a resident wizard back during your dad's time?" he asked.

Mr. Carrey mulled it over. "I suppose there was," he admitted. "Pappy didn't trust in magic that much either."

"Well, I have a pile of work orders from you, and I can either carry them out and make your life easier, or, if you'd prefer, I can come back another time and—"

"Ehh, ehh," Mr. Carrey said, waving Wil off. "Do what you're here for. But if any of my goats end up with a second head…"

"Then the Midsummer Faire will get a lot more interesting," said Wil, flashing the old man what he hoped was a charming grin. Mr. Carrey sniffed, unimpressed, but he didn't object.

Wil shivered. Back at the academy, everyone was happy for a chance to access the potent natural leylines winding through the school, but access to them was restricted, and for good reason. It didn't take much to become addicted to the power and the ease with which it could be accessed. Top researchers fought over the right to use the leylines, and here Mr. Carrey had one just lying in the center of his property. He didn't know how lucky he was.

The first thing Wil did to access the power was open his mind and magic up to it. Wil had never been struck by lightning, but he imagined it feeling very much like tapping a leyline. More power than his body could safely channel flowed nonstop, oblivious to the world around it. Next, he extended his senses into the earth itself, feeling the soil and the crops and the animals. Farther and farther, stretching for acres in all directions until the very ends of the property were fuzzy and Wil nearly lost himself among it all.

The leyline flowed right through him, through the earth and the worms and critters living inside. Wil flexed just a portion of that power, causing a ripple through the soil. At its core, earth magic was about the connections between living things and the planet they lived on. A skilled earth mage could feel where the soil and plants became one and touch deep inside. Wil did that, guiding a tiny trickle of the leyline's power into all of the land.

Life bloomed, rising in intensity. Wil let it flow throughout the entire farm, directing the energy to blanket the land with just a little taste. This was where being a spellshaper came in handy. With a strong enough will and clear enough imagination, all he had to do was whisper a tiny hint of encouragement: *grow*. Grow big and strong and fast, drink deep of the earth and its bounty, and give back to the world. The crops were already hale and hearty, but now they would be something else entirely.

The work wasn't done. With his sense of the land stretched to its limits, it wasn't hard to pick out the hundreds of sheep and goats off on one side of the farm. He mentally divided the land into sections and imagined a fence separating the crops from the animals, and the animals from the rest of the world. Just a gentle encouragement to stay inside hanging in the air to keep them safe.

Wil opened his eyes to find them watering and his legs wobbly. With a gasp, he released the energy and fell to his knees, panting. The world in front of him swam and black spots erupted in his vision. He nearly passed out then and there. His connection to the world wavered and for a second he didn't know if he was Wil or the land or even the goats, but then it faded. Leylines were not for beginners.

"Criminy, boy," Mr. Carrey spat. "What're you doing on the ground? Bad enough you stood around like a jackass for fifteen minutes, no matter how many times I hollered, and now you're lying down on the job? Shoot, what're they paying you for, anyway?"

Wil held up a finger. The emptiness where his expanded consciousness had been screamed silently. It took another half a minute before he was ready to speak.

"Job's finished," he said, climbing to his feet and dusting his knees off. "Took a lot out of me, is all."

"A lot out of you?" Mr. Carrey scoffed. "You just stood there!"

Wil sighed. "Would you just sign this work order?"

Not all of the residents were as crotchety or untrusting as Mr. Carrey, but a decent number of them viewed him, someone they'd known almost his whole life, as suspicious now. Not many people left Harper Valley unless they enlisted, and fewer came back changed, as Wil had. Maybe it would get better with time, but sometimes Wil couldn't help but feel hopeless.

"What's wrong with you?" Sarah asked as he trudged his way into the kitchen. She sat, leaned over a drawing in progress. "Weren't you supposed to be gone all day long?"

"Pulled a muscle," he grunted, dropping his work bag by the table and collapsing into a chair. "Did some major spellwork and it was a bit more than I could handle."

Sarah looked up at him, malicious mirth in her eyes. "I thought you were a master wizard or something. Helping farmers out too much for you?" She returned to her artwork. A foreign warrior in a white robe, his hair in a topknot, held a sword and snarled at the viewer.

"You try casting multiple spells over a couple hundred acres at the same time. Hey, you're getting pretty good at that." Wil pulled his chair over obnoxiously close to look over her shoulder at the drawing. "Is that what you've been doing the entire time I was gone?"

"Maybe," Sarah allowed. "Beats doing farmwork, and it's not like the old days," she said, twisting her face up and thickening her accent, "where Ma and Pa would find me a good husband so I could pop out enough kids to work the land." She snorted and drew out the last few lines. "No way I'm staying."

"I get you," he said. "I mean, I came back, but once you get out of here and feel how much bigger the world is, you just want to see more of it. What would you do, if you had your choice?"

Sarah, his bratty sister, considered him seriously for the first time in a long time, if ever. Eventually she shrugged and signed her name to the warrior. "I'd travel and draw. Dunno what else, but I know I want that."

Wil nodded, thinking about it. "Plenty of things you could do with that. You still good with animals?"

Sarah scoffed. "Of course I am."

"Well, good. You could always lean into that. Study animals and get good at drawing them for scientific studies and medical diagrams. Make entire books of them, even!"

"That's your solution?" Sarah made a face. "Be a nerd like you?" She paused. "Maybe. That could be fun," she admitted. "Maybe I will."

As far as Sarah went, it was a complete victory. Even calling him a nerd just seemed to be reflex at this point, and she seemed to actually consider his words. Good enough. Wil patted her on the shoulder and got himself some lemonade.

"Hey," said Sarah. "You want to play some cards?"

"Cards?" Wil asked, surprised. "Sure."

For the next hour or so, they went through all the card games they used to play as a family. From blackjack for no stakes to cutthroat Bullshit, crazy eights, and war, the time passed by in a flash. Things weren't the same, but she didn't treat him any differently than before. Before either of them knew it, it was getting close to dinner. After a hard day magically wearing himself out, Wil welcomed the reprieve. But it wasn't to last.

Jeb came in, pouring sweat and covered in dirt. He went right past the two and got himself some lemonade. He drained half the glass in one long guzzle. Turning around, he stuck the cool glass against his forehead and considered his siblings. "Good to see us all hard at work," he said.

Wil didn't know if it was pointed at him or Sarah, and he didn't care which. He opened his mouth to say something but Sarah beat him to the punch. "Screw you, Jeb, I did all my chores before noon. And Nerdboy here apparently pulled a muscle doing some magical crap."

"Oh, really?" Jeb narrowed his eyes at Wil. "This a real pulled muscle or the kind of pulled muscle that would conveniently appear and allow you to get out of work? Being town wizard a bit too draining for you, Wilbur?"

Irritation warred with sadness. Wil didn't want this. "Yeah, it's been a rough few days. I'll get used to it. Want to take a break and join us?" he asked hopefully.

Jeb sneered. "Naw. Some of us got real work to do." He finished his lemonade and went back outside.

Sarah turned to face Wil. He didn't recognize the look on her face for an embarrassingly long time. She felt bad for him. "He's gotten a bit of a stick up his ass since you didn't come home on time. He'll get over it. Eventually."

"Yeah, I hope so," said Wil.

"Or," Sarah added hopefully, "it'll drive him mad and he'll try to burn you like back in the olden days!"

"Even better," Wil said with a smile. "Next game?"

"Sure!"

CHAPTER 8

No Cuts!

After a full week had passed, Wil believed he understood his job a bit better. The most important part was getting tasks done. The more tasks he accomplished, the more he could prove that he was worthy of the job and that his presence made Harper Valley better. As critical as the work itself was, he still had to worry about the paperwork. Something that could've been going better.

The county jail wasn't the most comfortable place to work, but it turned out to be necessary when dealing with the residents of the valley. Not everyone was happy just dropping off a work order and leaving it be. Some needed to talk to him directly, and some of those people were the most aggravating pains in his ass. Worse than that, it meant dealing with Sheriff Frederick.

He stared. A lot.

Sheriff Frederick was a big, red-faced man with a droopy mustache and watery, suspicious eyes. His desk sat on the far side of the room, next to the one big holding cell Harper Valley needed. It was clear on the other side of the room from Wil's desk and a couple of cabinets, but every time Wil stepped in, the sheriff stared at him. He didn't ask Wil any questions, he just watched him like a hawk. Never before had Wil felt so guilty for no reason.

"Is there something wrong, Sheriff?" Wil finally asked one afternoon. He set down the report he'd been working on and faced him.

Sheriff Frederick shook his head, a simple left-right, and then went right back to watching him. To make it worse, it was dead silent in there. No one talked, there was no radio playing music or the news, and both of the men sat completely still. Wil because of the creeps running up his spine, and Frederick for reasons only the gods knew.

"Then why do you keep staring?" Wil pressed. "It makes it really hard to concentrate. Have I done something to bother you?"

"I'm curious 'bout something," said Sheriff Frederick, steepling his fingers together. "What kinds of crime can you commit with that magic of yours, boy? What're you capable of that no one else here is?"

Ah, so it was fear again. Wil took a deep breath, trying not to sound too annoyed. "If I were to put my mind to it, a lot. Is that what you're worried about? Me going around and being a criminal? I have no reason to. I'm here to serve the community, same as you."

Sheriff Frederick made a harsh sound that Wil took too long to realize was a laugh. His watery eyes narrowed. "It ain't about thinking you're a criminal. It's wondering what I could even do if you decided to go bad. That's what I hate about you wizards. Ain't no law I could enforce on you if you didn't want it. No check to that power 'cept other wizards."

"Sheriff," Wil began patiently, "I'm not a battlemage or spellstriker. I'm not like them, and I have no interest in breaking the law or hurting anyone."

"But you could," the sheriff said.

"No, I damned well couldn't!" Wil snapped. Breathing evenly, he smiled and said, "If I did, my ma would kick my ass."

For a second, the sheriff kept on staring. Then his focused frown warped into a smile Wil found unsettling.

"Well, at least there's someone to keep you in check." The sheriff leaned back in his chair, arms over his chest and feet up on the desk. For the first time all day, he looked away.

Finally, Wil could relax. He picked up the report and went back to reading what he'd written. Three sentences later, the door to the jail opened, and a wiry woman in her sixties limped inside. She made a beeline for him, clutching an oversized purse to her chest.

"You the wizard?" she demanded. Just seeing old Mrs. Potter gave Wil the start of a headache. Before he could answer, she continued, "I've been waiting all week to see you! Why haven't you come by my house and helped me out? What the hell are you doing with your time?"

Wil went dead inside. It was easier that way. He stood and bowed his head respectfully to her. "Good afternoon, Mrs. Potter. I hope you're well, and—"

"I'll be well when you get the work I asked for done! I know who you've been helping out," she said, jabbing a finger into his chest. "Helping out rich bastards like Jonjon and Carrey first! Well, when are the rest of us going to matter? You ever plan on showing up for the little people or did all of our tax dollars go toward a servant to the rich?"

Explaining it would be pointless. He knew that, and still Wil wanted to try. Worst of all, she had a point. He had focused on them first. But it wasn't as if he'd skipped over important things just to help out those who had helped him most.

"I have a priority system," he started, "and I've been taking care of some of the biggest jobs first. Let me take a look and see where you are, okay?"

Mrs. Potter sniffed. "Fine. Let's see how far back I am, then!"

Wil sat back down and pulled out his large folder. It took only a couple of seconds to find her file. Ah, that was why. "Mrs. Potter, it says here you want me to do something about the heat and something about your food spoiling. I've been helping out people who have critical problems first." It was mostly true, at least. The first day, he took it easy, and after that, he focused on getting the big stuff done first.

"Oh, so I'm not important enough to be seen in a timely manner?" she sneered. "What do I gotta do to bump me up a few spots? I'm suffering here!"

"I can't just let you cut in line," said Wil, holding up his hands. "If I did that, I would be doing exactly what you complained about me doing, just in your favor. I'm trying to be as fair as I can about this. I promise I'll get to you. At this rate, it'll be either the end of tomorrow or first thing Thursday morning. I give you my word."

Mrs. Potter stared him down. Her steely gray eyes shone with pure malice, but before she could go on another tirade, the door opened again, and his mother walked in with a basket. She looked at the situation, understanding almost instantly.

"Hey there, sweetie," she said, stepping up beside the older woman. To Mrs. Potter, she said, "Hello, Penny. My son been treating you alright?"

Mrs. Potter puffed up. Gathering a storm around her she said, "No, Sharon, he has not! He's been downright rude and unhelpful! *Apparently*, I'm not a high enough priority to help until almost two weeks in!"

It had been nine days.

Sharon clucked her tongue sympathetically. "I know I raised my boy better than that, Penny. I am so sorry, and you can bet I'll be having some words with him over this. Don't you worry, I'll take care of this."

After making a show of thinking it over, Mrs. Potter nodded. "Yes, thank you, Sharon. I know you'll straighten this out." To Wil she said, "And I expect to see you at my house with solutions in hand, young man! It's been way too hot out, and I can hardly stand it."

Wil sighed. "Yes'm."

Mrs. Potter gathered herself up and stormed off, head held high. Sharon waited until the door slammed shut before bursting out laughing. "Ahahahaha! I am so sorry, honey. That woman has got her head up her own ass." She sighed and set the basket down on the open corner of his desk. "Lemme guess: you tried being reasonable and she got mad."

"Yep."

Sharon shook her head. "Not going to work with people like her. Better just to smile and nod and let them wear themselves out, and then go back to ignoring them. Or better yet, do what she says as fast as possible to get her off your back."

"I don't want to do that," Wil protested. "I'm trying to be as fair as I can. Her request is really low priority."

"Which means it would be quick to deal with, right?"

Wil frowned. "Yeah, but—"

"Hey, Wil," Sharon said, smiling wide. "Would you take a look at the flowers when you get home? I'd really like to have a couple of them mature early, and you said you could do that."

Wil blinked. "Uh, yeah, of course, Ma. I'll do it when I get home."

Sharon snapped her fingers and pointed at him. "So you're willing to bump me up to the front of the line? Why not get it over and done with? She's a miserable old biddy, and bossing others around is the only joy she gets. Might as well keep her from fussing or getting more miserable."

The worst part about coming back home was remembering how easily one's parents can reduce you to a dumb kid all over again. Wil sighed, holding his hands up in playful defeat. "Okay, okay, I get it. I don't like it, though. What kind of message does that send people? That I'm okay with being bullied by anyone willing to be an obnoxious jerk?"

"You don't do it *every* time, you goof! You pick and choose your battles carefully. You don't help the hateful old biddies because they need you more, you do it because they have nothing better to do with their time than harass you. You help the rich people out first because they can owe you a favor later. You help family out because we're family. There's always a reason, but you have to choose carefully."

Wil raised an eyebrow. "Wow, Ma, that's really cynical of you."

Sharon smiled, shrugging. "Who do you think plans things out for this family? Your dad's good at managing the farm, but I manage the business. You're not being corrupt by prioritizing Mrs. Potter. You're taking care of an elderly member of society. How does that sound?"

"Hah, okay, yeah. I think I can live with that. What did you bring me?" He pawed at the basket.

Sharon opened the lid. It contained an enormous sandwich and a bottle of beer. "I thought you might want something from home since you haven't gotten paid yet. Glad I came in. I was just in time to bail your ass out."

"Thanks, Ma." A beer was exactly what he needed to head off the looming headache, and he'd never turn down a sandwich from Mom. Wil allowed himself to relax, grabbing half and biting into it. He flopped backward, moaning.

"Don't be weird! Anyway, I'll see you when you get home. When you get done eating, go take care of Mrs. Potter, is that understood?"

"Hah, yeah, fine. I promise."

"Attaboy." Sharon blew him a kiss and left.

Sheriff Frederick stared at him silently.

"What?" Wil demanded.

The sheriff snorted and pulled out a book. "Corruption's a funny thing, son. It starts out small, and soon the rules are inconvenient and you end up on the wrong side of the law."

Wil chewed on his sandwich thoughtfully. He cracked open the beer and took a drink. "Are you saying that me helping out a cranky old lady is a slippery slope that will lead to me being a vicious criminal you have to hunt down?"

"Mm." Sheriff Frederick opened his book and finally, for the first time all week, ignored him. Wil noted that it wasn't a no to his question.

He returned to his sandwich, taking another huge bite. His eyes fluttered at the perfect blend of meats and cheeses brought together with a layer of spicy mustard. Just like how he liked it. The job was a bit more of a pain than he had expected, but it was nice to work close to home.

It'd be even nicer when they finished his house.

CHAPTER 9

Great Expectations

Once Wil had learned it was possible to talk to animals, it was one of the first things he made a real effort to practice on his own back in school.

Hours upon hours of learning how to connect with an animal, and how to manipulate his magic to then communicate as if they were speaking together. It was one of the trickiest spells he'd learned and it took two years to master in his time off—before he realized the tragic truth about talking to animals: most of them weren't good conversationalists.

Sure, it was interesting to know how a horse felt as it galloped across the plains or to know how inescapably hungry dogs were, but Wil soon learned that most animals were simple and had one-track minds. Some animals, like crows and cats, were intelligent enough for him to consider full people, but others were honestly kind of dumb. Like Carl the bull.

"It hurts!" Carl whined. In actuality, he was mooing and making a bunch of nonverbal gestures and reactions that made up his body language, but the spell and experience translated it into something Wil could understand. It was a very difficult spell to maintain, and it was wasted at the moment. "It hurts!"

"I understand it hurts," said Wil, running his hand along Carl's back, "but can you tell me where it hurts? How it hurts?"

Somebody snickered. Wil heard the sound of someone being smacked, but that snicker passed through the Kline family. Wil sighed. It must've looked ridiculous, talking to a bull bellowing in pain. Two years of mastering the ability to bridge the gap between man and beast and he looked like a total dork while using it.

"It huuurts, make it stop hurting," Carl moaned, flopping dramatically against the ground. Wil jumped back to avoid getting nicked by his horns as he thrashed.

"I'm trying to help, but you need to take a breath and calm down, Carl. I've got you."

"Don't worry, Carl, he's got you!" someone stage-whispered, before they all descended into laughter.

Wil turned around. The Klines weren't the owners of the land, just the custodians of it. Carl was the lead stud on the ranch, and his sudden collapse and crying out in pain seemed emergency enough to bring Wil in after the veterinarian had declared Carl would need expensive surgery. Now that he was trying, they treated it like a stupid joke. None of them would meet his eyes.

"I know how weird it looks, but it's working," he said to the Klines. "Now, Carl, I need you to hold still."

Carl moaned loudly and flopped over. Wil took his chance and put his hands on Carl's sides. This close, he did look to be a little swollen. Wil extended his senses outward and did a quick mental scan of Carl's body. He pressed further on the connection, diving into where his mind met Carl's and the spell allowed them to communicate.

It wasn't that he could read Carl's thoughts. They were oddly both too simple and too complex to read like he could a person's. It was more like getting a feel for everything Carl sensed at that moment and taking a mental picture of it. His gut screamed with pent-up, high-pressure pain. Wil released it before the pain could sink into him and take hold of him.

"There's an obstruction," he said, rubbing his stomach about where it would be on Carl's body. "It's causing some pretty severe backup and that's what's causing him pain. I can deal with this, but I'm going to need your help."

The Klines looked at each other, and then back at him. "Whatcha need from us?" Konner Kline asked for his kin.

Wil motioned with his head to Carl. "I'm going to need you all to help hold him down. This isn't going to hurt, but it's going to feel weird, and I don't need him goring me to death while I'm trying to help him, you know?" He smiled, but that just seemed to make them more concerned.

"You fixing to get us gored instead?" Konner scoffed, but he did as he was asked and motioned for his boys to help him. They gathered around the fallen bull and took hold of his big head and his legs. The poor bull was too weak to give much more than a token resistance.

"Alright. This will be no problem." This was one of many spells Wil had learned specifically for helping out with animals, or even people if the situation called for it. He put his hands on Carl's side and vibrated the air around and inside Carl's body. It made a low buzzing sound that grew deeper and deeper until it could no longer be heard.

True to Wil's word, Carl jerked violently, but the Klines were ready for him and kept him down. It took only about half a minute of generating that low rumble deep in Carl's guts for it to work. A piece of the obstruction broke off. And then another one. And another. They made themselves evident, coming out of Carl's backside along with a great deal of rancid brown liquid. Wil held on, gritting his teeth and ignoring the splash and unholy smell. The last of it broke to pieces and he dropped the spell.

By unspoken agreement, the Klines all backed off, leaving Wil alone against Carl's heaving, violently expelling form. Still, Carl mooed in alarm. Wil patted his side reassuringly, keeping it up and practically beating the bull as he let it all out. Finally, there was nothing left but a slow brown trickle. Wil stood up, hands held out in front of him.

"Does someone have a towel?"

After checking with Carl and finding the bull was now just tired, Wil went straight home. As tempted as he was to go straight up to the shower, he stopped outside by the well and drew up some water. He turned the bucket over his head, soaking him to the bone. Sure, there were spells that took care of the filth itself and even stuff that helped with the smell, but there was no substitute for a good soaking. This was only stage one.

"That kind of day, eh, Wil?" Bob came from the nearest field and stood a healthy distance away from him. "What happened?"

"Carl was constipated," said Wil. "I helped, and it got messy. You wanna know more?"

"Nope." Bob climbed the steps up the porch and sat down in his rocker. He watched Wil from there, waiting a bit before asking, "So, a week in. How're you liking the job? Is it everything you hoped and expected?"

Wil just groaned, letting the bucket fall to the ground. Grabbing his bag, he went over to his rocker and plopped himself down, dripping wet. "I like it. I really do. But some parts I'm having trouble with."

"Oh, yeah?" Bob took a drink of some lemonade that had been left out, and made a face. "What're you having the most trouble with?"

It was hard, at first, to decide what the hardest part could be. The hours, the pressure, the need to be creative to solve problems…

"The people," said Wil. "They're good people, but nobody trusts or respects me. They all seem to think that something's going to go wrong and ruin them. They don't understand what I'm doing, and half of them give me trouble when I'm trying to *help* them."

Bob nodded thoughtfully. "Yeah, I can see that. The way I figure it, two big reasons for that. To some of them, you're still my boy. A little bookworm too shy to go on adventures with all the other kids. You're different now, and they're still getting used to the new you. We all are, you know. In some ways, it's like the boy I sent off to school came back a different person. Not a completely different person, but it's still jarring in some ways."

Wil said nothing at first, giving it real thought. He rocked back and forth gently, enjoying the late afternoon warmth and the pleasant breeze keeping it from being too oppressive. He was happy to be home, but how different could he be?

"I know I'm different," said Wil, "but I don't feel different. I just feel like...me."

"And that's exactly it," Bob said, pointing at him. "You're more of yourself. When you were a teenager, you were a timid little thing and you were always on the outside, looking in. Now you're not really a kid anymore, you're good at what you do, and you know things, but nobody knows you. You just gotta keep at it, be yourself, and people will eventually get used to you. And if they don't, they can kiss your ass."

Wil chuckled. He looked out down the road. Far off in the distance, a horse-pulled cart became smaller and smaller. Time had passed, but his dad still felt like his dad to him. But even if he said he didn't know him anymore, he at least accepted him and was willing to see what kind of person Wil was now. Everyone else seemed so suspicious.

"That doesn't bother me as much as how many people think I'm either going to be dangerous or incompetent. It's the fear that bugs me. Everyone seems scared of me now. I did all of this for them."

Bob made a sympathetic noise. "I know that. But they don't. Harper Valley's a good place, and the people in it are generally pretty decent, a few bad apples aside. But they're simple people, and you can do stuff no one else can. Everyone's probably wondering why you would stoop so low as to be the town troubleshooter. Not many people are that altruistic."

"I'm not altruistic, I just want to contribute and help people."

Bob shot him a look.

"Okay," Wil said, sighing. "But it shouldn't be weird to want to help out. When I help out someone, I help out all of us. I just thought there'd be some kind of respect for the role. I don't expect people to sing my praises or worship me, but the least they can do is not fight me the entire time."

Bob got out his pipe and packed it. "Well, a couple days from now there's that welcoming potluck the mayor announced in your honor."

Wil made a distressed noise. "In my honor. I don't want people to make a big to-do about me or anything like that. Feels weird, like he's going to parade me around to show me off. The last time we spoke, it was about his reelection chances. He's going to make sure everyone knows he made this happen."

"That's just politics for ya." Bob shrugged. "Why don't you look at this as an opportunity? This could be your chance to show off, maybe do a couple of tricks, and meet with people without having to work. You know, let them get to know you a bit better so maybe they'll stop being a bunch of small-town jerks!"

Wil grunted his doubts, but he still gave it some thought. "Maybe you're right. Couldn't hurt, at least. And worst-case scenario, I get some free food out of it."

"That's the spirit." Bob lit up his pipe and took a puff. He blew it out slowly and turned, considering Wil carefully. "What is it you want out of this job, Wil? One thing. The biggest thing you want out of it."

It was a hard question, but one Wil had been asking himself all week long. "To know I made a difference. That I made things better. Having a comfortable job is nice, but I really could've gone anywhere. If I'd run away, no one would've been able to find me. And some friends of mine at school, they offered, you know. To take me in, and we'd go traveling and on adventures together."

"Were you tempted to say yes?" Bob asked.

"Of course I was," Wil said with a laugh. "But I couldn't. Everyone did so much for me. It's a good place, and I think it could be even better. And once I get into the swing of things, I can start traveling to nearby towns, too, to give them a bit of help. If I ever did want to travel, I'd still be doing this—I'd be just going town to town to do it."

Bob puffed away, letting the silence settle in comfortably. Wil was starting to get a bit cold from being soaked, but it was nice on a warm day like this. He'd still need a shower and a change of clothes, but it hadn't been a bad day, exactly. He'd gotten some work done and helped poor Carl clear out a major blockage. Bit by bit, the pile of work orders shrank.

"I think you're right," said Wil. "The potluck will make everything better. Things will get better in no time. I just gotta be patient."

"Attaboy," said Bob.

CHAPTER 10

Passable Potluck Portents

While Harper Valley wasn't the biggest town around, there were more than enough people to make a big event crowded and claustrophobic. Or maybe it was just Wil, terrified by how many families were packed into the big activity center and amphitheater. They were on the southwest side of town, right before civilization turned to forest and mountain, and you couldn't get around without bumping into people or sliding past them.

And all of them were here because of him. Nothing could be more nerve-racking.

"How're you doing there?" Wil asked for the hundredth time that day. This time it was to Lance and his wife, Sharlene, and their kid, Conrad. Conrad had been five when Wil had last seen him, fat-faced and energetic. Now a preteen, he stared sullenly at him.

"Fine, just fine," Lance said. Wil didn't know them that well, but they were familiar enough that his indulgent laugh grated on him and felt false. "This is some shindig you got going here," he said, looking around at the hundreds of people all around them.

"Yeah, you're a pretty big deal now, aren't you?" Sharlene asked, eyes narrowing. It didn't sound like a good thing coming from her. "Not every day we have a big party for just anybody."

"I didn't ask for it," Wil said bluntly. He made a show of looking around, an exasperated expression on his face. "But it's as good an excuse as any to see all the families of the valley, right?"

"Right," Lance said, unconvinced. Conrad continued to stare.

"Hey," said Wil, "watch this." He held out his hand. A miniature firework launched up a couple feet into the air, exploding into colorful sparks with a subdued pop.

Conrad's eyes lit up. He grinned and looked eager for more, but Wil simply waved at them and continued down the line. So far, this was about how it went for most families. Some familiar faces, friends of the family, were a welcome sight, but mostly it was wary interest from the adults and excitement from the kids after he did a little trick for them. It was hard not to feel like a cheap performer, begging for applause.

"Well, lookee here!" Jonathan Johnson and his family were next. Darlene sat next to him and sighed, looking up at Wil with a silent apology. Jonathan's wife, Angelica, looked somewhere near where he stood but said nothing. "I gotta say, boy, whatever you did at my house worked perfectly. We haven't seen a single mouse all week long, and just today, a brick bounced off my window!"

"Yeeeah," Angelica slurred, sounding vaguely enthusiastic. "Thass some good work, Wilbur!" She clapped awkwardly. Darlene looked like she wanted the earth to swallow her up. Wil was about to respond when Jonathan spoke up again.

"Not sure if it's worth how much money we poured into your schooling, but it's a good start," Jonathan said with a laugh, not breaking eye contact with Wil.

"Dad," Darlene groaned. "Since when do you not know the difference between short-term investments and long-term ones? He's been at it one week."

Jonathan's face twisted in anger, but Wil cut him off before he could turn on Darlene. "I'm really grateful for all your help, Mr. Johnson. It was my pleasure to fix your house up and I hope to be useful for decades to come." At this point, reassuring people was making up at least a third of his night so far.

Angelica pointed at him, finger coming uncomfortably close to Wil's face. "S-see that, Jonjon?" she demanded, hand wavering. "He's a good boy, and alwayss hass been! You were gettin' grumpy for nothin'."

"Dammit, woman, I'll be grumpy about whatever I damned well please! He was supposed to be home two years ago, and—"

Oh gods, this again. Wil stood there, letting the man get it all out of his system. He caught Darlene's gaze and she gave him a crooked, long-suffering smile. It was hard to focus on anything after that.

Wil found himself speaking, interrupting Jonathan's rant. "Hey, do you want to get lunch tomorrow?"

Jonathan looked between the two of them, as incredulous at the request as he was at the interruption.

Darlene's face lit up. "I'd love to. Say, noon at Mack's Shack?"

"Perfect." Wil smiled brightly and used that opportunity to slip away and catch his breath.

He actually did it. He asked his crush out. It wasn't like it was a date or anything like that. Wil wasn't an expert on dates, but he was pretty sure it required something in the evening and maybe dinner. This was nothing like that, but it'd be a great way to actually socialize with someone outside his family.

He knew he should be making the rounds more and trying to get as much goodwill as possible, but frankly, he was tired. He liked the work, but being a public figure was harder than he imagined, and he'd barely been at it. Rather than go seek out more people and greet them, Wil found his family and joined them.

"You look dead inside," Sarah pointed out helpfully as soon as he sat down. Sharon smacked her shoulder.

"I made you up a plate, honey," said Sharon, pushing a full plate his way. Heaps of barbecued meats and fluffy mashed potatoes and fried onions and greens made him realize just how ravenous he was after a full day's work and an hour of meeting and greeting.

"Oh gods, thanks, Ma," he said, grabbing a rib and gnawing on it immediately. His father chuckled, shaking his head, but Sarah made a face.

"You're a savage," she said. "Nice to see school didn't make you any less gross."

"I've seen you eat," Jeb said to her. "You really think you got any room to talk, Princess?"

Wil blinked. It was the closest Jeb had come to defending him or saying anything positive all week long, and even then, it was more like putting Sarah in her place. Whatever it was, he'd take it. He nodded at Jeb gratefully, pulling a huge strip of meat off the bone. Jeb grunted and sat back, draining the rest of his beer. It was almost like old times, until Bob opened his mouth.

"How you holding up, dealing with everyone? Crowds have never been your thing, have they?"

Wil shook his head, taking a bite of potatoes. They were even fluffier than they looked. He sipped some lemonade and made a face. He brought the big mug up to his mouth and blew out frost, chilling the liquid. "Worth it for the food."

"That's my boy," Sharon said, laughing. "If we ever need you to do anything, we've always known how to bribe you." At Jeb's snicker, Sharon jabbed a finger in his direction. "That goes double for you. No one in the house eats more than you."

And so it continued for a while. Wil just enjoyed being around family with some good food. After a few minutes of letting himself be and not being the star of the show, some of his earlier tension faded. The reactions to him hadn't been bad, but they were enough for him to wonder if a welcoming feast was really the best idea. Maybe after a year or two, people would be different. Gods, he had so much time and work ahead of him.

He was lost in his thoughts when he realized his family had gone silent and were staring past him. Bob stood up and nodded his head respectfully. "Mr. Mayor," he said.

"Bob, Sharon, Wil," he greeted everyone, more or less. Jeb scowled at being overlooked but Wil sincerely doubted Sarah cared. "How's your night going so far?"

Wil stood up, wiping his mouth off and suddenly self-conscious. "Not bad, sir. Was just taking a break from the meet-and-greet to grab some food. Should I have not?"

Mayor Sinclair laughed it off. "No, no, you're good. Just figuring that before people get too fat and full, we might want to get on with the speeches."

"S-speeches?" Wil's face dropped.

"Oh, this is gonna be gooood," Sarah sang.

"Speeches!" Mayor Sinclair confirmed. "I figure I'll go out there first, warm the crowd up and introduce you, and then you can go and say a few words about the position and how excited you are and all that. It'll be good for the town to see you up there by my side and to know they can count on the two of us to take care of them."

No one had told him about any damned speeches! Rather than complain about it, Wil swallowed hard and nodded. "Yeah, sure. No problem. Just give me a couple of minutes to finish this?"

"No problem! Come on up when you're ready, and I'll get things started." Mayor Sinclair patted him on the shoulder and retreated.

"What a pompous jackass," said Jeb, snorting into his drink. That earned him a smack from Sharon.

"Be respectful, he's the mayor!" she chided.

Bob grunted. "He's a civil servant, Sharon," he said. "Respect is one thing, but none of us should be kissing his ass. Least of all you, Wil."

Wil shrugged and finished the last of his onions. "I don't plan on kissing his ass, but I imagine he could make things pretty difficult for me. I'll play nice for now."

He got up and found an outhouse. It stank, but it was dark and the clamor of the crowd came through muffled. Perfect for getting his head on straight and taking a breath before he went out and faced the entire town. Relieved and with a cooler head on, he went up to the stage at the far end of the activity center.

It was used for almost all of Harper Valley's social functions, and often they had live music on the stage or a play or show down in the amphitheater. Tonight, it was pared down to just a bunch of food and conversation. When Mayor Sinclair saw Wil, he nodded and went onstage, behind the podium.

Sheriff Frederick was nearby and blew sharply on a whistle around his neck. The families sitting nearest to the stage, usually the richer or more powerful ones, fell quiet. And then so did the next group, and the next, until almost everyone's attention had turned to the stage.

"Good evening!" Mayor Sinclair said loudly, to be heard over the last remaining whispers from kids who didn't care what he had to say. "Thank you all for coming out here and blessing us with your delicious dishes. I tell you, I can't see myself ever leaving the valley. The food's just too damned good!"

That earned him a few polite chuckles and the odd whoop from those with an excessive amount of town spirit.

"Today I am pleased to say that after six long years of hard study and working his way up to the position of master wizard, Wilbur McKenzie is finally home!"

A polite smattering of applause, and hundreds of eyes on Wil. His entire head radiated heat. It wouldn't surprise him if he looked like a human beet. No, he couldn't say he liked the attention, but what could he do?

"I'm proud to say that we're the only town in the Le Guin Basin to have our own wizard, here to help solve problems and defend against the weather and wandering monsters. Not that we have much to worry about there," the mayor added with a laugh. "I've spent some time with Wilbur, and I gotta say, I can't think of anyone I'd rather have helping us out. In just two weeks, he's answered dozens of requests, and he's got a long, busy life ahead of him serving Harper Valley. You wanna come up and say a few words, Wilbur?"

Oh gods, no, no, he didn't, but Wil didn't see that he had a choice. Everyone watched him, some with clear doubt in their eyes, others with interest. He caught Darlene's eye and she flashed him a reassuring thumbs-up. Sighing, Wil climbed the stage and took the podium to another polite scattering of applause.

Rather than yell, he just cast a quick spell. "HELLO!" his voice boomed, louder than he intended it. The people at the nearest tables jumped with a start. "Hello, sorry about that. Hi, I'm Wil. McKenzie. Um." Gods, please let the earth swallow him up. Wil took a deep breath. "Look, I'm really bad at speaking in public, so please bear with me."

There were a couple of chuckles and one loud cheer from his mother.

That wasn't embarrassing at all. Wil pushed it out of his mind. "I'm sorry I wasn't here sooner, but I'm here now and ready to serve. When I was a little kid, my father would tell me that the greatest thing a person can do is help someone else. That kinda stuck with me. I was lucky enough to be born with a rare gift, and I believe it's my responsibility to use that gift to help others.

"And that's what I intend to do. I'm going to be the best wizard Harper Valley's ever seen. I believe that we're already pretty great, but if we all work together and help one another, we can be the best town in the basin. You all helped me. You sent me to school, you gave me the chance to discover who I could be if I put in the hard work. I promise I'll repay that, even if it takes my entire life. Thank you."

The applause came louder now. It seemed as good a sign as any that he hadn't completely messed up. He waved and released the spell on his throat, hopping down from the stage. Hard as it was, Wil managed to ignore the weight of so many stares on his way back to his family. He sat down and buried his face in his hands.

"Well," said Sarah brightly, "that could've gone worse!"

"Hush," said Bob. "You did well, Wil. Give it another month, and everyone'll love you."

"I hope so," he muttered.

CHAPTER 11

Totally Not a Date

Wil showed up to lunch early. A nervous habit, and something he'd done ever since he was a child.

Few things rankled him like being late, and after making the mayor wait over Wil's choice of fashion, he was downright paranoid about it happening again. Making the mayor wait embarrassed him; making Darlene wait would be a nightmare. It was good enough that she agreed to come see him and have lunch and—

He shook himself out of it.

Mack's Shack sat in the middle of town, not too far from the train station. Like most of Harper Valley, it had started out small and expanded unevenly throughout the years, with more sections built on haphazardly in a bizarre mishmash of different looks. "Shack" was the only reasonable word for it, though not many shacks were this big. It had been too long. Wil smiled and walked through the doors.

"Welcome, I'll be with you in a sec!" a familiar face called out.

"Hey, Candy!" Wil said. If he remembered right, Candy had about ten years on him but had been one of the few people to never hold his bookish nature against him. She was a pretty redhead just a little shorter than him now, unfailingly friendly. He always did like her. "Take your time."

She flashed him a grateful smile and glided on past to refill coffee mugs at a couple of tables. After returning the carafe to its spot, Candy met him at the entrance and finally realized who he was.

"Wilbur!" she exclaimed, looking him up and down with a big smile. "It was great seeing you last night. I meant to talk to you, but you looked super-busy."

"Kind of was," said Wil, making a face. "That's one thing I wasn't expecting and I'm going to have to get used to. How have you been? You still singing on the weekends?"

Her face dropped. "Ahh, sort of. I've been doing it a bit less, I guess. Not many places to sing around here that haven't gotten sick of me yet, you know?"

Wil shook his head. "No, I don't know. Who could get sick of you? Your voice is stunning!"

"Ha, you're sweet. You want a booth or to sit at the bar?"

Damn, what would Darlene prefer? Bar stools were nice and casual but weren't as comfortable. Booths were comfy, but would that make it seem more like a date? Because it wasn't. "Booth, I think. Darlene Johnson's meeting me here."

Candy's warm smile turned wicked. "Darlene Johnson, eh?" She grabbed a menu and led him to a booth in the back, away from most of the other customers. "She finally notice you back?"

Wil's cheeks burned red hot. "Not like that. It's not a date. We're just grabbing lunch, going to chat." He slid into the booth, forcing himself to relax.

"Well," said Candy, setting the menu in front of him, "anything I can get you for this not-date? Coffee? Tea?"

"Coffee," said Wil, smiling.

"Coming right up." Candy came back a minute later with a mug of steaming coffee along with a small bottle of milk and bowl of sugar. She flashed him another smile and left him.

Wil inhaled the rich, dark scent of the coffee. At the academy, they favored tea, but no son of a hardworking farmer could ever give up the stronger drink. He put in two teaspoons of sugar and a splash of milk, and mixed it up. He took a sip. Hot enough to scald, just how he liked it. Before he knew it, Wil had sucked it down and asked for another.

After cup three, Darlene showed up. Lightning coursed through his veins, and Wil found himself nervous and jittery, but also excited and enthusiastic. He waved his hand vigorously until she noticed him. He stood and greeted her. "Hi!"

"Hi, yourself," she said, a half-smile on her face. Closer up, Wil had reason to panic. Darlene wasn't made up for a date, he didn't think. But her short, dark hair was spiked perfectly and her blue eyes were so bright. And unlike him, she had dressed to look good instead of comfortable.

He immediately regretted his work clothes—not as junky as what he wore when on the farm but meant to remind people he was one of them. The thought of an apology crossed him and he dismissed it. This wasn't a date. They sat down together and Candy came by.

"Hey, sweetie," she said. "What can I get you to drink?"

"Coffee sounds good," said Darlene.

Candy turned to Wil, but he was ready for it. "Water now. Too much coffee."

Darlene snickered. "Is that why your eyes are darting all over the place? And here I thought I just made you nervous."

"Why would you make me nervous?" he asked, laughing nervously.

"Because you've had a crush on me since we were, like, twelve." Darlene's smile was smug, teasing, and clearly said, "Ball's in your court."

"I'll go get that coffee, then!" Candy said, suppressing laughter at the stricken look on Wil's face. She disappeared.

"Was I that obvious?" Wil groaned.

Darlene raised an eyebrow. "You used to stare at me when you thought I wasn't looking. Kinda the same way you're looking at me now, only not as self-conscious and terrified."

Wil buried his face in his hands and groaned again. If there was a way this could be more humiliating… Well, the day wasn't over yet. "So if you knew and are just teasing me, why did you come?"

Darlene shrugged pleasantly. "I dunno. I thought that if you still had a crush on me after all this time, that's kind of sweet. Or maybe stalkerish. I haven't decided yet. Either way, I figured why not give you a shot? Here I am. Impress me!"

Candy came back with a steaming mug of coffee and a fresh glass of water. She pulled out a notepad. "You two know what you want?"

Wil looked at Darlene. She smirked at him and took the lead. "Country-fried steak and eggs, scrambled. Thanks."

"I'll have the same." Wil couldn't remember the last time he had had a good, hearty, deep-fried breakfast. Candy winked at him and put their orders in.

"So," said Darlene, leaning forward and resting her face in her hands. "You've got me here. What do you want to talk about? Want to tell me all about that school you went to?"

As much as people asked about it, Wil still wasn't tired of talking about just how wonderful, if grueling, the experience had been. But maybe he talked about it too much.

It was nervous, jittery energy rather than consideration that drove him to say, "Naw, I'd rather talk about you. You said you wanted to start your own business. What would you do if you could?"

Darlene blinked at him. Then her face split into a genuine smile. "Most people don't ask me that, even when I say I don't want to work at the general store for the rest of my life. They just sorta laugh and expect me to follow in my dad's footsteps. Honestly? I don't know. It could be anything. I've been doing my best to learn the ins and outs of running the store and reading about start-ups and all the hidden costs of business. At this point, I think if I can handle the store, I can handle just about anything in the valley, or even the basin."

"What about beyond that?" Wil asked, leaning forward as well. "Think you might leave the Le Guin Basin sometime? Become a famous captain of industry?"

She burst out laughing. "No, no, my dreams ain't that big. If I don't even know what kind of business to start just yet, no way I'm going to get super-huge or rich. I don't even want to be rich. Dad does well, and people hate his ass. I just want to build something out of my hard work that's mine and pays the bills and gives me enough time to do the things I love."

"Like what?" Wil pressed.

"I dunno. Drinking cocktails on the porch, going to concerts, dancing." Her eyes lit up. "Why are you asking about me leaving the basin? Aren't you here to stay for, like, the rest of your life?"

Wil broke eye contact, shrugging. "I dunno about the rest of my life, but maybe for the next twenty years or so at least. Build up some savings, maybe experiment and see if I can contribute something else to the world."

"Oooh." Darlene sat back, spreading her arms along the edge of the cushion. "Experiments, huh? Making potions and wands and turning goats into monsters?"

"Why is everyone here worried about me messing with the goats?" Wil said with a shake of his head. "Potions, yes. Wands, maybe. I was never really good at wandcraft. Takes way too much precision and patience for me. But enchanting could be fun. As much as I can help people by showing up, if I can start making better tools and stuff for others, it could save me a lot of work."

Darlene made an inscrutable sound and considered him for what felt like forever but was probably only ten seconds. "You talk a lot about helping people. And that's nice and all, don't get me wrong, but what about what *you* want? What're you gonna do for yourself?"

Candy returned with a plate balanced on each arm. She set the identical dishes down in front of them and straightened up. "Here you are. If you need me, just wave me down!"

"Thanks, Candy," Wil said, grabbing his fork and knife. He breathed in the brunch. Hot, savory, deep-fried beef and fresh, fluffy eggs smothered in thick gravy. He cut off a piece of steak and his eyelashes fluttered closed at the explosion of taste.

"Hey, you don't get to dodge the question that easy!" Darlene teased him, grabbing her own silverware. "What about you?"

Wil swallowed and said, "I dunno. I don't really need or want much, you know? I really do want to help people. Other than that, I'm pretty simple. I want to eat good food, listen to good music, and be around good company. Two out of three is pretty good right now."

Darlene looked up from her plate, an amused gleam in her eye. "That was almost smooth."

"Almost?"

"Yeah, you're still dodging my question, you silly bastard!" Darlene speared a bite of his eggs and ate it, grinning at him.

"Right." Wil chuckled and thought about it for a second. "I want to make cool things. The type of wizard I am, complex enchantments are hard for me. But I bought this really nice rug from Mrs. Anders and I was thinking about seeing if I could make it fly. That's what I want to do, I guess. I want to be able to fly over the valley and maybe even to other towns instead of using a carriage. And if I do it well enough and can do a good enough job here in town for a while, maybe travel.

"Once you get out of here for a while, it's crazy how much bigger the world is. Bigger than anyone can ever imagine. And I'm happy to be home and I want to stay here for a while, but I don't think I could resist going back out there and seeing what I can do in the world after I've had some time to sharpen my skills and get better at dealing with people. The hardest part of the job."

Darlene took a couple of bites and chewed thoughtfully. "Flying sounds incredible," she admitted. "I don't want you to think I'm just hanging around you on account of your vast magical powers or anything, but I would *love* to go flying sometime if you can make it happen."

Maybe it was how relaxed he found himself after getting used to the idea that Darlene wanted to be there, maybe it was the coffee making his mouth faster than his brain, but he couldn't help himself. "I'd be happy to take you once I get it working. Maybe that can be a real date."

"Real date?" Darlene smiled wickedly. "I thought this was a real date. You just toying with my heart, Wil?"

"What? No, I'm..." he trailed off when she started laughing. His cheeks burned, but it wasn't as embarrassing this time. "This was totally not a date. Just treating an old-school friend to lunch. Why? Would you be interested in a date?"

She smiled, and he couldn't for the life of him read what was behind it. "Well, I'm not seeing anyone and you seem sweet enough. Like a big puppy trying to be a good boy."

Okay, maybe just a little embarrassed. "Gee," he said, "thanks."

"No problem! So, yes, I'd be interested in a date." She took another bite, grinning at him. "But I've got a question. If this isn't a date, does that mean I can't get dessert?"

"Sorry, those are dates only," Wil said with a smile of his own.

"Alright." Darlene nodded. "Then I guess I have no choice. This is a decent first date, and I demand a milkshake after."

"Well, I guess I gotta, then." Wil couldn't find it in himself to complain.

CHAPTER 12

A Day Off

After two weeks of working every day, Wil finally realized he desperately needed a break. It hadn't been so bad at first. The people of Harper Valley worked hard, so that meant Wil had to work at least as hard. He'd wake up, grab breakfast, then consult the work orders and plot out his day before carrying it out. Some days he even finished all of his tasks before the sun set and his family had dinner. Others…well, a lot of work carried over to the next day.

It came to a head one night when he arrived late for dinner and collapsed into his seat at the table. A plate full of food waited for him, but everyone else had finished.

"Another rough day?" his father asked. Wil could only groan. "It's good to see you givin' your all, boy, but maybe take a day."

"Yeah!" Sharon agreed. "You're no good to anyone if you're too tired to take care of yourself."

"But people need me," Wil protested.

"Where was this kind of hard work *before* you went to that school?" Jeb snarked, but his comments were fewer and farther between as people ignored him and he realized no one else had the same problem with Wil.

Even Sarah backed up their parents, sort of, by saying, "If you work yourself to death I'm taking your room."

So that decided it. That night, Wil relaxed on the porch with his father and the pipe, and in the morning, he slept in. When he got up, everyone had already eaten, but a covered plate of pancakes waited for him. He heated them up with magic and ate them, trying to think of how to spend his unexpected free day. It would have to be something restful, something relaxing, something to reinvigorate him for work the next day.

Wil found himself in the fields, helping Jeb harvest wheat. His older brother approached things methodically, swinging his scythe line by line before gathering up the fallen stalks, bundling them up, and sticking them on the cart. Meanwhile, Wil picked the next field over and stood in the center. He took a deep breath and extended his senses. He breathed in and out for a minute, gathering up some power. He released it in a low wave of sharpened force. A ring making up over half the field fell to the ground.

"The hell are you doing?" Jeb shouted. He jogged over, looking at the destruction with disgust in his eyes. "Why did you do that?"

"Just trying to help!" Wil said brightly, clapping his hands and rubbing them together. "You see how fast I can clear the field? I haven't been doing nearly enough for the family, so I thought I'd—"

"I was trying something with this field," Jeb said. "Each row had a different mix of fertilizer. I was going to measure up each line against each other. Now look at it!" He tore his gloves off and stuffed them in his pockets. Pulling at his hair, he groaned, the sound turning into a growl.

"I'm sorry," Wil blurted. "I didn't know. I was just trying to help. Since when do we do that?"

"Since three years ago," Jeb snarled. Wil flinched, which seemed to break through to Jeb. His older brother took a deep breath and shrugged. "It's fine. It's done. Now, please stop helping me."

More than anything, Wil wanted to ask Jeb how long he'd stay mad. Was this ever going to end, or did the extra two years at school and no visits mean a permanent rift between them? Wil hated how much it affected his brother, and he couldn't bring himself to blame him for his anger.

"You got it," said Wil, slinking back toward the house.

His next attempt at finding something to do involved bugging Sarah as she drew in the kitchen while Sharon started assembling sandwiches and homemade potato wedges for lunch. Sarah sat hunched over her drawing as usual, blond hair forming a curtain around it. Wil looked at the drawing upside down.

"Hey, nice dragon," he said.

"Mm."

Sarah was always hot and cold; Wil could never predict her moods. Seemed like this wasn't the best time to bother her. So, of course, as her older brother, he had to. Bit by bit she connected the lines on a really good if inaccurate dragon.

"You know dragons don't have six legs *and* wings, right?" he teased.

"Oh? And how many dragons have you seen?" Sarah shot back at him without looking up from her drawing.

"My favorite professor had a dragon skull hanging above his desk," said Wil.

"So, none, then."

Undeterred, Wil waited until she was mostly finished with the drawing before he had a bit of fun with her. Illusions were often considered a less useful field to go into, but Wil loved them. A whisper of power and the dragon on Sarah's page came to life, crawling off the paper and across the table. It let out a roar and a blast of two-dimensional fire over the white tabletop.

"Stop it!" Sarah glared at him. "I worked really hard on that. I don't need you showing off just because you can." She got up and stormed off upstairs.

Wil collapsed back in his chair, frowning. Sharon came over with his sandwich and a tall glass of lemonade. "I didn't mean to make her mad," he told her. "First Jeb, now Sarah. I'm making a mess of everything."

Sharon just shrugged. "Wasn't today supposed to be your day off? Why not spend it lazing around, maybe read one of those books you love."

Wil took hold of the big roll filled with ham and turkey and bit into it. Sandwiches never tasted this good when he made them. Moms could make sandwiches like no one else. "I'm restless," he said with a full mouth. "Do you need help with anything?"

"Nope. I need you to relax and stay out of my hair for a bit, how's that?" She laughed and went back to the counter for the other sandwiches, which she balanced along with two lemonades in her grasp. "Why don't you walk around town, maybe see Darlene? Or do something for yourself. Didn't you say you couldn't wait to do experiments once your house is ready? Why not do one here?"

There was an idea. "Yeah," he said, "okay. Thanks, Ma."

"Anytime."

After lunch, Wil headed to the garage with a bag of magical tools. Waiting for him was the big rug he bought. Making it fly wouldn't be the hardest thing in the world. He'd seen it done at the academy with other things like brooms, and even an entire ship, so there was no reason it couldn't work for a simple rug. There were plenty of stories about wizards on the other continent using them, at least. If nothing else, having a flying carpet would make traveling across the valley easier and faster.

The rug had been made for someone's living room and took up a good chunk of the garage's available floor space. He had to pull a couple things off it before he got to work, but it remained in good condition. It was eight feet by eight feet with a simple border of black geometric shapes and big flowers on the corners, and a lion and a tiger roaring at each other in the middle. Half the charm was just how ugly it was. Wil sat down in the center of it.

Making it rise into the air was easy. All Wil had to do was push against the ground from beneath the rug itself. He rose three feet into the air, wavering as the amount of force changed. The cloth rippled along the edges. It worked but wasn't stable, and wouldn't be. The trick wasn't to constantly push against the ground so much as make it so the carpet stored several spells in order to do it for him, with the ability to alter how much push or pull it had at any given time. More than anything, enchanting was a massive headache.

If nothing else, it killed time. Wil spent the next hour getting a feel for the material and using his own magic to make it move and see how it felt. The two hours after that were spent with his head in one of his schoolbooks on enchanting, giving himself a refresher on all the most up-to-date methods and different possibilities. Crystals or a wooden framework beneath it were out of the question. He ended up deciding on rune thread, but that would get expensive.

Sharon came out before too long with another glass of lemonade and left after watching him float for a couple of minutes. She was the only one to come into the garage while he worked. Eventually, Wil came to the conclusion that he couldn't do much about it that day. It'd take a bunch of money and ordering out for supplies, but before the summer was out, he'd have a working flying carpet, dammit!

Just as he called it quits, Wil heard a knock at the door. At first, he didn't think anything of it, until his stomach twisted and flipped. It threw him for a loop—a familiar but new sensation. Seconds before the garage door opened, he recognized it as the feeling he got on the train before the bandits' ambush. He looked at his mother. She wasn't alone. Next to her was Mrs. Lane, red-eyed from crying.

"Wil! Mr. McKenzie!" she started. Oh boy, that felt weird.

"Wil is fine," he said, stepping forward. "What's wrong? How can I help you?"

Mrs. Lane was in her mid-thirties and lived on the north side of the valley, right between the Stellan River and Harper Forest. She wrung her hands together and said, "My kids, they were playing up in the forest. Jack came home alone after getting separated from the others. Sally and Ralph are still out there."

His stomach did another flip. As far as Wil knew, that meant danger of some kind. At the very least, it filled him with a sense of urgency he couldn't ignore. "I'm on it. Get back home and I'll meet up with you as fast as I can."

Mrs. Lane nodded, the motion so hurried it made her bun wobble. "Jimmy's organizing a search party right now. I just thought that maybe you could...you know."

He did know, and Wil couldn't help but feel a little good that his skills were finally recognized, even as guilt hit him for the thought. "I can. We'll get your kids home safely, Mrs. Lane. I promise."

Tears filled her eyes again. She nodded and rushed out of the house.

Sharon looked at him and said, "We should probably get your father and brother for this too."

"I'll go get them."

Wil went outside. Far in the distance, his father and brother were tiny specs working different fields. Walking would take too much time, he decided. He held his hand up and a blindingly bright light launched up into the air. Once it made it about a hundred feet up it detonated in a searing flash and crackle of noise. They ran to the house.

Jeb made it there first. "What's going on?" he demanded, wiping sweat from his brow.

"The Lane family's lost their kids up in the forest," Wil said. "They're organizing a search party right now, but I know a way to find them. I'm going to need your help. Everyone's help."

For once, Jeb didn't give him any crap. He just nodded. "You got it. I'll tell Dad, and you do…whatever it is you need to do."

A look of understanding passed between them. Wil liked to think that Jeb, despite his resentment, understood this was a task Wil could do better than anyone. But he couldn't do it alone. They were going to need some tools, some simple enchantments, and a minor ritual. Thoughts raced through Wil's head as he came up with a plan. He rushed to his bag in the garage and pulled out five simple wooden wands. He stuck them in his pocket and returned.

His family waited for him in the living room.

"C'mon," said Wil. "I'll tell you the plan on the way."

As one, they followed his lead.

CHAPTER 13

Lost and Found

The search was already underway when the McKenzie family arrived at the Lane residence. Wil supposed they were late, and it was his fault. His parents had understood he needed time to prepare, but both Jeb and Sarah grew impatient with him and didn't understand why he needed time to carve a bunch of weird lines into a bunch of sticks. Even after telling them they were magic wands, it still didn't really register for them how or why they would be useful, and Wil was too focused to explain much.

The house crawled with friends and neighbors coming up to the main house to coordinate with the family and take on the forest in groups. The McKenzie family strode up to the house together, Wil and Jeb carrying Wil's bags. Mrs. Lane tapped her husband on the shoulder and pointed to them as they came up.

"Mr. Lane, Mrs. Lane," said Wil, getting right into it. "I can find your children, but I'm going to need something from you first."

Mr. Lane scoffed. "Are you extorting us? While our children are missing? Why, I ought to—"

"For Pete's sake, Jimmy, listen to yourself," Bob piped up with a scowl. "Why would you think he'd be out to get you? You know us better than that."

Jimmy had the good grace to look ashamed. His eyes slid back over to Wil, who shrugged. At this point he understood and was used to it, but it still stung. "I get that people don't trust me, but I can help. I can find your kids with magic but I need something for the spell. Nothing more."

Mrs. Lane nodded vigorously. "Anything you need, Wil. Please, just get them back."

Wil took a deep breath, knowing how his request would sound. "I'll need a piece of clothing for each of them, something they've worn a million times and have a connection to."

"Right, no problem," said Mrs. Lane.

"Aaand I'm going to need a few drops of your blood."

Silence, then Mr. Lane barked out, "Are you out of your damned mind? What do you need her blood for?"

To Wil's surprise, it was Jeb who spoke up in his defense. "Do you want us to find your kids or not?" he demanded. Gesturing at Wil he said, "This is your best chance for finding them before they get lost and some critter eats them. You really going to stand here and argue or are you going to do as he asks?"

Sarah decided to be helpful and added, "He's too much of a dork to do anything mean using your blood. Seriously."

The Lanes traded a look. Mr. Lane nodded and disappeared inside the house. Mrs. Lane held out her arm, making a face.

"If you need my blood, then take as much of it as you need! Anything to get my kids home safe."

Wil smiled. "I appreciate that, but I'll only need a few drops. You've got nothing to fear. We've got this." He tried to be as soothing as possible. This couldn't be an easy time for them, and the unknown quality of magic didn't help things. He might even have made it worse when he rummaged through his bag and brought out an athame. Mrs. Lane gasped at the ritual blade, but she set her jaw and thrust her arm out again.

"This won't hurt at all," said Wil as he pressed the blade against the crook of her arm.

"I'm a parent, Wil," Mrs. Lane said with a crooked smile. "I know that lie."

If nothing else, Wil tried to make it painless. Just a quick little dip of the grooved bone blade opened Mrs. Lane's skin with little more than a sharp intake of breath. He collected the blood he needed and dripped them over the four magic wands he had carved and brought with them. Even without him opening his senses further, the power thrummed off the runes carved into the wood. The introduction of blood brought them to life.

Mr. Lane came back outside to find his wife clutching her arm and Wil holding a dagger. Fear, agony, and even rage crossed his face but a quick shake of her head stopped him. The farmer suppressed his growl and thrust the children's clothes over. A shirt and a little dress. Jeb took them from him, grunting defensively.

Wil switched out knives, cutting off strips of cloth from each of the clothes and tying them to the wands. He closed his eyes, feeling the connection between runed wood, blood, and now the possessions of the children. The power thrummed without him, and it took very little for him to push a little bit of his own magic to lock them all together and anchor a spell to the wands. A spell with one command: *search*.

"Okay, it's done," said Wil. He let out a deep breath and handed the remainder of the clothes back to Mr. Lane. Then he passed out the wands to his family, everyone but his mother, who had taken it upon herself to step outside and direct newcomers over to where the sheriff passed out lanterns.

Jeb jerked uncomfortably when the wand touched his hand. "The hell is this?" he said, holding on tight as it seemed to want to leap out of his hand. "It's pulling on me!"

Wil couldn't help but smile like the nerd he was. "That's the spell. It'll lead us directly to the kids if we follow them. It'll home in on them using the blood and clothes as a guide. We've got plenty of people to spread out and search the mountains, but we'd better group up with one wand per group, just in case they ran into trouble. Sound good?"

All around him, people stared. Sarah took a wand from him and held it up. The tip dipped and aimed across the river and through the forest up to the mountain. "Dibs on a wand. Who wants to be in my group?"

They split up into different groups. Bob went with Sarah and took Sharon with them. Mr. Lane took his son Jack and two of their nearest neighbors with him. One wand went to the sheriff, who took it with a suspicious grimace, but he and Deputy Duran headed to the mountain together. It left Wil and Jeb with the last wand, still in Jeb's hand.

"I guess it's just us then," said Wil. "You want to hold the wand?"

Jeb made a face. "Is it going to keep pulling me the entire time?"

"Probably."

"Heh. Neat. Let's go, then."

Jeb took one of the remaining lanterns and together they crossed the river, heading up along with the rest of the search parties. Wil stayed in step with him, holding a glowing ball of light that illuminated everything within fifty feet or so. It made Jeb side-eye him, but it gave off way more light than the lantern. They reached the outskirts of the forest and made the trek upward.

Before long, the incline grew steep as the path led them through the forest. They remained mostly quiet as they walked, and Wil was grateful for it. A few weeks into being home and Jeb had never been this accepting or supportive. That saying nothing at all was an improvement stung a little, but Wil couldn't bring himself to care too much. For a little while, at least, he had his big brother back.

If it hadn't been for the missing children and sense of urgency, it could have been fun. Just Wil and his brother, walking through the forest and climbing higher and higher. They were just over the mountains, which cast them in darkness save for the light they brought with them. As they followed the trail around a fallen log, Wil found himself grinning.

"What's got you in such a good mood?" Jeb asked after a few minutes of silence. "It's annoying."

"Nothing," said Wil, still smiling. "Remember when we used to go up in the woods? We never got lost like this."

Jeb snickered. "Not for lack of trying. I tried to lose you in the woods a few times, but Sarah would start crying and shouting, and I'd end up coming back. Longest I ever made it was, like, fifteen minutes before I got tired of the whining and had to come get you."

Wil's smile faded. "Did you hate me back then, too, and I just didn't notice?"

"Hate you?" Jeb faced him, eyes narrowing. His features softened and he shook his head. "I don't hate you, Wil. Just think you're a bit of a bastard, and too big for your britches. You could stand a good couple smacks upside the head, but hate? Naw. You're not worth it."

He said it so casually, Wil stopped in his tracks. It took a few seconds for Jeb to notice and turn around. He sighed, and said, "What now?"

"What happened, Jeb?" Wil asked, hating how broken up he sounded. "I'm sorry I didn't come home. I'll be sorry about it for the rest of my life. I'm sorry it hurt you so bad, but—"

"Me? Hurt *me* so bad?" Jeb let out a harsh, fake laugh. "I don't give a damn, Wil. Doesn't hurt me at all. Now, Ma and Dad? They were hurt. And that's why I can't forgive you. You broke their hearts for six years, and then you come home and say, 'Oh sorry, my schooling was more important,' and act like they should understand. I can't believe they think you're the smart one."

He held up the wand and let it pull itself nearly out of his grasp. "C'mon, I think we're getting close. This thing is pulling pretty hard now." He continued in that direction.

Wil stayed a few seconds, heart pounding. He didn't think it would be this bad. How could his brother think so little of him, when he thought the world of Jeb?

Wil jogged to catch up, light from his magical orb bouncing with the movement. He turned around a tree and nearly bumped into a stopped Jeb. The wand lay flat in his hand, pointing to a tree branch a few feet from the ground.

A scrap of bloody clothing hung from the edge of the branch. Just a little torn piece, stained through with blood. Jeb swallowed hard. "It's pointing here, but..."

Wil took the wand from him, trying to calm himself down as well. One of them had to keep a level head. "It doesn't mean anything, necessarily," he said. Stepping around the branch, the wand spun around to keep pointing at the blood. "We can use this," he said.

"How?" Jeb asked, looking around, as if the Lane child missing a piece of clothing would be right around the corner waiting for them.

Rather than answer, Wil plucked the scrap of bloody cloth from the branch and wrapped it around the tip of the wand, tying it off. "We now have a better source to track," he said, holding the wand up. It pointed farther up the mountain. "C'mon, they could be in danger!"

He took off running, Jeb just a few feet behind him. They wound their way around trees and logs and brush, climbing ever higher up the mountain. He ran out of wind before Jeb did, slowing down after just a couple of minutes. Jeb snatched the wand from him.

"What's wrong, wizard? Spend too much time in classrooms and not enough staying fit?" Past the edge, there was a playfulness underneath the smile. He put on a burst of speed, leaving Wil behind as he continued on. Wil followed the flickering light more than anything as his brother put more distance between them.

The trees grew thicker and thicker the deeper they went, and soon Wil had to brush branches out of his face and leap over enormous roots. A scream pierced the night, and that gave him the second wind he needed to keep going. He went around a particularly enormous tree and nearly crashed right into Jeb, who stopped and hid behind the tree.

"What're you do—"

"Shh!" Jeb hushed him fiercely. He motioned for Wil to get rid of his ball of light, then pointed around the tree. Wil did as he was told and then peeked out.

The good news was, they found the children alive and in relatively good condition.

The bad news was, they were up a tree and a massive Nullbear sat at the base, a demonic growl rising in its maw at the sight of an easy meal.

"Shit," Jeb groaned. "Now what?" Angry as he may have been before, he turned to Wil for the answer.

Wil swallowed. "I...I got this." He hoped.

CHAPTER 14

Bear-Faced Aggression

I'll distract it, you go for the kids," Wil said, already regretting his words.

Jeb looked at him like he was crazy. "You better be careful, because if you get yourself killed, Ma's gonna blame me."

Wil flashed him what he hoped was a confident smile. "You'd deserve it after the way you've been lately, jerk."

"Seriously?" Jeb cycled through annoyed and impressed before he growled, shaking his head. "Fine. Give me some time to get into position, and then…do your thing, I guess."

As Jeb skulked to the side, keeping his head low, Wil peeked around the tree. Even knowing it was there did nothing to stifle the raw fear the Nullbear instilled in him. On all fours, it stood six feet tall and would be a good fifteen feet if it reared up. Its fur was a shaggy, reddish brown, and its two front paws were thick and topped with bone and huge claws capable of deflecting magic or cutting through enchantments. Nullbears were rare, dangerous, and almost always irritable.

Ralph and Sally were about twenty feet up on a solid branch, holding on to each other for dear life. Tears streamed down their faces as they screamed in fear of the nearby predator.

Unfortunately for them, that just attracted the Nullbear's attention. It tilted its head up at them, inhaling through two huge nostrils, huffing in their scent. A low, rumbling growl Wil could feel in his bones even from a dozen yards away made him want to scream too. He looked to the side, trying to catch sight of Jeb. Nothing yet.

The Nullbear rose on its hind legs, its massive head nearly as big as each of the children. It sniffed again and licked its chops. Wil cursed under his breath and acted.

"Hey, assface, over here!" Wil cried out, jumping out from behind the tree and waving his hands around wildly. The beast began to turn, but it wasn't fast enough for his tastes. He launched a flash of exploding light at the Nullbear's head. Right as it should've detonated, it crackled and fizzled out instead. A lower, deeper growl sounded from the bear.

Wil swallowed hard. Looking up at the towering monster, he was reminded of just how small he was, and how utterly screwed he could be. Even at the best of times, Wil wasn't great at combat magic, let alone against a beast famous for being able to prey on other magical creatures, including wizards. Hell, there weren't many other options.

"Okay, how about this?" Wil formed balls of unstable energy and threw them at the beast one after the other. The first one hit it in the snout and detonated, making it blink and recoil. The next two it swatted out of the air with its famous anti-magic boned braces. It roared in anger, and Wil very nearly wet himself.

He followed his instincts and took off running right as the Nullbear launched itself forward, colliding with the even bigger tree Wil had been hiding behind. It connected with the wood, making it creak dangerously. One claw the size of Wil's entire body swiped at him, coming up short by less than a foot.

Wil stumbled but caught himself before he fell. He held up his hands and went for the second most basic spell. Flames shot out of his hands in a cone, wrapping around the Nullbear's claws and fading out before it could do any damage. The great bone braces glowed with absorbed magic. The beast charged forward, knocking down the smaller tree in its way. Wil ran out of sheer reflex, only belatedly realizing he was going down a path with no trees. The Nullbear leaped again just as Wil ducked sideways, back into the tree line.

Wil vaulted over a fallen log as he ran, trying to keep as many trees as possible between him and his pursuer. Seconds later, the bear smashed through that log, slowed but not stopped as it tore down several trees in its rampage.

Wil circled around, heart pounding, brain racing. He could think only of his fear. Planning, goals—all of that was forgotten; all he could focus on was running away from the monster that would devour him the second it got close enough to do so. He didn't even realize he'd led it back to the clearing where the children were.

Jeb was halfway up the tree, helping Sally get down. Ralph stood on the ground, pointing at the Nullbear and screaming again. Wil cursed and Jeb shot him a panicked and yet still somehow dirty look and motioned for him to go. He nodded.

Wil threw another volatile missile at the tree nearest the Nullbear, detonating it early and sending chunks of bark into its eyes. It bellowed with pure rage, blinking violently and running in a straight line. Wil got out of the way as it crashed headfirst into a tree. The bear's body kept going for a few seconds before it caught up with the knock on its head and crashed to the ground with an earth-rumbling tremor.

"Oh my gods, I think they're up there!" a voice called out. The other search parties' wands had them up here as well, finally. A dozen faces came through the trees in the clearing, where Wil stood next to the fallen Nullbear.

"Get back!" Wil called, motioning with his hands. Jeb managed to get Sally down and she and Ralph ran out of the clearing and into the arms of their parents.

The Lanes gathered for a big, smothering group hug, seemingly oblivious to the fact they were still very much in danger. Wil frantically looked at the rescue party and the Nullbear, now climbing to its feet in a daze. It blinked unsteady, cluttered eyes in Wil's direction. He held very still until it inhaled deeply and a fresh growl spilled from its slavering lips.

"Run!" he shouted, ready to do the same himself. The Nullbear swiped at him. Wil ducked out of the way, but not in time. The claw caught him in its massive soft pad, sending him careening into a tree. It was like being hit with a cushioned battering ram and then hitting a wall. His entire body jolted with a white flash of pain as his wrist creaked on landing.

Wil groaned as he fought to get to his feet. The bear reared up in front of him. There was no escape now, no time to get out of the way when it launched itself at him. He had one idea, and it was more out of desperation than anything else.

"Cover your ears!" he shouted. Without ensuring anyone did or even doing it himself, Wil licked his lips and blew, focusing his magic. The shrill whistle that emerged was louder and higher than anything he could produce without magic. The sound of it made his eyes water and the world grow fuzzy on the edges.

But it worked. The Nullbear recoiled, falling ass over ears as the sound hit its much larger, more sensitive ears. Wil cut the whistle off. The beast looked around wildly. Wil aimed another, even sharper blast of sound at the bear's face. It might have been able to swat away his fire and volatile missiles, but it couldn't do anything against an illusory sound.

Wil climbed to his feet, cradling his arm against his body. He tried to ignore the pain, from his wrist and his ears, and adrenaline did the trick, keeping him on shaky feet for a few seconds longer. He blew one last, long blast, so high-pitched it made him want to stop and sob.

The beast roared in pain and took off in the other direction, crashing through the trees and farther up the mountain. Wil kept the sound up for another few seconds before dropping it. A second later, he fell to his knees, shaking violently. He had nothing left.

"Wil!" he dimly heard behind him. The voice was almost as loud as his heartbeat, going a mile a minute.

Jeb crashed into him a second later, making Wil groan and clutch his battered wrist tighter to himself. His older brother pulled him into a crushing hug that would've been welcome any other time.

"You crazy, brave bastard!" Jeb cried, laughing. He helped Wil to his feet and dragged him back to the rescue party, letting him take his time as his rubbery legs fought to keep him steady.

His mother and father greeted him first, grabbing him and Jeb into a tight hug. Sharon started fussing over him immediately. He heard the words but registered none of them. He did hear his dad pull his mom away and then usher him down the mountain.

The rest of the trip passed by in a flash. Wil found himself too tired, too shocked, and too stressed to remember much of it. When they plopped him down in a chair in front of the Lanes' house, he was beyond grateful and settled in with a loud groan. Everything hurt now.

"Awright, out of the way. Out of the way! How're you feeling, Wil?" a familiar voice asked him.

Wil focused his eyes, swallowing hard. The shakes had only gotten worse, as did his nervous sweats. He held his wrist up to whom he now recognized as Doc Hawkins. The silver-haired doctor took his wrist and carefully turned it around.

"This might sting a little," said Doc Hawkins as he twisted it. Wil clamped down on the cry of pain, suppressing the worst of it. "I know, I know," the doctor clucked kindly as he turned it around. Wil bit his lip and stayed silent as Doc Hawkins squeezed the area. Then he released it and nodded.

"Just a sprain," he said, smiling. He pushed his glasses up on his nose and continued, "We'll wrap it up. You should avoid straining yourself for about a week, and then you'll be good as new. Unless you're good at healing spells, I guess." He didn't sound too confident about the idea of magic doing his job for him.

Wil shook his head. "No, I'm garbage at medical spells. Crap, I've got a lot of work ahead of me still. I can't afford to take a week off!"

Doc Hawkins chuckled. "After what you just did, I'm pretty sure no one in town could give you any guff for it. Relax and take it easy. Doctor's orders. Now, let's get you wrapped up."

It didn't take long for Doc Hawkins to splint and wrap up his arm tight as could be, and then give him a couple of painkillers he had on him. Wil washed them down and then wandered out to the Lanes' backyard, where the rescue parties had gathered and returned lanterns. Now that the danger was over, it had become a small party.

The conversation faded to nothing as soon as he staggered out. He blinked, uncomfortably aware of the dozens of people watching him. Then Mrs. Lane came up and hugged him tightly, crying once more. Wil awkwardly put his good arm around her.

"Gods, thank you so much, Wil," she said, sounding on the edge of losing it again. "You saved my babies!"

"No problem," said Wil, awkwardly patting her back. "Just part of the job, right? I'm just glad we were able to find them in time. That Nullbear was really close to—" He realized his mistake too late, as she broke off into a sob and hugged him even tighter.

"It's okay now, Mary," Mr. Lane said, mercifully pulling his wife away. He shot Wil a grateful look, complete with The Nod of respect. Wil thought that'd be the end of it, until Mr. Lane spoke up again. "Let's all hear it for Wil McKenzie!" he shouted.

All around, their backyard voices rose in unison, cheering him on, some whistling and screaming raucously. Wil looked around like a panicked animal, surprised and almost confused by the reaction before he allowed himself to relax. He caught the eyes of his parents, who couldn't have looked prouder.

Even Jeb and Sarah applauded and looked happy for him. That alone made it worth it. Wil raised his injured hand and waved, soaking in honest praise for the first time since he had returned. It felt good.

CHAPTER 15

Hero for a Day

Wil hadn't intended to take more than one day off, and now he faced the prospect of taking the better part of a week easy. When he woke up the next day, the first thing that greeted him was a dull, throbbing pain in his wrist that got worse if he tried to move his arm. As much as he wanted to get back to work, the pain of just getting dressed told him to take a break.

He'd slept in and missed breakfast, so Wil ventured out into Harper Valley for the day, intending to grab a bite to eat and just not stay cooped up as he recovered from dealing with the Nullbear.

The first thing he did was head to the diner for a bite to eat. Candy greeted him warmly. He found breakfast a little harder to eat than normal, but the coffee was as good as ever and the food tasted great. Nothing seemed different, until he went to pay for his meal.

"Oh, that's not necessary," said Candy, pushing his money back to him. "It's already been taken care of."

It took Wil a few seconds to register what she meant. "It is? Why? It's not because of last night, is it?" Wil's cheeks bloomed red.

Candy shrugged, flipping a strand of red hair behind her ear. "Probably! All I know is Harry over there paid for your breakfast. Didn't tip, though, so if you wanna do that…"

Wil took almost all of his money back, leaving a ten on the table. "He didn't have to do that. Chances are I make more money, anyway. Where is he?"

Candy pointed to an average-looking man with slicked-back black hair and fairly nice clothes. Wil thanked her and made his way over to the man. He stopped a couple of feet away. Harry noticed him immediately and beamed at him as if they were old friends.

"Hi," Wil said awkwardly. "Did you pay for my breakfast?"

"Sure did!" Harry said brightly. "Those were my niblings you saved last night. If anything had happened to them, Jimmy and Mary would've been destroyed, and so would I. It's the least I could do!"

Wil had no idea how to feel about it. On the one hand, it was nice to finally receive a bit of recognition for his hard work and passion for helping. On the other, getting gifts felt weird and wrong. His mother's voice whispered in his head, telling him to mind his manners and just deal with it. "I appreciate it, but I was just doing my job, you know?"

"Maybe, but I'm still thankful." Harry offered his hand, switching to his left when he realized Wil wouldn't be able to shake it easily. "If you ever find yourself in legal trouble, you come to me and I'll take care of you, okay? Harry Ansem."

"Sounds good," said Wil, shaking his hand. "Thanks. Wil McKenzie, obviously."

He left the diner puzzled and a little embarrassed. After a few weeks of being the town handyman and gofer, getting a measure of respect didn't feel right. He tried to put it out of his mind and just walked along the road, heading toward the town square to browse the shops for a while.

If any part of Harper Valley stayed busy, it was the town square. That's what they called it, at least, but over the past couple of decades, it had become a busier, more urban-looking area compared to the rest of the valley. The streets were well cobbled and kept, and no carts or carriages were allowed through, only foot traffic. It kept things feeling homey and like a community instead of just a bunch of buildings to pass by.

There, his strange day continued as he walked past people staring at dresses in Elizabeth's Wardrobe. A few young women in their late teens or early twenties tore their attention away from the intricate gowns in the display to stare at him as he passed. Whispers followed him, making his skin crawl. It was almost as bad as the feeling of their eyes on him.

"Hey, Wil!" said an older gent with a sun-beaten face and a cap on, inclining his head respectfully.

"Mr. Wizard, want a frozen treat?" Olly the ice cream vendor called out. Wil did, but he only smiled and waved, walking a bit faster.

"Mr. McKenzie!" a little kid said. Wil wanted to scream. He forced a smile and all but ran directly to the general store, one of the oldest and largest buildings in the region. Jonjon's business was essential to the community, and for all basic needs and necessities, it was hard to find a better source or better prices. It wasn't empty, but at least there was a familiar face.

Darlene stood at the counter, ringing stuff up on their heavy metal register and making change so fast Wil doubted she had to think about the quick math as she did it. A line waited in the front, but the moment Darlene saw Wil, her eyes lit up. She finished with her current customer and then put a "Be Right Back" sign up on the counter.

A groan rose among the people in line. The register to the right was open, but the cashier had white hair and trembling hands and moved about as fast as molasses. Mrs. Beckitt had worked there as long as Wil had been alive, and she worked at the same speed now as she had when he was a child.

Darlene greeted him with a punch on his arm. "Hey there, 'hero.' Enjoying the attention?"

Wil shook his head vehemently. "No, not at all. It's weird!"

She smiled, shaking her head. "Wanna grab a drink? I could use a break."

They grabbed a couple of bottles of fruity soda and headed into the back room, where there was a table and chairs, a couch, and a radio warbling some old-timey big-band music. Darlene sat at the table, popping the top off her orange soda and taking a long drink, wincing at the burn of the carbonation. Wil joined her, clinking his bottle of grape soda against hers.

"So what's weird, then, Wil?" Darlene asked.

"Everyone's staring at me more than usual, and some guy paid for my breakfast," Wil complained. "People I don't know are greeting me and being nice."

"The horror!" Darlene smirked.

Wil slumped in his seat. "Okay, when you put it like that, of course I sound silly!"

Darlene took another sip, not hiding her mirth. "You mean when you're being silly you sound silly? Go figure. Everyone's talking and you're a hero. You really going to tell me you're not enjoying it at all?"

Wil shrugged wildly. "I don't know! When I was young, either I was invisible or people laughed at me for being bookish and quiet. And then when I got back, it was mostly suspicion, you know? And now I don't know what to think. It hasn't been too ridiculous, but it's...I'm not used to it."

"Well, tell you what, Wil. Next time you have a chance to save a couple of children from a rampaging monster, I'll tell you to just let them die so you don't have to deal with this." Darlene's smile couldn't get any bigger if she tried.

Wil squirmed, grabbing his soda. "You have a hell of a way of putting things into perspective," he said, drinking. "Thanks."

"Anytime," she chirped. "Honestly, I'm really happy for you. Seems like you needed a win after the way people were giving you crap. I know what you told me, but you should've heard the things people were saying about you beforehand."

Oh no. "What were they saying?" Wil asked in a voice just above a whisper.

Darlene waved him off. "Not important. What's important is they've turned around, and maybe things are going to get better. I mean, you fought off a Nullbear, didn't you? They aren't exaggerating that any, are they?"

"'Fought' is a strong word," he said. "Mostly I distracted it while Jeb got to the kids, and I led it around on a little chase. Got a bit banged up before I managed to scare it off, but I didn't fight anything. I mostly blundered around and got lucky. It could've been *so* much worse."

That just made Darlene shake her head. "Do you think anyone else could've handled the bear on their own? Anyone in town?"

Once again, Wil's face heated up. "Feels egotistical to say no." He sulked. "But probably not. Would've taken the entire militia to deal with it and there probably would've been a loss or two. But the Nullbear lived and might still be up there for all we know. The danger's still there."

Darlene raised an eyebrow at him. He sighed and held his hands up in surrender. "Okay, fine. Thanks, Darlene," he added with a smile.

"Anytime," she said again. "Always happy to keep your ego in the sweet spot. If your head gets too big, I promise to shrink it. Besides, you're getting me out of work. For a few minutes at least. We'll call it even today, but next time, you owe me more dessert."

Wil left the general store feeling a lot better about the whole thing. Out on the streets, people still greeted him, but this time Wil waved and tried to be as friendly as possible. All it took was ignoring the natural suspicion others' interest raised and a willingness to embrace the fact that maybe he had done something good for the community. Even if he wished people would focus on the kids' safety rather than his part in it.

He spent the better part of the morning just walking around, enjoying the summer heat and the break from work, after all. More than anything, he treasured not just staying at home and sleeping in his spare time. Harper Valley was a beautiful place with good people. Now that he was no longer a shy teen, he had no reason to be a hermit or avoid enjoying himself in public.

Eventually, Wil thought about heading home or maybe grabbing lunch somewhere, when he made eye contact with Sheriff Frederick, who made a beeline for him.

"McKenzie!" the sheriff called out from twenty feet away, as if worried Wil would bolt upon seeing him. If he were honest, the thought had occurred to Wil. "The mayor wants to talk to you."

"The mayor?" Inside, Wil groaned. He had an idea of how it would go and he wanted no part of it. "What does he want?"

"Well, you'd better go find out then, shouldn't you?" Sheriff Frederick scowled at him, watery eyes boring into him.

"Right. Thanks, Sheriff," said Wil, backing up from him. Briefly, he considered grabbing lunch first, but maybe it was better to get this over with. He went straight for the town hall, where the secretary waved him through with the same impatient look on her face as last time. Today he wasn't even late for anything!

"Wilbur McKenzie." Mayor Sinclair beamed, shaking his injured hand vigorously. Ten seconds in and Wil was already exhausted and wanted to be gone.

"Mr. Mayor," he said, biting back a wince of pain and pulling his splinted hand back. "How can I help you today? I'll get back on those work orders as soon as my arm gets better, I promise. The doctor told me to take it easy for a couple of days."

"Well, I'd say you earned it, haven't you?" the mayor chortled. He paced in front of his desk excitedly, saying, "You're the talk of the whole town! Your rescue prevented a horrible tragedy, and I think it's only right that you're rewarded. I was thinking of maybe a ceremony—"

"No!" Wil surprised himself with how vehement he was. "No, no. That won't be necessary, sir. I'm afraid I'm a bit shy, and as far as I'm concerned, it was just part of the job. When my arm heals and I get through the backlog I'll undoubtedly have, I should spend some time in the mountains making sure it's safe and that other magical beasts don't venture too close to town, you know?"

His words came out fast, tumbling from his mouth until he all but gasped for air in the end. Mayor Sinclair watched him curiously, shrewd eyes looking right through him. He nodded slowly.

"Alright, then, I know a bad idea when I come up with one," he joked. "You're not a man to hog all the spotlight, and I respect that. Is there anything we could do to say thank you?"

Wil pretended to think about it and then shook his head. "No, I'm honestly just happy to help, sir. No need for anything special or grandiose."

The mayor grinned at him. "Well, how about a bit of good news, then? Your house is just about ready. You should be able to move in as early as tomorrow. How does that sound?"

Of all the things the mayor could have told him, few could have made him as happy. "Really?" Wil asked. "That's fantastic. Tomorrow? I should probably go home and pack." As happy as he was, he welcomed any reason to get out of the mayor's office faster.

Mayor Sinclair reached into his desk and fished out a keyring with a couple of heavy iron keys on them. The old-fashioned kind no longer used in most homes or even buildings constructed this century. Wil loved them. He took them from the mayor, spinning the keyring around his finger.

"Keep up the good work, Wilbur!"

CHAPTER 16

Housewarming Party

It took another two days for Wil to move in. His injury could've been so much worse, but the prospect of moving his few belongings into a new house as well as securing some basic furniture proved to be overwhelming. Luckily, with the help of his family, he came up with a plan and decided to make a day of it. Moving day would be part work and part housewarming party as they set Wil up in his new home.

But first, he had to check it out on his own.

It looked so much better this time, his lone house on the hill. Standing at three stories high, and with repairs and fresh coats of blue and white paint, his new home looked perfect. The leftmost corner was a rounded room Wil already knew he'd make into a study, but the other side was a long rectangle, including a sprawling covered porch that wrapped around the back. Up top, the third story had exactly one room, and in Wil's mind, it made for a perfect wizard tower bedroom.

He let himself in, looking around. It smelled like wood dust and fresh paint, but more than that, it smelled like home. Or it would, once he got his things moved in and made it his own. Before now, Wil wouldn't have considered himself especially mindful of interior decorating. He had his bedroom with his family, and there had been his dorm at the academy. Both were just one room with little chance to branch out. Now that he had an entire house to himself, Wil's brain overflowed with ideas.

The area he marked for his study would be the perfect place to set up all his books. A desk and a couple of chairs meant he could do resident wizard business in his house instead of at the jail. It would mean people coming in and out of his house, but it beat Sheriff Frederick's eternally watchful eye and offered a more personal touch in taking care of the community.

He only briefly checked out the kitchen, which looked good enough to him. In all honesty, with his extravagant pay, Wil figured he'd spread the love around and eat out for most of his meals. A way to give back to the community—and not at all because he was too lazy to cook his own meals.

What really interested him was the basement, its entrance in the spacious backyard. He'd be able to have a garden if he wanted to, and with just a bit of his talents, it would almost take care of itself. The basement itself looked like a good place for a lab for alchemy and enchanting. He was an expert at neither, but Wil fully believed that one's education never ended, and he had a whole life ahead of him to improve and become the best version of himself. His basement had space for that and then some.

Finally, he went up to the tower, first to the second floor which had a couple of bedrooms and a bathroom, and then to the third story. Right away, Wil knew that the large room at the top of the house was his bedroom, even if it would be a pain to get furniture up there. It was practically a single-room apartment on its own, with a huge closet and a large bay window overlooking the town square in the distance. He stood there for an embarrassingly long time just soaking it in.

Wil was so caught up in the sight, he nearly jumped when he heard a knock at the front door. He hurried down two flights of stairs and opened the door for his brother.

"Jeez, must be nice," Jeb snarked, shouldering the door open. His arms were full of Wil's suitcases of clothes. "You really get all of this and don't have to pay for any of it? Must. Be. Nice." He grinned.

If Wil had known that all it would take to make his big brother treat him like family again was driving off a dangerous magical beast, he would've made it happen weeks ago. Things weren't back to normal, but mainly because there was no normal anymore. Not yet.

"You're one to talk," Wil shot back good-naturedly. "The farm's already paid off, and you get it when Ma and Dad kick the bucket. Poor Sarah's the only one who has to worry about getting her own place."

Jeb snickered. "Naw, that'll be solved when we find her a nice man and marry her off so she can start a family."

They both made a face and burst out laughing. Jeb schlepped the suitcases over to what would probably end up being the living room. "Ma's still fussing over which dishes and silverware to give you, but Dad's on his way with Percival."

"You think he'll survive the trip? Is this going to be it?" They laughed again. Poor old Percival was ancient by horse standards but still fought to go for walks and lug things around whenever he could. They'd need a new horse soon, but no one had the heart to retire brave, hardworking Percival just yet.

Wil brought his suitcases up both flights of stairs with the simple hovering spell, and when he came back downstairs, Jeb looked impressed indeed.

"I was only jokingly jealous before, but now I'm real jealous. This place is really nice. Too much for just you, though."

"I don't disagree," said Wil, walking around the first floor. Each room other than his new study was connected via a wide walkway, giving the place a pleasantly open feeling. "I don't think I'm gonna be starting a family anytime soon, but once I get it set up, this'll be a great place for get-togethers. You know, me and my oodles and oodles of friends."

Jeb shook his head, smiling that same insufferable grin he'd had since arriving. "I dunno, Wil. After saving the Lane kids, I think everyone's gonna wanna be your friend. Have they started asking for autographs yet?"

"Kiss my ass," said Wil, laughing again. Gods, it felt so much better to be back to good-natured snipes at each other. "I'll be happy when that dies down. We did a good thing, but that was the point, right? They needed help. Not like I was trying to show off or anything."

"And yet you had an audience at the end. Damned good timing, if nothing else." Jeb shook his head and went to the kitchen. Finding the icebox empty, he grumbled, "You came here early and you didn't even bring beers to stick away for later?"

"Ma said she'd take care of everything food- and drink-related today!" Wil said, heat rising to his cheeks.

"Ma ain't here yet, now, is she?" Jeb scoffed and headed for the front door. "I'll get us some beer. No need to thank me!"

Wil just chuckled and waved him off. With Jeb gone, he spent the next few minutes wandering around, imagining the furniture he'd get and what everything would look like in the end. As much as he loved playing with illusions, Wil was no artist, but even he thought the walls looked a little bare. Maybe he could go around and get paintings and other art from the residents of the valley.

From one of the big windows along the sides of the house, he saw his father arrive. Bob led Percival up and around the gently sloping path that connected Wil's house with the rest of town. It was just out of the way enough to be comfortable, and a little bit of a journey for the ancient horse. Wil met his father outside, accepting the big hug his father had for him.

"It's a huge day for you," said Bob, slapping his back enthusiastically. "I remember when I first bought the farm. Your ma was pregnant with Jeb and we had some money and all the hope and promise in the world that we were unstoppable and we'd make it. We did, and I'm even more confident for you. I'm proud of you, m'boy."

"Thanks, Dad," said Wil. He tried not to look too pleased. "It feels like a bit much to have just for me, so I guess I just have to live up to it, huh? I'm going to have my own library and basement laboratory!"

"Thank goodness," Bob joked. "Our house is going to look half as full with all your books gone. I imagine it'll pretty this place up real good. Seems like it might get a little lonely, though. You know our door's always open, right? And we expect you for dinner at least once a week!"

Wil beamed at his father. "More than once a week. I haven't learned to cook yet, and I'm not about to start now. I'm paid enough to eat at a new place every day and still save up."

"Sure, if you wanna get fat and complacent. And you know what? That's your choice, son. Gimme a hand with all this."

Bob hefted an old, battered table that they'd used in the kitchen years ago, before they'd upgraded to the one they used now. Wil helped him right it and pull it up the steps and into his house. Maybe he could've made it lighter and easier to carry, but that felt like cheating. For now, it was nice to just work with his dad and his hands, even if he still had to take it a bit easy.

The act of slowly taking each item out from the cart and bringing it into its new home made it real. As the cart emptied, the house filled, and Wil could see the start of a brand-new life, all his own. Before too long, Jeb came back and stowed the beer away before lugging in chairs for the dining room, as Bob and Wil brought in a couch that was as comfortable as it was hideous. This time, Wil did lighten the load, but only a little.

They were almost finished when Sharon and Sarah came up the drive with a couple of full wheelbarrows. Neither looked heavy but they were too full to carry their contents by hand. Sharon looked as happy and proud as Bob, while Sarah didn't seem too happy to have to help out. In some ways, that just made it better.

"I got everything you need to make your kitchen yours," Sharon said, stopping to hug Wil. "Including some of the first cookbooks I learned from! It's not like Sarah wants to learn," she said, shooting daggers her daughter's way.

Sarah just shrugged and said, "Look, I'm not going to be a housewife. As far as I'm concerned, I'll bring home the bacon, and whomever I end up with can cook it for me." She peeked in through the front door and made a face. "Big, but that's how you're gonna do it? You're hopeless." Sarah went inside and immediately changed the way his ugly couch faced. It did look better.

"She's got a hell of an eye, doesn't she?" Wil said to his mother, as Sarah continued tweaking the layout of the room and making it look so much more alive. "I think she'd do well in Manifee City, if given the chance."

Sharon clucked her tongue. "Expensive, though. We're doing well, but I'm not sure we're doing *that* well."

"I could help…" Wil tried not to sound too eager. He must've failed because his mother glared at him.

"We appreciate it, but she's still our responsibility and you've got your own life to worry about. I'm gonna go fill your kitchen up, okay? You can rearrange when I'm done but for now, I'm just gonna make it like home."

Wil smiled. "That's how I was going to decorate it anyway, so you're doing me a favor."

An hour passed in the blink of an eye as they completed task after task, and step by step, the house became a little closer to home. By the time they had emptied the cart and wheelbarrows, Wil and his family were pleasantly drained and hungry. He offered to treat them all to dinner in whatever restaurant they wanted, but Sharon wouldn't hear of it. She'd brought enough stuff to outfit his kitchen, and by the gods, she intended on cooking for them.

After conscripting Sarah into helping her despite numerous protests, that left Wil, Jeb, and Bob alone to relax with the gifts Wil valued above all else: two rocking chairs for his porch. He and his father took one while Jeb leaned up against the wooden railing. Each of them nursed a beer and enjoyed that perfect feeling of silent companionship. That satisfaction of a job well done with no need to speak when they could just all soak in their efforts.

Jeb raised his beer and the other two followed in his example. "To Wilbur," he said with a smirk. "Harper Valley's finest wizard, and now a homeowner. Let's see how long before he blows the place up."

Bob and Wil laughed, but they clinked their bottles and drank.

The School Bully

Wilbur never had many friends in school. It wasn't that he was unpopular or disliked. Sometimes, some kids just found themselves on the outside more often than not, never quite rejected but never embraced either. As a middle child and a bookworm in a rural area full of much more active kids, he'd ended up falling between the cracks and mostly was just invisible, compared to everyone else. With one notable exception.

No matter how much Wilbur kept to himself, Abraham Stevenson Junior somehow saw him and hated his guts. It had started so simply, back when they were twelve years old. As far as Wilbur could remember, he hadn't done anything to the other kid, but everything he did seemed to offend him.

"Why are you reading?" Abraham had said, blocking Wilbur's sunlight. When he looked up, the bigger kid sneered down at him. Puberty had hit Abraham early and given him the awkward combo of being very tall while still carrying all his baby fat. The result was a nearly man-sized angry child who dripped menace and disdain.

"Because I like to?" Wilbur answered, unsure of what the problem was. Being invisible could be lonely sometimes, but it also protected him from the worst of others.

"Reading's stupid," Abraham scoffed. "What's the matter, not good enough to play baseball with everyone else?"

It was then that Wilbur realized what was happening. Unfortunately, he had no idea how to react. So he just shrugged and returned to his book. That just egged Abraham on.

"Yeah, you look like you suck at sports. I wouldn't want you on my team either. Bet you'd just stand there and stare off into space." Abraham twisted his face up into a parody of dreamy and wistful. "Oh, can't wait to go back to reading!" He mimicked getting hit by the ball and keeling over before laughing.

It wasn't the words themselves that irritated Wilbur so much as the knowledge that Abraham meant to hurt or bother him. He didn't care for it. So Wilbur just looked him up and down and said, "You're not playing baseball yourself, so I guess nobody wanted you either." He went back to his book.

A second later, Abraham slapped it out of his hands. Wilbur had enough time to squeak before the bigger kid grabbed him by the front of the shirt and dragged him to his feet.

"What're you doing?" Wilbur asked, suddenly just the tiniest bit afraid. Maybe saying no one had wanted him hadn't been the best idea.

Abraham's eyes had a manic, wild look to them, and a few unshed tears. "I lost *one* ball and they said I was too big. I bet they'd never even want you to play!"

Wilbur did his best to shrug. "I really don't care," he said. "I don't want any trouble, I just want to read."

He didn't know why it was the wrong thing to say, but apparently, Abraham took exception to it. The next thing he knew, the bigger kid had slugged him in the nose. Wilbur stumbled backward and landed on the ground. The pain came a few seconds later, numbed by the pure shock of being decked in the face.

"What'd you do that for?" Wilbur demanded, touching his lips. He came away with a bit of blood on his fingers. Seeing that blood, funnily enough, made him want to cry way more than the feeling of being punched.

Abraham picked up his fallen book and paged through it. A horrible smile took over his face as he glanced over at Wilbur. "You like reading, huh?" He snorted. Then he grabbed a fistful of pages from the middle and tore them out.

Wilbur saw red.

Later, he didn't actually remember doing it, but he remembered how he'd felt as it happened. As if his head had caught on fire. As he struggled to breathe, he grew aware of something new underneath and inside him. His nerves shrieked as this new sensation pulsed.

"Aww, did that make the little bookworm sad?" Abraham taunted him, throwing the ripped papers into the air. A breeze carried them off across the field outside the school. Wilbur remembered those words coming in clear, and everything going white a second later.

He remembered the way it felt to push on that new sensation, that feeling of power, and let it loose. Abraham Stevenson Junior became the first person in Harper Valley to experience Wilbur McKenzie's newfound magical abilities. He discovered the hard way not to bully smaller children, as raw force carried him through the air and he landed hard on his arm with a crunch.

That horrible crunch stayed with Wilbur, even as the effort of magically throwing Abraham sapped his strength until his consciousness abandoned him.

He woke up at home a few hours later, surrounded by his family, Doc Hawkins, and his teacher, Mrs. Mann. He had a splitting headache, a fresh burst of fear from the looks on everyone's faces, and a new problem in his life as he became the first person in Harper Valley to show signs of magical prowess in decades.

Abraham Stevenson Junior got a broken arm, a stern talking to, and an ass-whipping from his father that only served to cement his hatred of Wilbur. After that, Abraham kept a healthy distance while his arm healed but took every opportunity he had to insult Wilbur and laugh at him in front of everyone.

Whenever Abraham caught him reading in class instead of doing work, he made sure the teacher knew and always sent him this awful insufferable smile to remind Wilbur who had done it.

For Wilbur's part, he tried to stay out of the way and stick to his studies. It became much harder to care about the other students when it was clear he had a different future ahead of him. And rather than drive the other students away, as his bully hoped, his new magical powers made him stand out more among his classmates, who cheered him on during lunch as he made his sandwich float and twirl in the air or somehow lured every bug within several feet to land on his hand.

For the first time in Wil's life, he stopped being invisible. At home and school, his family and teachers paid more attention to him and gave him extra instruction and care he'd never before known. It would've been great, the ultimate satisfaction a middle child could ever have, were it not for people like Abraham, and even Jeb, growing resentful of his new abilities and attention. What started out as novel became overwhelming and isolating.

The years went by much like that, and the animosity between Abraham and Wilbur grew, though the fledgling wizard did everything in his power to avoid the bigger kid. He didn't want trouble or a fight, and he didn't want to accidentally hurt Abraham ever again. It became a game of cat and mouse, a dance of trying to avoid the bully while he studied and tried his best to enjoy his life with an increasingly alienating skill marking him as different.

Abraham never hit him again, but that didn't stop him from throwing things, tripping him, saying horrible things about him to others for a laugh, and doing everything he could to use his superior size to order others around and be the classroom king. Where school had once been Wilbur's favorite part of the day, by the time he finished with it, he resented everything about it.

On the day Wilbur left for Saint Balthazar's Academy of Magic, a handful of his classmates saw him off at the train station. Some might've been jealous, but plenty of others cheered on the idea of one of their own becoming a powerful wizard and even coming back later. Abraham was, mercifully, not invited and didn't show up later to crash the event.

And after that, it became very easy for Wilbur to put the bully out of his mind and focus on his new life and a never-ending pile of books that demanded his attention and focus. By the time he had graduated and returned to Harper Valley, he hadn't thought of Abraham Stevenson Junior in literal years.

Until now.

CHAPTER 17

Public Servant Number One

Maybe it would be dramatic to claim that everything changed after he saved the Lane children and got his own house, but it felt true enough to Wil. Enough stories went around about the Nullbear that distrust and good old-fashioned rural suspicion gave way to open-armed acceptance in the blink of an eye. The work remained largely the same, but it came a little easier.

When Mr. Higgins's favorite goat escaped from his enclosure for the tenth time that year, Wil located him and talked some sense into him.

"What's the problem?" he asked the goat, Jimothy. Mr. Higgins had a strange sense of humor with names. "Aren't you happy there?"

The goat bleated, and Wil's spell gave him the impression of a gruff older guy shaking his head vehemently. It was easy to imagine the goat's beard belonging to a man, and his strange rectangular pupils were more intelligent and passionate than Carl the bull's had been. Goats were the superior conversationalist.

"Not anymore," Jimothy moaned. "Everything was fine until *she* appeared. It's downright intolerable!"

"Ahh." Wil nodded, plopping himself down on the ground next to him. He'd found Jimothy near the river, getting a drink. The goat never ventured too far but once every couple of weeks got out and wandered around some.

"Women troubles? Wanna talk about it?" Not that Wil had any expertise on the subject.

Jimothy bleated neutrally. "What's there to talk about? Henry and I had a good thing going, and then he ruined it by bringing her home. Now she annoys the hell out of me, and just... She does everything wrong, and I was here first!"

Definitely not his wheelhouse, but Wil could deal with it. "If she's really that bad, maybe I can talk to Mr. Higgins and see if he's willing to sell her to another rancher. He's really been sad about all your escape attempts, so I bet he'll listen."

"Good!" Jimothy huffed, making his beard bounce. "I hate Barbara, and I'm tired of how much time he spends with her."

"Oh. Crap." Well, Mr. Higgins wasn't going to break up with his girlfriend just because Jimothy didn't like her. Probably. Still, he could work with that. "How about this, Jim? We'll go back and have a talk with him and figure this out. Just you, me, and him."

"Fine."

Walking home with Jimothy was more fun than he expected, as the shaggy goat ended up being playful and spent half the time racing with him. It made Wil wish he'd been better at transmutation—turning into a goat and playing with him would've been a great way to soften him up before the talk. Instead, they got back and he managed to pull Mr. Higgins away from his girlfriend and explain the situation.

"Is he serious?" Mr. Higgins asked, jaw slack and eyes screwed up. "He hates Barb? She's been nothing but good to him!"

"She has not," Jimothy countered when Wil translated for him. "She doesn't feed me the right stuff, she scratches the wrong part of my neck every time, and her voice could curdle milk. Either she goes or I do."

Mr. Higgins stared at him. From the outside, it must've looked and sounded super strange, the two of them bleating and baaing at each other. Either way, Mr. Higgins mostly hid his discomfort, and before long, they had hashed it out. Barb would no longer have anything to do with his care, and when Jimothy wanted to go for a walk, he'd wear a vest to mark him as safe to travel and come back before nightfall.

"Thanks a bunch, Mr. Wizard," Mr. Higgins said, shaking Wil's hand after they were done. "I never thought this'd be the problem, but I'd rather Jimothy be happy with me. He's my best friend."

"All in a day's work," said Wil.

Mr. Wizard. More and more people called him that now, and it sounded a hell of a lot better than Mr. McKenzie. It gave him the willies every time they called him that. "Mr. Wizard" had respect and maybe even a little playfulness he could appreciate. It was better than "Ain't you the McKenzie boy who ran off for six years?"

After a quick lunch downtown, he made his way to Mr. Tre's place. The man kept chickens. Foxes kept getting into the henhouse, and aside from the loss of a good few hens, the nighttime intrusions stressed out the rest of the bunch to the point that they had stopped laying eggs. With a bloody feather as a focus, a quick divination spell allowed Wil to relive the chicken's abduction and murder.

Not the most pleasant experience, if he were honest about it, but it made it easy enough to set a trap for the fox. Tomorrow, he'd check back in and use the fox's bones to make a bunch of wards—and he'd have a gorgeous fox pelt to keep or maybe give to someone. Win-win, if a bit morbid. He marked it as a job half done, and then returned home to handle the paperwork and see whom he'd help next. The work never stopped, but now he enjoyed that.

It took him only a couple of weeks after moving in to outfit his house. People were more than happy to help him, and with his pay, he could buy anything he'd conceivably want or need in Harper Valley. All thanks to the job, but it was his hard work and dedication that made it all work. Now that he'd been at it for over a month, it felt earned. He went into his lovely home, kicked his shoes off, and headed to the study.

Now that he had his own office and office hours, the paperwork was not as necessary, but a part of him craved the stability of it and having good records for all the work he did. Every finished project went into a big pile he totally didn't count once a week. He may or may not have completed one hundred and thirty-four tasks in his time as resident wizard, and his pride would only go up as the number did. Wil added another two completed slips to the pile and grabbed a book from the shelf.

He'd be the first to admit his office hours were a bit wonky, but he genuinely believed it worked out for the best. He started his days off with breakfast out of the house as he went over jobs for the day. Then he completed a couple of work orders, had office hours, then lunch, then got more work done, and then put in some office hours again. The first few days, people waited outside his house awkwardly, until he put up a sign making things clear.

After two weeks, the complaints were finally starting to die down as people got used to his hours. He offered the public four hours total each day, in two-hour chunks. That was fine, right? Wizards were meant to be eccentric, and this gave him a chance to catch his breath and read when no one actively needed him.

When the day's surprising visitor showed up, he'd been rereading through a textbook on advanced transmutation, trying to make it make sense. The knock on the door made him stick his bookmark in and look up, only to freeze in place.

The man stood at a staggering six and a half feet or so and was built like a grain silo. He wasn't fat so much as just naturally heavyset and too big. Even hunching in place and trying to minimize himself just made him appear even larger. He wore dorky round spectacles, kept his long hair in a ponytail, and looked familiar. Wil couldn't place him immediately, but every instinct screamed at him to kick the man out.

"Um..., hello," the man rumbled in a voice like a rockslide.

Wil stood slowly, eyes locked on the man. "Hello," he returned. "I know you, right?" He knew he did. He didn't know why.

"Uh, yeah…, unfortunately." The enormous man took a deep breath and let it out slowly. "We knew each other as kids. I'm Abraham Stevenson. Junior."

Long-dormant memories over the last decade flooded Wil. Each time Abraham had mocked him or spit in his food or talked about what a weird nerd he was. All the times Wil could've struck back but had to be better. All the times he hadn't used magic to get revenge or win fights or defend himself unless it was an emergency, no matter how nasty or cruel others were. Over a hundred instances of the bigger kid coming after him, when all Wil wanted was to be left alone.

"Abraham Stevenson Junior," Wil repeated flatly.

"Bram, to my friends," said Abraham, smiling sheepishly.

A million responses came to Wil then. He had trouble not laughing in Abraham's face, not asking him if he actually *had* any friends. But he had a duty to do. He took a deep breath and said, "Mr. Stevenson. What can I do for you?"

Abraham winced but didn't look surprised. He sat down in one of the chairs at Wil's desk. It creaked dangerously beneath him, which made Abraham wince again. "A lot, I hope. But first, can I just say, about when we were kids—"

"No," said Wil, fists clenched so hard his nails dug into his palms. "Let's not talk about that. It was a million years ago and not relevant to whatever you're here for, I'm assuming." Wil didn't sound convincing, even to himself. "What brings you here today?" He remained standing.

"Well, I've fallen on some hard times," Abraham started, wringing his hands together. "I'm…I'm going to lose the farm."

"And you want my help saving it?" Wil couldn't suppress the disbelief in his voice. He nearly did laugh then, and his scorn must've been obvious.

"No, it's too late for that." Abraham sighed, bowing his head. "Another couple of weeks and it's going up for auction. Nothing I can do will change that." His voice thickened like he was trying not to cry. "The place has fallen into serious disrepair. I've not been able to keep up with it, and with Mom getting sick and needing all our money to go into that, we couldn't afford any extra hands, and…" He stopped, swallowing hard.

Of *course* the jerk had a sob story. Maybe he felt he needed one, coming to Wil after all the crap he'd pulled. Years of being awful, and now he thought he could just come in and cry and get some help? Wil struggled to keep his breathing even, reminding himself what his job really meant.

"So what is it you want from me, Mr. Stevenson?"

Abraham's shoulders slumped. "Please just…help me clean the place up so we can sell it at a decent price. Mom's medical bills really ate into our savings, and now I can't afford to keep the place or turn it around. If I can sell it for a good price, maybe I can start over and do something else."

"Like open a bookstore, maybe?" Wil snarked at him. His patience only lasted so long.

"Y-yeah, maybe!" Abraham said, making Wil's blood boil. "I love reading, and it'd be nice to be able to spend all day reading and organizing and making sure I connect people with books they'd like. That would be a great fresh start. Not what I was thinking, but—"

Wil couldn't help it. He burst out laughing at the pure absurdity of it all. Harsh, unrestrained laughter while Abraham's face fell and he tried to make himself smaller in his seat. "I thought reading was stupid," Wil heard himself say. Why did he say that? "What happened, you keep some of the pages you ripped out of a book and find out it's fun after all?"

Gods, Abraham actually had tears in his eyes. "I'm sorry," the man said, standing up. "You've got every right to be angry. I just...I can't do this on my own. Here." He pulled out a folded-up work order from his pocket and set it on the desk. "Take a look. If you don't want to, I understand. I'm sorry," he said again before turning around and squeezing through the door.

Wil stood there for a few seconds, pulse pounding in his head as years of built-up anger, forgotten until now, came bubbling up and battled within him for control. He didn't consider himself an angry person. Not really. Maybe that was why actually feeling real anger, deep and personal, made him sick to his stomach and ready to scream.

He took the work order in trembling hands and looked it over. Out of every work order he'd handled, this one had the most demands. This could've been three or even four work orders, something he'd handle over a long period of time. Doing it all would take Wil the better part of a week, at least.

And here this jerk came and just added the order to the pile, expecting it could get done. As if Wil didn't already have dozens of other things to do and only so much time to get it done before summer ended and fall arrived.

Wil took another breath. This was the job. He couldn't afford to pick and choose whom he helped, even if he could rightfully claim it came in last in line. Wouldn't be his fault. Wouldn't be his problem.

About two minutes of thinking that way, and Wil realized how awful he felt about it. With one last look at the creased work order packet, he realized he needed an alternative point of view. He locked up and left in search of some perspective.

CHAPTER 18

Voices of Conscience

The problem with finding perspective was that Wil didn't know whom to ask. Some of the more obvious people stood out as wrong choices or he already knew what they'd say. His mother would no doubt tell him to let it go and help out. His father would probably say the same thing, come to think of it. And while he wasn't looking for people to tell him to *not* help out Abraham, he at least wanted them to understand why he didn't want to.

So maybe it was a mistake, but he went to Sarah first. He met up with her that evening before supper, bringing with him a bribe of a fresh notebook and pencils. His sister accepted these gifts with all the suspicion and distrust of a younger sibling.

"What do you want?" she asked, after flipping through the brand-new blank book.

"Can't I just bring you gifts because I want to support your artistic endeavors?" Wil flashed a winning smile.

Sarah's eyes narrowed suspiciously at him. "No, not really. Mom and Dad like to give me things. Jeb likes to give me crap about them giving me things. You…well, you've been gone, so I really don't know how you do things anymore. But in over a month of being back, you haven't gotten me a single gift, so why now?"

Wil deflated. He sat down on Sarah's bed, looking at all the pieces of personal artwork she had put up throughout the years. She really was improving, and he did want to help encourage that, but she wasn't wrong about his motive. He needed to be better.

"Alright, you got me," he said. "But I really should be giving you more gifts. You're my sister and I love you and you deserve respect."

Sarah gagged, really emphasizing the dry retching. Wil laughed, and soon after, she did too.

"But seriously, though. You're way cooler than you get credit for. And I want your advice on something. Remember Abraham Stevenson Junior?"

Sarah rolled her eyes. "You mean the guy who ripped up your book and tormented you? The guy who bullied you for, like, five years straight? The one who tried to give me crap once before Jeb beat his ass? Naw, can't recall."

Wil's expression darkened. "He tried to bully you too?" he said, voice just above a whisper. Well, that made his decision much easier.

"Once." Sarah shrugged. "Jeb set him straight, and after that, he even apologized. I think he thought we were closer than we are."

"We're family," Wil protested. "Man, either you're not giving me any breaks, or I have a lot to make up for."

Sarah patted the new notebook. "This is a start. Keep it coming and we'll talk. Anyway, what about him?"

Wil took a deep breath and tried to figure out how he could word it. He needed to make it clear without sounding petty or childish about it. "He came today with a huge work order for me. His family's losing his land and he wants me to help him clean it up so it'll sell for more at auction."

"Huh," she said, picking up a pencil. On the first page, she started sketching out some lines, well-rounded and soon vaguely human-shaped. "Sucks to suck. What, you don't want to do it?"

"Well, no," said Wil. "He beat me up and then spent years treating me like crap. Why should I have to help him?"

"Don't ask me. I wouldn't. I'd laugh in his face and tell him to cry about it." Sarah grinned, and Wil had no doubt she'd do just that. Little sisters were brutal creatures. "Are you looking for permission to tell him to piss off?"

"I guess so. Maybe. No, I'm just trying to figure out what I should do, and I'm at a loss. It was years ago, but he kept trying to ruin things whenever I was happy in school."

A knock at the door interrupted them. A second later Jeb stepped inside. "Dinner's ready," he said, eyes flitting between the two. "What's going on in here?"

Before Wil had a chance to answer, Sarah piped up. "Wil got a request from Abraham Stevenson Junior to help repair his farm so he can sell it, and we're talking about telling him to go eat—"

"I don't know if I want to help him out," Wil interjected. "He made things tough on me and now he comes begging for help? I don't know."

Things had largely gotten better between him and Jeb. His older brother still liked to tease him and still had some bitterness over the years Wil been gone, but it had settled into something familiar and even brotherly again. Now, though, he looked like he wanted to strangle Wil.

"Question," Jeb said. "You got a list of people you're willin' to help out?"

"No?" Wil cocked his head to the side.

"What about a list of people you won't help out? You got a list like that?"

When Wil shook his head, Jeb snarled, "Then why the hell do you think it's okay to tell *anyone* you won't help them? You didn't sign up to just help out your friends and family, you're supposed to be a big powerful wizard for the whole damned town! And what, you wanna tell somebody in need to go to hell just because you had problems when you were kids?"

"Man, I don't know who you are, Wilbur. I'm no saint, and I got plenty of people I wouldn't spit on if they needed to wash up, but if somebody asks you for help, you help them. The fact that you're even *thinking* of saying no...Ma and Dad raised you better than this." With one last baleful glare, Jeb slammed the door shut and stormed downstairs.

Wil stared at the door, heart pounding in his chest and a whole lot of shame whispering in his ears. Sarah didn't help.

"Wow, he destroyed you!" she said, continuing her drawing. "Bet you he's telling Mom and Dad right now."

Wil looked down at her notebook. She'd drawn a fairly good sketch of Abraham as a teen, still fat instead of just huge all over, but lumpy and kind of goofy too. Like someone people in the academy would bully if they saw him.

"I gotta go," Wil muttered.

"Thanks for the art supplies!" Sarah called after him.

Rather than go down and face his parents' judgment over his momentary crisis, Wil ran out the front door and down the lane and on the road leading into town. Running felt good, or at least better than the guilt and shame gnawing at him. Jeb was right, but worse than that, Wil still didn't want to help Abraham. He wasn't sure he could bring himself to, but if that meant dealing with his parents' disappointment, what choice did he have?

Wil had no particular destination in mind at first. It was enough to simply run and let his lungs burn and his muscles scream to drown out the storm of thoughts brewing. He just ran and ran, letting his feet take him downtown to the general store, where if nothing else he had at least one friendly face.

He burst through the door, panting. This time of night, they were about to close and only two people were in line. Darlene paused partway through ringing up someone's milk. "You alright, Wil?" she called out.

Wil shook his head, sucking in as much breath as he could.

"Alright, then, just gimme a couple." Darlene finished with the older woman's order and motioned for the next person to come forward. A few minutes later, she flipped the sign on the door and dragged him over to the break room and sat him down in a chair. She leaned against the table.

"Alright, what's got you hot and bothered?"

Wil frowned. There was no easy way to say it without looking like the bad guy. So he didn't even try. Starting from the time Abraham beat him up and destroyed his book to all the years after, then forgetting him, and then him coming hat in hand to beg for some help, the words tumbled out of him like a mudslide. When he finished, he fully expected her to act like Jeb and tell him to grow up and just do it.

"Can't say I blame you for not wanting to help," Darlene said with a sigh, running a hand through her spiky hair. "Abraham was a real jerk when he was younger. I used to hate him too. At least he never hit me or did anything other than hit *on* me a few times. But if I were gonna be mad about that, I'd probably have to kick you out as well."

He chuckled, shrugging. "Sorry about that."

"No, you're not," she said with a smile. "Not your fault I'm smart, funny, charming, and good-looking. Aww, yiss," she said, cackling as he turned red, "I love making you squirm. Point is, I used to hate him, but now I don't. Haven't in years, in fact. Mostly I just feel bad for him."

That startled him. "Feel bad for him? What on earth could possibly make you feel bad for him?"

Darlene's smile disappeared. "What do you know about Abraham Stevenson Senior? You ever really get a chance to meet him?"

"Only the once," Wil admitted, eyes darkening at the memory. "He tried to get Sheriff Frederick to arrest me for breaking his son's arm. Called me an unnatural menace and loudly yelled that if I ever used magic on his son again he'd kill me. Kinda left an impression."

"Yeah, sounds about right." Darlene nodded. "He was a pigheaded, narrow-minded, angry sumbitch who didn't have a kind word to say to or about anyone. He drank, he threw away his money on any kind of get-rich scheme he could, and when that failed, he took it all out on his son and wife. Probably did it Abraham's entire life."

As eye-opening as that was, it didn't really change how Wil felt. It explained things, but it didn't undo anything. "You said 'was.' Did he die?"

"Four years ago," said Darlene. "Drank himself to death. The farm's been in a state ever since then. After Abe Senior died, Bram lost it and kind of became a nervous wreck. Like he couldn't believe his daddy was gone and kept expecting him to come back and whoop his ass for doing anything differently. A couple years later, his mama, Addie, fell ill. He's spent the last two years taking care of her and watching her circle the drain.

"Comes in here every few days to pick up food that's easy for her to eat and to see if we've got any extra stock of medicine. He stopped asking for medicine not too long ago, so…yeah. If he's wanting help selling the place, I don't think Addie's gonna be around for much longer." Darlene sighed and looked him in the eye.

"I'm not telling you what to do, or whether you should get over your grudge or forgive him or anything. That's on you, Wil. What I'm saying is that he's had it rough longer than you think, and maybe he's at a cracking point. Might be good to show a little kindness, even if you don't think he deserves it. Like it or not, he's a part of this community. Maybe for just a little bit longer before he leaves and finds a better life elsewhere."

Wil stayed silent for a minute, mulling it all over. Guilt and shame threatened to overwhelm him. Worst of all, the anger didn't disappear, even if it had been cowed into submission temporarily. Mostly, he felt unclean after all of it.

"I didn't know," he said finally.

Darlene patted him on the shoulder, managing to come off as sympathetic rather than condescending. "No, I didn't think you did. So I thought you ought to. Maybe that'll make your decision a bit easier. And if not, maybe *this* will. You help clean up his farm if you want to go out with me again sometime."

Wil smiled despite himself. "I thought you'd go out with me regardless," he said.

She shook her head. "I would've, before this. But if you're the type to not help, then why would I want to? It's not a bribe or threat—just telling you how it is. I don't want you to do it just to go on a date with me, though. I just have no interest in dating anyone who'd let someone suffer because of what happened as children."

He flinched. She and Jeb together could bring anyone to their knees. He was glad his mother hadn't gotten a chance to jump in on it, or Wil would've been dead on the spot.

"You raise a good point," he admitted. "And you're right. I do want to help out, more often than not. So I will. I'll clean up his farm and make sure he's not screwed, but I don't see myself forgiving him or liking him. That's not gonna happen."

Darlene smiled and leaned forward to plant a kiss on his forehead. "Wasn't asking you to. All I'm asking you to do is help out. Be the kind, dorky wizard who just wants to help out. We aren't kids anymore, so let's be adults about it."

Wil sighed but smiled too. Abraham had been a real jerk, but maybe helping him would mean he'd leave forever and Wil would never have to see him again. He could do that much, at least.

CHAPTER 19

Common Ground

Although Wil decided he would help Abraham, he didn't show up at his property until the afternoon.

It wasn't out of spite or wanting to make the other man sweat and think he was being ignored. Wil still had wards to put up on multiple houses, and he needed a plan. Abraham's work orders were extensive and would probably take the better part of a week to get done, but they couldn't be all Wil did for the next week while other work piled up.

As Wil spent more time on the job in general, he came to understand how to juggle it all, and he realized that not everyone would be understanding. In Abraham's case, the young man had no choice but to be understanding. The way Wil saw it, he did owe it to the community to serve each and every one of them as they needed it. But that didn't mean he'd tolerate abuse. Abraham had a chance, and if any of his old behavior showed itself…

Wil tried to tell himself he wasn't looking for an excuse to drop the job. As he headed to the Stevenson farm, he even started to believe it. That was, until he saw the state of the land.

Deep in the valley, tucked away at the base of the mountains to the northeast, the farm looked all but abandoned. What had been fences were now just collections of sticks and wire, consumed by overgrown grass and wild wheat way past harvest time. There were four fields around the house, and all of them told the same story, save for one field that remained empty, the earth blackened. A large barn looked to be barely standing, as if a strong gust of wind or a loud curse would collapse it.

It took Wil a couple of minutes to drink it all in—all his plans for getting stuff done had jumped out of his head and run for the hills the moment he saw the mess. Not everyone had it good in Harper Valley, but rarely did he see it get this bad. He took a deep breath, walked down the lane, and knocked on Abraham's door.

Half a minute later, Abraham appeared. Seeing it was Wil, he adjusted his glasses and waited to be addressed. Hell, he looked borderline scared of Wil, or maybe more scared of Wil telling him no.

"This place is a mess," Wil blurted, looking over his shoulder. "I can help, but how did it get this bad?"

Abraham winced. "Long story," he said. "I'll tell it, but maybe over a cup of tea?"

Wil blinked. Maybe Darlene was right, and Abraham was a different person. Wil found it hard to reconcile their troubled past with this shrinking giant in front of him. "Yeah," he said, "alright."

Inside, boxes were piled everywhere, some open and filled with books or trinkets, plenty more with a load of trash inside. It all smelled vaguely wet and like bad cabbage. The house remained in better repair than the rest of the property, but not by much. Abraham led him past a stack of old newspapers and into the kitchen, where he cleared trash off two chairs at the table.

Wil sat while Abraham filled the kettle from a sink overflowing with dishes. He put it on the stove and came to the table, sitting down with a heavy sigh.

"Are you okay?" Wil surprised himself by asking. His eyes darted around the place.

Abraham opened his mouth and then closed it. He laughed, a series of breathy inhalations and exhalations without sound. Then he shook his head and slumped over the table dramatically.

"No," he moaned. "I am not."

All that pent-up anger over the years, back as though it had never left, hit a brick wall and fell flat. How could Wil be angry at someone this sad? He didn't really pity Abraham so much as feel a guilt over all that anger, lingering pain from a lifetime ago.

Sighing, he reached forward and patted the man's shoulder. "Do... Do you want to talk about it?" he asked, knowing he'd regret it.

His former bully raised his head and rubbed his eyes. "Yes. No. It's just..." Abraham gestured at the room. "I can't do it all. I can't take care of Mom as she lies dying, while cleaning up, packing, throwing things out, fixing fences, growing crops, selling things, doing the bills, and just..." He let out a strangled cry as he pulled on his long hair.

"I try to do it all and I get overwhelmed and just do...nothing. Nothing but take care of Mom, and read to try to stay sane." Abraham deflated. "I wouldn't blame you if you walked away. I let it get this bad, and you don't owe me anything. Not after the crap I said and did."

"I considered it," Wil admitted. "Not right now, but yesterday, when you came in and I realized who you were. I was real tempted. But I talked to Darlene Johnson and she told me a few things."

Abraham flushed. "What kinds of things?"

"Well, a bit about the hardships you've faced. That your dad was a bastard and he died, and your mom was sick. Those sorts of things. She's why I can't say no to this, mostly. My brother's the other reason. It'd be like kicking you while you're down. But you gotta tell me something," Wil said, fighting back a smile.

"What's that?"

"When the hell did you go from thinking reading was stupid to being a bigger bookworm than me?" Wil pointed at the boxes of books everywhere.

Abraham's face split into a wide grin. Then he started laughing, big belly laughs. "It's so weird, isn't it?" He guffawed. "All of this trouble over me being a jerk to you and now..." The laughs dissolved into a sigh. "It was my dad. He didn't like me reading instead of being outside and fighting or playing with other kids, or anything like that. Kept worrying I'd end up a sissy if I did, and unable to take care of the farm."

"Good-ol'-boy logic, right?" Wil said, scoffing. "Gotta work yourself to death to feed your family, and anything other than misery is slacking off or weak."

"Yep. Didn't like that I didn't like most of the things he did. I never liked hunting, or fishing, or anything like that. So I think he just sorta...punished me for it. Until I faked it for him." He bowed his head. "Doesn't make what I did to you right."

It gave Wil a lot to think about. He imagined his own father acting that way. Or at least, he tried to. Bob McKenzie wasn't a perfect man, but no one would ever accuse him of not caring about his family. He was closer to Jeb and Sarah than he was to Wil, but there had never been a time he'd doubted his father's love or thought he was being punished just for being himself.

"No," said Wil, shaking his head. "It doesn't. But I could either hold it against you for the rest of my life or just try and move on. Like I said, I don't aim to kick you while you're down."

Abraham looked grateful and opened his mouth to say something when a loud, wet cough came from upstairs. "Excuse me a second," he murmured and went upstairs. The stairs creaked with every step, and Wil found himself curious but unwilling to follow.

Through the floor, Abraham's deep voice came through muffled, just on the edge of hearing. His mother must've been the other voice, and Wil could barely pick it up at all when he tried. He knew it was none of his damned business, but he couldn't help his curiosity. So he did something bad.

Wil cast one of his more difficult spells, twirling his wrists together to give himself a better mental image and feel of a magical orb. He poured power into it until it linked with his sense of sight. Then he let it drift up through the floor and into the bedroom to spy on Abraham and his mother.

Her bedroom may've been the only room in the house not a complete mess, but it was also mostly bare. Addie Stevenson lay in a bed way too big for her, with only a simple dresser and portraits of family on the wall to keep her company. Jars of medicine littered the nightstand, as well as a glass of water with a straw in it.

Abraham sat on the side of his mother's bed, helping her into a sitting position. Her skin was a vivid yellow and she trembled. He quickly turned around to get her a pill and the water. He put the pills directly put in her mouth and then brought the straw up for her. With tremendous difficulty, she swallowed it all and motioned to be put back down.

Addie's eyes fluttered shut and her lips moved. Wil could still hear just the barest bits of sound from his position down below, but the spell didn't allow for sound to come through unless he really taxed himself. Abraham took her hand and squeezed it. Whatever he said to his mother, it looked calm and reassuring, even as he blinked tears out of his eyes. He kissed her hand and gently set it down before tiptoeing downstairs as quietly as a man of his size could.

Wil released the spell just in time to look natural, though everything in him burned with shame for capturing such a private moment. It was none of his business, but he had to know. Now he did. The rest of the anger evaporated, leaving only sympathetic pain in its place.

Abraham never got a loving, supporting father, and it wouldn't be long before he lost his mother. He'd spent years having to deny himself and had lashed out violently at others for it. And if Wil were to guess, everything had probably changed when his father died and Abraham no longer had to fear him. Everything fell apart around him just as he tried to stand on his own and discover himself. Wil didn't have to be friends with him, but how could he hate him?

"Sorry about that," Abraham said, going to the cabinet and getting a couple of mugs now that the kettle had started to whistle. He grabbed a couple of teabags and plopped them in, and then poured the water. His hands shook the entire time.

"Think nothing of it," Wil said. "How is your mother doing?"

Abraham stiffened at the counter. Wil knew immediately it wasn't a good question to ask. Abraham sighed and brought the mugs over to the table. "She's not. Doc Hawkins is surprised she's lasted this long. The only relief is that it'll be over before the auction. Gods, that must sound awful."

Wil shook his head, taking the cup of tea and pulling on the string, dunking the bag a few times. "It doesn't. I've never had to deal with this kind of loss, but I know how bad stress can destroy a person. At the academy, we discussed and dealt with a lot of mental strain. When times are tough, it's really easy to go cold and think in terms of practicality. It's also common to freeze up."

For a couple of minutes, neither of them said anything. It could've been awkward, but somehow it wasn't. Wil figured Abraham needed time to think, time to decompress and relax. He'd likely need it off and on over the next while, which could make things difficult. As for Wil himself, it gave him time to come up with a plan and think carefully about what he wanted to say.

"I'm going to help you, Abraham," said Wil. "We'll get the fields fixed up, and I can fix the fences and do all kinds of magical touch-up on the land itself. But I can't do it alone. I'm probably going to ask my family to help, and I'm going to need your help too. I can't deal with all the little things in the house like you can. My mom could help you with the actual cleaning, but the trash and packing has to be all you. You can't stay frozen for it."

Abraham nodded thoughtfully. "You're right. I can't. But it's been really hard. I'll do my best, but I can't control it all the time."

Wil took a sip of his tea. Awful, but he pretended to like it before setting it down. "I understand. The point is to keep trying. Together we'll clean this place up and get you a second chance at life."

Then Wil did something he never expected to do. He held out his hand to his former tormentor. Abraham took it and shook it.

"Thank you, Mr. Wizard."

CHAPTER 20

Hard Work and Hangovers

It didn't take much to convince his family. Wil took a day to get as many work orders done as possible, and then the day after that, he and his family descended upon the Stevenson farm with tools, cleaning supplies, and carts of fresh lumber and nails, paid for by Wil himself. It made a small dent in his monthly pay, but not enough to worry him.

The look on Abraham's face when they showed up nearly made the whole thing worth it. The enormous young man immediately teared up out of gratitude and welcomed them all in. Sharon made them all breakfast while Bob and Jeb led in detailing their plans and in what order they'd tackle it all. Wil was happy enough to sit to the side and listen to the professionals handle it. An hour later, they were all hard at work.

The first major task was breaking down the rotten remnants of the old fence and carting it away. Wil could've just used a bit of magic to blow it all down and into a pile before they did away with it, but he didn't.

He joined Abraham in methodically breaking and moving pieces of wood to the cart while Bob and Jeb measured and built the new fence to replace it. At first, Wil fully expected Abraham to falter or drag a little, but he gamely brought armfuls of wood and detritus over to be disposed of, and even pulled the cart himself to give poor Percival a break.

While the Stevenson farm wasn't even close to the largest in the valley, the majority of that first day was spent on just the fences. They stopped work just before sunset, having cleared away all the old and put up just over half of the new. Then they broke apart for the day, and Wil went home with his family for dinner, before calling it early and sleeping for a good twelve hours.

The next day was most of the same, though putting up the fence didn't take as much time as expected. They finished one section before noon and Jeb and Bob took a much-needed break while Wil went to work putting his own touch on the wood.

"What is it you're doing?" Abraham asked him, mopping sweat from his brow. He leaned against one of the fences Wil had already worked on, which probably explained why the wood didn't buckle or creak.

Wil chiseled some careful lines in the wood, hands as steady as he could make them. "Runes," he said, finishing the design. A quick gust of breath and wood dust flew up from it. "Small, long-lasting spells I can cast that will anchor themselves to an object and just feed off ambient magic around it to keep going. It helps that there's a very minor leyline running across your property that feeds them on their own."

"Runes. Neat!" Abraham practically brimmed with enthusiasm. "What kind of spells are you putting on the fence?"

"A bunch of them," Wil answered, carving out the start of the next. He waited until the outline was complete before continuing. "An anti-weather spell to keep it from getting too wet or dry. A minor pest repellant, to keep away bugs, mostly. And something to make it extra sturdy and hardy, difficult to move. If I were to layer up a couple of these babies, a bull could charge it and bounce right off."

"Oooh." The larger man all but danced in place. "That's so cool and will be great…for the next guy who owns the place," he realized, voice weakening.

An unfortunate truth. Wil smiled and said, "Maybe, but for a few days before the auction at least, your home is going to look better than it has in years. You any good at woodcarving?"

"One of the few things I *am* good at," Abraham confessed. At Wil's signal, he came closer and took the wood chisel from him. "What do you want me to carve?"

Wil tapped one of the two runes already there. "Make a copy of this one. It's the rune for strength, and I'll tie in a couple of spells to that. But you have to be very precise."

Abraham faltered. "You sure you want me to do it, then? I don't want to screw up your hard work."

"You'll have to be careful then, won't you?" Wil grinned and got out of the way. Abraham took his place and studied the rune carefully. Very carefully.

"If you mess it up, I can fix it, so give it a try," Wil suggested.

Finally, screwing up his face and sticking out his tongue, Abraham made the first cut. The wood chisel peeled back wood in a gentle curve downward. He did the same motion from the other side, making the two ends meet at a careful point before closing the design up at the top. The strength rune happened to be one of the simplest runes to carve, and it took only another minute or so before Abraham climbed to his feet.

"How bad did I do?" he asked.

After a quick inspection, Wil nodded. "Not bad. My senses tell me it'll work as is. I *could* probably make it a tiny bit better, but I won't. Let's call it you leaving your permanent mark on the place. A piece that will always be yours."

That seemed to make Abraham happy. They finished with the work that day and then promptly took another three days before they continued. The McKenzie family still had plenty of work to do on their own farm, and Wil focused on making sure his other work orders didn't pile up too high.

The next time Wil and his family went over, they were pleasantly surprised by the inside of the house. The old, decaying wallpaper had been scraped off and all the walls repainted a neutral beige color. Jeb fixed up the cabinets in the kitchen and Sharon did a magical job cleaning every square inch of the downstairs. It looked like a brand-new house.

The upstairs they left alone, to try not to disturb Addie any more than they already were. Abraham swore she was fine—just resting and on a lot of painkillers. Wil only heard her voice muffled a few times, sounding weaker each time. Occasionally, he thought he heard Abraham crying, but no one in the world could blame him under the circumstances.

As the work continued and the McKenzies brought goats over to devour the overgrown fields, Wil spent more and more time with Abraham and found himself almost forgetting what had happened between them for years. It was easy to hold a grudge and just stew in it, but when he saw how much of a different person his former bully had become, it was like hating one person for the actions of another.

Even weirder than that, Wil thought he could even like the guy. Maybe even be friends. For being as large and intimidating as he was, Abraham seemed more like a nerdy, nervous wreck than even Wil had been before the academy had built up his confidence. They both had a passion for reading and stories, they both grew up in the valley and had plenty of shared history that wasn't all bad, and as it turned out they both had a love for the finer things in life.

"This is what I'd do," Bram said, and then he let out a belch almost as large as him. He set the empty beer bottle down on the kitchen table, where he drank with Wil and Jeb.

"Get drunk after a hard day's work?" Wil scoffed, letting out a much smaller burp.

"No, dumbass, he means make beer," said Jeb, who never passed up a chance to enjoy a few drinks if someone offered. "Right?"

Bram nodded enthusiastically. "Brew my own beer. It was one of the few things me and Dad did together that I actually liked. I haven't done it since, but

I miss it. Maybe when I sell the place I can buy up a small house and turn the basement into a miniature brewery."

Wil thought about it, taking another drink. "We've already got a brewer in town, but I think Old Brown's gotten too cushy without competition. What all would you need to get going?" It was an honest question, nothing extra behind it just yet, though Wil's gut tingled in a way that made him take notice.

"Ten thousand zynce's worth of equipment." Bram sighed.

"Damn." Jeb shook his head and downed his beer. "Didn't think it would be cheap, but getting started in any business is going to cost a lot."

"I have the money—technically," Bram hedged, clearly wondering how much to share with them. Wil didn't push it. After a few seconds, Bram groaned and said, "Mom still has a bit of a nest egg, just not enough to save the place with the debt we've gotten in. Most of it's just to the state, and the auction will forgive that debt and I'll get to keep the difference. It might be possible."

"But this equipment," Wil pressed, "that's all you really need?"

"Well, that and some good ingredients. Wheat, barley, hops, and good clean water. There's other stuff that can go into it too, but those are the basics. Not hard to find in the valley when that's what half the people are growing, anyway." Bram chuckled and gathered up the empty bottles. He wavered when he stood but then tossed them into the trash.

"Hell," Jeb said, grabbing another two beers from the icebox at his feet. He set one down in front of where Abraham sat. "It's a damned shame you gotta sell the place. You could grow all of that right here and be a self-sufficient brewery. You could do it all in one place. If you weren't selling it."

That dropped the mood a little. Still, that tingle in Wil's gut didn't go away. It almost felt like that weird drop he'd felt when the bandits had stopped the train or when Mrs. Lane came to ask for his help. This wasn't as urgent, but he couldn't ignore it and just followed where his instincts took him.

"Any chance of getting personal loans and then trying to keep it and build up a business that way?" Wil asked.

Bram sat back down, his chair protesting until the wood settled. "I dunno. I never thought about it. I was too busy just..." His face fell as he thought about it. "Taking care of my mom and freezing up's kind of eaten up all my time. I could've maybe saved the place if I hadn't wasted time. Kinda shot myself in the foot, didn't I?"

"Sure did!" said Jeb, toasting him.

Wil shot him a dirty look. Jeb just shrugged, unable to keep the drunk smile off his face. "Maybe, but you still have a future," Wil said. And Bram did, if Wil trusted that tingle in his gut. The only question he now faced was whether or not he'd be okay with putting himself on the line for someone he almost hadn't helped.

Pfft. As if that was even a question. Maybe Bram would freeze or not make use of the opportunity once given, but if Wil could give him that opportunity, didn't that mean he owed it to him to try? Being the resident wizard meant more than just filling out work orders and serving the people. It also meant watching out for everyone and doing what he could to improve everyone's lives. He understood that better now.

"What's got you smiling so wide?" Bram asked. "We still got a mountain of work ahead of us. You guys coming back tomorrow?"

"No, sir, I've done my share," said Jeb. And he had, mostly without complaint. Wil couldn't argue with the results. "Tomorrow I'm going to take a day to myself before we get back to our own damned chores."

"I've got a date tomorrow," said Wil, receiving the obligatory high-pitched "oooh" from his brother and new friend. "Yeah, yeah. With Darlene. I've been so damned busy lately, I haven't gotten a chance for a real date yet, so I figured maybe I'd treat her to steak and a few drinks. Show off my ostentatious wealth and all that."

His ostentatious wealth he could be using for so much more. Yeah, he had to see Darlene, but maybe she'd be able to help him out and brainstorm a little. They had only a little over a week left until the auction was scheduled, so he'd have to work fast. Wil smiled and raised his bottle.

"A toast," he said. "To hard work and the hangovers we'll have tomorrow."

Laughing, the three men clinked their bottles together.

CHAPTER 21

Definitely a Date This Time

Harper Valley was growing fast, but it was still largely a farming community. No matter how big things got, that would always be true. So when it came to fine-dining establishments, Wil and Darlene couldn't afford to be picky. There weren't any good places to try foreign foods, for example, and more than anything Wil would've loved to have shown Darlene the many noodle dishes of the Ramenia, but that wasn't an option.

So they settled on steaks.

Danson's Steakhouse might be considered fine dining—if one were to cross their eyes. The richest and most powerful people in the valley ate there regularly, as did anyone out for a special occasion. Jeb had to put up with babysitting Wil and Sarah during date nights for their parents plenty of times. It felt a bit funny going there for a date for the first time, but mostly it was exciting.

"You ever come here on your own?" Wil asked as he and Darlene stood outside the doors, arm in arm. Wil had dressed in his best school uniform again without the jacket. The moment he saw Darlene wearing a nice black dress, he kicked himself about not making time to get fitted for good clothes.

"On my own? No, that sounds like it'd be lonely and sad," said Darlene, eyes twinkling with mischief. "With others, though? Plenty of times with my parents, and three times on dates, before now."

"Oh," said Wil, deflating a little.

Darlene nudged him. "You'll never see me say no to a fat steak and a plate of potatoes. Relax."

It did make him feel a little better. Together they walked inside and Wil blinked at just how cool it was inside compared to the heat from the last enduring rays of the sun. Fans overhead spun fast, and the restaurant had an open feeling to it. They went up to the host.

"Lovely to see you again, Ms. Johnson. Two of you this evening?" he asked, looking over them both. Wil's skin crawled from the way his eyes lingered and his nose wrinkled at the sight of him.

Darlene nodded. "Yes, thank you, Emile." She smiled at Wil as they followed the host over to a table.

Wil remembered almost too late to pull her chair out for her before he sat down, and then again to put the napkin in his lap. The rest of the rules for not making an ass of himself were gone, as if they'd never been there in the first place, but he could remember those two things at least.

"Would you care to get started with some drinks? A nice wine perhaps?" Emile said, clasping his gloved hands together.

"Uh, sure," said Wil, fighting a small panic. "What do you recommend?"

"The Deveraux 1870 is a favorite choice with all our cuts of beef."

"Sure, that." Wil smiled nervously.

"And for the lady?"

Darlene smirked at Wil. "I'll have a beer. Something dark and nutty."

"Excellent choice," said Emile, bowing his head and ducking away.

"H-hold it," Wil said, catching him just in time. "Actually, I'll have what she's having."

Emile quirked an eyebrow at him. Wil wanted to squirm. After two uncomfortable seconds, the host smiled and nodded, disappearing.

"You really want to impress me, huh?" Darlene laughed.

Wil shrugged. "I mean, I don't *not* want to impress you. I'm bad at stuff like this. I don't have the foggiest clue what I'm doing."

"Well," said Darlene, leaning forward and resting her elbows on the table. "You could start with a compliment. Not just telling me I look nice, though."

He thought about it for a second and smiled. "You're really good at making me second-guess myself, and I can't seem to relax around you."

"I make you uncomfortable, huh? Fantastic compliment, Wil." But her own smile told him she wasn't mad.

"It's more like I feel like you see right through me," Wil said. "Like, no matter what I say or do, you seem to see me pretty well, and I can't hide from you."

Darlene's mouth made a silent "O". She nodded, smiling and trying not to seem too pleased. "Now that's a pretty good compliment. I'll take it and bask in it for a bit. In the meantime, what've you been up to the past while?"

Wil fell back in his chair and groaned. "Helping Bram clean up his place. We've been at it for a week now, and we're mostly done."

"Bram, huh? So I'm guessing things are going better than you expected?"

Once again, she had that piercing, knowing smirk that tormented Wil in the best way.

"Look," Wil started, before they both descended into laughter. "He's not the same guy he was. I guess neither of us is the same. It's weird to see but feels good. Expectations are rough, especially when you end up becoming someone completely different than expected."

Darlene's smirk fell, turning into a more natural smile. "Don't I know it. My mom and dad both have some specific expectations of me, and every time I tell them I want nothing to do with it, they get so mad. And I know you must be dealing with a lot of it, right, Mr. Wizard?"

"Exactly right. What you said stuck with me, so I decided to give Bram another chance. And now that the work is almost over, I'm actually pretty worried for the guy. But I can only help him so much, I guess." Wil fiddled with the napkin in his lap. "I wish I could do more."

A uniformed woman came by with their drinks, poured into glasses for them already. Darlene took hers and sipped, eyes fluttering shut at the taste. Wil tasted his and had to admit, it was a good nutty brown ale.

"Hi, I'm Erin. Do you two know what you want?" the waitress said, sounding perky. The steakhouse wasn't too busy that night, and it was still early.

"Yeah, give me the rib eye, rare, and the baked potato and broccoli," Darlene ordered, handing over the menu. Wil realized he hadn't even looked at it.

"Excellent choice. And for you?" Erin turned to him.

"Um, same."

Bowing, the waitress took his menu as well and moved on. Only a few seconds later, Darlene snickered.

"What?" Wil demanded.

"Two dates in a row, you just ordered the same thing as me. What's wrong, Wil, afraid to make your own choices?" she teased.

His cheeks burned. "Actually, I just really like figuring out what people like and why. By getting what you're getting, I'm trying to see a little more of you."

"Huh. You're not as much of a disaster as you think," she said, eyes twinkling. "You keep surprising me with little bits of sweetness."

"Oh good, you bought it." They laughed and Wil finally let himself relax some.

"So, back to Bram, what more would you do, if you could?" Darlene pressed him, taking another sip of her drink.

How could he explain something he didn't fully know himself? He'd had plenty of thoughts on how he could help Bram, but none of them seemed realistic or sensible. His ideas reeked of fantasy and optimism, when he knew that wasn't how the world worked.

"Find a way so he doesn't have to sell," said Wil with a sigh. "He fell into a dark place and things got bad. But just last night we were talking about what he'd do if he could, and he wants to start a brewery. Wouldn't that be fantastic, having a second brewery in town? His farm would be perfect for every part of it. We'd just need to build a new barn and convert the basement, maybe."

Darlene raised an eyebrow. "That's awfully specific. But maybe not out of the question. How much does he owe on the farm?"

Wil wondered if he should share or not. They weren't his details to pass around, but if she could help him, maybe that made it okay. "Something like fifty thousand zynce to the city. That's why they're repossessing the farm if he doesn't auction it off."

She did some quick math in her head. "That's rough," she said, "but maybe doable. If you wanted to do something big, you could probably offer to buy the debt off whoever's in charge. Probably the mayor. He seems to like you well enough."

Oh, gods. He probably *could* get it done that way without much hassle. But relying on the mayor felt gross and humiliating. And like the man would hold it over him for a favor later. He hadn't done that to Wil before, but he seemed the type. Then again, if it meant saving Bram's farm and giving him a second chance, wouldn't that be worth it?

"I might do that," Wil said. "But I'm a little bit worried about it. If I do this and Bram doesn't pull through, that's a lot of baggage for me to deal with."

"Yeah, there's always a huge risk going into business with friends. There's not just labor to worry about but also operating costs, overhead"—Darlene listed things off on her fingers—"distribution. It's a lot to consider, even before you get into risking your personal relationships."

Of course! The answer was staring him quite literally in the face!

"You've done a lot of study on what it takes to run a business, right?" Wil asked, trying not to sound too excited.

Darlene scoffed. "It *is* kind of what I've been focusing on my entire life. I've read books, I've handled everything in the general store for Dad for the past few years, I've come up with all kinds of plans and—oh," she paused, understanding. "I just said there's a huge risk going into business with friends and you want to drag *me* into it as well?"

Wil winced a little. "Okay, when you put it like that, it sounds bad, but think about it. You've been wanting to branch out and get away from your dad's business, and here's the potential for starting something of your own. Between my ridiculous pay and your savings and know-how, we could probably make a brewery happen. You'd share your expertise, and if you ever wanted out, I could buy out whatever you paid into it. In time."

"You're not wrong," Darlene admitted. "It does sound appealing. And like it would be the perfect test run before I do something on my own. Something with a little less risk. But if we're going to do this, then Abraham's gotta be on board with it all, including being a one-third partner and not fully in charge. You think that'll be okay?"

"Okay? He'll be so relieved he won't have to stress about it all on his own." Wil laughed. He couldn't say he knew Bram well, but after a long, dedicated week with him, he thought he was learning. "This is fantastic. Here I am enjoying drinks and steaks with my crush while planning on how to uplift my bully."

Darlene raised her glass to that and they drank. "Now that business is out of the way, let's focus on us, huh?"

Wil flushed but nodded enthusiastically. He had a job he loved, a new friend, and maybe a girlfriend. Life was only getting better and better.

CHAPTER 22

Death and Rebirth

Addie Stevenson's funeral took place on a blistering Sunday, attended by only a handful of people. There might have been more, but before his death and Addie's sickness, Abraham Stevenson Senior had driven away many of their loved ones. With her health failing, Abraham had neither the time nor the energy to mend bridges and get back in touch. Just another tragedy in an already tragic life.

"To the earth we return, where we will nourish the next generation. A life has ended, but life goes on," the priestess finished, and Wil repeated the prayer along with the others. Then the priestess bowed her head in silent contemplation, and Wil did as well, trying not to wipe the sweat from his brow.

All funerals took place outdoors, where the living celebrated the dead's life and mixed their ashes into the soil to fertilize the future and keep giving back to the world that nurtured them. Addie Stevenson had loved flowers, and the small gathering took place in the newly cleaned up garden in front of the house Bram had prepared to sell.

Bram took the urn with her ashes and lifted them up. The McKenzie family, the Johnson family, and the mayor stared back at him. Tears falling freely from his rough face, Bram opened the lid and gently poured the ashes around the flowers, grabbing a claw and working them into the earth. He took his time and Wil appreciated the care he put into the motion. Beside him, Sarah fidgeted.

Finished, Bram stood and cleared his throat. "I know as her son I should have a speech or something prepared. I don't. I'm not good at that. All I can say is, it wasn't fair. She died too young—married to a bad man who treated her poorly and falling ill before she could ever live for herself. She deserved... deserved better!"

He wept openly. Wil's heart ached for him, but it seemed to do Bram some good, being able to let it out without judgment. After only a couple of seconds, Sharon took it upon herself to break the separation between Bram and the other mourners and pulled him into a big hug. He wrapped his arms around the much smaller woman and just let himself sob.

Wil wasn't one to cry, more often than not. A middle child had to have a certain level of toughness to get by, and it was easier to bottle things up and deal with them later. Seeing Bram lose it made his eyes burn and sting and water. Darlene squeezed his hand, and he smiled at her. She motioned with her head and Wil followed her to give his mother and Bram some privacy with their grief.

"You doing okay?" Darlene asked him.

Clearing his tightened throat, Wil said, "Yeah. I can't imagine losing my parents. They need to stay alive as long as possible, preferably until I'm an old man."

"I think it's different for you," Darlene said, half smiling. "You'd be mourning good relationships. Bram is mourning relationships he'll never get to have. I think that's where I would be too, if it were mine who died."

"You don't have *any* good relationships with your parents?" Wil asked, only a little surprised.

Darlene shook her head. "Not really. Dad wants me to be more like him and then gets mad when I am. Mom's barely there, even when she's there. No siblings, so all their hopes and dreams and fears and insecurities are all on me."

"I can vaguely understand that, if not personally. I'm very fortunate," said Wil, for once feeling it to be absolutely true. "Do you think it's a bad time to talk to him about our plans? Think we should wait?"

"Absolutely. He's going to be raw and busted up today. No need to stress him with talks of business until at least tomorrow. At least."

The heat continued to assault them. Now that they were no longer in the service itself, Wil mopped the sweat from his brow and flung it at the ground. Darlene made a face and moved away from him, but he couldn't blame her. It was too hot to be too close to anybody.

Wil studied the sky. Clouds hung not too far in the distance, fat and gray. Another week or so and it could've been a light storm, but that would take too long. Opening himself up to the feeling of the land, Wil gently tapped into the small leyline running through the property. Charged with more power than he'd have on his own, he reached up for the nearest cloud and sent a firm invitation.

It didn't hurt, pulling the cloud down over the house, though it felt like it should. Teeny, tiny, little Wil McKenzie put himself between a cloud with a million pounds of moisture and the earth itself and pulled on both ends, and somehow it didn't destroy him. Though after a minute of it, the physical tax was like having run a mile nonstop. But he wasn't done.

With a burst of strength he felt through the earth to the flower patch. The ashes were there, full of death waiting to be brought back around and used to give life. He drew them into the earth and directed a little trickle from the leyline to the flower bed. And then he released it and let it do the work himself. He panted for breath but when he opened his eyes, the sky above the farm was a dark gray in a sea of open blue. Rain started falling, slow and ponderous. Everybody stared at him.

"S-sorry," Wil said, shrinking a bit under the attention.

"What did you do?" Bram asked, eyes red and face swollen from crying.

Rather than answer, Wil pointed over to the flower bed, where even now the start of a flower poked through the dirt and grew before their eyes. Slowly but steadily it grew to full size over the course of half a minute or so. Then bright blue and purple petals bloomed, larger than normal. Soon, the entire flower bed was a riot of color.

Bram looked at Wil and then the flowers. The next thing Wil knew, Bram charged him and scooped him up in a bear hug. Wil's bones creaked dangerously, but he did his best to hug back as Bram shook more with silent sobs. Which only brought Wil closer and closer to crying as well. He slapped his friend's back until Bram finally released him.

"T-t-thank you-hoooo." Bram swallowed hard, face screwing up as he tried not to cry more.

Wil pat his arm one last time. "It's nothing," he said. Nothing compared to the pain Bram was clearly going through.

Mayor Sinclair stepped up. "Aw, how modest. That's our Wilbur, always helping others and pretending it ain't a big deal. Real mind for service, that one." He smiled, and Wil already regretted asking for his help. "Good afternoon, Mr. Stevenson, Ms. Johnson. Aside from our tragic circumstances, I trust you both are well?"

Bram sniffled and that was all the answer he needed to give. Darlene, on the other hand, put on a forced smile Wil recognized, the same he wore whenever around the mayor.

"As well as can be. Just here to support a friend," said Darlene in a 'please leave me alone, I don't want to deal with this' tone. The mayor either didn't notice or didn't care.

"And what support you're giving! I'd say that you two are probably the best friends young Abraham Junior here could have."

Oh no. He wasn't going to—

"Yeah?" Bram looked at them curiously. "I agree, but what makes you say so?"

Before Darlene or Wil could stop him, Mayor Sinclair chuckled and said,

"Well, they're taking a hell of a risk on you, aren't they? Not many people would put tens of thousands of zynce of their own money toward helping a friend. But when Wil came up and asked me for a favor, why, your story moved me so much, I had to help."

Bram just stared at all of them. Darlene looked at the ground.

Wil sighed. "We hadn't told him yet, Mr. Mayor. We were going to wait until tomorrow, not when he's raw with grief."

The expression on the mayor's face froze. He cleared his throat, straightening his tie. "Ah, then I fear I may have…may have misspoken. Pardon me. Harper Valley grieves with you, and I'll leave you to it and not bother you further. All the best, Mr. Stevenson." He beat a hasty retreat, going off to talk with Bob.

"What is he talking about?" Bram asked, the suspicion cutting through his grief.

"Look, it was technically my idea, so if you're mad at anyone, be mad at me," said Darlene. "Wil may have bought the debt to your house. For pretty cheap, actually. So you can keep the farm, and we could maybe make it a brewery."

Bram blinked. He looked at Wil. "Is this true?"

Wil squirmed. "Yes. After we talked the other night about fresh starts and a brewery, I ran away with it a little. I know how much crap you're going through and didn't want you to lose your home too. And I figured, if you wanted a fresh start with a brewery, me and Darlene could make that happen. If not, you can still auction the land, but do it without fear of losing your home if someone lowballs you."

Silence. Wil badly wanted to take Darlene's hand, as if she could protect him from the consequences of his own good intentions. They'd intended on asking Bram first if he wanted to go along with it, but then his mother died the day after their date, and time melted away as Bram dealt with her funeral and everything else. With only a few days away before the potential auction, Wil had to leap on it. Now that it was revealed early, he didn't know what to expect.

But maybe he should've expected another bone-breaking hug. Bram grabbed both Wil and Darlene in his arms and pulled them in for the biggest and sturdiest group hug Wil could ever remember being a part of. Bram kept it going until Darlene squeaked in pain, and they broke apart suddenly.

"I can't believe you two," Bram said. Luckily he wasn't crying anymore. He looked like he wanted to, though. "You didn't have to do that. I know I wouldn't take a chance on me, knowing what you do about me failing and freezing the last few years."

"You're mistaken," said Wil, not hiding the smile on his face. "This is purely selfish. I want my own source of beer but I don't want to go through the effort of actually making it. I'm getting you to do the grunt work for me while I enjoy the fruits of your labor."

"Yeah, same," said Darlene brightly. "I just want to own a business and you're convenient. It's not like I care about you or anything."

Bram laughed, and oh gods, what a relief. He laughed hard and long. Wil expected to be dragged into a hug again. The big man refrained, though he did keep a hand on both of their shoulders, both grateful and clinging to them as lifelines.

"I...I don't know how much you're willing to put in, but I've got some savings still, and will get more now that Mom is...gone. We'll need so much to get started."

Wil nodded. "Already thought of that. We'll put in an order for all the equipment you said we'll need, and while it takes time getting delivered, we'll build up a new barn and make sure it's sturdy and warded against critters getting in. Maybe set your basement up for storage, now that a lot of your dad's old crap is cleared out."

"We're going to need to buy local ingredients first," Darlene added, just as swept up as they were. "But with Wil focusing on handling the farming stuff himself, we could get in a harvest or two before summer's out and can have a decent enough stock for the first few batches of beer as you get the hang of things. You won't see any profits for a good long while, so I hope those savings are enough to get you through a year."

Bram did some quick math, and not for the first time Wil saw that aside from the nervous, emotional wreck he'd become, the massive man was smarter than people gave him credit for. "Without having to pay for medicine, I could last for a couple years comfortably. " Grief struck him again, but he pushed it down. "Thank you, you two. I don't think I would've bounced back without a plan, and you two just...well, thank you."

Wil spared another glance at the flower bed, now overgrown and lush with bright life. No matter how much he wanted to feel good about things, it still felt selfish, helping Bram. But maybe it was okay to be selfish if you were still helping people. Everyone deserved a chance, and Bram had showed him people could change.

"Not a problem, my friend."

CHAPTER 23

Food, Friends, and Fatherly Advice

After the funeral, the three of them were inseparable. Bram took it upon himself to come over to Wil's house every day and help with the paperwork, now that they no longer had to rush to finish cleaning the property all the way. Wil didn't need the help, but having the company turned out to be nice enough that he didn't feel the need to tell Bram to stay home.

Darlene tended to pop in around lunchtime or after her shift at the general store, and they'd get a bite to eat together. Sometimes, Bram tagged along and they made it a group outing. There wasn't much to be done until the equipment arrived, and Wil had already done a lot of the initial planting of wheat, barley, and hops.

A new day found them all meeting together at the McKenzie household for an extended family dinner. Which was nice, all things considered, but Wil had something important to do, and it wasn't something he felt comfortable doing around too many witnesses. As far as Wil was concerned, it was between him and his father, and anyone else being in on it would've been uncomfortable. He was open with his ridiculous wages, but getting help on top of that…Wil put it out of his head and tried to focus on the positives.

Like the incredible smells wafting out of the McKenzie house as the three of them stood on the porch.

"Gods, that's incredible," Bram said, all but openly drooling. Being a very large man, Bram could put away about as much as anyone expected of him, possibly more.

"I never get home cooking anymore," Darlene moaned. She inhaled deeply.

"Y'all are weird," Sarah said, opening the front door and gesturing for them to come in. "You act like none of you have eaten before."

"Each time I taste your mama's food, it's like I haven't," Darlene said with a grin.

"Can you really blame us?" Wil asked, getting a whiff. "Who could resist a good platter of fried chicken?"

They all went inside, where Bob sat in the den listening to the radio. He raised a hand in greeting but kept his attention on the baseball game being broadcast two towns over. A loud hiss and crackle came from the kitchen. Wil peeked his head in to find Sharon flipping over strips of chicken in hot oil. Beside her, the family's biggest serving platter was nearly full.

"Wil, get in here and handle the potatoes!" she barked.

Darlene and Bram snickered at him, but Wil just shrugged and stepped up. Grabbing a couple of pot holders, he drained the boiling potatoes and grabbed the masher. He dumped in what felt like an appropriate amount of salt, pepper, garlic, and butter, and then just a splash of milk, and mashed away for all he was worth. He probably could've done something to make it go faster, but there was an honest joy in the work he didn't deny.

"Lookin' good," Sharon said, finally getting a second to check over Wil's work. Then she turned around and brought her hands together in delight. "Bram, Darlene, so good to see you two," she said, beckoning. "C'mere!" Bram went in for a massive hug. Sharon kissed Darlene's cheek casually. "You two looking forward to dinner?"

"Been looking forward to it all day," Bram exclaimed, doing a tappy little happy dance.

Wil shook his head, chuckling. The big man wore his heart on his sleeve.

"I haven't had good fried chicken in years!" Bram said.

"Well, we're going to have to load you up and send some home with you, now won't we?" Sharon beamed at him.

"Anything I can do to help?" Darlene asked brightly.

Sharon pointed at the final burner in use. "Check on the corn and keep it mixing together. Sprinkle in some salt, pepper, sugar, and butter, and when it looks like it's just starting to get crispy around the edges pull it off."

Darlene joined Wil at the stove and did just that. Together, they worked quietly while Sharon and Bram talked. Wil let himself relax and enjoy the moment. A few seconds later, Darlene lightly hip-checked him. He chuckled and then did it back, just a little harder. Soon they were pushing against each other while they cooked, acting like children and loving it.

"Get a room, you two," Sharon teased as she pushed through and took out a piece of chicken with some ancient tongs.

The three of them finished up dinner together and brought it to the table, where Sarah had just finished setting it.

"Bob!" Sharon called out. A long-suffering groan and the creak of his chair told them he was on his way.

Before too long, everyone but Jeb had gathered around the table and served themselves. Jeb had decided to spend the night at the pub with friends rather than fighting to fit around their table with everyone else. After how hot and cold he'd been the past couple of months, Wil didn't mind much. Instead, he just made sure there would be enough leftover chicken, garlic mashed potatoes, corn, and green beans for him to get food-drunk off of.

The beginnings of a good dinner like this had very little talking. Mostly, people just grabbed at food and funneled it into their mouths while occasionally groaning or complimenting Sharon on her cooking. It was enough to just share in good company while indulging in the senses and sense of home that came with a good meal.

It wasn't until at least halfway through before someone spoke.

"So, what kind of beer are you guys going to brew first?" asked Bob. "You got any recipes handy, or what?" He speared some green beans on his fork and shoveled them into his mouth.

Bram chewed faster and swallowed hard, eager to answer. "We bought enough equipment to have four batches going at once, so we're going to try a bunch of recipes and see which ones we like best and how much we'll need to tweak them. And then from there we'll get a recipe or two down and see about mass producing and if any local places want to serve it. We know we can probably get the general store, right?"

Darlene made a face. "Probably, but you don't want to count on that. My dad's a little pissed at me for branching out into a new business. He's been giving me all kinds of crap about not focusing as hard on the store as him."

"That's Jonjon for you," said Sharon, clicking her tongue. "No offense, sweetie."

"Oh, none taken. I agree."

"We're a good match," said Wil. "We all bring something pretty critical to the mix and I think together we can really make this work."

"And what do you bring?" Sarah snorted at him. "A bunch of money?"

"Sarah," Bob warned, but it was too late. Wil's cheeks heated up dangerously.

"Wil's going to be handling the crops for the next little while," said Bram, using a fork and knife on his chicken, instead of just spearing a piece and biting hunks off like the rest of them. "It's four fields, but we're not filling them all the way. Just enough to have a good stock of wheat, hops, and barley for the winter batch. Once we get going, we'll be able to hire some people to do the fields for us."

Darlene nudged Wil's leg with her own. "Wil's handling the farming and ingredients, I'm going to handle all the bookkeeping and budgeting, and Bram's going to be fiddling with the recipes and handling the actual brewing process."

"But do you know what you're doing?" Sarah pressed. "You ever make beer before?"

"With my dad," Bram muttered, shrinking in his seat. "Before he died, we'd make our own beer every season. And now I'm going to do even better. Maybe make him proud."

No one said anything about what a bastard Abraham Senior had been.

"I think it's a fine plan, and one I'm glad to be a part of," said Bob. "Even if only distantly. You put your mind to it and work hard, you'll get it done. The hardest part of brewing beer, from what I hear, is the waiting. All the work is front-loaded to getting a batch ready and then you just wait for a couple of months. Isn't that right? What're you gonna do when you've got all the work done and are just waiting around?"

"That's something we worked out together, actually," Darlene piped up. "It takes four to eight weeks for most simple beers, right? We're going to stagger them out so that a new one's done every two weeks. That way there's always some work to be done so there isn't a bunch of dead time."

"You're not gonna let things get bad again like before we cleaned, right?" Sarah asked gracelessly.

"Sarah!" Sharon snapped.

Wil was already on top of it. "No, it's not going to happen. That was a one-time thing that's understandable, given the circumstances." Bram shot him a grateful look, nodding and keeping his head down in leftover shame.

"Besides, he's got too much on his plate to stop. Aside from brewing and keeping the machinery clean, we're going to have to go around and sample our competition and take notes, right?"

Bram came back to life, vibrating with excitement. "Absolutely. And if there's one thing I love, it's tasting things and taking notes."

"I can see that," Sarah said, finishing her chicken with a smirk.

"How about you help them out, Sarah?" Bob said pointedly. "They're going to need a good logo for their brewery when they're ready. Maybe you can help out with that."

"Depends," said Sarah. "Am I getting paid for it?"

Before either of their parents could give her any trouble for it, Wil said, "Well, obviously. Your art is fantastic and we'd never treat you as anything less than a professional, now, would we?"

The rest of the meal tapered off from there. Their collective appetites appeased, it became all too easy to just linger around the table drinking sweet tea or cold beer. Just when Wil thought to offer to help clean up, Bob pushed his chair back. "Thank you for the wonderful meal, Sharon. It was perfect, like always. I think I need to step outside for a few."

"Oh, phooey. You're just going to go take a post-dinner nap," Sharon accused with a smile. Bob just shrugged.

"There's actually something I wanted to talk to you about," Wil said, standing as well. "In private, if that's alright."

Bram and Darlene looked at him curiously but just shrugged. "I'll help clean up," Bram offered, taking a few mostly empty plates. Darlene joined him, and Sarah took the opportunity to slink away up to her room. Wil and his father stepped outside, and sure enough, Bob pulled out his pipe. When he offered it to Wil, Wil waved him off.

"Naw, if I smoke I really will fall asleep, and I don't think Darlene or Bram need to wait on me to wake up," he said, chuckling.

Bob packed a bowl and sat down in his favorite rocker. "S'no problem. It's nice to see you with friends. Well, friend and girlfriend, I guess. How's that going?"

Wil joined him in the rocker next to him. "Well enough. Slow, though I think part of that's introducing business into the mix. I'm a bit worried about that."

"You should be," said Bob, lighting the pipe and puffing away. "Mixing business and pleasure's often a good recipe for disaster. But you're good kids, and this is a good opportunity for y'all. I think you need each other, honestly."

"Yeah?" Wil thought about it and then took the pipe from his father for one puff after all. "I really appreciate the help you've given, Dad. I don't think we'd be able to pull it off if it wasn't for you."

Bob took the pipe back, shrugging a little. He looked off into the distance, toward the sun setting over the mountains in the west. "Eh, what're dads for? I know you're good for paying me back."

"I am. In fact…" Wil fished inside his pockets for an envelope. He handed it over to his father, saying, "This is the first payment I owe you. It's about a quarter of my share of it. I wanted to get it to you early, to show I'm serious and I appreciate your help. The rest will come over the next four months as I get paid."

Bob took the envelope and stuffed it into his back pocket without looking at it. "I appreciate that, Wil. Not necessary, but I know you're a worrier. That'll serve you well over the next while. Having your own business, it's a huge responsibility. So long as you keep your head on straight and don't let petty arguments wreck you all, I think you can do it."

Wil took a deep breath and let it out, rocking gently on the porch. "Do you have any specific advice? For keeping a business going. You and Ma have done pretty well over the past thirty years, right?"

"We sure have," Bob said with a hearty laugh. "Three wonderful children and food on the table every year. We're comfortable but still have plenty more we could be doing. It's a nice spot to be in. You want advice? I think that's what you should go for: Do enough to keep you guys hungry for more, but don't be afraid to rest and make sure you got enough energy for the future. Don't burn candles at both ends.

"If and when you get mad at your partners, and you will, don't do anything rash. Always sleep on any major decisions, and remember that above all else, you're friends, and that comes first. This business is gonna mean more to Bram and Darlene than you, I think. Don't forget that.

"And most importantly, have some damned fun. Y'all are in the prime of your lives and have so much room to live and make mistakes. Do it, and don't be afraid to have fun. You get me?"

Wil got him. "Thanks, Dad, we will." He grinned. "If nothing else, it's an excuse to drink beer every night and try out every place to eat and drink in the valley."

Bob scoffed. "Like you needed an excuse."

They laughed, and rocked on the porch for a little while longer.

CHAPTER 24

The Midsummer Faire

Handling all the chores at the Stevenson farm could've been a backbreaking amount of labor had he been any other person. Luckily for Wil, he got to cheat the entire time. The little leyline let him safely tap into almost the entire property and till the land through an expenditure of will. A minor localized earthquake and minor telekinesis meant he could plant his seeds without having to get his hands dirty or his back bent.

The hardest part, funnily enough, was making sure everything got proper amounts of water. Lifting water magically wasn't much easier than lifting it physically, and conjuration had never been Wil's strength. It came easiest when Wil could make it rain, but some days were easier than others.

Wil stared up into the hot, cloudless sky. Deep in the heart of summer now, they were between rainy seasons, with endless blue and just a few scattered white clouds staring back down at him. He reached with his senses, trying to gather moisture from the air to coalesce into a cloud. Nothing happened.

"I thought this was easy for you," Bram said from behind him, making Wil jump out of his skin.

"No," said Wil as he clutched his chest, "not easy. Not unless there's already rain or some serious cloud coverage. If there's already a storm? Oh, no problem. I just reach into the storm and can make it bigger or smaller with some effort. Bigger's usually easier. Days like this? I might as well piss on the crops to water them."

"Gee," Bram said with a smile, "hope you're hydrated enough. But seriously, it hasn't been too hard so far, managing all of this on your own?"

Wil shook his head. "Naw, it's been easy enough. I've had to take it a bit easier for work orders, but now that I'm, like, two months in, some of the excitement's worn off and people are getting more patient, knowing I do good work. Besides, today's my day off, anyway."

"True, true. You going to work any more on that rug of yours?" Bram didn't hide his excitement. Ever since Wil had told him of his plans, he very badly wanted to ride a flying carpet.

"You know, I just might. After I finish watering the wheat. Already took care of the hops and barley. We're lucky I can help speed things along some because there's no way we'd be able to plant and harvest enough without it. How're the current batches coming?"

Bram's eyes lit up behind his glasses. "I bottled the first batch today. It'll just take a few more weeks until we're ready for a taste. I've been keeping extensive notes on all the little differences between our first few batches, and I'm really excited to see how they all turn out!"

Wil grinned, then turned back to his work. There was always the possibility of drawing water up from the ground, but in the middle of summer, that could have all kinds of complications and consequences. One didn't mess with the natural order of things willy-nilly.

Probably for the best he did not. Sighing, Wil motioned for Bram to follow him. He led them up to the pump and a couple of big watering cans.

"Looks like it's classic hard work for us today. Fill yours up and start on the east side, we'll meet up in the middle."

As fun as it could be to cheat, Wil couldn't deny the appeal of honest work and toiling under the sun. The upside of it all? As hot as it was, when Wil approached the bottom of the watering can he just dumped it over his head to cool off. At first, Bram looked at him like he was crazy and then did it himself, laughing as they refilled at the pump and finished up the last bits of work for the day. They still had another five hours until dusk, all to themselves.

They spent it indoors under a slow-turning ceiling fan, with cold drinks and open books. One of the best things about his new friendship was how much Bram really did read these days. And now that they were friends, he'd even started going through Wil's schoolbooks. He couldn't do any magic himself, but he remained in awe of every bit of the education and often asked Wil questions. That usually ended with Wil explaining, in general terms, how magic worked and even, he believed, led to him understanding the subject better.

It was during one of those back-and-forths about the nature of magic and specifically telekinesis that a knock at the door disturbed them. Wil let Bram get it since, despite how often he was over, it wasn't his house. A few seconds later, Bram called him over anyway. At the door was a local teen, Tanner, who sometimes ran messages for a couple of zynce here and there.

"The mayor wants to see you," he said when Wil came to the door. "Said he wants to talk to you about something."

"Why didn't he send me an invitation to a chat in the mail or something like that?" Wil asked.

Tanner scowled. "He did, but you apparently don't spend that much time at home or don't open your damned mail."

"Are those your words or his?" Wil cocked his head to the side.

"Whatever. Message delivered. Go see the mayor." And then the surly teen turned around and trudged up the lane, away from the house.

"Well," said Bram, "it's great to see that good manners are being fostered in the youth. Yes, I know I don't have much room to talk. What do you think the mayor wants to talk about?"

"Probably the festival," Wil answered. "It's coming up next week—there are posters about it all over town. Honestly surprised he hasn't tried talking to me sooner about it, considering how ecstatic he's been to parade me around and show me off."

"Maybe he has," Bram snickered, "and you just don't check your mail often enough."

"Look, most of it is work orders, and I focus on those. Only other mail I get is from people who want money from me. I better go. You want me to leave the book here?"

Bram wiggled his fingers eagerly. "If you don't mind."

"Sure."

Not too long ago, Wil would've stopped by home to shower and get better dressed before meeting up with the major. It wasn't so much that he no longer respected the man as he no longer feared him. Mayor Sinclair was a boisterous, self-aggrandizing bag of wind, but he wasn't that bad overall. But Wil treasured the hard work he did, so why shouldn't he show up dressed in farmer's work clothes with a healthy coating of dirt?

The receptionist looked down her nose at him, again, even after all this time. Wil did his best to ignore her and waited the ten or so minutes it took for the mayor's meeting to end. The door opened and Wil jumped to his feet. Mayor Sinclair shook hands with a well-dressed middle-aged man Wil didn't recognize. The man nodded to Wil on his way out.

"Wilbur McKenzie, you're a hard man to reach!" the mayor boomed, clapping his hands together.

Wil sighed on the inside and smiled. "Just been really busy lately. Sorry it took me so long." He walked into the office and remained standing in front of the desk. "What did you need to see me for, sir?" Wil asked.

Mayor Sinclair went around to his seat and sat down, getting comfortable. "It's about the upcoming Midsummer Faire," he said. Wil nodded and motioned for him to continue. " I seem to recall your family always having a bunch of fun. It's gotten big since you were away. There's a lot more food stalls and entertainment now, not just the animal show."

"Yeah," Wil admitted, "I've always loved the Midsummer Faire. I was looking forward to being able to wander around with more money than when I was a kid. Not going to lie, sir, I'm going to eat enough sausage pastries to make me sick."

The mayor let out a polite laugh before he leaned forward on his desk, fingers steepled together. "Well, it's been a few generations since we've had a resident wizard, so you've never gotten to see their contributions to the festival. As one of the major fixtures of Harper Valley, it's now on you to help us put on a show celebrating the town."

Wil blinked. "What? I was...not really expecting that. Or prepared. It's a week away and you're telling me I have to think of a good show to put on for people?"

"To be fair, I sent a letter nearly a week ago."

Wil pulled at his hair. He took a deep breath and forced it out slowly. "What kind of show are we talking? How long, how complicated, how...I've never put on a show before in my life. Even in school when we were supposed to do a play, I had to duck out and have the understudy take over!"

Mayor Sinclair laughed. "Ah, being a kid is scary. But I'm certain you'll rise to the occasion. I don't have the foggiest clue what you should do for a show, I just know it should feature your special gift and be something about Harper Valley. The rest is up to you. If you'd like, take a break from all work orders until you've got something done. Anyone complains, send them at me and I'll take care of it.

"And it's not like we're asking you to do this for nothing. As one of the biggest contributors to the Faire, you'll be paid a tidy sum for the show you put on. Enough to help that burgeoning business of yours."

Or, more likely, enough for Wil to finish paying his dad off that much sooner for the loan he took to buy out Bram's debt. Either way, it didn't entice him any further. All in all, it just made things more stressful, knowing money was in the picture.

"I'll do it," Wil groaned. "I don't think I've got much choice, do I?"

"Not if you want to remain in the people's good graces," said the mayor, an empty smile on his face. "I've been talking around and people are really excited about what kind of show you'll put on. Word is we're going to have plenty of people from the neighboring towns show up to get a good look at what you can do."

"Oh, so no pressure," Wil deadpanned. On the inside, he screamed endlessly.

"That's the spirit!" Mayor Sinclair snapped his fingers. "Remember, eight days from now. We were thinking you'd open the Faire, and then after, we'd have a band playing through the night. I'm sure whatever you come up with will make a perfect opener for the night's festivities."

Wil left the town hall with a pit in his stomach, growing by the minute. As much as he loved magic and goofing off with it, the idea of performing for thousands of people…He took his time going home, trying at once to both think of what he needed to do and not think of how much would be riding on him.

When he got home, he fixed himself a drink, drained it, and screamed.

CHAPTER 25

Brotherly Brawl

Maybe putting on a show wouldn't be so bad. Wil repeated that to himself when the panic set in, and his skin crawled. It didn't help. The problem was he knew the kinds of things he found interesting and funny, but as much as he loved Harper Valley, he didn't fully fit in. Whatever he might like would probably just be boring or weird to the rest of the citizens, and they were the audience.

The first step ended up being admitting to himself that he was out of his league and needed help. After that, things got easier. Mostly.

"Why're you asking me?" Jeb asked as he cracked the reins. Poor Percival lumbered forward, a contraption of three blades lashing behind him, lazily turning circles and cutting the wheat down. "Do I look like the kind of person who has time to think about putting on a show?" He didn't sound angry, just incredulous.

"Well, no, but you love this town as much as I do, right?" Wil walked along patiently.

"If not more. I didn't leave for six years without visiting."

Wil took a deep breath. "Then why not help me think of something to do? Please. I wouldn't be asking if I thought I could do this all myself. This is your chance to give back to the community and do something that'll make a lot of people happy."

Wil had only just started begging and even now he felt tapped out when it came to his big brother. Jeb might not have been the ideal first person to ask, but that just made it more important to ask him. His older brother had lived here his entire life without leaving the basin even once, and as far as Wil knew, he planned on digging his roots in deeper and staying there until he died and the farm passed on to his kids. Who else would best know what the community needed or wanted?

"Do you want to make something good or do you just want to avoid embarrassing yourself?" Jeb asked, keeping pace with the horse.

"Both," Wil groaned, "but mostly the first one. I want to give the town something worthy of them. I have no clue what to do."

Jeb looked over his shoulder with a horrible, smug smile. "You could always pull rabbits out of hats and saw people in half. Ta-daaa." He let out an annoying, braying laugh.

"Screw you too, pal," Wil grumbled.

"I helped you with your new best friend, didn't I?" said Jeb. "I helped clean up that land and build new fences. You want my help on this too. I'm really kind of busy here, Wil." He snapped the reins again. Percival whinnied in irritation.

Wil stopped in his tracks. "Seriously? I've tried helping you once and you got angry at me for ruining your fertilizer experiment or whatever. You want some help now? Here." Wil turned toward the rest of the field. The power came when called, and he didn't even have to make a formal spell. He just gathered power and swept his leg across the ground and pushed. A force fired from his position and cut down a huge line of wheat.

He did it again and again, little bits of power thrown around like it didn't matter, and the rest of the field, save for a few spare stragglers, cleared. He didn't stop there. One field over, potatoes launched themselves from the ground and landed in piles. Huffing for breath, Wil turned toward his brother with a nasty smile.

"How about now? That's two fields taken care of. Still want to ignore me? Got time to talk now?"

At first, Wil didn't understand Jeb's expression as he dropped the reins and stepped down. It wasn't anything he'd ever seen before on his older brother. Then Jeb put both his hands on Wil's chest and shoved him to the ground.

"What the hell?" Wil demanded, standing back up. "What'd you do that for?"

"You think you're so damned special, don't you?" Jeb demanded. "You just *love* to rub my nose in how much easier you have it, don't you?" He shoved Wil.

"You think I've got it easy?" Wil scoffed. "You've been doing everything you can to make things hard on me! I don't know what I've done to you that's made you such a jackass, but I'm sick of it!" And then he shoved Jeb back.

The two stared at each other for about two seconds before Wil let out an enraged war cry and the two crashed against one another gracelessly.

Fists flew until one of them, neither would be able to say who, grappled the other and they went tumbling to the ground. For the first time since Wil had come home, they were no longer familiar strangers. They were just two angry brothers throwing punches and rolling around on the ground like children. Not once did the idea of using magic to end the fight or win cross Wil's mind. Nothing did, except finding the perfect leverage to break free of Jeb's grasp and slug him in the face.

The two continued like that until his older brother used his superior size and strength to get in a good hit that left Wil sprawled out on the ground. Jeb got to a sitting position, huffing and puffing. His lips and nose bled slowly, trickling down his chin. He wiped his face with the back of his hand, getting hay stuck to his face.

"You're a real bastard, you know that?" Jeb demanded. "It's not bad enough you left us all, but now that you're back, it's all about you. You need help, you got a problem. What about the rest of us? When's the last time you checked in on us and saw how we're doing? But no, putting on a stupid show is the most important thing in the world."

Groaning, he got to his feet and staggered off, leaving Wil on the ground. Soon enough Wil got up too, pain radiating from his face and ribs. He knew he looked a mess, but he couldn't bring himself to go into the house and clean up as he might've done when they were still children. His parents might see him and then he'd have to explain.

Percival stood there, staring at Wil with tired eyes before he snorted and bent over to eat some straw. Later on, Wil would be ashamed of himself, but he just left Percival there and walked home. If Jeb wanted to abandon the job after attacking him, then he could deal with Percival being loose with the contraption on his back.

Wil tried his best to ignore the people he passed on the way to his house. Enough people stopped and gave him funny looks that he knew his face was likely a complete mess, and dirt and straw covered his body. He put it all out of his mind and just trudged home. Inside, he wiped away the blood and grabbed a cloth and filled it with ice, and pressed it up against his sore jaw.

Everything hurt, but not as much as knowing his brother seemed to well and truly hate him. He'd thought things were getting better, but apparently not. And even as much as Wil wanted to get in another few good shots to make up for that last punch Jeb got in on him, he still loved him. He didn't want to be this angry or upset, and it made his stomach twist and churn.

Worst of all, he wasn't any closer to figuring out what he should do for the festival. But he knew someone else who could help him. One of the only people who'd always been a help since he'd returned. When the ice had mostly melted, Wil headed to the general store.

Darlene must've been getting used to his visits in the middle of her shift, but this was the first time he wandered in looking like tenderized meat on legs, so she stopped in the middle of ringing up Mrs. Maron and gaped at him.

"What the hell happened to you?" she gasped. The rest of the people in line turned to look at him.

Wil's face burned. He pointed at the back. "I'll just be back there. Take your time." And then he went to the break room, confident he'd be allowed back there at this point.

The presence of Jonathon Johnson told him otherwise.

"Hoo, boy, you get into a scrap today?" Jonjon laughed like an obnoxious mule.

Wil just sat down across from him at the break table. "Something like that," he grumbled. "Just here to see Darlene, I won't be here for that long, I promise."

Jonjon's eyes narrowed. "You the reason she's been taking a bunch of breaks and closing the store up? That's costing me some money, Mr. Wizard."

Wil's patience barely existed. "So bill me," he said, staring Jonjon down.

Jonjon grimaced and said, "Maybe I will. If you're here for Darlene, I might as well take the front so we don't have to close down entirely." He got up and left Wil. After about a minute, Darlene came in.

"What the hell happened to you?" she asked again, grabbing a chair and dragging it next to Wil so she could take a closer look at his face. He tried not to wince when she touched a sensitive area.

"Jeb happened," he said, and then told her everything. From the meeting with the mayor to asking Jeb for help, to him using magic to clear the field, and Jeb punching him. While talking about it did make him feel better, he got a nasty surprise when he finished speaking.

"Well," said Darlene, leaning back with a huff. "You probably shouldn't have used magic to make him feel small. I can see why he got mad."

"What? *What?*" Wil's eyes bugged out. He gestured to his face. "Are you serious? He wasn't listening, so I helped him out so he'd have time to talk to me."

Darlene wasn't impressed. "Were you trying to help him, or were you proving a point? You ever think about how embarrassing it must've been for him for you to just do all his work with a wave of your hand? You trivialized his problems while begging for help with yours."

She might as well have smacked him. "It wasn't like that," he insisted.

"Maybe not for you," she said. "But things are different for him. He's clearly got some unresolved anger toward you and you just kind of brushed it off like it was nothing. You didn't do it to be mean, I don't think, but you still did it."

Wil just grunted in response, looking pointedly at his lap.

Darlene chuckled and put a hand on his shoulder. "I'm just guessing, mind you. I don't have any siblings, so you'd know better than me. And for what it's worth, for the Midsummer Faire, you should just do a bunch of impressive magic. You like illusions, right? Maybe do a bunch of cool illusions to wow and impress everyone, and call it a day."

"That's a good idea," Wil said, still not quite looking up.

"Thank you, Darlene, you're always so helpful," she said, laughing as she leaned forward to kiss the top of his head. "What would you do without me?"

"Probably be crabby about my brother and panic about the show," Wil admitted, trying not to smile.

"There you go. Now, I don't know what you're gonna do about Jeb, but at least you've got the start of a show idea. Maybe you can try to talk to him later. But for now, I think I gotta go back to work, okay?" She kissed his forehead again.

As she turned to leave, Wil said, "Thanks, Darlene. Really. You've been the best part of coming back."

Her face lit up, and the entire day was worth it just for that. "That's sweet of you to say," she said. "Make it up to me with another nice dinner sometime. That's the low, low cost of my priceless advice."

Wil stood, wincing a bit at the aches and pains. "I'll happily pay it." They walked back out, and he headed out the door while she returned to the register, ignoring the looks Jonjon gave them.

This little stop had solved one problem, but the fight with Jeb haunted Wil. He didn't think he could go back to work like this, so he didn't. He went off for a walk, heading to the mountains.

CHAPTER 26

A Short Hike

The mountains surrounding Harper Valley were a place all the kids eventually explored. The McKenzies had spent plenty of time wandering through the forest, getting higher and higher as they got older and bolder. For Wil's tenth birthday, Bob took him and Jeb up to the lake at the peak of the western edge of the Skalet range.

It was a core childhood experience that had changed Wil's life and seared itself into his memory. Everything about the walk up through Harper Forest had been magical. The easy, winding trail up through the woods, the way it got rockier the higher up it went, before it flattened out at the top. Animals of all kinds living their lives just a stone's throw from civilization. The air tasted different, and it had made young Wil realize for the first time that new places could make you into a different person.

As the bookish middle child, he went largely unnoticed until he developed his gift. Always in between Jeb's firstborn pride and Sarah's baby status, for the longest time, Wil didn't know if he even had an identity of his own outside of reading and being quiet.

Going to Skalet Peak had showed him for the first time that he could be quiet without being invisible. He could be at peace and just exist unnoticed and still feel connected to everyone and everything around him.

Wil didn't know why he hadn't visited since returning, but after leaving the general store, he made his way up to the peak. There were still a good four hours of daylight left, and unlike most people, he wouldn't be unsafe in the dark alone. The need to collect his thoughts and come up with a show nagged at him, but the call of the peak was greater.

Of course, going up the lazy, winding trail from the western edge of town, he realized that he still hadn't quite gotten back into the shape he'd been in before school. No matter how hard he worked, he had nothing on the energetic teen who went hiking with a pack full of books and a snack. But this just meant he got to take his time and enjoy the sights.

Like the family of deer who ran in front of the trail, stopping just long enough to stare at him before dashing into the trees. Or the skunk who waddled just off the trail. Wil kept his distance, even knowing he could probably handle the smell if the worst happened. As mundane as it was, he had to stop and look at mushrooms growing on the side of a massive tree that had cracked in half and fallen over some time ago.

Out in nature, Wil was the guest, and he welcomed the chance to just slip into the background and appreciate the world around him. Step by step, he got closer to the peak, and his state of mind mellowed out. When he began the last stretch before the top, Wil readied himself to think about the fight and how to make it right.

Everything Darlene had said made sense. Jeb had plenty of reasons to resent him, but Wil hadn't known it could be this bad. He knew he had a lot of apologizing to do for not visiting home and for being oblivious sometimes, but he'd hoped he could make it up in time. But two months later, Jeb seemed to oscillate between friendly and hostile depending on the day. He'd never expected it to lead to a fistfight. Then again, Wil had thrown the first punch. He racked his brain trying to find some unifying thread linking the moods and situations.

All he could remember were the kinder moments being spent with family. As long as they were all together or all unified on something, Wil belonged and Jeb didn't treat him like dirt. Anything focused on Wil or his gifts tended to put Jeb in a sour mood. Everything in Wil's gut screamed jealousy, but that didn't sit quite right with him. How could Jeb be jealous when he had everything he wanted already?

The lake came into view, vast and murky. The trees stood around it in a ring, making Skalet Peak look like a private sanctuary, just for him. The only things up here were a massive log cabin technically owned by the mayor, sometimes rented out for occasions, and a well-maintained dock.

Wil went all the way up to the dock and breathed in the smell of the lake.

Jeb's behavior hurt, but Wil couldn't help but think it was on him to make things right. His absence had caused the rift, his gifts caused resentment, and everything he did seemed to annoy or hurt Jeb in some way. Standing now at the top of the mountains with a gentle calm in place of the earlier anger, all of that sounded wrong. Would he have to spend the rest of his life apologizing for who he was?

Nothing about it felt right, and for the life of him, Wil couldn't figure out what to do. So he stopped trying and just breathed. In and out, surrendering himself to nature and just letting himself be. A bird let out a loud, repetitive call from above. He saw a handsome, bright-red fellow on top of the log cabin.

On the ground lay a few fallen feathers. Wil picked one up and used it as the focus for his spell to speak to animals. The loud, sharp calls warped into something recognizable as words to him.

"Ladies! Ladies! Ladies! Hey, ladies! I'm here! I wanna dance, come dance with me. I got some pretty sticks for you! Laaadies!"

Wil let the feather fall to the ground. Well, that was a conversation he didn't care to have just then.

"Wilbur?"

He turned to find his father standing just a few feet away, a little red-faced but less obviously tired than Wil had been when he reached the peak. "Dad? What're you doing up here?"

Bob approached, face falling when he saw the bruises and crusty blood on Wil. "I saw Jeb and talked to him. Figured since you weren't home or at Bram's place, you must've come up here to think. Just like you used to when you were a kid. You doin' okay, Wil?"

Wil thought about it. "As well as can be expected, I guess. Before you say anything, I hit Jeb first."

That just made Bob laugh. "Trust me, I know. Even if Jeb hadn't pointed it out, I'd have known. He's been picking fights with you for a while now. It's about time you fought back. You want to talk about it?"

"Not at the moment, honestly."

Bob nodded. "Then we don't have to. We can just stand around and enjoy how nice and cool it is up here. I'll give you some space and when you want to talk...well." He nodded and headed back to the edge of the peak.

Wil did take some time to himself. Not more than a few minutes, mostly just to collect his thoughts and figure out what he'd say when he *was* ready. He went to stand beside his father and looked down the mountain. From up there, the entire town was visible, including his house, slightly apart from everyone else's land. Near the center of town but alone. That had to be a metaphor for something.

"I'm trying," said Wil. "I am. I'm doing everything I can to try to be a good wizard, a good man, a good brother. I don't know what I'm doing wrong there. I know I messed up by not coming home, but I don't get why he hates me so much."

"He doesn't hate you." Bob sighed. "He might think he does, but he doesn't. Not really. He'd probably list off a bunch of reasons, but if you ask me, they don't really matter. I hate how much this hurts both of you. You're being pricked anytime he feels insecure and this situation's bringing out the worst in him. He's been more sullen and moody than I've ever seen him since you got home. This can't continue."

"What should I do?" Wil asked, heart dropping. "Tell me what I need to do to fix things, and I'll do it."

Bob cautiously put his hand on his son's shoulder and looked out over the town. "Not sure it's your responsibility to fix. But if you want to do anything to maybe make things better, you might need to have an uncomfortable heart-to-heart with him. Talk it out and come to an understanding, for better or worse. If he'll let you."

"That's part of why I asked him for help in thinking of what to do for the show," Wil said. "I wanted to just talk to him and do something cool with him. Include him. I...I care what he thinks, even if he doesn't believe it. I was going to ask you and Ma and Sarah too."

"I know, son," Bob said. "You got no idea what to do for a show?"

Wil shook his head. "All I know is I'm going to use some illusion magic and I want to do something that honors Harper Valley. I don't want the show to be about me. I want it to be about the town. Something for everyone."

Neither of them said anything for a few minutes, but Wil didn't doubt his father was listening. Bob wasn't the type to talk just to fill the silence. Sure enough, after about five minutes he grunted. "You really do love this town, right? So find some way to show that. You've always been a sharp, observant kid. Good eye to you. Find a way to show the people your love of Harper Valley through your eyes, and it'll all work out. No doubt about it."

Wil took some time to process his father's words. He did have good vision, and even from up here he could see so many details of the town clearly. It was almost like a big painting, and—there it was.

"How do you always manage to know what to say?" Wil blurted out, laughing with relief.

Bob just shrugged. "It's a magic of my own, boy. Something all parents learn to do, if they're worth a damn. Why, what did I say?"

Wil pointed out to the town. "Show them my love for Harper Valley through my own eyes. What if I could bring this view to everyone as part of the show? And not just this, but so many more things all around town. Familiar sights, things everyone knows and loves mixed with a bit of razzle-dazzle. I think...I think I'm going to need Sarah's help."

"I'm sure getting her help will be easier than getting Jeb's." Bob chuckled.

"I'm going to need Jeb's help too. And yours, and Mom's. If you're all willing, I think we can make it a family thing, and do something really special." If nothing else, things were better when they worked together. Maybe doing this as a family would help that sink in for Jeb.

"Well, you know you got me and your Ma's support for sure," said Bob, hugging Wil with one arm. "Dunno how you're gonna get Sarah, but you're going to have to talk to Jeb about this. He might not be willing."

Wil took a deep breath. "I know. But I gotta try, and I want to make things right between us. I think I got a way to do it all in one go and maybe fix things."

Coming up here had been the right decision. A good walk always helped clear the mind, and it showed just how well his father knew him, even if sometimes Wil felt invisible and forgettable. The tranquility of the lake and a sense of distance from the hustle and bustle of the town filled him with a sense of peace. And determination.

He had his show, now he just needed his brother back. And since he didn't think Jeb was likely to apologize to him or try to fix anything, that meant Wil had some work to do. And if he tried and Jeb didn't listen...well, it would be his brother's problem and loss.

CHAPTER 27

Sibling Unity

They made it down the mountain shortly after dark and headed straight for home. It was funny that Wil still considered the house his home, even after moving out. Then again, he was returning with a bloody nose and lip after his dad had gone out and got him from a quiet thinking place. The entire stupid fight had reduced Wil to being a kid again, in trouble for fighting with his big brother.

Sharon waited for them at the door and took Wil's face in her hands, clucking over the bruises and fat lip. "Oh, he did do a number on you, didn't he?"

"Yeah," Wil grumbled, looking down. "I got in a few good hits of my own. He probably looks way worse than me!"

"Oh, hon. No. He beat the crap out of you." Sharon kissed his forehead before releasing him. "You look *way* worse."

"So that means he gets in trouble and I don't, right?" Wil said smiling.

Sharon shook her head. "Neither of you is in trouble. We're not angry, just disappointed it's gotten to this point. We know there's nothing we can do to change it. This is your and Jeb's problem. Mostly his. So all I can say is I hope you boys can make up and not let this hurt you too badly."

It already hurt plenty, and his mother probably knew that. Still, Wil fully intended on trying to make things right if he could. He patted her on the shoulder and took a deep breath to steady himself. With a heart heavy with apprehension, he went down the hallway to Jeb's little wing of the house.

As the oldest and the heir, over the years Jeb had gotten some extra room, with upgrades, to himself. It was something Bob had insisted on once Wil first showed signs of having the gift. At the time, Wil thought it was unfair. He showed a special gift, and Jeb got rewarded for it? What a load of crap. But time brought perspective, and now he better understood giving Jeb something more.

Music echoed down the hallway. They'd all learned an instrument when they were younger, thanks to their mother insisting. Jeb playing was either a good thing or a bad thing, and Wil didn't know which. He crept forward, listening closer, before just thinking 'screw it' and knocking on the door.

The twangy sounds cut out.

"Come in, I guess," Jeb called out.

Steeling himself, Wil stepped through the door.

Jeb lounged on his bed, pillows stuffed under his side as he half lay, half sat there with a guitar tucked under his arm. Upon seeing Wil, he grimaced but didn't immediately tell him to leave, so it could've been worse. Not once taking his eyes off Wil, he strummed a little tune, waiting for him to speak.

Wil didn't, at first. He just looked around, realizing how long it'd been since he was in Jeb's room. In many ways, it still looked like the room of a broody teenager, as haphazard as it was, with posters of traveling performers littering the walls and clothes strewn about the floor. The bedroom had to be twice the size of Wil's and Sarah's, and even had its own private bathroom.

"I've always liked your room," he said finally. "It always seemed so big to me, like your own little house."

Jeb snorted. "You say that, having an actual huge house."

"Yeah," said Wil, "but that's new. All these things about me that are making you so mad are new. For most of my life, I looked up to you. I was jealous, even."

That earned Wil an incredulous look, but nothing else. Jeb continued to play his guitar lazily as if waiting for him to just get to the point. It irritated Wil, but he pushed it aside for now.

"Hard not to be jealous. You were the oldest—you got to do everything first and impress Ma and Dad. You got to do adult things while Sarah and I were still just kids, and you got your big room while Sarah and I had our little rooms upstairs. You got everything new, and then I got all your hand-me-downs eventually, and of course, Sarah got her own stuff because she's the baby and the only girl."

"Did you really come to cry about how unfair you had it?" Jeb demanded, setting the guitar to the side.

"No, I'm trying to explain something," said Wil, heat rising straight to his head. He blinked rapidly, fighting to avoid saying something he'd regret. "Something important to me. I was a nobody and always lived in your shadow. And then one day I showed my gift, and things changed. And ever since then, things have been bad between us. For something I have no control over."

"Oh, please," Jeb sneered. "Ever since then, you've gotten everything you wanted. You got to be special, you got to spend more time with your damned books, and you got to go to that big, expensive school and get the hell out of Harper Valley. Maybe you did have it bad for a little while, but everything's been going your way since. You going to keep complaining?"

Wil let out a strangled yell. "I'm not complaining, you thick-headed ass, I'm trying to—" He blew his breath out, taking in another to calm down. "Are you really trying to tell me you're so jealous of me that you can't just talk to me like a normal person?"

"I ain't jealous," said Jeb.

"Sure you aren't," Wil scoffed. "Ever since I got home, you've take every single opportunity to get a dig in on me. I can't do anything without you actively trying to make me feel bad. I'm getting real sick of it, Jeb. If you aren't jealous, tell me what the problem is. Tell me what it is I can do to make you stop hating me."

Jeb stood up, and for a second Wil thought he was about to get punched again. His older brother had a few inches on him and looked ready to throw hands, but then he just sighed and deflated. "I already told you last time we had one of these heartwarming chats, I don't hate you. I just don't like you very much anymore.

"You run around acting like every single thing you do is end-of-the-world-level important. How often do you check in on us and see how we're doing? How often do you ask us about what's going on in our lives? I'm dating Sheila Gibbs now. Did you know that?"

"No," said Wil, "I didn't.

"No, I didn't think you did. But did you ever ask? No. Whenever you come home for dinner, you talk about what you've been doing and ask how the farm is. Usually focusing on Ma and Dad. And that's it."

Wil felt a stab of guilt. "When did you ever give me a chance?" he scoffed. "You cut me off and walk away whenever I try to spend time with you. What about just talking about things going on in your life? Isn't that how everyone else did it for my entire life? Everyone used to talk over each other at dinner. Now that it's not all about you, you get mad?"

"Huh," said Jeb. "I guess I do."

Neither of them said anything, just stared the other down while breathing hard. Wil was about to give up and just walk out, see if he could do his plan with everyone else, when Jeb sighed and looked down.

"I don't know who you are anymore. You got to go on this big life-changing journey and learn something none of the rest of us will ever understand. You can go anywhere you want, do anything you want to do. You said you didn't like living in my shadow? How the hell do you think it feels to live in the shadow of your younger brother? Can you imagine how humiliating it is?"

"Humiliating?" Wil felt like he'd been punched again. "What are you talking about? You're Jeb McKenzie. You're tall, cool, good at guitar, girls always liked you, and you've always known what you wanted to do. How could anything I do humiliate you?" Wil's voice lost all its heat.

Jeb looked up, and to Wil's surprise, he looked lost. "Does it matter if I know what I want if I never really have a choice? There has never been a question of who I am, or what I'm gonna do. It's all been chosen for me. What kind of shadow is there to live under when my damned younger brother gets all the freedom I never had? If I did hate you, maybe that's why."

Knowing that, it made sense now. Jeb didn't resent him for having magic or going to school. He resented him for having choices Jeb himself would never get to make.

"It's terrifying, you know," Wil whispered. "Having so many options. I always envied how easy it seemed for you. You had everything planned out and just had to show up and be yourself and it'd all work out. School wasn't easy. I had to work hard to learn everything I can do, and the worst part of it was just figuring out what I wanted.

"And then hearing you constantly dump on my choice to come back here and help people. That's what hurts, Jeb. Every step of the way you keep making it out like I'm some diva who wants everyone to kiss my ass. I don't. I want to help everyone, and I did because that's what you'd do. And I've always looked up to you."

Wil was surprised to see a tear trail down Jeb's face. He took a breath in and had trouble, and realized his throat was tight and tears of his own were falling. They stayed like that for a few seconds, silently crying before Jeb suddenly laughed, desperate and unhinged. Wil joined him, and together they stood there laughing until they doubled over and had to help one another stay up.

"Still a big crybaby," Jeb teased, which made Wil laugh even harder.

"Shut up, hypocrite," Wil returned. Eventually, he sat down on Jeb's bed and Jeb joined him there.

"I guess I am a bit jealous," Jeb admitted after a moment. "Just a bit. It's not like I think you don't deserve nice things. I just wish I had the options you did. There was never a question of me taking over the farm, and I *do* want it. I just hate that there were never any other plans for me. It was always going to be this. It's hard not to feel trapped. I don't like feeling that way."

Wil nodded. "I never meant to make it worse or rub your nose in it. I'm just trying to live my life and do good. I meant it when I said I wanted your help because I know you love this town. I wanted to give you a chance to be in the spotlight."

Jeb winced. "Yeah. I'm sorry for…for everything, I guess, but especially for shutting you down so hard. I've been a real bastard, haven't I? I can help you think of something for your show. Not sure it'll be anything good, but I can try."

"And I'm sorry too. I'm not trying to be a big attention hog or show-off, I swear. I just wanna do what's right, like you taught me. Actually, I did think of something after you kicked the crap out of me," said Wil, brightening up. "I still need your help with it, though. I need the whole family's help if I'm going to do it right."

"Well, you got my help for sure," Jeb said. "And probably Ma's and Dad's. How're you going to get Sarah to help you?"

Wil smiled. "Leave that to me."

"You got it," said Jeb, slumping on his bed. "I'm going to try to be better. But I need time. This has been buildin' up for a while now. I don't hate you, though. But maybe you oughta hate me."

"I could never." Wil touched his bruised face and winced. "Well, maybe not *never*, but it'd take a lot more of this crap to do it."

With things better for the moment, the air cleared up fast. They didn't speak any more about their problems, but Wil did tell Jeb his plans. Jeb agreed to help out, and then Wil left him alone, trusting that everything would get better going forward. There was so much work to be done. Some on his side, so much more on Jeb's.

But there was only so much they could do in one night, so Wil headed up to Sarah's room and knocked on the door, entering when she beckoned.

"Hey, Sarah," he said. "I've got to put on a show for the Midsummer Faire and I need your help."

Sarah looked at him from her bed, where she was working on a new drawing. "What's in it for me?"

"I'll pay you two thousand zynce for your troubles."

Her eyes widened. She swung her legs off the bed and gave him her full attention. "Brother dearest, however can I be of service?"

And with that, his entire family was on board. With just about a week to put everything together. Hard, but with his family, he could do anything.

CHAPTER 28

Last-Minute Prep

Wil didn't know who was more distraught about the work they had to do for the Faire: Sarah or Bram. Sarah loved the idea of making a huge chunk of cash using her artistic skills, but going out into the world to do stuff over the course of the week irritated her. And when Sarah got irritated, she terrorized others. Her current favorite target happened to be Bram.

"Please, for the love of the gods, can you get her to leave me alone?" Bram begged Wil at one of their stops.

The three of them stood outside Mack's Shack. Well, two of them stood. Sarah, the demanding diva that she was, sat on a stool to do her work. Wil and Bram stood off to the side, Bram whispering constantly to Wil.

"C'mon, just ignore her," Wil whispered back. "She's just doing it because you give her a reaction. Just act bored instead of sputtering, and she'll stop bugging you."

Sarah stopped her work, looking up from the picture she'd been painstakingly working on for the past twenty minutes. Almost every detail looked perfect from where Wil stood, though Sarah could be finicky about whether something was acceptable or not. She let out an aggrieved sigh.

"Jenkins, I require a cool drink," she announced.

Bram's jaw set. He dwarfed both the McKenzies, and in his irritation he looked even bigger. Sarah just smiled at him, daring him to refuse her.

"Stop. Calling. Me. Jenkins," Bram growled.

"Wil, please cast a spell to make the butler obey."

Wil put himself between his sister and Bram, smiling apologetically. It'd be better if Bram didn't know how funny he found it. He fished in his pockets and pulled out a tenner and handed it to Bram. "Get yourself something too, and just chill. We're halfway down the list."

Bram looked past him, glaring at Sarah before he took the bill and headed into the restaurant. The moment he left, Sarah descended into a giggle fit. "Gods, he's too easy!"

"You could stand to cut him a little slack," Wil said with a sigh. "He's done nothing to you. Not since we were kids. Why do you have to pester him?"

"Because it's funny," Sarah said cheerfully. "You'd think he can take it, given all he's here for is to carry stuff for us and keep you company while I work. It's not like I'm saying anything *really* bad."

"You'd think, with the amount I'm paying you, you'd be able to afford to take it seriously and just…you know, *not*." Wil shook his head fondly. Sarah could be pretty funny when her brattiness wasn't pointed at him.

"You'd think."

Bram came back out with a couple of glass bottles. He handed a bottle of dark purple liquid to Sarah, who popped it open and took a long drink.

"Thank you," she said, looking up at him with big eyes. "I know how much of a pain I can be, and I just want to say I appreciate you sticking with us and lending all your help." Bram went from suspicious to pleased in just a few seconds. "You're a good man, Jenkins."

Bram sighed and trudged off to the side, drinking his soda. He had the look of a man with a broken spirit, and Wil gave him some distance and watched his sister work instead.

As annoying as Sarah could be, her art skills were some of the best Wil had ever seen. Several people at Saint Balthazar's had been big on art, and Sarah could've gone toe to toe with any of them. In about half an hour, she'd captured almost every line and angle for Mack's Shack, exactly how it looked to them. It was in black and white, and next would come the shading. It would be perfect for Wil's uses.

"You're doing a good job," Wil said to Sarah. "I don't think I'd be able to pull this idea off without you."

"So pay me more," Sarah said, picking up a red coloring pencil.

"No."

All around town they traveled, getting two or three pictures done a day. It was slow going, and Bram complained about lugging stuff around for them, but all he had to do at home was read and wait for beer to finish up in the bottles. The way they both saw it, he still owed Wil some help, and it could've been so much worse.

They'd started around the farm, getting a good vantage point of the whole thing, and Sarah sketched it out, adding colors and details over a couple of hours.

Then came a meal paid for by Wil, and then another picture. They got started late a couple of days, after Wil made time to finish a few work orders and meet with a citizen or two to listen to their needs and work things out with them. Then he, Sarah, and Bram were right back out in the world, getting more pictures for the show.

Eventually, moods soured and too much time spent together had everyone on edge. It happened, of course, right when they were about to finish up. Sarah found one thing in particular to complain about.

"I don't want to have to climb Skalet Peak," she said. "I hate making that trek. You and Jeb may love it, but there's nothing up there but a stupid lake and that creepy cabin. Are you really going to make me go up there and draw *another* pretty landscape? C'mon Wil, everyone in town knows how beautiful it is around here. They don't need you to remind them."

"She might have a point," Bram said. The traitor was not the kind of person to go on a hike, and ever since he'd heard Skalet Peak was their final destination, he'd tried to talk Wil out of it. "We've gotten so many good pictures of the rest of the town, maybe we can skip this one."

Wil rubbed his eyes. "We've been over it a thousand times now. This is the most important picture of all. This is the shot that inspired me to do all of it. If we don't get it, half the impact is gone. If I need to pay you both more for you to go, I will, but—"

"Hey, hey, no need for that," Bram said, face reddening. He'd taken pay for his help this week, but only after Wil had insisted. The subject of money would be a touchy one around Bram until he'd paid off his debts or just relaxed.

Sarah looked at each of them. "Fine, then I'll take whatever money he's turning down. Unlike you two clowns, I'm gonna get out of here for good."

Wil wished her the very best and added a couple hundred to her pay. Anything to get the best view of the town possible. With Darlene giving him direction and the talk with his dad making it clear what he should do, the fear of putting on a show in front of thousands had turned into excitement for Wil. Maybe this was one instance of showing off he could be proud of.

That just left making the actual climb. They packed for a day's journey, despite it not being that hard. Wil had to fight back the frustration from hearing both Bram and Sarah dragging their feet and complaining the entire time. It took until the tenth time Sarah griped about the bugs for Wil to do something about it.

"Thanks," said Sarah, scratching at her skin where even now she had several bites. "What did you do?"

"It's a repulsion spell," said Wil, fighting to keep a straight face. "I amplified your natural charm and now no living creature wants to be within five feet of you."

Bram guffawed and even Sarah smiled and clapped appreciatively. They resumed their trek up the mountain.

They ended up taking a short break halfway up for Bram to catch his breath and eat a snack. Wil pointed off to the side and said, "That's where the Nullbear had the kids trapped. See all the fallen trees?"

Sure enough, all the damage from the fight had left a scar in the forest of felled trees and crushed logs. In time, nature would reclaim the area and things would grow anew, but for now, it remained a monument to a situation that could've gone so much worse than it had.

"Did anyone ever find out what happened to the Nullbear?" Bram asked, swallowing hard. He looked around as if expecting to find a giant magical bear behind every tree.

"Yeah, the mayor sent some rangers out to follow the trail," said Sarah, taking a bite out of her sandwich. "I remember Dad said he heard the trail was farther up the mountain, away from the peak and along the range. We should be safe enough, right, Wil? If it shows up, we can always throw Jenkins at it and escape while he gets eaten."

"At this point, I'd welcome it," Bram muttered.

When they finally arrived at the peak just after noon, Bram all but collapsed onto the ground with a groan. Sarah bent over panting, and Wil was amused to find himself in the best shape out of all of them. He took the folding stool from Bram and set it and the easel up for Sarah while she rested a little longer. Then he just sort of wandered around, waiting.

It was only a few minutes before Sarah sat on the stool, getting her notebook out and preparing clean paper for her drawing. She looked out over the town and the paper, memorizing bits and pieces as she mulled over where to start.

"You okay?" Wil whispered to Bram, sitting down on the ground next to the massive man.

"I need to get out more," Bram said, flashing him an uneasy thumbs-up. "I'll be fine. I gotta say, I didn't want to come up here, but it's gorgeous. Maybe it was worth it after all."

"I like to think so," said Wil. Despite being in much better shape than either of them, he still found himself fatigued. Eventually, he grabbed his pack and used it as a pillow and closed his eyes. A few seconds later, two hours passed by and he woke with a terrible kink in his back.

He got up and saw Bram also napping. Sarah sat at the stool, picture mostly done. He joined her there, looking over it.

"This has been the hardest one," said Sarah with a grimace. "Everything else was easy, but there's just like, so much to capture. Why is this one so important?"

Wil pointed out over the town. "Just look at it. You can see everything from here. It's easy to think of Harper Valley as just a bunch of farms and small-town people, but just...look! We've got everything we could ever need, right here. And two days from now, during the Faire, I want to show everyone what I see. A beautiful, thriving community nestled in the heart of a bunch of mountains. A little slice of paradise, tucked away from the problems of the rest of the world."

Sarah looked at him, without making a face or obviously mocking him for a change. She looked as though she were considering his words seriously. Eventually, she frowned. "Do you really like this dump that much? Even after you got out?"

Wil nodded. "It's home. It was great getting to see new places, and I know I'll want to see them again, eventually, but...there was this call of home I couldn't ignore. And I want to share that feeling with as many people as I can. Ma, Dad, Jeb, they'll be super-handy during the show, but nobody can help me like you are now. No one else has the eye you do."

Her frown deepened. She looked out at the spectacular view. "I don't feel it," she said. "Not the same way you do. It's okay, I guess, but I don't want to spend the rest of my life here. I want to get out and try new things. I overheard you talking to Ma, saying you'd help send me to art school. Were you serious?"

"I was and am," said Wil. "I've got the money for it now. Ma and Dad don't want my help because they think they gotta do it alone, but if it means getting you out there and letting you experience the world, I'll do it in a heartbeat. Even if it's us going behind their backs. I want you to be able to find your own magic place that calls to you."

Sarah thought about it, then returned to work. Wil watched her take seemingly disparate strokes of the pencil and make the details come to life in a way he'd never be able to truly replicate. What he'd do during the Faire would be a cheap imitation, but hopefully flashy enough to impress people.

Another few minutes and she finished. "Done, I guess. And if you're going to pay for my school, then..." She looked at him, idly chewing a lock of stray blond hair. "I'd rather you hire me to do stuff like this than just pay for it. You got it? I don't need charity. I plan on earning my way out of here."

Wil smiled. "I wouldn't have it any other way, Sarah. You've more than earned the pay for this."

She smiled back, a rare one with no mischief or malice or mockery. "Thank you." Then, before he could savor the moment, she said, "Think we can leave Jenkins behind?"

"Sarah," he said warningly.

"What! It'd be funny! Oh fine, I'll wake him up."

Wil smiled and shook his head as Sarah crept up to Bram. She opened her mouth for a rude awakening, but no sound came out, thanks to a quick spell.

Wil burst out laughing at the betrayed look on her face, and that was enough to wake Bram up.

"What? What's going on?"

"Nothing," said Wil. "We're ready to go when you are."

Together, they cleaned up and headed back down the mountain.

CHAPTER 29

Mingling and/or Schmoozing

O ddly enough, Wil was grateful for the welcoming feast they'd done two months before.

It had been a massive pain in the ass and a bothersome waste of time featuring the mayor parading him around and shaking countless hands of people who mostly knew him better than he knew them. The night had left him drained and in no mood to socialize for days afterward, and had been perfect practice for the Midsummer Faire.

It wasn't all bad, or even that bad if Wil were being honest. He loved the Midsummer Faire, and going as an adult wasn't *that* different from going as a kid. He still helped his family bring their wares and contributions for their little stall, and he still made a beeline for one of the food vendors, where he bought two sausage pastries and a drink and devoured them fast enough to make his mother chide him for it.

"You're gonna make yourself sick!" Sharon said, nudging his shoulder. "At least space it out, or leave room for other things. There's going to be a million different options for food—are you really going to stuff yourself full of the same thing you get every year?"

"Yuh-huh," said Wil, washing down the last of his pastry with lemonade. Even in his newfound freedom of being a young adult wizard, it was too early for beer, and lemonade made the relentless sun a little less oppressive.

"And then I'm going to buy an entire bag full before they close and take them home with me. And there's nothing you can do to stop me, Ma! I'm an adult now!"

"That's right," said a smiling Sharon. "You're a big boy and can suffer through your own tummy aches. But if you complain around me, I'm gonna laugh at you, understand?"

"Entirely fair," said Wil, sipping his drink.

Just as he brushed crumbs off onto the grass, the mayor showed up. "Heya, Wilbur! You're good for the show later, right?" He let out a laugh that might've been nervous or pointed, Wil couldn't tell.

"I should be," said Wil. A bit of mischief struck him. "Unless I drink too much. If I pass out, I might not be good for the show, but if I *do* pass out, get Bram to dump a keg of water on me. That'll probably wake me up." He chuckled.

Mayor Sinclair stared at him, jaw slack. His face betrayed pure anxiety. Wil decided to throw him a bone.

"I'm kidding, sir. Seven o'clock, at the amphitheater. I've got a short show in mind that'll do pretty well, I think." Wil flashed a winning smile.

"Well, alright then," said Mayor Sinclair, patting his shoulder. "Seven o'clock. And in the meantime, if you could…"

"Yes," said Wil with a sigh. "I'll make the rounds and greet people and do little tricks. And make sure they know about the show and all that. Don't worry, sir, I won't let Harper Valley down."

"Attaboy," said the mayor, chortling as he walked off.

"You really don't gotta call him sir," Bob said from the stall, which he continued to set up while everyone else scattered. "Mr. Mayor is respectful, Mayor Sinclair maybe, but a man like that, you call him sir and he'll think he's some big shot."

"You're probably right," said Wil, "but I'm in too deep and I don't want to deal with the hassle of him being mad at me. Do you need any help?"

Bob grinned at him. "I wouldn't hear of it, Mr. Wizard. You got your audience to go around and greet on behalf of Mr. Mayor Sir, and I can't get in the way of *that* now can I?" He burst out laughing.

Wil waved his parents off and wandered around the fairgrounds. At first, only the people who knew him really recognized him. That was nice, not getting swamped immediately by people who wanted attention from him. Not for the first time, he toyed with getting an official wizard hat to serve as a mark of his office and show when he was active. It would at least make him stand out when he wanted to.

He had all of fifteen minutes of greeting people and making clouds of illusory butterflies and masses of snakes for children's amusement when the first big shot came up to him.

Mr. Carrey greeted him like an old friend, though the leathery old man was squinting, as always, with suspicion. "Mr. Wizard!" He took Wil's hand in both of his and pumped it energetically. "Thanks to you and that thing you did with those line thingies, I've had the best crops I've seen in *years*! It worked out real well!"

"Any two-headed goats?" Wil joked, but Mr. Carrey just stared at him oddly. "I'm happy to hear that, Mr. Carrey. It's really gratifying to know I'm doing a good job."

"You are, you are," Mr. Carrey said, still not releasing Wil's hand. He tugged and Wil allowed himself to be pulled in so Mr. Carrey could whisper, "But if you're helping everyone like this, then mine won't be so impressive, right? What would it cost to make sure you never help Old Bundy out on his farm?"

Wil froze. He pulled his hand away with more force than he'd intended. Mr. Carrey winced, knowing immediately he'd made a mistake. The wizard took a deep breath and let it out slowly.

"I'm going to pretend I didn't hear you say that, Mr. Carrey. I'm here to help everyone, and if I'm going to ignore any farms, it's likely to be those who ask me to not help others. I believe in community and helping each other out. You couldn't afford to pay me enough to not help out others. Good day."

Wil made it all the way to the other side of the fairgrounds before he realized just how much Mr. Carrey's request bothered him. He supposed it shouldn't have come as a surprise. While he felt most of Harper Valley's residents were good people, there would always be some who couldn't see past their next payday. The fact that he'd almost turned Bram down out of anger still haunted him.

"What's eating you?" Bram asked. His friend found him near one of the areas set aside for displaying prize animals, throwing feed at some especially fluffy and handsome chickens.

"Mr. Carrey," Wil grunted. He quickly filled him in on what happened.

Bram frowned, leaning against the fence until it creaked beneath him. "That's a bastardy thing to do. What're you going to do about it?"

Wil shrugged. "Nothing. I still owe him a lot for sending me to school in the first place, and I still intend on helping out. But if he suggests it again, he might find his leylines running dry when it comes time for spellwork. Ugh, I can't hide here forever. I have to make the rounds."

"Let me help," said Bram. "I'll be your personal assistant, and anytime someone bothers you for too long, I'll make it clear we need to go. I'll give them a look like this." Bram took his spectacles off and stuck them in his coat pocket. He scowled and went from looking like a nerd to the very image of intimidation, just like that.

"Very nice," said Wil, "I'll happily take you up on it."

And so for the next two hours, Wil made his way around the fairgrounds, largely performing for children and occasionally shaking the hand of someone he'd helped along the way. Some he even stopped to chat with for a bit, and Bram was great about reading his expression and either relaxing nearby or interrupting to keep them moving.

"It's time to go," Bram said as he pulled on Wil's arm. His face was all business and vague menace. The old lady who'd been chattering at Wil for going on five minutes paused.

"And who are you?" she asked, looking between the two of them.

"He's my bodyguard," said Wil, fighting back a smile. "Keeping me moving so I'm a harder target to get at."

"O-oh, I see." The old lady nodded and tottered off. They collapsed together snickering, and moved on.

Bram had to intervene only a couple of times after that. For the most part, it was actually nice talking to families and occasionally mentioning to stop by the amphitheater as the time dwindled and they got closer and closer to showtime.

Wil had just made up his mind to leave early and make sure he had a drink and relieved himself before he performed when he stumbled upon Darlene and her father, in the middle of an argument.

"And I don't understand why you can't just do what you're told!" Jonjon barked at Darlene in front of a small audience. "You think you're too good to continue the business?"

"It's not about being too good for it, Dad," Darlene said in a restrained voice. "It's about building something that's mine. I don't want to just coast along and live *your* life!" Her hands were balled up into fists at her side, her lips pressed together.

Wil paused, wondering if he should get involved even as part of him wanted to stay and listen. He didn't get to decide. Jonjon turned his ire onto the wizard.

"You!" He jabbed a finger in Wil's direction. "This is all your fault! You're the one who's gotten my daughter into that half-assed brewery idea! It's the two of you! I thought you were supposed to be serving the community. Well, I'm the community and you're messing with my business and starting your own!"

Wil looked around, suddenly chilled to the bone. He opened his mouth to defend himself and reassure anyone watching that it wasn't true, but Darlene beat him to it.

"Don't you dare drag Wil into this! He didn't force me to do anything, he showed me an opportunity and I decided to take it. He's given me a way out from being stuck with *you*. I've got my own business now with my friends, and there's nothing you can do to stop us!"

Jonjon's face darkened, going from his normal tan to an ugly bruised color with murder in his eyes. "Is that so?" he said, voice dropping. Wil didn't like that. "Then I suppose you don't need anything from Mom and Dad, right? Consider yourself cut off."

Darlene froze, looking unsure for the first time. "What?"

"Yeah, cut off," said Jonjon, an unpleasant grin radiating menace. "No more money, no more housing, no more nothing until you get in line and get back to work. But don't worry, I'll allow you to take anything you and your boyfriend can carry." He laughed.

Whispers sounded throughout the crowd. Jonjon wasn't exactly a beloved figure in town, but few believed he'd be this cruel openly, Wil included. The silence that followed was agony. For the longest time, no one said anything, until a whisper went through the crowd, picking up a life of its own. Darlene covered her mouth with her hand. Wil found his voice.

"Do we have your word on that?" Wil asked, stepping forward. "That we can take anything we can carry?"

Jonjon grinned and inclined his head. "Never let it be said that I'm an unfair man. You and Darlene can go through and get whatever you can carry off. Grab some clothes, maybe some keepsakes, anything you don't want to go in the trash. After that, she can be your problem, since you're so quick to take her in."

Wil went over to Darlene and put his arm around her shoulder and pulled her close. She clung to him gratefully, grip tight enough to hurt. He felt her shudder against him as everything sank in. He looked up and leveled his best glare Jonjon's way.

He enhanced his voice to project and sound a tiny bit deeper and said, "Then with all of these people as witnesses, a pact is forged. Any attempts to renege on your word will result in triggering the curse."

That froze the man in his tracks. "Curse?"

Wil stared him down. "Heed my words now, Jonathon Johnson. Soon, Darlene and I will come by for her stuff, and if you attempt to interfere or stop her from taking anything she wants, you will trigger the curse attached to this binding pact."

"I didn't agree to no pact!" the man said, a hint of panic in his voice.

"It's too late to go back, unless you wish to trigger the curse." Wil didn't have to fake his fierce smile. Jonjon shook his head vehemently. "Then leave now, and prepare yourself. And stay out of my way."

With one last parting look, Jonjon scowled and walked away. The crowd parted for him, and then eventually dispersed entirely now that the show was over. Wil ran a hand over Darlene's short hair in a way he hoped was reassuring. She hugged him tighter.

"I just...I can't believe he..." Darlene sputtered.

Wil kissed the top of her head without thinking about it or worrying if it was the right thing to do. "We'll take care of it. Together."

Darlene nodded and then broke down, crying.

CHAPTER 30

Home, Family, Community

Okay, okay, I'm good," said Darlene, wiping away tears and snot with the back of her hand. "I don't know what came over me, but I'm fine now."

"It's okay to not be okay," said Wil. "I'd be a wreck if that happened to me."

"Did you really curse Jonjon?" Bram whispered, looking in the direction the man went, though he was no longer in sight. "Like, actually curse him?"

Wil shook his head, laughing. "No, but he doesn't need to know that."

Darlene laughed as well, then heaved one last sob before she finally collected herself. "I can't believe he...just because I don't want to spend the rest of my life at *his* store."

"We won't let anything happen to you," said Wil. "You'll have a place to stay, no matter what. My home has space. Or if you aren't comfortable with that, my old room at my family's house. My parents would happily take you in."

"Or I've got plenty of spare rooms," said Bram. "Well, by plenty I mean two, but that's still one more spare room than you need, so."

Darlene shook her head, chuckling. "I appreciate it, boys. We'll figure it out later. We still have the rest of the Faire to get through, and you've got your show soon."

In the drama, Wil had almost completely forgotten the show. Now that Darlene was hurting, it seemed silly to even consider putting it on. "I can probably skip that if you need to get out of here sooner."

"Seriously?" After a week of lugging things around for Wil and Sarah, Bram looked like he wanted to cry.

"No, no, no need for that," said Darlene, and Bram clutched his chest in relief. "You've worked hard on it, and I kind of want to see what you've got in mind for it, anyway. I'll be okay for now. Thank you."

Wil nodded, then headed toward the amphitheater at a jog. People got out of his way, and he made it with several minutes to spare. His family waited in the orchestra section of the amphitheater, their instruments ready.

"There you are," said Sharon, cradling a fiddle to her chest. She didn't play that much these days, but he'd managed to talk her into practicing and performing.

Jeb was plucking his guitar. "I swear, if you were gonna be late after all this…" He shook his head, smiling.

"Everything okay?" Bob asked, picking up his flute.

Wil shook his head. "Darlene might need our help. We'll talk later. You ready with the pictures, Sarah?"

Sarah held up a stack of the drawings she'd spent the last week making. She thought his request was kind of weird, but if getting the rest of her money meant standing around and waving pictures in his face, she wouldn't argue. All that remained was waiting for the amphitheater to fill up.

And fill it did. Over the next ten minutes, every seat was taken, and plenty more people stood, waiting. More people than Wil could ever remember seeing at one time. Down in the front, the mayor flashed him a thumbs-up, mouthing something he assumed Wil could understand. Wil just gave a thumbs-up back as he tried not to freak out.

Thousands of people, all there to see him. The combined weight of their attention shook Wil to his core. There were more people there than there'd been during graduation, and he'd had to perform a speech there as well. Wil took a long, deep breath. He survived that, he'd survive this. All he had to do was let his magic do the talking.

He nodded at his family and expended just a little bit of energy to cover them and himself. Jeb plucked a chord on his guitar and led the family into a relaxing, friendly tune. Sharon joined in with the high-pitched cheer of the fiddle, and Bob's flute rounded them off, playful and lilting. Their music played loudly from above, as audible to those in the back as those up close.

But then Wil took that sound he heard and layered it with an aural illusion. Just a little touch to take that pleasant, familiar sound and warp it into something a little more ethereal and wistful.

Sarah held up the first picture she'd done with him and Bram. A landscape of the family farm from the end of the drive. Wil concentrated, taking every detail in as wholly as possible. Then, behind him on the wall, the picture came to life, thirty feet tall, every line and scratch and bit of shading. The amphitheater erupted with whispers. Wil put them out of his mind and spoke.

"My name is Wilbur McKenzie, and I was born and raised in Harper Valley. This is my home. Wonderful, isn't it?"

With a little push of his effort, the image narrowed in on the house.

"I grew up here with my parents, Bob and Sharon, and my siblings, Jebediah and Sarah. Just a simple farm family, working the land together."

Sarah followed her cue, switching to the next drawing. Wil's focus changed immediately, blowing the picture up behind him. This time, it was of his family. Bob and Sharon, fifteen years younger. They held a screaming, flailing Sarah while Jeb looked serious and Wil picked his nose.

"That's me in the middle. When I was little, I never dreamed I'd be much of anything, let alone in the position I am now. And I owe it almost entirely to a love for my community fostered by my parents."

Wil let the warmth he felt for them out, doing his best to make it shine in the picture, in the mood in the air. He couldn't broadcast his emotions like some wizards could, but he hoped that what he felt showed through in the images and his tone, and in the gentle music completing the mood.

Sarah switched the picture again and Wil grinned at this one. The entire valley got to see a picture of Bob and Sharon playing music together with Jeb while Wil covered his ears and Sarah played a kazoo in his face. Still images at first, until Wil focused and the figures on the wall moved and danced as his real-life family played their instruments.

"They taught me from a young age that community meant living together and helping each other. Community meant working with one another to build a better life for all of us. And with that in mind, I believe Harper Valley is something unique."

The next picture he displayed on the wall was city hall, underwear on the statue's head. Sharon sawed away on her fiddle, making a fast, goofy melody. That got a good laugh out of the crowd, but the mayor shot a disgruntled look his way.

Then he took everyone downtown, fully displaying one of Sarah's more artistic renditions and letting the lines move and draw the viewer in. He showed off a scene by the river, of people fishing and kids jumping in the water. One child hung frozen in the air, then he crashed into the water and a big splash came from the wall, illusory water crashing to the ground.

"I always felt so lucky to grow up here, where the land is beautiful and the people are kind and helpful. Where everyone's welcome, and even if we're all different, we can agree on one thing: we work hard so we can play hard. It's about family, the good and the bad. Life is about helping each other out and enjoying yourself."

Next came a series of quicker images, pulled out one by one by Sarah, just as they'd planned. The audience got glimpses of Mack's Shack, Danson's Steakhouse, the little strawberry stand on the south side of town that somehow always had the cleanest, freshest strawberries even when they were out of season. Smell was harder, but a gasp went through the amphitheater as everyone was enveloped in a strong whiff of strawberries. The music picked up in pace, slowly turning into a familiar tune often sung in the pubs, upbeat and playful.

Wil showed them all the places he loved in the town. He showed the audience the town through his eyes. Big, complex illusions that combined his sister's incredible artwork with his own imagination. Illusion after illusion, places and memories came to life. With his family playing a gentle, playful song in the background, Wil used all the magic at his disposal to share the best message he could think of: *home.*

"Life is all about having a full heart and a full belly. To live with nature and raise up the next generation to have the same love and respect for life we do," he said, swallowing hard. The amount of magic he threw around was a lot, and for something so trivial as illusions. He loved it.

"This Faire is about you, the people," he said, looking into the crowd. Magical power flowed between his eyes and the wall, capturing everything he saw and blowing it up to share. Every face he saw and focused on for even a second. More and more people, Wil took his time scanning the crowd. "The Faire is about all of us! Our friends!" Wil looked over at Bram, sitting up straight. He smiled at Wil, raising a hand in a half-hearted wave. "Our loved ones!" said Wil. Darlene showed up on the screen this time, her expression like a startled deer.

The pictures changed again, going over shots of different farms, goats frolicking, a sea of wheat, and the main road winding through town, well-used and iconic. And finally, for the last image of all, Sarah pulled out the landscape drawing she'd done on Skalet Peak. Wil let himself fall into the picture and brought it to life.

"Welcome to Harper Valley!"

With a final push of energy, Wil added one more thing to the picture behind him. From his imagination, he conjured his favorite large, scary illusion. The fiery demon circled lazily on leathery wings in the sky above the projected town until it caught sight of them. It flew closer and closer in the picture. Wil gasped and released the image, bringing a fully detailed, glowing red demon out of the wall and flying it around the amphitheater as the crowd gasped and cheered.

It flew around in circles, getting higher and higher until it stopped hundreds of feet up in the sky. Wil grinned and released the spell holding it together. The demon exploded into bursts of light and sound, like fireworks without the mess or smell of smoke. Pop by obnoxious pop, the demon's feet and tail disappeared in flashes of colorful light, continuing a chain up its body until only the head remained.

Wil detonated the head, and the lights trailed downward onto the stage. His family stopped playing their music, and Sarah ran up to Wil, who needed a hand staying upright. Soon his parents and Jeb joined in, and it became an impromptu group hug. Wil loved it. He was glad the show was over. It left him tapped out.

"That was insane," Bob crowed, slapping him on the back.

Wil grunted his appreciation and even gamely accepted his mom kissing him on the cheek in front of the entire town. Jeb at least kept his distance and just smiled at him, none of his resentment there at all. Maybe he'd liked the little show they put on, and being a part of it. He certainly didn't hate the applause that erupted—he took a bow while the rest of the family was occupied.

The mayor was approaching, and Wil broke apart from his family and looked around. Bram stood there applauding and grinning like a fool, but Darlene wasn't there. Wil pointed to where she'd been, but Bram just shrugged and pointed off to the side.

"Mr. Wizard," Mayor Sinclair called out. "Ladies and gentlemen, that's our very own resident wizard, Mr. Wilbur McKenzie. Let's all have a round of applause for him!" He shouted to be heard over the already present claps and cheers. He reached for Wil, but Wil pulled away.

"Sorry," he said, "I gotta go." He turned away and ran, his gut telling him to go after Darlene.

CHAPTER 31

Friends First

Wil ran after Darlene, ignoring the pounding in his head. He forced a smile on his face and waved at several people as he passed, wincing when they expected him to stop and chat and he didn't. After the day Darlene had, she needed somebody to look after her. Gods knew he should return the favor after all the times she'd bailed his ass out.

Outside the amphitheater, the fairgrounds were less busy than before. Several vendors sat or leaned against their stalls and food carts, enjoying a snack or drink and a much-needed break. Wil stopped at the first one he saw.

"Have you seen a woman with short dark hair and freckles go by?" he asked, eyes darting around.

A motherly looking woman nodded and pointed at the far-off end of the Faire. "Over there," she said. "Went barreling through. You just missed her. Poor thing looked broken up. Did you say or do anything to upset her?" the woman demanded.

Wil shrugged, eyes widening. "Gods, I certainly hope not. That's why I'm trying to find her!"

"Well, get on, then!" The woman laughed and made a shooing motion with her hands. Wil nodded and took off again.

Throughout the fairgrounds Wil ran, each step jolting his head and making it worse. It had been a while since he'd pushed himself that far magically, maintaining several complex illusions at once. If he'd been less experienced, some of those images would've faltered or bled together. He considered himself fortunate to be skilled enough to handle it all, but it did come with a cost.

The first time he tried to seek out Darlene with his magic, the backlash made his vision go black and his legs turn to rubber. He caught himself on a bench and sat down for a second. Wil breathed evenly. It cost him a couple of minutes, but it gave him time to catch his breath and think more clearly. He realized he knew exactly where she was going, so he didn't need to rush.

Darlene waited among the animals, leaning out over the children's petting zoo fence and feeding a fat miniature horse. Wil made sure to make a sound as he stepped up to the railing and leaned over it as well. She didn't say anything to him at first.

"You don't have to talk if you don't want to," Wil said softly. "I just came to make sure you're alright."

She nodded but took her time. When all the feed in her hand had been thoroughly slurped away by the mini-horse, she reached forward to scratch his head and play with the fluffy little mane. The mini-horse tolerated it, licking his lips and letting out a short whinny.

"How'd you know to find me here?" Darlene finally asked.

Wil shrugged, turned around, and sat on the railing. The sun had set a little while ago, and now they were in that first real darkness of the night, dimly lit by a nearby lamppost.

"I figured you didn't go home. Hard to right now, and I didn't think you were that upset. You didn't get a bite to eat. It's too dark and you're unprepared, so I doubted you'd go into the forest. Someone said you came this way, so I figured cute animals would cheer you up."

"Oh, the crying girl needs cute animals to cheer up? That's sexist, Wil."

Wil leaned forward. "Was I wrong?"

Darlene burst out laughing, shaking her head. The mini-horse neighed and trotted away. Apparently, they weren't very interesting if they didn't have food to give him.

"Then if it's right, I'm not sexist. That's just logic." Wil stuck out his tongue at her. She shook her head, rolling her eyes. "Did the cute animals help?"

"They did."

Wil finally had to ask. "What made you run off in the first place? My show wasn't that bad, was it?"

"No, no! A little hokey maybe, but it was sweet." Darlene smiled, and there was a new pain there. She put her hand on his leg and squeezed. "I was just a little overwhelmed is all. Dad losing his mind and throwing me out, and then me and Bram talked for a bit about me moving in before your show, and then... Why did you put me and Bram up on the wall?"

Wil blinked. "Because you're my friends?"

Darlene swatted at his arm. "No, I get that, but. Bram was labeled as a friend. And then I was under 'loved one.' Don't you think that's a little fast?

And then with you offering me a place in your house?" She hugged her arms to her chest.

"Ahh," said Wil, flushing. "Well, I got a few reasons for that. First, it just sounded good and had real impact. And it makes me look like a real adult with an adult relationship and everything. As a showman, I have to consider these things."

"Oh, right, right," said Darlene, seriously. "So that's it? Just showmanship and trying to impress people?"

Now he had to decide how honest he wanted to be. "Not just that," Wil admitted, trying to hide a smile. "I don't have many friends. You and Bram are it. And, well, I'm pretty sure you're my girlfriend now or something. Unless I'm wrong."

Her hand found his and closed around it. "No, I don't think you're wrong," Darlene said with a sigh. "Ever since you came back, you've been a new person. More confident. I don't think I thought that much of you during school, but I like who you've become. And not just because you're a rich and powerful wizard."

Wil burst out laughing. "Me? Confident? Rich and powerful? Please." He shook his head, an occasional laugh still spilling out. But then he thought about it. "I'm...one of those things. I suppose I am fairly powerful in my own way, but I don't feel like it. And I'm not rich yet, just well paid."

"Give it a few years," said Darlene knowingly. "You'll end up rich *and* confident, and then you'll be someone I can be proud to be seen with." She winked. "Though after that show, I think your popularity's rising, Mr. Wizard."

At that, Wil couldn't help but get excited. "Did you see the demon and how I made it explode in small pieces? That was particularly difficult. That was a couple dozen simultaneous illusions working both together and independently. That could've been my graduation project."

"Yes, it was very nice," Darlene said, like a mother placating her child. She couldn't keep a straight face and soon they both descended into laughter.

"So you're going to move in with Bram, you're thinking?" Wil asked, after another short silence.

Darlene nodded. "Like I said when you came in with a head full of steam about not wanting to help him, he's different now that he's alone. He's a good guy, and I think it'll do us both some good. I'd...I didn't want to take you up on your offer," she said, voice shrinking. "I don't want to have to feel like I owe you something, in case things don't turn out good for us."

"I understand," said Wil. "It's a good idea, and one I think will work out well. Besides, as often as I'm over there and you two are at my house, it's not like I'll be seeing you any less. A bit of space is good. I really like you, Darlene, and I'm not going to try to rush anything or push you into doing anything you don't want to do. I mean it."

She looked at him then, exhausted and drained after a demanding day. And she smiled and leaned forward. For a change, Wil felt no nervousness or fear or anything other than quiet pride and acceptance. He met her halfway, their lips gently brushing together, tentative and seeking. They broke apart after a few seconds.

Wil turned away, fighting his growing smile. "I'm happy to help. Especially when we get your things. Jonjon's going to wish he didn't do you dirty like that."

"Oh? What're you going to do?" Darlene's eyes lit up.

"Just give it a couple of days for me to recover, and then…"

A couple of days later, Wil showed her exactly what he planned on doing. They met up for lunch and Wil brought all of his empty suitcases and told her the plan. She loved it, and she went to work considering the targets she would go for and what to do if Jonjon gave them trouble.

They marched up to the sprawling house. Wil stayed back and let Darlene take the lead, banging on the door until Jonjon answered.

"Well, well, well, it's time, then?" He wore a smug, terrible smirk. "This is your last chance to reconsider and drop that brewery nonsense."

"I'd say this is your last chance to kiss my ass, but there will be plenty of others," Darlene said brightly. "Move."

Jonjon scowled and threw open the door. He motioned with his head for them to come in. Darlene did and Wil followed with four massive suitcases dragging behind him. Jonjon seemed content enough to just ignore Wil and focus on hounding his wayward daughter.

"Hey, babyyy," Darlene's mother, Angelica, slurred from the couch. She had a large glass of a toxic green liquid in one hand and an expensive cigarette in the other. "You stop fightin' with your father, now. Juss come home and stop this."

Darlene ignored her. Wil followed her to her room. Darlene paused in the doorway, looking around. "Okay, the bastard didn't move anything on me or go through my things. I guess there's that, at least. Alright, I'll start grabbing things, and you do your thing!"

"You got it." Wil opened up two of the suitcases and dragged out more, miniature suitcases. He released the spell shrinking them and they expanded. Soon the number of actual suitcases had doubled. It would be difficult to carry them all.

He grabbed one and set it on the bed, right as Darlene unloaded a drawer full of clothes onto it. One suitcase filled up with clothes, and then another. Then she focused on getting pictures, knickknacks, journals, and jewelry. They had enough room for all of it and then some. They were in there for the better part of twenty minutes, working quietly when Jonjon showed up again.

"You planning on hauling all of those out yourselves? Won't that be a sight?

The town wizard and my horrible traitor of a daughter having to drag all these across town. You're just gonna embarrass yourself and me if you do this."

Wil turned to Jonjon. "I have magic, you half-wit. Do you really think it's going to be hard? I could pack up your entire house into these suitcases if I wanted to. Don't test me."

Jonjon paled. "Now, you don't get to touch anything that ain't hers! We had an agreement!"

"You're right, Dad," Darlene said, closing one suitcase and getting one small bag off the bed. "Now, I'm going for my inheritance and you're not going to stop me."

"Now hold on just a damned minute!" Jonjon protested, blocking the door with his body as she approached him.

Wil held up a hand and pushed the air. Jonjon wasn't thrown back so much as roughly shoved by raw force. Darlene headed for her parents' room, her father quickly scrambling behind her. Wil tied the suitcases together and made them float along behind him. Together, it was about as hard as dragging a wheelbarrow full of dirt. Not the easiest, but not hard either. He dragged them to the entryway and then met up with Darlene in her parents' bedroom.

"I told you, you could have anything that's yours, but that jewelry ain't yours! Not yet." Jonjon looked seconds away from putting his hands on his daughter. Wil almost wished he'd try.

"Grandma wanted me to have them after she passed," said Darlene, emptying rings, necklaces, and earrings into the bag. "She'd be rolling over in her grave if she knew you thought you were going to keep them from me."

"Enough of this," Jonjon said, finally putting his hand on her arm. She fought to get out of his grip, but he wouldn't let go. "Put it all away. Come back to work and we'll pretend this never happened. Stop this right now!"

"You had your chance," Wil said, coming up from behind. "She's leaving, she's taking the jewelry, and you'll get out of the way." He had no idea where this calm came from. He couldn't remember ever being so quietly angry and wishing to unleash what he could do, but it came out evenly and almost detached. "Step aside or I'll make you."

Jonjon's face turned an ugly shade of purple. He thrust his finger in Wil's face, opening his mouth to start yelling. Wil lost his patience and removed Jonjon's ability to speak.

"JONATHON JOHNSON," Wil bellowed with a deeper, enhanced voice. "YOU DO NOT WISH TO HAVE ME AS AN ENEMY. STAND DOWN, OR I WILL UNLEASH MY WRATH UPON YOU!" All it took was channeling his best impression of his elderly enchantment teacher, Professor Figgis. The melodramatic old bastard would be so proud of him now.

Jonjon stumbled back, bravery faltering. Wil pushed his advance in his normal voice. "Think of everything I've done for your house and how easily it would be to take it back. I don't want to be your enemy, but if you don't treat your daughter better, I will be a villain. *Your* villain."

Darlene tugged on Wil's arm. "C'mon. Let's go." With one last contemptuous look at her cowering father, she let her hand slide down Wil's arm until she had his hand in hers. Together they left, picking up the luggage and dragging it out. They set off for the Stevenson farm, leaving the Johnson residence behind.

"You'll be a villain. *His* villain?" Darlene snickered.

"It worked, didn't it?" Wil smiled, pushing his anger aside. He didn't need it anymore. For the most part, he wanted to be as fair and kind a wizard as he could, doing everything in his power to serve the community. Threatening someone was new for Wil, but he wouldn't take it back, and he'd do it again if he had to. Especially if they moved against his few loved ones.

For now, it was time to take Darlene home, and to a new, hopefully better chapter of their lives.

The Storm Dragon

O nce upon a time, dragons covered the land. Before humans moved in from the east, the dragons ruled over half the world, crownless kings of a seemingly endless domain. No one knew how long they had been there, just that the western continent, not yet named, had more dragons than Albetosia, and more than the far east, even. That vast stretch of paradise, untouched by man, would eventually be called Calipan by the time Wil and his family lived in the western reaches.

As people came and spread across Calipan, their numbers grew while the dragons dwindled. Huge, powerful, mobile, and magical, at first the dragons defended their homes fiercely, with an intelligence humans tended to underestimate. The taming of Calipan took centuries of fighting back until the humans could not only hold their own, but win.

Bit by bit, the dragon population dwindled until only the most cunning or powerful survived, hiding in territories too harsh or dangerous for man to thrive. Occasionally, they'd steal out of their lairs and venture out for food and treasure, but as the years went on they spent more and more time to themselves.

Nowadays, sighting a dragon could be seen as an omen.

Whether that omen was good or bad depended on who you asked and what type of dragon it was, as they were as varied as the humans and other magical beasts across Calipan. Most flew, some swam, and others even tunneled, finding homes deep in the mountains and quarries of the world, hidden from eyes until the next time humans decided to dig deep for precious metals.

Inevitably, even today, dragons were occasionally roused from their long slumbers and peaceful lives and had to relocate. Some dragons, those who were sick or ancient, found themselves returning to their former homes when it seemed like their time was near.

Like the enormous silver dragon, flying just above the clouds on his way west. He was an old dragon, though not the oldest. He still had at least half a millennium left, if he survived that long. At over a hundred feet long with a wingspan that could blot out the sun, the silver dragon had few peers left in the world. His scales, hard and almost metallic after a lifetime of rolling in treasure and fighting for his life, blended in with the rain clouds beneath him.

Upon closer inspection, someone would be able to see the rain moving with the dragon, as if he were resting on a cloud as he drifted farther and farther west. Indeed, if anyone were able to be up at his level and to see his face twisted in pain and his eyes cloudy with sickness, they'd realize the rain centered on the dragon as he lazily headed from one coast to the other, drenching the earth below.

The sun set over the horizon, and while the dragon had excellent night vision, he was exhausted. With a low, rumbling growl audible only to himself, he sank beneath the clouds, losing altitude as he flew slowly in circles. The clouds came with him, sinking lower and lower until he landed, and rain came in a deluge, surrounding the massive creature in a several-hundred-foot radius.

The dragon inhaled, his breath hitching. He couldn't remember how long he'd been flying, or even why he flew on his journey. All of that seemed so far away, so unimportant. As did the storm soaking him and the meadow he landed in. All that mattered was getting home. Then he could rest. Truly rest. He exhaled and lightning pooled in his mouth, crackling with ozone but not leaving.

The dragon curled up and fell asleep, dreaming of his youth and better times. As he slumbered, the rain carried on without end. Water flowed downhill, more than even the greedy earth could drink up. The rain went on and on until the water reached the river and joined it. The river raged, winding around the meadow downhill to the town below.

No one thought anything of it, at first. Early autumn storms weren't uncommon, and the occasional flashes of lightning off in the distance seemed normal. That was, until the lightning went nowhere, striking the same patches of meadow again and again. Thunder cracked open the sky, rolling and rumbling the earth and getting the townspeople out to investigate.

It may have been the only thing that saved their lives.

The river ran through the town, the lifeblood of the community. When the new surge of water came rushing in, an old man with a fishing pole saw it first. It swept away his rod and drenched him as the sides of the river surged up with increased momentum. He stared blankly at the torrent of water before he ran to the town proper.

"Flood, flood!" he cried, but the river arrived before he did, destroying the old bridge that split the town in half, while lightning flashed and thunder roared.

They were no strangers to floods, but one this fast and furious would've taken anyone by surprise. They had enough time to evacuate their homes before the flooding got worse, spilling out into the streets and covering the town in a rising layer of water. Families grabbed what they could carry and headed for the hills. No one wanted to be around to see how far it would go before it was over.

It was a wise choice. The relentless storm raged all night long, and then into the day. The river never stopped, and by the time the following evening arrived, the entire town sat in water five feet deep. Those too stubborn or too weak to run were left behind. The lucky ones took refuge on their roofs, watching the disaster play out.

Eventually, some got in their heads that the storm was unnatural and bore investigating. So a few groups of people braved their way up the hill to the meadow nestled up at the halfway point of a small mountain. No one could miss the halo of clouds hanging low in the sky, endlessly pouring water.

When they got closer, no one could miss the enormous slumbering dragon either.

It didn't take more than a quick discussion before everyone understood the dragon was to blame, and that the town might not exist for much longer if they didn't do something about it. They gathered all the able-bodied men and loaded them up with whatever available weapons could be scrounged. No one had any illusions about being able to harm the dragon, but after a full day of flooding and fear, they were ready to try anything.

The meadow itself was flooded with all the water that had yet to make its way down the river. The would-be dragon hunters had to wade through water, trudging their way toward certain doom.

They made it to the dragon easily enough, and surrounded him, each of them armed with axes, picks, hammers, and knives. They looked at one another, trying to summon the bravery to be the first to slay a dragon and save their town. That bravery somehow held, even with lightning striking nearby trees and turning them into splinters, and thunder so loud it made their ears bleed.

One of the men shouted a war cry and attacked, and the others followed shortly after. Dozens of puny humans, striking a beast that dwarfed them and barely noticed the attempt. The townspeople gave it their all, and one of them managed to land a good hit, driving his ax into the dragon's nose horn.

The dragon awoke, his reptilian eyelids peeling back and focusing on his attacker. The human left the ax there and backed up, eyes wide with regret. Blinking, the dragon became aware of all the little strikes on his armored form. He stood, throwing several people down into the rising water. As he woke, the storm around him intensified.

He didn't understand why these humans had attacked him. All he wanted was to sleep off this terrible feeling, this cloudiness in his head. He had to get home. Maybe then he'd recover and the storm would end and no longer drain him. He flapped his wings, and the gusts sent humans sprawling backward.

Again and again the dragon pumped his wings, inhaling and exhaling, and getting ready to lift off. He kicked off the ground in a flash of lightning and took to the skies once more. Still exhausted, but a little better than before. He flew off, leaving a few dozen confused humans behind.

More importantly, he took the storm with him. It was too late for the town below, which would need to be rebuilt, but at the very least, the flood hadn't completely swept everything away. No one would be grateful for it; instead, they would curse the dragon for years to come for the destruction he had brought with him.

The dragon paid the humans no mind and continued his trip west, riding his clouds across Calipan. He didn't care how slow he moved, or that he'd need to stop and feed soon. He had only one thing in mind, which pierced the fog of sickness and fatigue.

He had to get to what was now known as Harper Valley.

CHAPTER 32

Test Flight

Wil had just finished up the last touches on his project when the basement door opened behind him. He looked up to find Darlene in the doorway of his laboratory. Tables on which he used alchemical equipment and kept his enchanting tools lined the walls. The middle of the room was open. It had to be, for his project. He raised a hand and waved.

"There you are," she said, coming to him. The dim lighting from luminescent crystals overhead made her pale skin all but glow. "I was wondering why you weren't answering the door. Working on this old thing again, huh?" She nudged the big rug with her foot.

She had no idea. Wil extended his senses toward the rug and did a sweep. It thrummed with magic, flowing from point to point in the rug in one continuous circuit. Enchantments had never been one of Wil's strengths, but with enough time and effort, nothing could stop him. Smiling, he stood up and posed triumphantly.

"Nope. I am *done*! As far as I can tell, this thing's ready to go. It only took me all summer. Watch this!" Wil stepped off the rug and snapped his fingers. The rug rolled itself up as tight as it could get.

Darlene shook her head, chuckling. "Very impressive, Mr. Wizard. You have a self-rolling rug. But will it actually *fly*?"

Wil grinned. "Only one way to find out. Care to join me?"

Amusement turned to uncertainty. "Depends. How likely am I to get hurt falling off?"

"Depends," Wil echoed. "How much do you trust my skills?"

A month and a half had passed since the Midsummer Faire that saw Darlene kicked out of her home and moving in with Bram. A month of starting over for her, and life as usual for Wil. In that time, a great lot of nothing happened. Not that he was complaining. It gave him time to get through work orders, be with family and friends, and, of course, to finish a complex enchantment.

The dying days of summer blanketed Harper Valley with enough heat and humidity to make the town a big soup. Every day, the leftover heat lingered while autumn and its storms drifted in lazily, a lingering promise for later. It didn't rain, not yet, but the entire basin would be happier when it did.

It may have been warm, muggy, and getting close to sunset, but to Wil that just meant it was a perfect day for flying.

"Alright, so we'll take it nice and easy at first," said Wil, dropping the rug on the ground and unrolling it with a flick of his wrist. He sat down in the front, patting the spot next to him.

Darlene gave him the side-eye but did as he asked, sitting cross-legged. "I feel like a kid again. Any chance of making something with proper seats?"

"If this works, I could always see about making you a flying bike." Wil winked and pulled up the front edge of the carpet. "Now, stay still. We'll stay low and see how it feels first, okay?" She nodded at him, swallowing hard but apparently trusting him. Well, he'd just have to prove that trust wasn't unfounded.

Once more, he extended his magical senses and felt for the series of enchantments on it. There wasn't just one enchantment telling it to fly—he'd done a few dozen small enchantments woven around a much larger one, with everything from altitude to turning covered and linked together. Best of all, if he didn't push it too hard in one go, the carpet would recharge itself just from not being used.

Wil took a deep breath. It was time.

On the front edge of the rug, he'd installed two leather loops, laced with glowing green threads like wires. Wil gripped these and pulled back. The magic came to life and the rug rose in the air slowly, just four or five feet. It hovered in place, almost completely still. The barest of movements it made came from Wil's hands on the handles, not quite steady.

"Oh my gods," Darlene said, half crashing into Wil as she moved away from the sides. "It works. It works!"

"So far!" Wil said cheerfully. With a gentle tug of the leather straps, they swayed from side to side in the air, the carpet tilting just the slightest amount. Left and right, tilting higher and higher until Darlene let out a little shriek and threw her arms around Wil.

"Stop it, I don't want to fall!" she cried out.

"You don't? You're *really* not going to like this then," he said, twisting the handles to the left. They rolled in place quickly. Darlene couldn't notice it, but

Wil couldn't miss the way a new spell kicked in, grabbing both of them by their rears and not sticking them to the rug so much as telling reality that they were right side up and didn't need to fall after all, thank you very much. It had its limits, but it worked.

They turned right side up and Darlene huffed and puffed in fear. She turned to Wil with murder in her eyes. "You *jerk!*" She smacked his arm and chest repeatedly. It hurt a little, but maybe he deserved it.

"Hey, it works—you didn't fall. That's a good thing, right? So, what do you say? Shall we go for a ride?"

Darlene looked at the open area around Wil's house on the hill. From there they could see downtown. She smiled then and nodded. "Yeah. Show me around town, Mr. Wizard."

"As you wish." Wil pulled up on the straps and they rose. He pushed down and they fell a bit. Good enough for him. That just left one direction. He tilted his wrists and pulled forward. They shot forward at a decent speed. Darlene jerked back but neither of them fell off the rug. Everything worked.

Higher they climbed, topping out at about thirty feet, just to be safe. Any higher and Wil couldn't guarantee stopping them if they fell. He kept it fresh in his mind, but the rug came equipped with an emergency spell if all the others failed. So onward they sped off, getting faster and faster the harder Wil tugged.

They did a lazy circle around downtown, where at this time of day shoppers milled around. It didn't take long for someone to notice them and point up. Soon, they had an audience as Wil directed the carpet around. He dipped down and Darlene waved at a little girl looking up at them with awe.

"Evening, folks!" Wil called out as he accidentally dive-bombed them a little, pulling up at just eight or so feet off the ground. They zoomed around in tighter and tighter circles until Wil stopped them in the center of the square.

"Any chance you'd be willing to sell that flying carpet?" one of the richer farmers, Wayne Cox, called out. "I'd pay a lot to be able to fly!"

"Talk to me after all the fall chores are done and we settle in for the winter," Wil called back.

From the general store, Jonjon came out. He looked up at the two with a mixture of irritation and awe. Darlene waved at him before turning her hand around and dropping every finger but one. Laughing, she nudged Wil and they took off high into the air.

Wil risked going higher until the entire town lay beneath them in a beautiful sprawl, each farm's field a big square of gold or green. The wind rushed through their hair and made their clothes flap wildly. Beside him, Darlene shivered.

"You okay?" he asked, raising his voice to be heard over the wind.

"Just a bit cold," she shouted back. "We're gonna need some better jackets and maybe goggles if we're going to be flying."

"Goggles?" Wil snickered. "No way. I'd look too dorky in them."

"You always look dorky, Wil," she said, fluttering her eyelashes at him. "It's part of your appeal."

Wil released the leather loops, ready to grab them again in a hurry if they fell. They didn't. The spells held and they hung in the air above the great Stellan River that split the town east and west. He let himself relax and carefully turned to face Darlene. He grinned at her until she squirmed.

"What?" she demanded, looking away.

"Just realizing how romantic this could be," Wil teased, taking her hand in his. "Just the two of us up here in the sky, no one around, with the greatest view anyone in the valley could have."

"Hmm. I suppose so," Darlene said, corners of her lips twitching, but she didn't break yet. "I bet you say it to all the girls you bring up here."

"As a matter of fact, I do."

Wil broke first, laughing until Darlene had no choice but to join him. She squeezed his hand and leaned forward. He met her halfway and they kissed, soft and sweet. It still surprised and made him giddy that he could do this whenever he wanted, and she wanted it back. They were still taking things fairly slow, but they were part of each other's lives now, and that felt incredible.

"I'm glad I got to share this with you first," said Wil, smiling like a dopey goof.

"Me too," said Darlene. Her smile turned wicked. "Because as soon as he knows it works, Bram's going to want to come up here as well, you know. It'll be plenty romantic then too." She laughed as he rolled his eyes.

"So, how's that been going so far?" It had taken everything Wil had not to ask the question before now. It would be so easy to come off as overbearing and overprotective, when Darlene was a fully capable, intelligent young woman who didn't need his help. He loved that about her. She welcomed his input and respected him, but she didn't *need* anything from him.

"Pretty well!" Darlene perked up. "I thought it would be weird at first, but other than seeing him in his underpants a couple of times, it's been really peaceful. We both have our work to do and I've been helping him get more and better brewing manuals and possible recipes to check out, as well as balancing out our books. That's actually why I came to see you today."

"Oh, yeah?"

Darlene turned around on the carpet, looking out at the Stevenson farm in the distance. They could see it from there, but only just barely. "It's time for a taste test and Bram sent me to come get you. I was going to tell you when I came down to your lab, but this seemed more important. And fun."

"Taste test!" Wil's eyes lit up. "You made the right call. If I knew the beer was ready we would've gone right over there first thing."

Darlene chuckled. "Thought so. We've got four different batches of beer to try. That's why he wanted to wait so long. As he's said over and over again, more time in the bottle…"

"Gives the beer time to mature and get tasty," Wil finished for her. Both of them shook their heads.

Bram's excitement was infectious, even when it could be exasperating. With all of the work he had to do front-loaded, the giant of a man spent most of the rest of his time talking about their business and hyping it up, keeping them all excited and their heads in the game while the beer took weeks to ferment and carbonate just right. He was their biggest cheerleader.

"Well, we better not keep him waiting, then," said Wil. He took the leather straps in one hand and offered them to Darlene. "Would you like to fly us there? It's safe. Probably!"

She thought about it. "Not this time," she said. "You're getting pretty good, though. Why don't you take us there as fast as you can? While still being safe, I mean."

Oh, if that wasn't an invitation, Wil didn't know what was.

"You got it, Darlene. Hold on tight!"

She let out a delighted shriek as they took off like a shooting star.

CHAPTER 33

Flight Test

Bram was waiting for them on his porch when they flew in. He spotted them about the same time they saw him, a little dot on the horizon. He stepped forward, looking up with undisguised excitement. Wil decided to have a little fun, diving down near Bram and turning a tight circle around him before they slowed to a stop, settling on the ground. He released the straps and all the spells lay dormant, partially depleted and already sucking in more mana from the surroundings.

"You got it working!" Bram gushed, helping pull Darlene to her feet. "Is that what took so long? You went flying without me?"

"Yep," said Wil as he pushed himself to his feet. With a snap of his fingers, the rug curled up and he stuck it up against the front of the house. "Wanted to test it out with just the two of us before I take you up in the air. Gotta make sure about the weight limits. No offense."

"Yeah, fair," Bram admitted, though a hint of red came to his face. "Well? What're the results?"

"It works," Darlene answered. She grinned like a fool. "It was wonderful, and I can't wait for you to get to try it. But it might have to wait for a bit."

"Aww, why?" Bram tried not to look too disappointed.

"Well, aren't you about to pour us a few beers?" Darlene asked. "You really don't want to get drunk and then fly on a barely tested magical carpet do you?"

"I guess not," said Bram, but the mention of his beer made him excited all over again. "We've got all four batches ready and I've got it all set up waiting for us! It was real tempting to try it ahead of you, but I waited until we were all here for it."

That made Wil feel a smidgeon of guilt over the flight, but he couldn't bring himself to be sorry. A mixture of a successful experiment followed by hopefully a second just made this the best day he'd had in a while. So instead of apologizing, Wil just slapped Bram on the shoulder.

"Looking forward to it. Tomorrow we'll get you up in the air. Who knows? Maybe I'll make a second one to do beer deliveries with." The idea sounded ridiculous to him, which just made it even better. Who wouldn't want to have their beer delivered by a giant on a flying carpet?

Bram's eyes lit up. He made a high-pitched excited sound and did a little dance in place before rushing into the house. Darlene shook her head with a smile and motioned for Wil to come in with her. They joined Bram at the kitchen table, where he'd already set up four glasses each and had four brown bottles with different colored caps.

"Alright, Bram," Darlene said as she sat, "what've you got for us?" Wil sat across from his girlfriend, but Bram remained standing.

"We have four wildly different but hopefully equally impressive beers," Bram said, getting into the role of a showman. "From the weak but smooth to the dark and delicious, I tried a few different recipes, both old and new!"

He lifted one bottle and popped the top off. Starting with Darlene and working to himself last, Bram took the glass and poured the beer at an angle to keep the head small. A light gold liquid came out, and the one bottle filled three glasses about halfway.

"This is a simple wheat beer, the majority of what we'll be selling. A nice light lager, easy going down."

The next bottle he opened contained a dark, reddish brown liquid that looked great when the light caught it. When Bram poured it, Wil couldn't resist bringing it up to his face and inhaling. It had the usual bitterness he associated with beer, but also a sweetness to it that made him want to take a drink immediately.

"This is a red ale," Bram announced, setting down the empty bottle. "It's a nice halfway point between light and dark, with hints of fruit and caramel as its main flavors."

The third bottle poured out a liquid that was nearly entirely black. Darlene looked at this one with narrowed eyes, lifting up her glass and sniffing. She made a face that wasn't exactly bothered but overwhelmed. "Hoo," she said. "This smells strong."

"Barley wine!" Bram said. "This is the one I'm looking most forward to. This is an older recipe and it *is* strong. This is about as dark and potent as a beer gets. Take another smell. Molasses and toffee."

Wil did as he said, and his eyelids fluttered at the scent. It was everything Bram said—dark and complex. Wil licked his lips, itching to taste this one immediately, but he held out.

Bram took the last bottle. The beer came out a soft yellow. "Last and definitely least, this is a small beer. Nothing special, just wanted to try a batch of my own. Back before we were better at cleaning water and making sure it was safe to drink, this is what everyone would drink for every meal. It's low alcohol. Should taste okay and get you a little bit tipsy if you drink it all day, but without as much risk of a hangover."

Finally, Bram sat down. He lifted a journal he'd been keeping since he started brewing. "I've kept extensive logs on what ingredients I've used for each, how the mash came out, and how long we let them ferment and time spent in the bottle before serving. Together, we'll make sure they come out perfectly!"

"Sounds good, Bram," said Wil, looking over the four half-full glasses in front of each of them. "Does that mean we can drink now?"

"Almost!" Bram wiggled in his seat. "We should probably drink them in order of potency. Or maybe flavor profile. Flavor profile would probably be best, but if we do that, I should get us a palate cleanser. Maybe—"

"Bram," Darlene said, silencing him. "Order of potency sounds good. But I wouldn't say no to a palate cleanser too." She shot a playful smile at Wil, who returned it and rearranged his glasses so the small beer was first.

"Right, right!" Bram hopped back up and rummaged through his cabinets. The kitchen was a lot cleaner than when Wil first saw it, but it still looked a little run-down and like it belonged to someone else. Seeing Bram fumble around just reinforced that. He got out three more glasses and filled them with water from the sink, and pulled some crackers from the pantry.

Wil lifted his small beer and Darlene did the same. Once Bram was back in his seat, he raised his glass too.

"Cheers!" They clinked glasses and all took a sip of the small beer.

Wil smacked his lips, thinking about it. It took a while to get an impression. 'Small' as a word suited it. It had flavor but it was a light one, like a memory of a better beer. That didn't make it bad, just closer to water. He took another sip, just to get a better impression of it.

"Well?" Bram asked, looking around.

"Well," Wil said, looking at the glass, "I could see drinking this all day while working. But I don't think I'd drink it for fun with meals or on a late night."

"Yeah," said Darlene, "I think there could definitely be a market for it. We seemed to move away from it and into water as being, you know, clean and healthy, but I can see some farmers wanting a light drink. Especially if we made it more refreshing. Winter's coming, but I could see this in the spring being fruitier and satisfying that way."

"Excellent point!" Bram opened his journal and wrote down some notes. "This is weaker and smooth, so it would be an easy one to sell for cheap, maybe even to younger adults as a first drink."

Nodding, Wil took the lead and raised the glass of golden wheat beer. His friends did as well, and as one, they drank. This time, Wil drank a little more deeply, eyes closed as he focused on his sense of taste. He swallowed, smiling.

"Mmm. Not bad. Smooth, light, with a bit of a dry finish. Kind of tastes like lemony bread." More than anything, it sure was beer. It tasted good enough, but it didn't really stand out too much to Wil. He didn't want to say that out loud, but then Darlene did it for him.

"Not bad," she said with a shrug. "I like a little more body with mine, but it tastes pretty good and it's the easiest and cheapest to make outside of small beer, right?"

Bram nodded.

"Then this will make for a good basic beer to give out for samples and get people used to our taste, maybe even wanting more." She took another drink, nodding. "Yeah. This is a good start, though I'm not sure what could be better."

"Oranges," said Bram with a nod of his own. "A beer like this needs to be more refreshing and an infusion of some fresh citrus will do wonders, I think."

"Yeah," said Wil, just wanting to contribute. He finished his and set it down, picking up the red ale.

Bram took the first drink this time. Wil followed shortly after, making a sound. Now this was a damned good beer. It had a fuller body than the wheat beer, and a more complex, darker flavor. Wil couldn't stop himself from drinking the entire thing.

"Well, I love it," Bram admitted, keeping one last mouthful at the bottom of his glass. "Even if no one else does, I might keep making batches of this for me."

Darlene swirled her glass around and then took another sip. "This is going to be perfect for restaurants. I guarantee you I can get Danson's to sell this. And then finally I'll start earning my keep!" She let out a laugh and Wil joined her, but Bram didn't.

"You definitely earn your keep," he protested. "Without your help, I would've given up weeks ago. You do a lot."

"Well, thanks," said Darlene, shrinking in her seat. Her eyes remained on the table, lost and cloudy in a way that had been happening on occasion since her father had kicked her out of the house. "I try to be. I learned a lot, and before now, I think the stillness was starting to get to me. Starting tomorrow, I can start giving out samples and talking to business owners about selling the beers. You've already got the next batches going?"

"Yeah," said Bram, face reddening a bit. "I got a bit excited and as soon as these were bottled I did the same recipes again, just in case we did well and could sell something. Maybe break even for the winter. So far, doesn't seem like the worst plan."

"No, good call, Bram," said Wil. "You did a good job, and I think we all work well as a team. As far as the debt and money go, I figured this winter's a loss, and we'll just keep our heads above water as best we can. By this time next year, though, we'll have made it. Until then, if you want a bit of money, I was actually meaning to work on my alchemy soon. I could use some help with it and that could get you paid."

"Really?" Bram looked hopeful. Then he remembered himself, and he took his glasses off and cleaned them on his shirt. "I appreciate it, but only if you could use the help. I don't need any more charity, you know? I just wanna be helpful and do well, and maybe start to thrive."

Wil shook his head. "No, I could seriously use the help. There are some potions and mixtures that are always handy to have in the winter, and I figured maybe we could sell them on the side as part of our joint business. Stuff like cold medicine, anti-spoiling agents, and maybe some things to help winterproof houses. You don't need magic for most alchemy, just an attention to detail that you might be better at than me."

"I'd like that," Bram said quietly, and Wil's heart broke a little.

Poor guy really needed to feel useful after all the help he got—it was as if he didn't realize how much help he already gave. Wil resolved to tell him so later. Maybe after taking him around on a flight. The past couple of months had been way easier with Bram's help at the office, even with the added chores of Wil taking care of the Stevenson farm as they stocked up on ingredients for brewing in the winter.

Darlene lifted the final glass, the barley wine. "Then it's settled. Tomorrow we got plenty more work ahead of us. You two can fiddle with alchemy while I take our beer around and see who wants to buy. If we're not popular by spring, hell, I'll move back home and apologize to my dad!"

Together they laughed and clinked their glasses together, then drank. Wil took just a sip and swirled it around his mouth before swallowing. All around the table, everyone was silent.

"Gods, this is amazing," Wil groaned, taking another sip. Dark, bitter, complex, with just a hint of sweetness at the end. Full-bodied and thick, the barley wine tasted like the ultimate dark beer, exploding with flavors before the mellow, earthy aftertaste made him want even more.

Darlene made a face, but she didn't look like she hated it. "This is...oof, this *is* strong. I don't think I could drink too much of this in one go, but I don't think I'd have to. This is good."

Bram finished his barley wine with a face as similarly ecstatic as Wil's. "Might not even sell this one," he said, grabbing Darlene's and drinking hers too. "Might have to keep it all for myself."

"Hey!" she said, swatting his hand, but it was too late. Bram laughed, and then she and Wil did as well, though Wil held his drink close to his chest.

"That's two okay beers and two really good beers," Wil said. "I think we're off to a good start here, folks. So here's a toast. To a bright future!" He held up his barley wine while Bram and Darlene lifted the last of their wheat beer. They clinked their glasses together.

"To a bright future!"

CHAPTER 34

Autumnal Alchemy

Fixing up his carpet and enjoying a few drinks with friends proved to be the calm before the storm, and the last time Wil had a night to himself for a while. And that alone didn't bother him. He appreciated the hard work as the last hurrah of the year before people settled in for winter and turned their attention toward their hobbies and secondary jobs.

It was the six years at Saint Balthazar's that made it more difficult. At school, the workload reversed. Autumns were spent getting back into the swing of things, with the difficulty of lessons and exams getting downright grueling in the spring, followed by a break for summer. Well, a break for anyone not taking extra classes or working their way through paying off the extra tuition, anyway.

Wil had half a decade of getting used to easy autumns and tough springs, and then suddenly it was reversed and he had to get used to how they did things at home again. Which meant from sunup to sundown Wil hustled and bustled and had more work orders than ever to take care of. Luckily for Harper Valley, he found his rhythm and fell into it.

Wil couldn't help with every chore that needed doing before winter, but he had plenty of work. The first thing he did was get all the work orders asking for help with firewood out of the way. Many of them were from older people who no longer had the strength or family to chop wood for them, and felling trees and breaking up the wood into usable logs was trivial for someone of Wil's talents. He finished over a dozen orders in just one day.

Winterizing chicken coops, rabbit hutches, and barns was the next big task he put his mind to. This was almost as easy but required some actual preparation and work on his part. Some wards and enchantments and a bit of rune work heated up and protected farm animals all across the valley. Wil spent a few days on that, traveling from farm to farm and getting it all done. He'd usually eat dinner with a grateful family, then pass out and repeat it the next day.

Then came almost the exact opposite: checking cellars and basements to make sure they were cool enough for the meat that hunters brought in to be stored all winter long, as families ate off the same deer for a month or more. The two weeks he spent grinding out work orders tested his ability to channel heat to or from houses.

It was almost a relief when the next few work orders came from people just wanting help with the harvests. As Wil proved to Jeb on multiple occasions, he could clear an entire field in a minute, and that alone could save people half the time it took to collect their crops.

Even his own family had a work order for that, and Wil somehow managed not to rub it in Jeb's face. Probably for the best, considering how much better things were since their cathartic brawl.

The days were long even as the weeks were short, and soon Wil had time to focus on getting more personal projects done. He knew he could've possibly justified taking a day or two to make potions and oils, but waiting meant he could dedicate his time to teaching Bram.

"Are you sure this is a good idea?" Bram asked for the millionth time.

"Completely positive," said Wil, clasping the larger man on his shoulder. "You've got a good eye for detail, you're careful, and you're curious. I'd bet a hundred zynce you end up better at alchemy than I am."

Bram shook his head quickly. "No bet. I don't even want to think of how much money I already owe you."

"Well, don't worry about it. I'm paying you for your work here. You can choose to give as much or as little of that back as you want to clear the debt. At the moment, I'd settle for more of that barley wine. You brought some, right?" Wil added hopefully.

Bram barked out laughter. "Yeah, of course. I figured we could use a few drinks after we see how bad I am."

That turned out to be not at all. Just as Wil expected, once he had instructed Bram on all the basics of the equipment and ingredients, he was a natural. At first, all the different glass instruments intimidated Bram, but this wasn't the first time Wil had tutored someone on the finer points of his education. It just happened to be the first time he taught alchemy, and it helped refresh him on basics he'd nearly forgotten.

That first day was just getting Bram used to the lab and all the equipment. They spent the second day on ingredients and how to prepare them and store them properly. So many magical herbs and beasties' body parts would go bad at the wrong temperature or if cut or smashed too soon before being added to the mixture. Wil ended up making a cheat sheet for the potions he needed to mass produce for the winter, and that's all Bram needed in the end.

By the time three weeks had passed since their night of flight and taste testing, they had a healthy stockpile of necessary potions. Cold and flu medicines, ointments for hypothermia, and nutrient-rich broths for the small population of homeless Harper Valley residents who might find themselves in danger as the weather turned for the worse. Any and everything Wil thought might be useful for the community.

Naturally, Bram loved helping out, and soon it became completely normal for Wil to find Bram already in his lab hard at work before Wil woke up. The biggest surprise was when Wil showed up in the late afternoon one day after doing another half-dozen work orders, to find Darlene there as well, helping out as if she'd been there the entire time.

"Hey, stranger," Darlene joked from one of the two alchemy stations.

Once the surprise wore off, Wil just smiled and waved. "What're you doing down here? Don't tell me Bram roped you into helping. We're nearly finished for a while." He shot a look at Bram, who stayed focused on his work and didn't turn around.

Darlene's bright blue eyes were alight with excitement. "He did, and I'm glad he did. I think you're sitting on something great here, and I don't want you to miss this opportunity."

Wil raised an eyebrow. "I am? What opportunity?" He came up behind her, looking over her shoulder at the bubbling liquid going up one glass tube and dripping out another.

She added what looked like fine silver dust to the pot, which frothed even harder. "Bram told me about that anti-spoiling agent you made."

"Yeah, a friend of mine in school came up with that. He was a real brewer, and graduated top of the class the year before me," Wil said, smiling at memory. "William Jackson. Great guy. Shared his recipes with anyone who asked, and I went through a minor alchemy phase during year four. What about it?"

Darlene looked at him like he was slow. "It's autumn. Everyone's going to be packing their food away for the winter, and most of them are going to pickle veggies and salt their meat to hell and back. You've got a great alternative here that doesn't make things taste awful. We gotta leap on this, Wil!"

Wil looked at Bram. "She got you in on this and you didn't tell me?"

The giant shook his head without turning around. "Darlene's way better at selling things than I am. I figured she'd make a good argument and I'd just support her after."

"Coward," Wil said with a chuckle.

"And how!"

Wil motioned for Darlene to continue.

She cleared her throat. "You've been working your ass off helping people, and at this point people mostly trust you, right? You're going the extra mile when you have the chance, but these potions aren't officially requested, right? Which means they're a good business opportunity. Not just for you, but for all of us here at Wiseman Brewing."

"Wiseman Brewing, huh? You like this name too?" Wil looked at Bram.

"I don't hate it," Bram admitted, finally spinning around in his seat. "I like doing the work, but I absolutely should never be the face of the company. Not if we want it to succeed."

"So you think I should be?" Wil scoffed.

"Well, duh," said Darlene. "You're Mr. Wizard, the beloved handyman of Harper Valley. And other nearby towns have been talking about you, even. Since you two have been busy, I've gotten a lot of samples out and have the interest of some people who want to sell our beer, but we need a recognizable name, and that one stands out."

"Okay, fine," Wil said with a nod. "All of that makes sense. But where does my alchemy come in?"

"You can sell it too," Darlene said with a sigh. "You're doing all of this in preparation for when things get worse in the winter and people get sick and need extra help, right? This isn't part of your normal duties, this is extra."

"Correct."

Darlene gesticulated wildly. "So make use of it! Everything. Your reputation, your resources, your friends. We can combine this all to have a stronger start to the business, right? We get the beer out under that name, and then we also start pushing potions and medicines, and suddenly *we* are the go-to group for anything that needs brewing. It gives us a clear future."

As far as plans went, Wil didn't hate it. That didn't mean he believed in it, but he at least could give it a proper chance. The more he thought about it, the fewer problems Wil had, until just a few remained.

"The thing is," he said, "I'm not actually *that* good at alchemy. At this point, Bram's probably better than me at the process itself, even if he isn't as knowledgeable."

"Aw, thanks!" Bram said, his face lighting up. "I've been working really hard on getting things perfect. You can see a difference between my most recent batch and my first few tries."

"Do you really need to be great at alchemy if you're the only game in town?" Darlene pressed. She stood up, checking her station one last time to make sure it was a good time for it before taking his hands in hers. "Think about it, Wil. We've got doctors and vets and they've got their own medicines and products that work, but you offer something different. And if we don't try to compete but instead *supplement* their stocks, we could not only fill an important niche but also normalize your magic."

Wil opened his mouth and closed it again.

Spotting weakness, Darlene leaped on it. "Fair prices for fair products that will make people's lives better. What could be better for the community than that?"

It wasn't fair, having a girlfriend so good at convincing him of things. Then again, Wil didn't see much of a reason to protest now. Not when she had a point. Adding in the hopeful look on Bram's face, Wil realized he didn't have the heart to refuse them. He just sighed, which made both Darlene and Bram let out a victory cry.

"See? I win, don't I? I totally won this." Darlene beamed.

"Yeah, yeah," said Wil. "You win. But I want you to approach this like you did the beer. If you want to do this so bad, then you're going to need to get samples out so people know what we're offering, and you'll want to do it soon, before they seriously start canning fruits and vegetables. Which is probably why you're here today to talk to me about it, I guess.

"Most importantly, though, we're *not* going to price gouge. I'm happy having my hand in a business, but..." Here came the guilt, same as always, when he thought about it. "I didn't go into this to get rich or anything. I just want to help out. I figure if we charge anything for it, we charge mostly for the materials and enough so *you two* can make a living off it. Anything I get, I think I'll want to reinvest it into the community."

Darlene wrapped her arms around his neck and dangled off of him, grinning pleasantly. "And that's one of the things I love about you, Wil. You're a complete sap when you aren't being dumb about things." She kissed him and Wil found himself unable to complain about any of this. When she broke away, he looked at Bram.

"Look, I agree, but I ain't kissing you," Bram said, laughing so hard his belly jiggled.

Rolling his eyes, Wil broke away and looked around his lab. *Their* lab, he supposed. "If we're going to do this, we're going to need gallons and gallons of the anti-spoiling agent. A little bit goes a long way, but this might be something everyone wants or needs, and it's better to have too much than not enough. This won't get in the way of the beer?"

Bram shook his head. "Next batches are well underway, and I can mostly just wait. Anything I have to do, I can balance it all. We can make this work, Wil. Wiseman Brewing!"

Wil couldn't help but wince at the name. "I get that it's a play off 'wizard,' but I sure don't feel wise. You got a logo and everything ready too?"

"Naturally," said Darlene. "Sarah made it for us." She reached into her pocket and pulled out a slip of paper. Wil took it and unfolded it to find a silhouette of a man with a wizard hat stirring a cauldron.

"Dammit." Wil knew he was beaten. "I love it. Alright. Wiseman Brewing. I'll drink to that. You two get back to work while I do that."

Bram and Darlene laughed and turned back to their stations. With one last look around the dimly lit basement, Wil couldn't help but smile. How could he not be pleased with the way things were playing out? Time went on and things kept getting better for them all. What could be better?

Another barley wine, maybe. Wil went upstairs to get one and relax for the night, thinking about where to treat his friends for dinner when they were done. Together, they were unstoppable and were going to take Harper Valley by storm.

CHAPTER 35

A Slice of the Pie

With the three of them working together, things progressed much faster. Wil and Bram spent their time brewing enough potions to fill up nearly all the spare space in the lab, making Wil very grateful he'd finished the flying carpet and no longer needed the space. The vast number of crates filled with their medicines and mixtures took up so much space they had a specific path leading through them to their two workstations and outside. Not the safest way to do alchemy, but these were simple, safe mixtures. Mostly. The crates wouldn't stay there for too long.

Darlene handled what felt like everything else, running herself ragged every day as she bounced around town. She procured jars and bottles, labels to go on their beers and potions, and the crates as fast as they needed them. Free samples went to all the major business owners, save her father. While Wil felt tired and burned out, Darlene kept on going as if she didn't need to sleep or eat.

It paid off soon enough. With all of their work done and autumn in full swing now, the time to finally make a showing was at hand. They took out an advertisement in the town newspaper and arranged for a spot in that week's two open market days, which just so happened to be on Wil's chosen days off.

It took them several trips at the crack of dawn with the McKenzie family cart and Percival to bring everything, but by the time the market officially opened, they were ready. Wil magically held up wood they brought and Bram hammered it together so they even had a stall to work at.

"We should've brought shade," Bram muttered as they all sat around waiting for customers to come their way. "Any chance of you gathering up some clouds above us?"

Wil looked at him, a crooked, incredulous smile on his face. "Well, haven't you gotten used to the perks of a wizard friend fast? I could, but I'm saving my energy for a long day. You should get a hat." He pointed up to his floppy wizard hat, something he wore only on occasion. Today seemed like one of those days.

Darlene reached down into the icebox they'd brought with them and pulled out three bottles of small beers and passed them out. "Summer's over, but markets like this are all about endurance. Stay hydrated." She grinned and flipped the cap off with a bottle opener and took a swig. The boys chuckled and did the same.

Turns out that was the best thing they could've done. One of the handmade signs advertised their beer menu, but seeing them drinking their own beer really got people's attention. Or so Wil decided to believe, because not five minutes later, their first customer showed up.

Lance Barrington came up to them and peeked inside their stall. "Hey there, Wil," he said. "Wiseman Brewing? Since when?"

"Since now," said Wil, leaning forward in his seat. "You thirsty?"

"Always! What's the strongest stuff you've got?"

Bram pulled out a cold bottle of barley wine. "Dark, full-bodied, and guaranteed to knock you out."

"Just how I like my women." Lance grinned.

He was the first, and then the three of them didn't have nearly as much time to sit around and talk, as a line quickly formed. Although it was early, most people were there for the beer, and Bram had to take Percival and make a run down to his farm to pick up more. His own bad luck for being the strongest. Wil and Darlene stayed with the stall and their dwindling stock.

They were down to their last few bottles when an unexpected person showed up. Angelica Johnson stepped up to the stall, somehow looking both embarrassed and terrified.

"Hey, baby," she said, with little of her signature slur in her voice.

Darlene sighed. "Mom. You here for our beer? How much have you had today already?"

Angelica winced. "I haven't had anything yet. I came here to see how you were doing. I saw the advertisement in the paper and I thought I'd drop by. How are you?"

Wil looked at the two of them and wisely decided to stay out of it. Darlene had an iciness to her eyes and voice unfamiliar to him.

"What makes you care all of a sudden?" Darlene demanded. "I've been out of the house for two months, and *now* you want to check in on me?"

Again, Angelica reacted as if she'd been struck. Tears filled her eyes and her voice grew thick. "It's not like that, baby! It's your daddy. He's been awful about it and won't stop saying horrible things about you. Each time I wanted to go check on you, he'd know somehow and stop me. I've been worried sick about you this entire time!"

Darlene took a long, deep breath. "So you've checked up on me and I'm clearly doing well. You thirsty, or do you need medicine?"

Angelica ended up buying one of each of their beers and an anti-hangover potion before she left. Wil watched Darlene carefully, but she very pointedly did not look in his direction or bring up her estrangement from her family, so he let it lie.

Before too long, Bram returned and they were back in business. For lunch, they took turns wandering the market, turning some of their earnings into food and a parasol for Bram, who didn't seem to think anything of being a giant with a tiny pink shield against the sun. If anyone thought it funny, they kept it to themselves rather than snark at the six-foot-six teddy bear.

It was after lunch that their star product got noticed. Still worked up after the surprise visit from her mother, Darlene went around with the preservative potion and handed out free samples to the farmers and cooks and others who'd brought food and produce they'd either sell or throw out by the end of the day. She demonstrated how it worked—just one part potion to nine parts water— and told them it would stop things from spoiling for a long time.

She told them to dip their vegetables in the mixture and then leave them out overnight. A tiny rinse would get rid of the potion and the food would be fine. Some people were incredulous. Some laughed. Even Wil and Bram were unsure of her strategy, but she just told them to wait until the next day.

Sure enough, by lunchtime the next day, the line was even longer. Now people bought potions at the same rate they bought beer. They sold out before dinner and went home. With all of their various costs that added up, ingredients and containers, they broke even. Not something Wil felt like celebrating, until Darlene brought up a good point.

"We broke even on our expenses and still have tons more stock back home," she said, throwing an arm around Wil's shoulders as they walked home from the market. "That means next week we'll be making pure profit. The first real proper payment for Wiseman Brewing."

"I still can't believe they like our beer. Love it, even!" Bram gushed, doing a happy dance along the road. "If we do this every week, we might actually run out before the next batch is done!"

"And at that point, we'll be able to expand and get bigger!" Darlene crowed. "It'll finally be time to replace that run-down barn of yours with something that won't fall over if you curse too loudly near it."

After that was another week of hard work, but now that they knew their products were desired, it didn't seem so bad. Every batch of potions Wil and

Bram made came just a little easier, and Bram could largely handle things on his own. It would've been so easy for Wil to forget about his actual job and focus solely on setting up the brewery, but he didn't let himself.

Every day, he went from farm to farm, helping people bring in their crops. It just so happened to give him the chance to tell them about his alchemical mixture and how good it was at preserving food for long periods of time, without that awful aftertaste other preservatives left. He even brought samples with him, at Darlene's suggestion. It worked like a charm.

The week passed swiftly, and when they set up their stall again, they had no need for advertisement: a lineup had formed before they finished unloading the cart.

Hours of meeting with damned near everyone in the valley and selling some much-needed cold medicine, insomnia cures, ointments, preservative potions, and alchemy finally overtook beer in sales. It was near the end of that day, right as they were about to sell out, that an unexpected visitor stopped by.

"Evening, Wilbur!" Mayor Sinclair cut in line the second Wil finished with a customer. "You look to be doing pretty well for yourself!" His big smile didn't meet his eyes.

"Seems so," Wil returned, instantly on guard. "It's been keeping me incredibly busy. How are you, Mr. Mayor?" Darlene and Bram exchanged a look Wil didn't miss, but they stayed out of it.

"Oh, I'm alright. I was hoping to talk to you in private, though, if you've got a moment." Mayor Sinclair's false smile deepened.

"Go for it," Darlene said when Wil looked her way.

"We got this covered," Bram added.

Wil led the mayor away from the market grounds and out into a nearby field between farms. One of the few pieces of land in the heart of the town not used for anything. He hoped they kept it that way as long as possible. Once the dull roar of the market had faded away, Wil looked at the mayor.

"What's on your mind, sir?" Wil tentatively asked.

"Your brewery," said the mayor as they continued to walk, his hands clasped behind his back. "You seem to be a smashing success and I'm really happy for you, son. Old Brown could use some competition. Maybe now, after a few decades of being the only brewer in town, he might update his recipe, or at least lower his prices to compete." He chuckled a little.

Wil said nothing, waiting for the other shoe to drop.

"It's your medicine that has me a little concerned, Wil. You're making it as part of your office as wizard, correct?"

This sounded like a trap. Wil looked over his shoulder, where his stall was the size of a grape in the distance. Darlene would know what to say. "I don't know about that," he said, forcing a laugh. "I'm rolling it together as part of the brewery. The processes aren't too different, and I've mostly been showing Bram a few things so he can contribute more."

"That's a very valuable gift you're giving your friend, Wilbur," said Mayor Sinclair. "That schooling of yours was expensive. Very expensive. And you're just giving the knowledge away for free, huh?"

Definitely a trap of some kind. "I'm a firm believer that knowledge is meant to be shared and shouldn't cost people a fortune to be able to better themselves," Wil said carefully. "I learned some valuable things, and the more I pass things on, the more good we can do in the world."

The mayor grunted. "That doesn't change the fact that you learned these skills while we paid for your schooling, correct?"

"Four years of it, at least," said Wil. "The last two years I paid for myself through tutoring and—"

"Let me get to the point, Wil," the mayor said with a sigh. "I'm thrilled that you have a successful business, but I don't know how I feel about you using something we as a community paid into together to make a profit alone. You're offering some revolutionary preservatives, I hear."

"Oh, that's not mine," said Wil. "A friend of mine made it and shared the recipe."

"Is he going to mind you using his recipe? Where is he stationed?"

"Oh, gods, like, three hundred miles south of here?" Wil tried to remember. "He's out on the southern frontier, near contested territory. He won't mind me using it. He'd be tickled that I'm using it."

"Yes." Mayor Sinclair's lips drew back into a sneer. "About that. I can't help but think that I could be a great help to you. You won't have any problems selling to the people of Harper Valley. At this point, it looks like there's no stopping you." He chuckled again, a forced, dead sound. "And it's a great thing you're offering to a farming community. But it's not the only community out there. We're surrounded by other towns that'd make great use of your potions. And that's where I come in. I have the resources, the know-how, and the connections to sell your potions directly to the other towns. At a much higher price. From what I understand, you're practically giving this stuff away."

"It's not that bad," said Wil as he glanced around. He couldn't bring himself to look directly at the mayor and keep a straight face. "We could probably charge double what we do now and it'd still be affordable enough to be worth it, but I have no desire to do that. I'm not out for profit, sir. I just know something that could help people while making enough to make it worth Bram's and Darlene's time. I probably *would* give it away if I could."

Wil knew that was the last thing Mayor Sinclair wanted to hear, but he could tell where this conversation was likely to go, and he didn't care for it. The mayor's tone and body language had him on edge.

"I respect the altruism," the mayor said through gritted teeth. "But think about what you're throwing away. Look, I'll be straight with you. You're doing a great job, and it's been a massive PR payoff for me. But the fact is, when you're at the top, you have to keep an eye on everything and make sure everything is on the up and up.

"Part of the point of the government is to regulate pies, let's say. We make sure the best ingredients are used, and that no one is getting hurt making these pies, and when it comes time to sell each pie, we get a slice of each one. You learned this skill through others paying for you, and now you're profiting off your own very special pie, but where's the government's piece?"

Wil clenched his teeth. "I'll pay taxes, same as everyone else," he said.

"Ah, but that's just a bite of the pie. Not an entire slice. I put a lot of personal money toward sending you to school, Wilbur. All I'm asking is a return on my investment. Here's what you could do to make things right. Wiseman Brewery can still be the business doing it, but if and when you want to distribute your medicines and preservatives to the nearby towns, you do it through my office. We increase the price so you and your little friends all get a good cut, and so does the town.

"It's only fair, isn't it? You owe everything you have to Harper Valley and those who paid your way. It's only right that you give back and help keep things running smoothly and efficiently. Harper Valley's growing, and there are plenty of public works a cut of your potions could pay for."

Wil understood. "I think we can handle it on our own, Mr. Mayor. Everything I do is an attempt to give back. This is a personal project and I'm not letting it get in the way of my wizarding duties. And I'll—"

"Look," the mayor cut in. "Take some time to think about it. I've done everything to make things easy and smooth for you. A bit of gratitude would be welcome, or at least not spitting in my face. Think about how you want your future in Harper Valley to go. Together, we can make this city greater than it's ever been. But alone...well, you're still new and inexperienced, Wilbur. I'm just trying to look out for you and make sure you don't make any mistakes that could hurt your future. Give it some thought and get back to me." With one last fake smile, Mayor Sinclair nodded to Wil and headed back to the market.

Wil stood there in the field, anger and frustration boiling over until he wanted to scream. The mayor had just threatened him, and he didn't have a single idea what to do about it.

CHAPTER 36

McKenzie Versus Sinclair

W hen Wil returned to their stall, both Darlene and Bram looked everywhere but at him. Their unspoken question loomed above them all, taunting him. He ignored it and collapsed into his seat, staring at the ground. He'd be thinking about a solution now if he wasn't replaying the conversation in his head, over and over and over again.

That look of frustration on the mayor's face as his patience wore out and he stopped being subtle. The way Wil's blood boiled at the demand and the threat. Everything just repeated on a loop. Wil couldn't run from it or hide; he couldn't distract himself or even try to talk to someone. He just had to suffer through it until it ran its course.

Luckily, his friends were smart enough to read the look on his face and left him alone. Bram even repositioned his chair in front of Wil's to block him from sight from potential customers who wanted to chat with the wizard while making their purchases. At some point, Darlene popped the top off a barley wine for him. He drank it gratefully.

Eventually, Bram engulfed his shoulder with a gentle hand and shook him out of his stupor. The market had ended and most other stalls were either empty or emptying now.

"You okay?" Bram asked carefully. Darlene looked up from the icebox she had been filling.

Wil shook his head. "No. I...I guess I have to talk about it because it involves all three of us."

Darlene reversed course and pulled out another few bottles and set them aside. They packed up the cart except for their seats and drinks and then sat in a triangle. Bram and Darlene waited patiently until Wil was ready to talk.

"The mayor threatened us," he blurted out.

"What?" Bram jumped, his spectacles falling from his face.

Darlene's eyes widened. "Really? Why?"

So Wil told them everything. From the guilt trips to the polite suggestions to chewing Wil out for not playing ball from the start. Bram looked increasingly horrified, while Darlene grew as angry as Wil, if not more so.

"And I don't know what to do," Wil finished, finishing off his drink. The mild buzz from a few drinks throughout the day helped loosen him up a little without ruining his judgment. As far as he could tell. He knew he was probably off-balance, but it didn't feel that way. This had to suck as much as he thought.

"What to do? I think the answer's obvious," Darlene scoffed.

"Yes," said Bram. "We do as he says."

"What?" Both Darlene and Wil turned to Bram, who winced and tried to make himself look small.

"Look, I know how it looks, but it might be the best choice here. I don't like it either! But if he can make trouble for us, shouldn't we avoid trouble if we can?"

"No!" Darlene snapped. "Absolutely not. We need to call his bluff and make it clear that we won't be pushed around."

Immediately, Wil was grateful for Darlene's unquenchable fire. He raised an eyebrow at Bram, who looked like he regretted speaking up. Still, with both of them staring, Bram had to continue.

"Unless it's not a bluff. Do you have any idea what he could do to make all of our lives harder? And our business too. He could probably find a reason to shut us down or throw all kinds of hurdles for us to jump over. And for what? We sell to our neighbors at a severely reduced price and the other neighboring towns have to pay more. The mayor gets a slice and we make more money. What's so bad about that?" Bram gestured wildly, eventually pointing at Darlene. "Isn't that good business sense? Don't make unnecessary complications, and sell for a profit. I thought you'd be all over that."

Wil didn't know what he expected from Bram, but being cold about it, prioritizing business over honor, wasn't it. Then again, he supposed it made sense. It was the path of least resistance, and despite Bram's childhood and size, the man didn't want trouble or a fight. He wanted things to go smoothly. And it looked like Darlene had just changed her mind.

"You're not seriously considering that, are you?" Wil asked.

Darlene made a face. "It's…damn, this is tricky," she admitted. "Money and being able to continue operating is kind of important. But if we do this, we're letting him know we can be bullied into doing whatever he wants. All he has to do is push and we'll obey. And men like him will never stop pushing.

"Trust me, my dad's like that. People like him, they never stop testing boundaries. They wanna see exactly how far they can push you. So whether we give in now or not, he's going to keep coming. There's no hiding or running from this. Eventually, we'll have to fight. So why not fight now?"

Gods above and below, that's how he felt. Wil knew he wasn't much of a fighter, but everyone had their limits. He didn't want to be the mayor's pet wizard, even if Sinclair had organized the fundraising for his education. Where did it end? *When* did it end?

Then again, the more Wil thought about Bram's side of it, the more he sympathized. Part of him would always be that quiet middle child who got overlooked and just let it slide and did as he was told. It'd be easier to just shrug and accept that he could make more of a profit if he did as the mayor asked. Bram and Darlene could have all the extra zynce, for all he cared.

Pure profit wasn't the point. Helping others and making it on their own, that was the point. Wasn't it?

"So what are you going to do?" Darlene finally asked, after the silence grew to be too much.

"I'm going to take Percival and the cart back to my parents' house and think for a bit. I'll have an answer by tomorrow."

Bram nodded. "I understand. Whatever you choose, we'll back you up," he said, grimacing. "Even if that means going up against the mayor."

"Going to fly home after?" Darlene asked with a smirk.

Wil chuckled. "Any excuse to use it. I think I got all the little kinks worked out, and it flies like a dream, but if I use it for more than a couple hours, it runs out of magic and needs to rest for a bit."

Darlene walked up to him and grabbed him by the front of his shirt. "Fly carefully, and take it easy tonight, okay?" She gave him a quick kiss and let him go, joining Bram as he walked away.

Wil watched them go until they were out of sight before climbing up to the seat at the front of the cart. He snapped the reins to wake Percival and they went on their way. Wil had plenty of time to think on the way to his parents', and he ran through two conversations now, weighing Bram's and Darlene's points against each other and his conscience. At least he'd be able to get more opinions, though he knew which way he leaned.

Bob and Sharon were happy to see him, even with the look on his face telling them something was wrong. Once Percival was back in the barn and properly rubbed down and taken care of, they all congregated on the porch. Bob had a pipe full of staggerleaf ready. Sharon just rocked quietly until Wil sat down, politely turning down the offer of the pipe.

"Well?" Bob asked, lighting up. "What's got you looking so haunted?"

Wil jiggled his leg restlessly, rocking back and forth. "The mayor paid me a visit today," he started. And then he went over the story again, getting no less angry about it this time. He told his parents about Bram's and Darlene's opposing advice and the pros and cons of each one. To his surprise, his parents weren't unified in it.

"Of course you're going to tell him to piss off," said Bob with a hearty laugh. He took a big puff and blew it out as a ring. "Darlene's right: you're going to need to stand up to him eventually or else he'll own your ass. We didn't raise you to back down to a bully."

Sharon swatted his knee. "It's not that simple," she said. "If he makes a real accusation of you using your office for personal gain, that could hurt."

"Yeah, but he's clearly using it for personal gain himself," Wil protested.

"Yes," said his mother in a patient voice, "but the difference is, he's had years of practice getting away with it and masking it. Everyone expects a politician to grow fat off the office, but you're younger and you have something no one else here has. It'd be real easy to turn that jealousy on you. Might even be able to run you out of town or make you pay back all that tuition if there's a big enough stink."

"I'd be happy to do that," said Wil, cheeks heating up. "I've always felt bad about it and dreamed of giving the money back. And with jerks like the mayor and Jonjon giving me crap about it like I'm gonna owe them for the rest of my life, maybe I will. I'll get an itemized list of everyone who put in for me, and pay them back from my wages. Put that to rest once and for all."

Bob puffed away, nodding to show he was listening. "That's not a bad idea, son. It shows you care and you're not using people. Doesn't help you right now, though. You still got this problem to worry about first."

"He'll have more than just this problem if he gives in," Sharon said. "There'll be that and whatever else Sinclair decides to cook up to put pressure on you. I'm not saying to roll over and bark for him. I'm saying maybe take some time, put yourself in a good position, and *then* knock his ass off his high horse and into the mud."

"That would be the smart thing to do," Wil admitted, although he'd already made up his mind. All the logic in the world couldn't beat that low simmering anger, the outrage and disgust that nearly choked him. "But I'm not feeling too smart right now. I'm angry and I don't wanna be pushed around by him or anyone."

"Attaboy!" Bob barked, laughing triumphantly. "Don't take crap from anyone you don't respect. And Sinclair's proved he doesn't deserve respect."

"You gotta be smart about it," Sharon insisted. "If you're going to turn him down, how do you plan on doing it?"

Like all of Wil's best-laid plans, it came to him in an instant—he'd work through the details afterward. Just a flash of inspiration, and then all it took was making it happen.

He smiled. "I'm going to make up a bunch more stock, and then me, Bram, and Darlene are all going to go to neighboring towns and offer up our products for cheap. Give everyone a taste this fall to help them out. Maybe we'll raise the price later on, but for now, we're going to do it honestly. And we're going to do it and tell Mayor Sinclair about it afterward."

Bob looked pleased by the announcement even as Sharon grimaced and said, "If you're sure, then we'll back you. But I don't think Percival will make the trip. You're going to need multiple carts, and to not go alone. It's dangerous out there."

"I can take care of myself," said Wil, pointing a finger and making a little jet of flame appear out the end. "Nobody's going to stop me."

"Yes," she said patiently, "but what about Bram and Darlene? Are you all going together, or are you going to split up? How much product are you taking with you? How much money do you intend to make from a full batch, and how are you going to secure the money on the way home? How many supplies do you plan on taking with you?"

"Oh," said Wil, sitting back.

"Oh," Sharon echoed. "There's a lot that goes with traveling and selling. The mayor, bastard though he may be, was offering to handle all of that for you. Which is why the price would go up. Shipping makes the cost go way up, as everyone along the way needs to get paid. You want to do this on your own, you're going to have to put a lot of your own time, money, and energy into it. You understand?"

Wil thought he did. It meant going all in on the business and making sure he could protect Bram and Darlene from his decision. It meant going up against the mayor and expecting retaliation later. It meant, more than anything, that their business was real and to be taken seriously. That, more than anything else, decided it for him.

"Yes," said Wil, looking at his parents. "I'm going to do it."

"Well, then," Bob said, nodding approvingly, "we'll do everything we can to help. Both now and when the mayor comes for you. I'm proud of you, boy."

That alone made it the right decision.

CHAPTER 37

Road Trip

It took them two weeks to get ready to travel, and it was the busiest Wil had ever been. He thought that had been the case the two weeks before, but soon ate his words. Some of it was the same as it had been for the last two weeks, brewing and bottling when he didn't have work orders to fill. He almost always had work orders to fill. After a few months of it, each job finished quicker than ever, but it never ended.

Once again, Darlene proved to be the best at organizing. It may have been largely Wil financing the venture, but it was Darlene who rented horses and wagons to transport their stock. The schedule they put together was initially hers and then later refined, and included who went where. They even sent out letters ahead of time to the mayors of the towns, letting people know to expect them.

They planned three trips, each within a few days of each other. Bob and Sharon left first, taking their wagon north. They had to go up over the hill that led down to the town of Orangeville. It wasn't an especially hard trip, but it required more care going downhill, and Bob had plenty of experience handling a horse. They took enough supplies for a few days and would be back in a week or so.

The next trip was for Bram and, to his immense displeasure, Sarah. She'd agreed to help out for a tidy sum, and Wil promised her extra if she behaved on the trip and didn't drive Bram completely nuts. They headed east, down to the other end of the basin, to Gallard Springs. It was the shortest, easiest of the trips.

"Are you sure?" Bram had asked, trying very hard not to sound relieved. "I can go south if need be. I'm big and no one's going to want to mess with me on the road." Tall as Bram was, Wil could practically see his knees shaking.

"I'm positive," Wil had said, patting his arm. "If there's any trouble, you'll be outnumbered. North is safe because it's too hazardous for trouble, and Gallard Springs is safe because it's, like, a day and a half away. Mostly, it's just going to be boring."

"Right. About that," Bram grumbled, "any chance I could go alone? I really, really don't want to go with Sarah."

Wil grinned. "No can do. I already paid her, and you'll want someone giving you a hand with the money. You know the merchandise, and Sarah's tough. Together, you'll do well."

Bram thought about it and shrugged, sighing. "I am three times your size, but I note you say *she's* tough. Fine, we'll get started."

That left Wil and Darlene to go on the most dangerous trip. Not that it was actually very dangerous, but Appleton was a few days south with a long, winding road running parallel to the railroad. If anything, the railroad was the problem.

Appleton had once been a thriving town, larger than Harper Valley. Famed for their apple orchards, cider, and logging industries, they had the rotten luck of being between two railroad stops. People still made the trek north and south and stopped at Appleton, but businesses and most passengers passed it by as they went to Harper Valley and beyond the mountains, north to the metropolis of Kappala, where the railroad went east all the way to Cloverton on the far coast. Too far south to be close to the city, too far north to be part of the southern frontier.

The once thriving town stagnated with the coming of the railroad. Times got harder, money a little tighter, and the residents of Appleton found it easy to be overlooked and forgotten, a small town in the middle of nowhere special. Wil didn't expect any trouble going out that way, but he hadn't expected trouble coming home from school and the train had stopped for bandits.

"Relax," Darlene chided him as they got ready on the morning they were set to leave. "It'll be fine. They'll get by without you. It's during your days off, anyway."

"And then one more day after," Wil corrected darkly. "You can be sure people will notice *that*. Not to mention I'll have the mayor to deal with when we get back. Not looking forward to it."

She shot him a look. "Well, if you're having second thoughts, it's a bit late for that."

Wil shook his head and magically stuck a piece of paper to his front door, a short letter describing where he was going and how long he'd be out, as well as an invitation to insert more work orders through the mail slot. Chances were he'd need to push a mountain of orders out of the way when he got home.

"No second thoughts. Just…going on this trip makes it real. Yes, more than Mom and Dad and Bram and Sarah already being gone did. After this, it's going out of Harper Valley for the first time as a master wizard on business. Can you blame me for being nervous?"

Darlene attended to their two horses, feeding one a carrot and rubbing just above his nose. "No, but I *am* going to tease you about it. Mr. Big Bad Wizard is afraid of going on a little trip. Do you know what we're in danger of, Wil? Dying of boredom."

"You're probably right," he said with a sigh. Finally, seeing no other reason to drag his feet, he climbed onto the wagon. Darlene joined him and handed him the reins. He took them and cracked them gently. With a lurch, the wagon moved onward. They took the wider, winding path out of town and down toward Appleton.

They started the trip in high spirits. The Le Guin Basin was a gorgeous place year-round, but in fall especially. The leaves on the trees displayed various shades of orange and red and yellow. Those that fell provided them with a colorful road to travel down as their two horses pulled them along and the hours melted away.

Before too long, they stopped for lunch and to give the horses a break. They'd spent much of the trip in comfortable silence thus far, but Wil had never spent a silent meal with another person, and neither had Darlene.

"You're crazy," she said, tearing off a piece of her sandwich and popping it into her mouth. "There's no way he'll make it another five years. He's too old."

"That's exactly why he's going to pull through," Wil countered. "Fritz is, what, ninety years old? At that rate, the only thing that can kill him is irony. He'll die a month before his hundredth birthday, just to spite everyone."

"You might be right," she admitted. "But I'm still betting he kicks it in the next year."

At no point did they talk about anything important. It was all gossip about their neighbors, speculation about their reception in Appleton, and which restaurant in town had the worst food on average. It was exactly what Wil needed to finally relax and let his guard down and just enjoy the trip.

The call of the open road had never been strong for Wil. He was a homebody. After returning home after six long years, it felt wrong to be leaving again so soon, even for a short trip. Darlene helped him keep his mind off it, and the lovely sights along the way helped. Even the small hiccup with their wagon getting stuck going uphill had been refreshing.

It hadn't taken much to get it moving again, just the two of them hopping out and giving a push. They walked for a time after that, Darlene in front with the reins and Wil in the back, helping keep things steady while they crested the slope leading them out of the basin. Then it was back to sitting for a while and passing the time.

"You know, I really thought there was a chance we could maybe get there in one day," said Wil, looking around for a good place to camp for the night.

"Fat chance, with as big as our load is," Darlene said. "These two poor boys are going to be so relieved when we return with a mostly empty wagon. Between that and it being downhill, we might make it back in one day."

The road had opened up into a wide field, with a forest to the east, a big hill dropping off to the west, and the railroad continuing around the hill, moving farther away from the town as it continued south. The forest being that close bugged Wil a little. Maybe they could venture on farther with a magical light and camp in the middle of the prairie. Some people might feel exposed camping out in the middle of nowhere, but to Wil it just meant being able to see trouble coming from far away.

"Here's good, I think," said Wil, tugging on the reins. The horses veered off the road and onto soft, thick grass. They continued for another hundred feet or so before Wil was satisfied.

"A little exposed, don't you think?" Darlene asked, looking around. They still had light, but not for too much longer. An hour, if they were lucky.

"Naw. This'll be fine. I'll know if anyone is coming." He hopped off the wagon and went to the back, where their camping supplies were.

"Oh? Going to make another one of those wards? Got a human skull handy for the spell?" Darlene nudged his ribs.

"You volunteering?" Wil grinned. "It'll be a ward, yes, but not one that repels. It keeps watch and if anything gets within a certain range, it'll let me know. No one will be able to sneak up on us."

"Neat!" And that was that.

They worked to set up camp as fast as possible. Wil cleared all the grass out in a ring and summoned nearby rocks for their firepit, which he lit up with fire straight from his hands. Darlene got their sleeping bags set up and dinner cooking while Wil set up the wards and took care of the horses. All the little tasks added up to a soothing ritual that further let him relax.

"This is nice," he said, once the sun had gone down. They sat in front of the fire, sausages turning on a spit above the flames as he lazily rolled his wrist and kept it going with magic.

"I'm surprised," said Darlene, snuggling close to him. "I figured you'd be more of an indoorsy kind of guy when left to your own devices. The outside might get your books dirty."

His face heated up pleasantly. "You'd think that, but I always had a sturdy pack to protect my books. I used to spend hours and hours out of the house, reading out in the woods or at the river by the waterfall. And I work outdoors five days a week. You can't think me *that* soft!"

"I don't," she said, twisting around to kiss him on the cheek. "I just like seeing you get flustered."

Sandwiched in the sweet spot between the two towns, they stared up at a night of open sky and endless stars, their campfire the only light in any direction. Wil wrapped his arm around Darlene and pulled her close, leaning against the wheel of the wagon. Their horses were fed, watered, and allowed to roam, a mild suggestion spell keeping them in range. Wil wasn't too worried.

"I never got a chance to thank you for how supportive you've been since I got back," Wil said to Darlene. "I would've been really lost without your advice and perspective. You've made coming back worth it."

She smiled, filling him with a warmth that rivaled their campfire. "You saying if I hadn't been there to help knock some sense into you, you'd want to leave? If you weren't serving Harper Valley, what would you do? Pretend you've been banished. Where does Wil McKenzie go next?"

Wil laughed and thought about it for a while. Long enough that Darlene looked away from him and just settled into cuddling against his side silently. There were too many options. A man with Wil's skill set could find work anywhere and do well without trying. Jeb hadn't been wrong to be bitter about that. Any wizard, let alone a powerful and educated one, could write their ticket.

"I've got a very specific skill set," he said finally. "I could've learned to do something different, but I focused on earth and wind magic, illusions, and some minor druidic and blood magic. I'm perfectly suited to taking care of farms, so that's probably what I'd do, no matter what. But," he added, seeing Darlene was about to protest, "I'd travel while doing it. Maybe go around from town to town, righting wrongs and helping heal the land."

"Oooh. Just like the heroes of your books growing up, huh?"

Wil flushed again. "Maybe. But with a lot less fighting. I never wanted to be a combat mage. It's stressful."

He'd no more finished saying the words when his stomach flipped and danced. He recognized it right as his wards went off. Again and again and again.

"Get up," Wil said, deathly serious.

"What's wrong?" Darlene asked, doing as he said and looking out into the darkness.

Wil scrambled to his feet, breathing hard. "We're not alone."

CHAPTER 38

Pirates of the Plains

A long, slow clap came from the darkness.

"Very good, we didn't even have time to finish our ambush!" an amused voice called out. "Why don't you come on out and we can do this all civilized-like?"

Wil doubted his version of civilized and theirs lined up. To Darlene, he whispered, "Get under the wagon. I'll handle this."

"I'm not going to leave you to—"

"Do as I say," Wil hissed. Darlene looked affronted but nodded. He tapped her head and cast the only spell he could think of that would protect her. She disappeared from view entirely, only a light shimmer in the air when she moved.

While he obviously couldn't see her, he felt her move away and heard the grass rustle slightly, telling him she'd hidden successfully. The spell would last maybe an hour. More than enough time for Wil to take care of things.

"Why don't you and your friends go elsewhere?" Wil called out into the darkness. It was telling that they hadn't just come up and swarmed him. Maybe they had an idea of how dangerous he could be. "I don't want any trouble, but if you push me, I'll be forced to oblige."

All around him, laughter echoed in the dark. Finally, one person came around the wagon, hands held up in the air, though he didn't look concerned. He was taller than Wil, broad of shoulder and big-bellied. He looked familiar, though Wil couldn't quite place him.

"Easy lad," the bandit said, "no use getting hurt when we can do this the easy way. We want all your money and anything valuable you have to sell.

Which, given your wagon, might be easier if we just take the whole thing and sort it out later."

"That doesn't work for me," said Wil, eyes darting around. It would be smarter to strike first, but he had no idea how many of them there were. "I paid a pretty high deposit on the wagon and horses, and I *really* don't want to get robbed *and* have to pay a fee. That's just kicking a man when he's down."

The bandit nodded appreciatively. "That *is* a problem," he said good-naturedly. "Unfortunately, it's not my problem. No one cared when we were down. They kicked us anyway. Just the way of the world, I'm afraid. But hey, if you cooperate, we won't hurt you."

Wil cocked his head to the side. "Are you so eager to cause trouble or hurt people? You have a run of crappy luck and now you don't care who you hurt so long as you get paid?" Wil took that opportunity to spit on the ground. The darkness muttered with irritation.

The leader glared daggers at Wil. "It ain't like that, son. But we don't expect you to understand. You came from Harper Valley, right? A bunch of fat farmers and their endless bounty. You bastards don't know how hard life can be. Why shouldn't we take from those who have more than us? Surrender now. We'll have a big chat about ethics after."

Well, there was an easy solution. Wil smiled and held up his hands. The image was fresh in his mind and had served him well the last time he'd dealt with bandits. Flames lit up the night on the ground in front of him. The earth rumbled and a giant demonic figure pulled itself out of the ground, letting out a night-splitting roar of hate and anger. The illusory demon lord stood twenty feet tall and wielded a fiery sword. With any luck, they wouldn't notice the lack of heat coming off it.

The bandit leader's eyes widened and he took a couple of steps backward. Then his gaze dropped to Wil and he burst out laughing.

"No wonder you seemed familiar!" he said. "You were the one from the train. The one who stopped our early summer payday. One of my boys stayed behind and saw your 'demon' turn into a unicorn. Get him!"

All around the edges of the campfire's light, faces appeared. Men, mostly, and women, anywhere from their mid-twenties to their late forties, wielded clubs and knives and even a few pitchforks. Wil tried not to think about how funny it would be to be skewered by a pitchfork after surviving school. They formed a circle and closed in slowly. He had nowhere to go.

"You sure you don't want to give up?" Wil asked, making the demon back up as well, an illusory shield for a very real problem.

"We're going to enjoy paying you back, wizard," the leader growled, all friendliness gone.

"I was afraid you'd say that," Wil said with a sigh.

It wasn't that he wasn't scared. This was honestly the most terrifying situation in his entire life, maybe with the exception of the Nullbear and dealing with finals. But as much as he enjoyed his quiet life of helping others, that didn't mean he wasn't capable of protecting himself. He just didn't specialize in it. Wil waited until they got close enough, and then smiled. He closed his eyes and detonated the illusion.

Searingly bright light exploded from the former demon, lighting up the night for one agonizingly long second. Even with his eyes closed and hands blocking them, the light hurt Wil. The bandits screamed in pain. Some dropped their weapons, clutching at their eyes. At least, Wil assumed that's what happened.

When he pulled his hands away, the night seemed darker, lit only by his little fire. The dozen or so bandits stood there in a stupor, most clutching at their eyes. A few were on the ground, sobbing. The leader looked around blankly, blinking furiously to get the afterimages of the demon out of his eyes. Wil decided to start with him.

There were many, many different spells one could use to fight with. Human nature being what it was, it seemed as if there were more ready-made or easy-to-adapt combat spells than there was everything else combined. It was easier to fight than to not fight, but it didn't come naturally to Wil. Too many of those spells would be lethal, and while he found himself irritated by the robbery attempt, he didn't want to hurt anyone.

Too badly, at least.

Mentally, Wil reached for the leader. He found him there with his magic, a human-shaped dullness in the world, no magic to him whatsoever. That meant he had little defense against what came next. Wil focused his magic, drawing in from the world around him before shaping it into a spell that could be described with one word.

"*Fear!*" Wil hissed.

Still blinking the long-gone light out of his eyes, the leader let out a blood-curdling scream and took off running in the opposite direction. He tripped immediately, cowering on the ground. There hadn't been even an iota of resistance to the spell. Unfortunately for Wil, that just galvanized the rest of them.

"He got Jerry!" one woman called out, as some of them got their vision back.

Wil thought fast, raising one hand and igniting the campfire. Flames shot up ten feet high and spread in a semicircle around him. It stopped the nearest people from charging and stabbing him, but Wil didn't stop there. He flung the fire outward, pulling back on the flames at the last second. The fire swept over several of his assailants, but Wil held it back from completely engulfing them in flames.

That took the fight out of some of them, but another three charged him again. Wil didn't have time for anything impressive or flashy or clever. His eyes widened and he drew in magic and produced a shield of silver light in front of him. It caught the pitchfork and a big man's body. Wil flexed and threw them back before the shield disappeared.

He stepped forward, swinging his arms and summoning a mighty gust of wind to blow the last few people backward, ass over ears. Any fight they had left in them was thrown away, along with their weapons. Wil was the only one standing, breathing heavily. So much quick, powerful spellwork drained him, but he still had plenty of fight left.

"Anyone else?" he demanded. "Anyone else want to pick an unnecessary fight, or do you want to just walk away? Here's your chance. I won't pursue, I won't hurt anyone. Just. Leave."

A rustling behind him caught his attention, a few seconds too late. Someone crashed into Wil from behind, sending them both to the ground. They scrambled back to their feet and Wil found himself face-to-face with a boy of about thirteen, holding a knife out and crouched in a fighter's position.

"Fix my dad right this second!" the kid snarled, slashing at the air. Wil ducked out of the way, hands held up. He was happy to defend himself from armed adults, but a scared and angry kid was simultaneously a fight he didn't want and more dangerous for being unpredictable.

"Drop the knife, kid," said Wil, eyes darting to the sides. The others didn't look in a hurry to attack, but he didn't like their numbers. "You've already lost this. All of you can stop this right now."

That just angered the kid even more. "Last chance," he hissed.

A second later he crashed to the ground, Darlene reappearing on top of him as she shoved him into the ground. He didn't waste any time and neither did the bandits. They rushed forward again as he sent a wave of raw force low. Most of them tripped and fell on their faces.

"Leroy!" the nearest bandit, a middle-aged woman, cried out. She reached for what Wil assumed was her son on the ground under Darlene.

That's when he decided to end the fight. Drawing up all of his remaining power, Wil extended his senses down toward the earth itself. There were no leylines here to aid him, the land wasn't his or familiar, but Wil was a spellshaper. What he lacked in refinement and nuance, he made up for in raw strength. The earth rumbled and groaned, cracking open around them as dirt vibrated and softened and swallowed the bandits' arms and legs. All at once it stopped, leaving the bandits all stuck in the ground.

With the angry child unable to move, Darlene climbed to her feet, kicking the knife to the side. She and Wil checked each other for wounds, sighing in relief when they were fine, if a little shaken and tired. Wil rested his forehead against hers as he caught his breath. The entire skirmish had taken only a couple of minutes, but it felt like an eternity.

From all around the remnants of their camp, groans and grunts sounded as people fought against their earthen restraints. Tired of being unable to see, Wil conjured a big ball of light and let it hang in the air, lighting up the plains like a miniature moon. The effort made him see white. He steadied himself, swallowing hard.

"I think we can all agree I won, and that you guys surrender, right?" he asked, mentally dispelling the terror from their leader.

Jerry was trapped on his back, stuck up to his armpits and knees in the dirt. He looked up at Wil, anger and resignation as bright as the light above them. "We surrender," he said with a sigh.

CHAPTER 39

Hurt People

S o, let me start by asking if you guys have any food," said Wil, clapping his hands together once. "I'm afraid you ruined our dinner, and I'm a bit mad about it. But also, if we're going to talk this out, my mom always said it should be over a good meal. Meals build bridges, don't you think?"

The bandits stared sullenly at him. Most of them. Some were half-buried in positions where they couldn't look anywhere but down or away. Plenty of them struggled to get free, but they would've had an easier time chewing their limbs off to get away. That suited Wil just fine. Trapped bandits couldn't hurt him or Darlene.

"Right. Kid. Leroy," said Wil, turning to the one bandit's teenage son. "Your family got an encampment anywhere near? Maybe some food we can cook together?"

Leroy looked him in the eye and told him exactly what he could do to himself.

"Leroy Jeremy Jackson, what have I told you about your manners?" the boy's mother scolded.

Darlene gaped. "You're worried about manners when you just tried to rob us? Are you serious?"

Jerry wriggled in the ground. "I don't like doing this any more than people like being robbed," he said.

"Doubtful," said Wil.

Jerry ignored him. "It's just about the only thing we can do to bring in money these days. Most of us lost our jobs and our homes once the kids got back from the war, and—"

"Wait," said Darlene, stepping forward. "Why would soldiers returning cost you jobs?"

The bandits all shared a bitter laugh. Wil and Darlene shrugged at each other and waited for the explanation.

"I guess you wouldn't know," the woman sneered. "Harper Valley's got the railroad and all that great land. I guess military recruiters aren't hitting you up constantly, promising you pay and world experience, before they destroy families. Every couple of years, young men and women leave for the military, and jobs open up. When they come back, there's less jobs than before and those 'heroes' push the unlucky ones out."

"And Appleton's veterans came back home recently?" Wil asked.

"Yes," Jerry said with a sigh. "Spring. They came back and a bunch of us farmhands and temp workers were told to hit the bricks. We took to the woods and tried to live there simply, but it's rough and soon we needed some zynce to get by."

"Why not just come to Harper Valley and find jobs there?" Darlene asked. "Or, if you know this area so well, why not guide people through them safely? Hell, some of you could even still pretend to be bandits just to make people know how necessary you are."

"Huh." Jerry nodded thoughtfully. "I dunno. Seems less honest than robbing people. Look, are you going to let us go or what?"

"That depends," said Wil. "If I let you out of the ground, are you going to try to make a move or are we going to all act like adults and chat over dinner?"

"The latter," said Jerry's wife. Sighing, she said, "I'm Danielle. Sorry about… everything."

Darlene smiled. "Darlene Johnson. And this is Master Wizard Wil McKenzie. He was the top of his class and he chose to be gentle with all of you. Remember that."

"Noted," said Jerry.

Wil felt for the magic inside him. While he borrowed heavily from the ambient mana in the world around him, a great deal of a spellshaper's power came from themselves. He was nearly depleted and if he drew too much in, it could be less than great for the land's health. Some wizards had private towers in barren wastelands, sucked dry by their projects. He had enough to release them, but then he'd need to draw on the earth if it got ugly again. So he hedged his bets.

The ground rumbled again. Jerry and Daniele pulled themselves out of the ground. No one else did. Looking around, Jerry nodded as if he understood. "Not risking more than just us for now? Sorry, lads, we'll get you out of here as soon as we can."

"This is really, really uncomfortable," came the muffled voice of a bandit trapped face down and his body twisted like a pretzel.

Wil relented and put more power into it. Soon, all of the bandits were out of the ground, dusting themselves off and cradling minor injuries. Mostly burn marks. Notably, none of them seemed anxious to get close to Wil, let alone try to attack him. Honestly, fantastic. He hated fighting, even though he now knew he could take them, even holding back.

"Right," Jerry said. "So, dinner. Mark, take Bruno and Leroy and bring something over to eat. We don't got anything good to drink with it," he said with a frown.

Darlene and Wil looked at one another, suddenly gleeful.

"That's okay," said Darlene. "Drinks are on us."

The entire time, Wil half expected the bandits to turn on them and make good on their promise to take everything they owned and possibly kill them. No such thing happened. With Jerry and Danielle suddenly friendly, the rest of them fell in line. Some even went out and grabbed the horses, who'd run off in the night. Wil hadn't even noticed through all the excitement.

Danielle and a portly man covered in sweat-streaked dirt worked on building their fire back up and cooking a stew for everyone. Another passed deer jerky around. Wil gratefully took a piece and gnawed on it slowly, enjoying the savory, salty meat while he and Darlene offloaded a few crates of beer. Before too long, Jerry, Danielle, and Leroy were sitting with Wil and Darlene while the rest of their crew sat a ways off, laughing and drinking their free beer and barley wines.

"You're saying you brewed this stuff? You?" Jerry finished his red ale, smacking his lips appreciatively. "It's been too long since we've had a good drink. Even if we walk away empty-handed, this was worth the robbery attempt."

Wil snorted. "Thanks. My friend Bram brewed it, though."

Darlene had a bowl of the stew in her lap as she sat cross-legged on the ground. The bowl looked like it had seen better and cleaner times, but Darlene wasn't some dainty damsel. She scooped out a taste and made an appreciative sound. "This is great, Danielle. Surprised it tastes this good if you're on the run and shaking people down."

"It's one of those things you learn," Danielle said with a shrug. "You learn what plants are edible and what makes for good seasoning and how to make the most out of any meat you manage to get. We're not bad people, you know," she added hastily.

"Never thought you were," said Darlene. That earned her a couple of laughs. "No, I'm serious. I think it's crappy that you're willing to take and hurt others to make a living. I can tell there's a lot of pent-up bitterness and anger there."

"Is not," said Jerry.

"Harper Valley is paradise, sent by the gods to bless a chosen few," mocked Wil.

Jerry's face immediately twisted into disgust. Then he sighed. "Okay, point taken."

"Point is," Darlene pressed onward, "you've got a lot of anger and were hurt. Hurt people often hurt others. It happens. Especially when money is involved. So I could either be mad at you people for your circumstances or I can hate the circumstances that led you to feel like robbing others was the only way out."

Jerry chewed on a piece of jerky thoughtfully. He pointed a finger at Wil and said, "You got yourself a special girl there."

Wil put an arm around Darlene's shoulder. "I sure do. Smart, passionate, and ethical. Minus suggesting you scam people while pretending to protect them. What was that all about?"

"Good business sense." Darlene leaned her head against his shoulder.

"It's not a bad idea," said Danielle. "Maybe we should've thought about it. But maybe it's time to move on. That's two foiled robberies due to you. Our luck's not been too hot, so maybe we should get going and find someplace else to call home."

For a little while, no one said anything. Wil kicked back and enjoyed the odd companionship and beautiful night. The stars continued to twinkle above them, and the moon hung high in the sky. It was the perfect autumn night, just chilly enough to need the fire. Good enough food, good drinks, and new friends? Well, they could be if he tried.

"What about going to Harper Valley?" Wil asked. There was a chorus of snorts and sneers.

"Why the hell would we go up to that town, full of frou-frou pampered pansies?" Leroy finally spoke up. He still hadn't forgiven Darlene for tackling and disarming him. He aimed his baleful glare her way, though she hadn't spoken.

"You know, I never thought I'd hear anyone describe Harper Valley that way," said Darlene, "so I am not sure how to respond to that. Oh, wait, yes I am." She threw her head back and laughed. Wil couldn't help but join in. It just angered Leroy more, but his parents just looked puzzled.

"We're hard workers," Wil insisted. "And we're a community." He thought then of Mr. Carrey and Jonjon and their bastardry. "Most of us. We care about each other and want to help out. We've only got a few people without a permanent home there, and most of them work odd jobs while staying in Harry Hardlin's inn.

"There's always work to be found, especially this time of year. You have no idea how swamped people are, trying to get their last-minute crops in and then treating the land for the winter freeze. You could easily get some work up there and make your way through winter at least. I'd be surprised if none of you got picked up for more permanent work."

Jerry reached for another beer before Danielle swatted his hand away. "I'm not sure it works like that," Jerry said. "In Appleton, they were glad to see us gone. Didn't want any outsiders there, begging for scraps. As if most of us hadn't lived there for years before times got as bad as they did."

"We're telling you, Harper Valley isn't like that," said Darlene. "How many of you are there?"

"Seventeen of us," Danielle said, brushing hair out of her face. "Used to be more, but once you summoned that demon in front of the train, a bunch of us quit and went legit. And now I guess we're talking about it too."

"You say that like it's a bad thing." Wil couldn't help but shake his head.

"Ahh, don't misunderstand us," said Jerry. "We don't want to be doing this. But there's a freedom to the lifestyle that being part of a community doesn't allow for. If we did go to Harper Valley and beg for jobs…well, *I'd* miss the freedom, anyway."

"Well," Darlene said, sitting up straight, pulling away from Wil. She began counting off on her fingers. "I know my father's probably in need of a register monkey. So that's one job. Mr. Carrey's a greedy old jerk, but he could probably use another few hands for the season. Let's call that three for him, so four people total. Mack's Shack is perpetually in need of more cooks. So that's another two."

"I see your point," Danielle said. "There's honest work available, but that's a temporary solution at best. We make it through fall with enough money to make it through winter, and then what?"

"That's up to you, isn't it?" Wil drank his nearly forgotten barley wine. "Stay, move on. You'll have all winter to think about it and make plans. I'd be willing to bet good money that you fall in love with the place and at least half of you will want to stay."

Jerry laughed. "Boy, if we had any money to begin with, we wouldn't be in this mess. But if you're so confident about it, fine, we'll give it a shot."

Leroy stood and stormed off without a word. They all watched him go and sit down with a different group of people.

"Aw, don't pay him any mind," said Danielle, waving him off. "He's had a tough life and doesn't like the idea of settling down with our rival town."

"Already forgotten," said Wil. He thought about it for a minute and decided his mood and goodwill were enough for it. "Honestly, if you like this beer, we could use some hands on our own farm getting the ingredients to make it. We're just starting out, but we plan on going big if we can get the momentum. I can't promise you the best pay in the world, but it'll be enough to get you food and shelter. Come winter, there's always some work in the mines or helping ship things. You've got options. Good options."

Jerry raised his drink in the air. "Alright, alright, you've already sold us. Can't guarantee everyone will go, but if they don't, that's less people to worry about finding a job for. Thank you, Wil. I'm glad we tried robbing you again."

Wil raised his drink and they clinked bottles. "Me too, Jerry." He let himself relax and trust these bandits, knowing either they'd slit his throat in his sleep or they wouldn't. He and Darlene had put in some good effort to help them out. That's all they could do. He leaned over and kissed the top of her head.

Darlene looked up sweetly at him for a second before leaning on his shoulder once more. They sat there together for another couple of hours before they turned in, side by side. And best of all, no one murdered them in their sleep.

CHAPTER 40

Appleton

They made it to Appleton just before noon, after getting a somewhat late start to the day. Breakfast had been another excuse to socialize and confirm their plans and the former bandits' general agreeability to honest work. Then it was just another couple of hours down the road, with two of their new friends, Jasper and Janet, a married couple, along to help with the heavy lifting and eyes on the way home. To Wil, it was mostly an excuse to make good on his promise to pay them.

Jasper and Janet sent their daughter, Jill, with the rest of the group to Harper Valley ahead of them. That seemed like another good sign to Wil that everyone was taking his offer seriously. The couple did their part well, walking beside the cart as they made their way up the final stretch of road to the town.

Appleton was mostly flat, with the tops of big family homes peeking out above the tree line. True to its name, there were apple orchards everywhere in various shades of red, orange, and green. Towns like this were best in autumn, and Wil found himself smiling widely as they approached.

"What's got you in a good mood?" Darlene asked, elbowing him in the side. She wore a fond, teasing smile.

Wil shrugged and gave the reins a light snap to speed up a little. "Just excited to do something good for our neighbors. And to maybe tweak Mayor Sinclair's nose a little."

"Funny how you both don't want to start a fight but somehow still very much want to start *something*." Darlene leveled a shrewd look his way. "What's with that?"

"My inner devils and my better nature, at war with one another," said Wil. "Mostly, though, I don't want to be pushed around by anyone. And I don't want to push anyone else around if I don't have to, but..." He nodded in Jasper's direction and lowered his voice. "I'm beginning to understand I need to push more sometimes."

Darlene nodded in understanding. "That's a good lesson to learn. I'm proud of you. If you stayed too naive and kind, it'd get old." She kissed his cheek. Wil just smiled, and they wound their way to the center of town.

This wasn't the first time Wil had been in Appleton. His parents had taken their kids to all the neighboring towns at one point or another, for festivals or to sell their crops, and on one memorable occasion, to see a play. He would never claim to be knowledgeable about the other towns, but he would've at least called himself familiar.

But now the buildings looked a little more run-down than he remembered. They weren't in poor repair so much as lifeless. The colors were muted, and a little dirty. The people they passed looked up at him with dull, resentful eyes. By the time they got to the market, Wil realized he hadn't been in Appleton since they had built the railroad in Harper Valley, when things apparently changed for the worse.

Nothing was explicitly wrong with anything. Wil just felt tense, and a quick look at Darlene told him he wasn't alone in that. A man with one arm stared at them as they passed.

"Man, Danielle wasn't kidding when she said the place had stopped being welcoming," Darlene muttered. "I don't feel unsafe or anything, but everyone looks like they're wondering why we're here, like we should go home."

"I noticed that," said Wil, looking around. He pulled over where the road turned into a large cobbled square bordered by a few big shops and boarded-up buildings. "What was it like when you guys lived here?"

Janet looked up at him, making a face. "Like this, toward the end. Everyone's so focused on trying to make things work and not lose what they've got. It used to be a lot happier and more relaxed than this."

Jasper scowled at the nearest people giving them the stink eye. "Careful about saying where you're from. They might not take it well."

"Like they might try to rob us?" Wil teased.

Jasper laughed. "Naw. Not openly. They might encourage you to turn right back around, though."

"That's a risk we're willing to take," said Darlene, hopping down from the wagon. "Let's get set up."

With Janet's and Jasper's help, and Wil making crates temporarily lighter, they managed to set up their wares between someone selling many different kinds of apple cider and someone who had pies to sell. So before they opened for business, Wil bought the four of them a couple of meat pies to share.

It gave their neighboring vendors time to understand they weren't going anywhere.

Because they didn't have their stall, they'd just turned the wagon sideways and propped up a wood sign with "Wiseman Brewing" and their logo painted on it. Wil and Darlene sat on a couple of crates with a rug set out on the ground in front of them, bottles of their potions and beer on display.

It was a good half hour before someone came up to them instead of just passing them by.

"What's this, then?" an older teenager asked, crossing his arms over his chest. "Magic potions?"

"Medicines and beer," Darlene replied, displaying their wares with a sweep of her arm. "Cold medicine, pain relievers, cough syrups, preservatives. You name it, we've got it."

His jaw set. "How much for cold medicine?"

Wil lifted a bottle of translucent blue liquid. "Twenty zynce for the bottle. That'll keep you for the season!" That had been the compromise price they'd decided on for needing to travel here. Darlene had estimated the mayor wanted to charge forty or fifty for it. No way that was happening.

The teen's face fell. "Oh," he said, turning away.

Wil and Darlene exchanged a look before Wil said to him, "What can you afford?"

He thought about it. "Ten?"

"Sold!" Wil handed the bottle over to the kid.

The teenager stared at it mutely, then looked back at Wil in confusion. Wil just smiled and waited, and eventually the boy fished out some bills and handed a fiver and five ones over. It looked like the majority of what he had on him.

"What was that?" Darlene asked after he left. "We'll only be breaking even if we charge ten."

Wil grimaced. "You see the look on that kid's face? He didn't ask about beer or want anything other than medicine. He needs it more than we need the money. I'd give this away if I could."

Darlene nodded, though she had a grimace of her own. "You're too soft for your own good," she said. "I love that about you, but you are."

"I know," said Wil. He hoped that never changed.

After that, a few more people made stops at the stall, and the next time someone asked about medicine, the price was fifteen. That sold, as did a few burn salves and painkillers. The painkilling potions and salves became hot items when several amputees and battered-looking men and women barely older than Wil and Darlene came by. But after a few hours, even that dried up.

"I don't think this is going to go that well," said Darlene, after a half-hour gap between customers. "I hope the others are having better luck than us. We might end up having to bring a bunch of this back with us."

That didn't sit right with Wil. He thought about how much it would hurt to actively give things away. Then, a better idea hit him. "I'll be right back," he said to Darlene. "Watch after her," he ordered his two new hires. Jasper and Janet both flashed him a thumbs-up.

At no point did Wil ever feel he was in danger while walking around, but he had the sensation of being watched at all times. To be fair, he got that at home as well, but it was different here. There wasn't that sense of familiarity in the attention, of recognition and even interest. More than curious, the citizens of Appleton were suspicious. It reminded him of his return to Harper Valley, only worse.

It didn't take long to find the town hall. Like Harper Valley's, it had a statue in front of it, leading Wil to think that maybe all town halls did. This one was of a child reaching up at an apple tree, with a pool of water below it. Wil threw in a couple of coins as he passed.

Whereas Mayor Sinclair's office often had people waiting to be seen, there was no one here other than a tired-looking older woman sitting in reception. She glanced up at him and then back down at the book she was reading.

"Can I speak to the mayor?" asked Wil. "I've got an opportunity for him I don't think he'll want to pass up."

With a sigh, she stuck the book face down on her desk. "Mayor Derr doesn't just take walk-ins off the street. If you want to speak with him, you'll need an appointment."

Wil supposed that if he was in charge of a dying town, he wouldn't want to be bothered by others either. But that didn't make it acceptable. "He'll speak with me," said Wil, putting some force into his voice. "Tell him the resident wizard of the Le Guin Basin is here and needs his time."

That got through to her. Recognizing who Wil was, her eyes narrowed but she did as she was told. She got up and went to the big door behind her, knocking before she opened it and stuck her head in. Wil waited patiently as they had a short conversation. She opened the door and motioned for him to go through.

"Oh, right, I got your letter. What can I do for the esteemed wizard of Harper Valley?" Mayor Derr asked with no small amount of bitterness in his voice. He was a man who must've been large in his heyday but now looked tired and shrunken.

"It's more like what I can do for you, Mr. Mayor," said Wil, inclining his head respectfully. "How is your town doing?"

"We're fine," the mayor growled. "Times are tough, but the people of Appleton are strong and hardy. We may not have all the amenities of other towns, but we're getting by. Why do you ask, wizard?"

"Call me Wil," he said, forcing a smile. "Things look rough to me. Last night marks twice I've nearly been robbed traveling from here to Harper Valley. I'm offering to deal with the bandits between the towns, and I have a load of medicines and painkillers and a really good anti-spoiling solution, all to be handed out to citizens most in need of them."

Mayor Derr frowned, looking him up and down. "And what would you want for such a generous offer?"

This is where things got hard. Wil wasn't the most worldly person, despite having spent six years in a decent-sized city during his academy years. He had learned a few tricks he didn't like using, but sometimes it seemed necessary. A man like this in a town facing hardship would never accept a gift without thinking there was something wrong with it. A trap, even.

So that meant Wil had to come up with something that would sound just selfish enough to be plausible. He did some quick math in his head for what they had left.

"I'm willing to deal with the bandits and give you all of my various potions for twelve thousand zynce and your word that you'll give the potions out to all the people who need them, and not sell them yourself."

Just as he thought, the number made the mayor flinch but it was still less than what the lot was worth. "That's no small amount," the mayor said. "Can I talk you down to eight thousand?"

Ah, perfect. Wil didn't have to fake his next smile. "Call it ten and tell me a nice place to grab dinner."

The mayor thought about it. "What guarantee do I have that your medicines even work?" he asked. "If they did, wouldn't you be selling them at home?"

Wil inclined his head. "I'm branching out and I want to make sure all the neighboring towns have a chance to try my products. The next batch won't be so cheap."

Grunting, Mayor Derr stood up and offered his hand. Perfect! Wil took his hand and gave it a little zap as he shook it.

"The hell was that?" the mayor demanded, clutching his hand to his chest.

"Oh, just the magical contract sealing," Wil lied. "If you try to go back on our deal or charge money instead of giving potions out, you'll face some unpleasant consequences. But don't think of that, Mr. Mayor. Think of all the goodwill you're buying next time election season comes around and people wonder what you've done for them lately."

Whistling, Wil walked away with a roll of wadded-up bills in a bag, the mayor and a few people following him back to the stall. Darlene was in the process of selling beer when they arrived.

"What's this?" she asked, eyes darting between Wil and the mayor.

"A bulk sale," said Wil, holding up the money. "I'll explain the details later. What's important is that all we need to do is sell some beer and then go home. The people of Appleton will get medicine."

Darlene understood, giving him a small smile. "Thank the gods. I didn't want to have to lug that all home again."

Wil started rolling up bottles in cloth and sticking them back in crates, and Jasper and Jill did the same, speeding it up considerably. Half an hour later, they were left with just a handful of bottles of beer left. Wil had decided they were better off keeping them and enjoying them on the way home.

"Good work, everyone," said Wil. The four of them had packed up the wagon just as the sun began to set. He pulled out a few bills from the bag he wasn't letting leave his sight until they got home. "Who wants steak for dinner?" The loud cheers from Janet and Jasper made it clear who wanted steak the most, but even Darlene looked excited.

All in all, a successful business trip. They hadn't made as much money as they could have, but when measured against helping people, Wil knew what he'd choose every single time.

CHAPTER 41

A Gathering Storm

They made it back to Harper Valley late the next day. Just as expected, a vastly lighter load and going downhill for half the trip made their return much quicker. That suited Wil just fine. They hadn't been able to get good accommodations in Appleton thanks to people negatively recognizing Jasper and Janet, so they'd ended up sleeping outside of town another night. They hadn't been robbed again, but Wil was no less tense for needing to guard their sack of money.

They wheeled in just before sunset, eager to get back but relaxed now that the edge of town was in sight.

"There it is," Wil said to his companions. "Home."

Jasper wasn't impressed. "Looks like Appleton but without so many trees in town," he said, keeping pace with the wagon still. He and his wife were used to moving around most of the day and didn't mind the walk.

Janet smacked his arm. "It looks homey and cozy," she said.

"No, it's okay," said Darlene. "It doesn't look like much, and half the time, it doesn't feel like much. But it *is* comfortable and welcoming once people get to know you. We'll make sure you guys have a smooth integration, but... look, I'm not accusing you of anything, but while you're here, you can't steal anything or threaten anyone. You saw what that did in Appleton when we tried to get a room."

Jasper ducked his head in embarrassment. "Sorry about that," he said. "I lost my temper. I'll find it and not let it out of my sight."

"I'll make sure of it," Janet confirmed.

The last bright rays of sunlight bathed the valley in their glow, and Wil felt a great weight come off his shoulders. He hadn't realized just how tense he'd been until he finally relaxed. The road took them between farms on the outskirts of town, and Wil raised a hand in greeting as they passed farmers and their field hands at work. Anyone who saw him returned the wave, all smiles and often with a shouted greeting.

Home.

First, they went to the McKenzie family farm, where the other bandits had been told to meet them. Wil didn't know what he'd expected to find when they got there, but a bunch of tents on the nearest field to the house wasn't it. They'd already harvested that field and there wasn't time for another before the season was up, so his parents must've set them up there for convenience.

Wil brought the wagon up next to two other wagons in front of the house. They were the last to arrive, more or less on time. Wil would have to take the horses and wagon back to the man he'd rented them from, but that was a task for tomorrow. After a few long days of traveling and stressing, it would be nice to have a home-cooked meal and a break before readjusting to life as usual.

"Ayyy, there they are," Jerry greeted, coming up and throwing arms around Jasper and Janet. "No trouble out there, I trust? There was none here. Your parents are good people, Wil. Took us in without a question. Your dad's even been sharing his stash of staggerleaf. Gods, I hadn't had good staggerleaf in months."

"Think this'll be a place to settle down?" Janet asked, extricating herself from Jerry's hug.

Jerry shrugged. "We'll figure that stuff out tomorrow. For now, we're just going to relax and enjoy Sharon's incredible home cooking!"

A cheer went up around the nearest people who, if Wil had to guess, had spent at least one full day enjoying his mother's greatest skill. If he knew her, she was probably exhausted and pleased with herself after getting to help so many people.

Wil hopped off the wagon and extended his hand to help Darlene down. She pushed his hand out of the way and jumped down next to him, grinning.

Jasper took the reins. "We'll handle brushing down your horses and getting them fed and watered," he said.

"Thanks," Wil said. "I should probably go talk to my parents about all of this." Jerry laughed, and Wil and Darlene went inside.

Bram was helping Sharon in the kitchen, running around surprisingly fast for a man of his size and gathering dishes for the sink as quickly as people brought them up. Sharon was pulling out a long chocolate cake from the fridge when they entered, and she caught Wil's eye. She set the cake down on the stove.

"There they are," she announced. A small cheer went up through the kitchen. Wil held up the sack of cash he hadn't let out of his sight in the past day. From the table, his father held up another sack, and Sarah had one resting at her feet as she leaned against a wall underneath a picture of the family from ten years ago.

"How did it go for everyone?" Wil asked, looking around.

"Uhh…, could've been worse," said Bram, scrubbing furiously at some plates. "Please never send me off with Sarah again."

From her spot against the wall, Sarah grinned mercilessly. She nudged the bag at her feet and said, "Made off like bandits, though. Metaphorical bandits. Not the ones you brought home."

"Yeah, that was a bit of a surprise," said Bob. "Not sure I know what you were thinking, making friends with a bunch of highwaymen, but they seem like mostly good people. Mostly."

"They just fell on hard times," said Darlene, putting her hands on her hips. "Most people would end up doing similar things if they were pressed hard enough. They deserve a chance."

Bob held his hands up in surrender. "No arguments here, just wasn't expecting it. I trust my son's judgment, and if there's anything we can do to help, we will. On that note, our trip was a smashing success. The people up in Orangeville loved the beer especially. They're going to want more in the future. We brought you home about eighteen thousand."

"Thirteen thousand here," Bram piped up. "Didn't quite sell all of it, but Gallard Springs wanted more medicine and enjoyed the beer well enough. I think they're mostly wine people, but I really don't want to branch out to wine just yet."

"No worries," said Wil, "we'll stick to beer. We brought home ten thousand. I may have cut a deal with the mayor. As you might've heard, Appleton isn't doing too well. Cleared out our stock for…not much, but I think we've done a good thing. A couple of good things."

Sharon looked up from where she was frosting the cake. "And that's what's important Wil. We're proud of you."

After they got the money squared away in Wil's old room, he helped with dinner and just enjoyed their company. As they all tore into a massive cottage pie, he couldn't help but feel an upwelling of love for everyone. His parents, who raised him to be kind and caring. Jeb, who could be a real jerk sometimes but had always looked out for him and helped him know right from wrong. Sarah, the chaotic little gremlin who always kept him on his toes. Bram, his former enemy and now closest friend, who was at least as in love with the work and books as Wil was. And Darlene, his girlfriend who challenged and inspired him and made him want to be a better person.

Just a few short months ago, he'd come home after a six-year absence. He'd been terrified that he wouldn't be accepted. They had every reason to have a grudge against him and only Jeb had resented him for not coming home once in that time. Wil felt right then how incredibly lucky he'd been. Life was good and he was just getting started. He had another hundred years, at least, of giving back to a world that had given so much to him.

Of course, just as he was at his most relaxed and content, his stomach had to ruin it. It did a twist and flip and Wil groaned.

"What's wrong?" Darlene asked as the conversation around the dinner table died down. Everyone stared at him.

"So," Wil said with a sigh, "wizards sometimes get a sense when danger or something big is coming. It's happened a few times since I've come home. It happened before our new friends tried to stop our train, it happened when Mrs. Lane's kids were in danger, and it happened again before we were surrounded on our way to Appleton. So now I'm wondering what's coming."

A knock at the front door made Wil groan.

"I'll get it," he said, pushing away from the table. He trudged over, dreading the worst. When he opened the door, he immediately wanted to close it again. Mayor Sinclair stood there, as furious as Wil had ever seen him.

"Wilbur McKenzie," the mayor said through gritted teeth. "You and I need to have a talk."

"I'm not sure we do," said Wil. He frowned openly at the mayor. He didn't want to have this talk, but he supposed that putting it off wouldn't help him any. He stepped out of the house and walked out past the porch. Sinclair followed him. The sun was almost all the way past the mountains to the west, a lingering glow illuminating the house and valley before the stars and moon came out.

"I thought I made it clear to you how things work, Wilbur. If you want to use your office to profit, then that means those above you get a cut of the action. And that's me. I'm above you. Do you have any idea how difficult I could make your life if you spit in my face like this?"

Wil took a long, deep breath. "I don't like being threatened, Mr. Mayor," he said in a quiet, restrained voice. "Please consider that I spent six years learning how to rewrite reality according to my will. The two things I am best at are illusions and mesmer magic. Anything you think you could do to me, I could pay you back in spades without ever hurting you."

"So now you're threatening *me*," the mayor said, laughing.

"Counter-threatening, more like," said Wil. "I don't want any of this. I want you to leave me alone, and for me to do the job I've been assigned to. I love doing it and I'm getting better and better at it. I've got a lot to offer Harper Valley, and I fully intend to give as much of myself to this town as I can. But I do mean to the town, and not you personally."

The mayor considered him silently. A storm of different emotions blew across his face. Anger, frustration, and even a glimpse of hate in there before Sinclair eventually got his head on straight. He took a deep breath.

"That's foolish, Wil. You don't get to do what you want around here. You're not in charge—you're a civil servant under my command. Remember your place. You're going to work through me in the future or find yourself without a job and needing to pay off all the tuition we paid for.

"Who do you think the citizens of this town will back? Their trusted mayor with nearly twenty years of experience running the town and keeping the most powerful people in it happy, or some uppity upstart freak?" Mayor Sinclair laughed. "You may be doing some good now and then, but no matter what happens, there'll always be a gap between you and everyone else. You'll always be the wizard, something to be afraid of. And that gets way worse if I make it. This is your last chance to take my hand in friendship before it becomes a fist."

Wil opened his mouth to tell the mayor exactly what he could do to himself in the privacy of his home when his stomach did another, harder flip. One that told him in no uncertain terms that the mayor wasn't the source of the danger. Wil looked up and blinked.

Off in the gloom of falling night in the east was a large black cloud, enveloping the entire sky and heading their way. The wind kicked up and even the mayor turned around and looked behind him. Light flashed from within the great black cloud, illuminating something massive in it.

"What the—" The mayor gaped.

"Storm," said Wil, as it all clicked. "We've got a storm coming in fast."

CHAPTER 42

Thunder

The black cloud stretched across the horizon, moving so fast Wil could see it getting closer by the second. Still a long way off but headed in their direction, relentless and implacable. Storms happened in the fall—that was a way of life. They didn't often happen after a full day of bright, clear skies, though. Instantly, the mayor was forgotten. Wil dashed back inside the house.

"Storm!" he called out, loud and clear enough to pierce the pleasant mid-meal fog. "Storm coming in fast! We need to get ready!"

For a second, no one said anything. They just stared as his words registered. Then Bob stood. "How bad's it look?" he asked.

Wil winced. "Bad. It's coming in from the east and looks as big and ugly as I've ever seen. Tonight's going to be rough."

Bob nodded. "Jeb, you get the animals squared away."

"You got it," said Jeb, wasting no time.

"Sarah, go around and close and bar all the windows. You know where the tools are." Sarah made a face but didn't argue. "Sharon, you—"

"I'll get all our guests safely in the cellar and make sure they've got food and water," said Sharon.

He smiled at her. "Exactly what I was gonna say. I'll make sure our stores are well protected and everything else is done, and then we all take shelter."

Except for Wil, he realized. He hadn't been given a task, but this wasn't a time for him to be told what to do by his father. This was a time for him to act, and he knew exactly what he had to do.

"Bram," Wil said, "you and Darlene head home as fast as you can. Secure the brewery and get in your cellar."

"What are you going to do?" Bram asked, letting out a breath of relief.

"I need to warn the rest of the valley about it. If I fly over, I can buy people some time, and hopefully we can get through this with minimal damage. And I'll see if I can divert the storm itself." Though a bit nervous, the greater part of Wil was excited. He'd always loved storms and how small they made him feel. Now he'd be a little insect fighting against nature itself.

"What about your house?" Darlene asked.

Wil shook his head. "Don't care. It'll be okay. We need to get you guys and the rest of the valley to safety first. If anything happens to mine, I can rebuild." And rebuy books, and set up another alchemy lab, and…Wil pushed it from his thoughts. He had his priorities.

Darlene got up and went to him. "Be careful out there," she said. "Don't do anything too brave or stupid, you hear me?"

"I make no promises," Wil said with a growing smile. Darlene grabbed him by the front of his coat and pulled him down for a lingering kiss. Sarah let out a high-pitched "WhooOOOooo," and they broke apart, laughing.

"I'll be careful," Wil amended. Then he bolted out the door, ignoring the mayor, who still stood in front of the house gaping at the storm. From the back of the wagon, Wil pulled out his flying carpet, which he'd taken with them to Appleton in case of an emergency. Well, this seemed like an emergency enough.

"What are you doing?" the mayor demanded as Wil laid the carpet out on the dirt.

"Warning the town. Threaten me later, but I suggest you get to shelter if you're not going to do anything to help." He shot a baleful glare the mayor's way and was delighted when the old jerk flinched. Then he got on the carpet and tugged on the leather straps. The carpet rose into the air. A second later, he took off like a shooting star.

Up in the air, the storm looked much worse. It took up the entire night sky, notably closer now than before Wil had warned his family. The black clouds rolled and swirled in a colossal lazy spiral, collecting other clouds along the way and growing. Another twist in his gut screamed danger, peril, calamity. Lightning flashed, and for one blinding second, Wil saw something in the clouds again. A monstrous form, coming closer.

He didn't know what it was, exactly, but he knew this wasn't an ordinary storm. And he had a job to do.

Looking down on the sleepy town below, some people saw the storm and pointed, but not everybody. He needed to warn as many people as possible, and going door-to-door would hardly cut it. The answer came to him at once, making him grimace at how unpleasant it would be for everyone involved.

He called, and his magic answered, coming to life inside him. Two days of relative rest made him fully charged and raring to go. Wil took a deep breath, in and out, and then conjured the most annoying wailing sound he could think of. Louder and louder it went, like a baby's scream, piercing and impossible to ignore.

Down he flew, closer to the farms, as he dragged that awful illusory scream with him. After a few weeks of playing with it whenever he'd had free time, the carpet answered his every call in an instant. He flew and maneuvered practically at the speed of thought, each little twitch and change in his grip on the straps controlling it along with his intent.

From their homes people came outside, covering their ears and glaring at him. Wil pointed in the direction of the storm and saw that anger quickly turned to fear and gratitude. They ran back in and he moved on. He did a loop around the town, all the way from the train station in the south to Mr. Carrey's farm in the north, scraping along the eastern edge of town and farther, to warn Gallard Springs as well.

The people of Gallard Springs didn't know him very well, and he rarely had reason to go there. It was a place for spiritual people, healers, and rich kooks to gather around the hot springs and commune with the gods. A lot of Harper Valley liked to laugh at them, but the thought of their closest neighbor not also preparing for the storm hurt.

"Storm!" Wil screamed as the agonizing wail continued on repeat. More and more people came out of their homes and got to work, quickly boarding up windows and heading for cellars. He continued to the edge of the basin, trusting the people to reach any neighbors who didn't hear his warning in time.

On the edge of town, Wil flew higher until the cold made his fingers numb and the wind buffeted and pierced right through him. He held on to the leather loops carefully, trusting in his spellwork to keep him on the rug. The edges of the storm crested the mountain, crossing over and bringing with it a torrent of rain.

Lightning flashed again, followed by thunder so loud he felt it in his bones. It made him realize how high up he was and remember that lightning tended to hit higher targets. He lowered himself to just over the treetops, blinking furiously as gusts of wind brought raindrops and mist to his eyes.

"Oh gods, no!" he heard from beneath him.

There were a couple of hikers holding a lantern between them. One of them stared at Wil, the other at the storm. Wil dropped like a rock, stopping just beside them.

"Get on!" he demanded.

"What?" a young, healthy-looking man about Wil's age demanded. "Are you crazy?"

"Not as crazy as you if you think it's worth turning down a way out from this crap," Wil shot back.

"Just do as he says," said the other hiker, a younger man with a strong resemblance. He climbed onto the back of the carpet, marveling aloud at how solid it was underneath him. The other man looked around, cursed under his breath, and then joined Wil up front.

"Hold on!" Wil commanded, giving them a chance to feel the carpet moving before he sped away. He headed west, away from the mountains, with the storm in hot pursuit.

The wind was at their backs, but the extra weight slowed the carpet down tremendously. With the wind came water, a few strong gusts of mist at first and then rain, soaking them as the storm overtook them. The winds pushed and pulled on the carpet. Wil fought tooth and nail to keep them flying straight, to keep them from being thrown and smashed against the ground.

Rather than drop them off at the first house they came to, Wil took them toward the town square. At this point, either his warnings had done the trick or the sky-shattering cracks of thunder had. People ran around desperately working on nailing everything down. Wil stopped in front of an inn and motioned for them to get off.

"Thanks," the younger of the two said. "Who are you?"

"Wil McKenzie, wizard," Wil replied. "Get inside, now!"

As soon as the two were on solid ground, Wil took off again. Ahead of the storm he sped, flying at an angle to keep up with it. Lightning flashed, one, two, three times back to back, until the night sky was as bright as day. Wil blinked furiously, a dark shape burned into the afterimages. He closed his eyes to see the image better and nearly gasped.

He knew that shape.

A massive, triangular head with horns. Great big wings, flapping ponderously slow and yet still somehow airborne. Four clawed limbs tucked underneath as it flew. The afterimage was a chaotic mess of darkness set against blinding white, but the shape was clear to Wil. He opened his eyes again and focused.

There, up in the sky, was a dragon. Wil knew the storm couldn't be natural with the size and speed in which it moved, but he never dreamed…Gods, looks like he got his wish. He was finally seeing a dragon in person, and it was majestic, powerful, and terrible.

The question was: What could he do about it?

CHAPTER 43

Rain

The higher Wil flew, the harder the winds blew. By the time the ground could no longer be seen through the darkness and rain, gale-force gusts were buffeting the carpet. Wil clung on for dear life, frigid hands already starting to go numb. Still, he had to get closer, he had to see for sure. He pushed harder and harder, willing the carpet to surpass its limits and make it to the center.

And he nearly got there. The swirling storm dragged him through the air as he fought against the current, stealing every last foot he could. The closer he got, the harder the winds threw him from his task, and the rug shook with the effort of remaining in the air. In the center, all was still. The dragon itself was the eye of the storm, covered in torrential rain.

As soon as Wil got a good look, seeing the dragon's silver, cloudy eyes and the way it moved through the air, Wil understood. It wasn't malicious, bringing a storm against humans to wipe them out. It acted as if it didn't even notice what it was doing, just lazily swimming through the air. Its serpentine body moved in a continuous wave, great wings flapping, and it drove the storm forward. Farther onto Harper Valley, far below.

Wil's stomach dropped like a rock, and then so did the carpet.

He hung on for dear life as the enchantments faltered, sending him plummeting to the ground below. The rug billowed around him. Winds from all over sent him twisting, barely hanging on to the rug as he fought to avoid panicking. Extending his senses to the dormant enchantments on the rug, he did a sweep.

The enchantments weren't broken, merely taxed and suppressed. Gallons of magical rainwater had smothered them and kept them weak. There was a solution to that. Wil closed his eyes, trying not to think of how close he was to hitting the ground. He felt for the carpet in his mind, mentally touching it and seeing the shape and counting every thread and tassel along the edges.

It was harder than it should've been, but he pushed with his magic and layered the carpet with a spell to repel water. It did nothing for the water already soaking it, but from that point on, water rolled off the carpet and into Wil's soaked clothing or onto the ground below. He opened his eyes and regretted it immediately.

He had only a few seconds left.

Wil pushed his magic into the enchantments he'd so carefully laid out over the course of months. Intricate, delicate spells all working together to carry out a shared task. With pure mental effort, he brute-forced them all into working. He shot forward and upward, coming within ten feet of the ground before shooting off into the night.

Gaining altitude was difficult after that initial burst of magic faded. Wil descended fast and crashed into the mud. The carpet skidded and slid into a stop. Breathing heavily, Wil stood on unsteady legs. He looked up.

The dragon traveled directly over him, continuing its way across the sky. The winds died down, but the rain poured on him as if the gods themselves were weeping. Wil stood there, helpless before such power, watching the dragon's massive body pass. He blinked drops of water out of his eyes and looked at his carpet.

He picked it up and waved it out. The water-repelling spell also kept the mud from sticking to it, but it was soaked. He focused on the moisture and did what he could to draw it out. It would've been easier if there wasn't all the other water around him. When he drew it forth, water from the ground and air as well as the carpet came together in his open palm in a water ball. He threw it to the side, and it exploded like the world's biggest waterskin.

"What the hell do I do against a storm dragon?" Wil asked no one, voice lost to another crack of thunder. He looked around, trying to figure out where in town he was, and if anyone was nearby.

As if anyone could help him. What could any of them do against the power of nature? There was always the chance he could change the weather, but that left the dragon. The difference between them magically was about as much as it was physically. With another few decades of experience and magical growth, maybe Wil could take on a dragon like this, but now?

"Gods…" Wil clutched at his hair. Taking a deep breath, he forced himself to calm down. There was no help coming. Only he could handle this—well, even if he couldn't, he had to try. It was part of the job, right? Right. He exhaled and looked around again.

This looked like the Lane farm, right at the base of the forest. The dragon continued northwest, up to Skalet Peak. As much as Wil hoped the dragon would just keep going and take the storm with it, the constant flips in his stomach told him otherwise. He knew without a doubt it was here to stay.

Wil set out the carpet again and sat down. He was cold, wet, tired, and terrified, but things could be so much worse, and would be if he didn't act. Taking the leather loops into his hands, he pulled and up he went, slower than he could but terrified the enchantments might fail again. They were already under half power.

The tips of the trees scraped the bottom of the rug as he flew up the mountain. Wil didn't dare to go much higher, and even that was a terrible thrill as he wove in and out of the tree line, more or less following the trail straight up the mountain. The higher he got, the lower he flew, eventually ducking down into the forest itself to shield himself from the wind.

Even cutting his speed, barely missing tree trunks as he swept by kept Wil wide awake and terrified that one slip-up would take him out and doom the town. It was a relief when the gaps between trees widened as they got closer to the top. Good news and bad news, as he once more fought against gale-force winds and lightning crashed down around him.

With another sharp burst of speed, Wil pushed past the wall of air and into the eye of the storm. The dragon had landed, and it took up most of the clearing itself. The cabin and lake stood between it and Wil, looking comically small in comparison. Water flowed off the beast's body like it was the source of the rain, streaming along the ground and coming up to Wil's ankles already.

Wil took a few steps forward, pushing against the swiftly rising water, waving his hands frantically in the air to get the dragon's attention. With a quick spell, he enhanced his voice and boomed out, "WHO ARE YOU? WHY ARE YOU HERE, DRAGON?"

The dragon turned its head, easily the size of a wagon, his way. Milky eyes stared unblinking. It heard him, but Wil had no clue whether or not it understood him.

"DRAGON! YOUR STORM IS GOING TO GET PEOPLE HURT OR KILLED. PLEASE STOP THIS!"

Water rose to Wil's calves. The lake overflowed and went downhill, past Wil and down the mountain, slow now but picking up speed. Just as Wil despaired over getting no answer from the dragon, it stirred.

"*Home*," it rumbled. A single, solitary word with the weight of the world behind it. Tired, sore, and melancholy beyond belief. Wil thought he understood.

"HOME? IS THIS YOUR HOME? THIS IS OUR HOME TOO. YOUR RAIN IS CAUSING A FLOOD. IF YOU'RE NOT CAREFUL, YOU'RE

GOING TO FLOOD US OUT!" Wil hoped he could get through to the creature, maybe reason with it. If he couldn't, what did that leave? He didn't have a hope in hell of doing anything to force the dragon to go.

The dragon lowered itself to the ground, curling around the cabin and the far end of the lake. Its milky eyes fluttered shut and it let out a low rumble. And then it was asleep, and the rain coming from above poured even harder. The water was up to Wil's knees now.

Wil swore. He held out the carpet and awkwardly jumped on it, taking it above the water. The enchantments throbbed in his senses in protest, but they held. He flew over to the edge of the clearing, where the ground sloped downward and water poured down the mountain.

The river was already overflowing at its source, flooding farmland. There seemed to be no end of rain coming from the now slumbering dragon, and if Wil didn't deal with the water now, entire farms would wash away and families would be ruined or even die.

He stared at the dragon in the clearing, racking his brain for some solution, wanting there to be an answer to jump out and solve everything for him. Wil closed his eyes and extended his senses. He found his answer immediately.

Skalet Peak was one of many places in the valley with a healthy leyline. It wasn't as vast as the one going through the center of the valley, through Mr. Carrey's land. It didn't need to be, to be useful. Wil tapped into the leyline and the entire mountain came to life for him.

Every rock and tree and creature lit up in the night, briefly illuminated in his mind as he felt the land itself and how and where everything went together. He had an idea then. A risky one, with definite consequences to it later, but he couldn't deal with the dragon until he was sure the town wouldn't flood. He reached beneath them, to the land underneath the carpet and gallons and gallons of water.

And Wil pushed.

Earth magic was one of the more difficult elements to learn. Everyone learned a bit of fire and air. Those were easy, as ever-present and easy to manipulate as breathing. Water was the next most difficult, so capricious yet malleable. Wil would've called earth the most difficult to manipulate if he didn't have a knack for it.

It was as simple and as difficult as reaching into the earth as a whole and sculpting it with raw power. The rain helped, softening the land and making everything much easier to move. With the power of the leyline backing him, Wil scooped out a twenty-foot wide gulf of land from the lip of the clearing, moving it all downward and to the sides.

He flew down slowly, pushing the entire time. The earth below caved and cracked and gave way to his will, thousands of pounds of dirt and rocks flowing like water. He pushed again and all the hard minerals were swept up along the edges so a new bottom and sides were formed as he continued his flight downward.

The leyline grew farther and farther away, yet Wil remained tapped into its strength. At a certain point, he had to mentally tug on it, and then yank hard as the land shifted beneath his power and so did the leyline. The leyline pulled back until Wil ripped it open, dragging the power with him. Downward, faster and faster, the twenty-foot scoop of land continued, digging deep and winding down the south side of the mountain.

Wil's heart pounded and his head throbbed from so much power coursing through his body, most of it not his. There would be a toll to pay, but if it meant saving Harper Valley, he'd happily pay anything. The pressure slammed against him as he flew down, until eventually, Wil found himself screaming from the pain and strain of carving a path down.

Just as his strength gave out, he reached the bottom of the mountain. He released the energy and collapsed onto the rug right as the swathe of earth split open and fed into the canyon below. Water roared past him, flowing from Skalet Peak and down into the two-mile channel he'd gouged for a brand-new river.

The world went dark and hazy at the edges. He crashed his rug into the ground again and rolled, darkness taking him under.

CHAPTER 44

Lightning

The deafening roar of thunder ripped Wil from unconsciousness. He woke with a jolt, coughing and sputtering water. He turned over onto his hands and knees, soaked up to his elbows, and hacked up the last of the water in his lungs. Looking around frantically, Wil tried to figure out how long he'd been out.

Then he remembered what he had just done.

The river roared past him, taking the excess rain from the mountaintop and flushing it away to the small canyon between mountain peaks. It was already a quarter full, and Wil didn't know if that meant he'd been out for long or if it had just filled that fast. Either way, he didn't have time for it. That dragon needed to be stopped.

The search for his flying carpet lasted all of ten minutes before Wil gave up. He had no clue where it could've gone. For all he knew, it had been flushed away by the river and he'd never see it again. He cursed under his breath and looked upward into the dark and dripping forest. He had to make his way back up there.

Just to test it out, he cast a simple light orb spell. About as easy as magic could get. It took him a couple of tries. He felt strained but not empty, like he'd run a marathon in one day, had a nap, and now the remaining energy could fuel him for another half-marathon before he collapsed entirely.

It was better than the alternative, at least. Sighing, he picked himself up and made his way alongside the new river.

Seeing his handiwork as he went made him wince. Trees, bushes, rocks, and even live animals had been thrown to the side and displaced as he dug his river. He ended up having to climb over a hill of mud and sticks and a few fallen trees that had gotten in the way. Now they lined the river and helped keep the water level from rising over the sides.

The light from his orb didn't do much in the darkness of the storm, but the lightning came on faster now, striking every few seconds somewhere on the mountain, keeping mostly to the peak. Wil would be trudging along, making good speed in the dark night, and then all of a sudden a flash would light everything up. Before too long, Wil got used to following the afterimages, treading carefully to avoid slipping in the mud.

Once he'd made some distance, Wil chanced looking out into the valley. The Lane farm had some flooding, but it could've been way worse. The roar of the river next to Wil was a comfort. Even if he couldn't fix things, he at least bought them a little time. Shivering and shaking from the wet and cold, Wil allowed himself a smile.

All around him, animals rushed by the underbrush, doing everything they could to flee the mountain and the heaviest rain any of them had ever seen. At one point, Wil had to duck behind a tree to avoid a pack of wolves scrambling to leave. For a second, Wil thought he'd have to defend himself, but the wolves wanted nothing to do with him.

After that, the climb was mostly the same. He'd made it dozens of times throughout his life, but never in weather like this. Never next to a landscape he had to reshape to save lives. The river served as a shocking reminder of what he was capable of. As Wil wondered about what he could possibly do to stop the storm, it helped him remember he was stronger than he thought.

Swirling winds told him he was getting close. The flashes of lightning were nearer now, the thunder roaring only a second or two later. It hurt his eyes and ears, and made him want to lie down and give in to the exhaustion and just take a nap. Let someone else deal with this until he had a chance to rest.

A time or two, he stumbled, and it took all of his willpower to get back up and keep trudging forward. Then he thought about his family, of Bram and Darlene, and everyone else in Harper Valley getting flooded or torn apart by the wind, and he kept going.

Wil crested the final hill, holding himself up next to a tree and panting. The next lightning strike happened too close, and he backed away from the tree. He was too drained to fully appreciate the danger, but part of him still knew trees were unsafe to be around. Yet every second of wading through knee-high water took him closer to the dragon and his probable death.

The dragon was still sleeping, its form lit up by lightning every so often. Wil pushed past the wind, arms flailing as he took the last few steps into the eye of the storm. Once there, he collapsed about fifty feet away from the creature, breathing heavily. With no wind here, even the rain didn't quite seem so cold and harsh.

But he had no time to waste. Wil picked himself up again and closed the distance until he stood just a few feet away. He held up his hand and, expecting the worse to happen, put it on the storm dragon. It was wet, solid, and radiating a much-desired warmth. It took all Wil had to not press himself up against the dragon and suck away every last bit of heat he could get.

"Why are you even here? What did we do to you?" Wil asked, mostly thinking out loud. He rubbed the smooth, beautiful silver scales reverently.

"This storm is yours, isn't it? I've read about your kind. Storm dragons travel under the cover of rain, capriciously giving and taking from the land. We would've loved seeing you in the summer, but..." Wil trailed off, biting his lip.

The dragon breathed deeply, snoring with little arcs of lightning sparking out of its nostrils.

Well, he wasn't going to get any help there. Wil extended his senses to the dragon and the storm itself. The two were connected. That much he knew for sure, and his senses told him that immediately. The dragon was the source of the storm, but it didn't seem in control of that. When he felt for the dragon's mind, it showed up as deep and wide and unknowable as the ocean. Wil had no hope of penetrating or changing it, but he could observe.

While the storm raged on outwardly, the inside was peaceful, minus the weakness. The dragon was dying. Wil could read that much, and feel it. The dragon was dying, and the storm was the cause of it. It drained and drained and never ended.

The storm was a curse.

Wil saw that and recoiled. Something had cursed this poor dragon to storm eternally at the cost of its health and whatever collateral damage it caused. He recognized it as spellwork, but curse-breaking had never been one of his strengths. Curses and combat magic had seemed so far outside what he wanted to work with that he had neglected them when he had the chance.

He laughed bitterly. "If I survive this, Professor Henderson's never going to let me live this down. I had to know better and choose not to deal with curses. Idiot." Wil rubbed at his temples.

While he didn't know how to break curses, maybe he could alter this one. Shrink it, maybe. Like trying to cover the sun with his body, Wil reached with his magic for the storm, willing it to shrink. He willed the winds to slow, the rain to cut off. He pictured the lightning flashing slower and slower, and then not at all. He pictured the storm in its entirety and tried to press in on it from all sides.

The curse magically bucked him off like an angry bronco. Wil recoiled from the dragon, coughing and sputtering as he tried to get his head back on straight. Then, because he didn't know any better, he tried it all over again. With the same result. Shrinking the storm just made it come back bigger and more uncontrollable. He remembered talking about this with Bram just a few weeks back. Storms were impossible for him to summon, but he could usually shrink or grow them. Growing them was easier, but what good would that do?

Just the same, Wil tried. He tapped into that storm at the heart of the dragon's magic and whispered a little encouragement. Grow. Get bigger, storm harder, and take up the entire sky. Almost immediately, the storm grew, and with it so did the eye.

Trees previously flailing in the wind settled as the force carried on farther, except for in the back of the clearing where the swirling gusts hit the mountains and crashed into nothingness. Wil's eyes widened and he let out a triumphant shout. That was it. There was no way to shrink the storm, but maybe he could make it grow and grow. If all of Harper Valley was in the eye of the storm, maybe it would get by. And if the storm was bigger, maybe it would drain the dragon faster and—

Wil looked at the dragon, heart sinking. It was beyond tired and didn't have much left to give. Would he do it? Would he kill a dragon to save his town? He already knew the answer.

"I'm sorry," he blurted out. "I'm so sorry for this. I don't want to, but …I'm sorry, I have to."

The dragon didn't answer.

Lightning flashed again, striking rock far outside the eye of the storm. When the storm grew, the lightning came down harder but farther away. That, more than anything, told Wil this would work if he tried it. He took a deep breath and stood up straight. Keeping one hand on the dragon's side, he lifted the other toward the storm.

And he pushed.

The eye grew, and with it, the rest of the storm. Winds picked up, tearing trees from the earth and flinging them. But not where Wil and the dragon were. Wil felt his teeth and skin itch before another blast of lightning touched the tip of the mountain just a few hundred yards away, a world-splitting crack coming after. And still, he pushed and pushed until the storm expanded. Wil poured in his flagging power until the storm was the only thing he could sense.

He pushed until the eye covered Harper Valley, and it was all he could do to keep it that size, to prevent it from shrinking and snapping back to where it had been. The curse pulsed in his mind, hot and oily. The dragon stirred, eyelids fluttering open. One huge silver eye, no longer clouded over, stared directly at him.

Wil kept on, using the last of his strength to tap into the leyline he tore open and which now bled magic. The power flowing into the storm doubled and then tripled. Wil screamed from the agony and ecstasy of all the magic flowing through and around him, more magic than he'd ever handled at once. His knees shook, his entire body burned hot and cold, and he wanted to laugh and scream and cry.

He held the storm in the palm of his hands, and he ripped it in half.

All at once the rain died down, followed by the winds. One last flash of lightning, and with the thunder, Wil collapsed to his knees. When he looked up, the dragon's snout was a foot away from him. Wil weakly reached for it and fell to his hands. His muscles burned, and it was all he could do to not fall face-first into the water.

"I'm sorry," Wil said again, though he didn't know if he was saying it to the dragon, his town, or his family.

His strength deserted him. Wil fell, but the dragon caught him easily in one massive claw.

"*Human*," it rumbled in a voice that was finally awake and aware. "*Thank you.*"

The last thing Wil remembered was the flapping of big leathery wings, and then a sensation of falling.

CHAPTER 45

Rest

The first thing Wil noticed was the pain. Not agony, or anything as spicy or memorable as all that. Just a full-body ache that made him stir from the deepest sleep he could remember. He had been floating in warm darkness, with no dreams or anything other than a sense of having done something great, something worth the rest. And then the pain came and dragged him into wakefulness.

"Ugh," Wil groaned, too tired to open his eyes.

"Wil, my boy, are you awake?" a familiar voice asked, sounding entirely too jolly for Wil's current mood.

"Ughhh," Wil replied, before once more slipping back into the warm darkness.

He awoke again to the sound of people talking. He had no idea how long he'd been out. Immediately, he recognized his mother's voice. She was speaking in her usual rapid-fire way, which he always had trouble keeping up with.

"And so, my boy, my sweet little goof of a boy, decided that he was going to follow the rules to the letter. We told him, 'No food outside the kitchen,' so the little brat stood right where the kitchen and living room met and ate his toast there. Every so often, he'd peek his head in on us listening to the radio, and I'd try to yell at him for it, but he'd just say, 'But, Mama, the food's still in the kitchen!'"

She let out a pleased laugh, and Wil heard Darlene join in. He'd heard the story a million times before, a tale from his precocious childhood. He didn't think Darlene had heard it. He could've spoken up, but that would've taken effort. All he wanted to do was go back to sleep, but this time, it seemed he would be awake for a while.

"That sounds like Wil," Darlene said. "Sometimes he and Bram will argue over the stupidest things, based on a technicality. It's like they're trying to see who can be more insufferable than the other."

"Who wins more often?"

"Neither wins. I just lose."

They laughed again, and even Wil had to join in. His laugh was weak and breathy. It got their attention immediately.

"Wil?" his mother gasped.

"Wil!" Darlene had to be the one hugging him—nobody smelled quite as nice as her. "You're okay!"

"Urk. That…" His voice came out a harsh, crackly whisper. A second later, Darlene drew back and pressed something against his lips. Wil opened his mouth and sucked water through the straw. Small, greedy little sips until his throat no longer felt like a desert and he could breathe without it stinging. "That remains to be seen," he said.

He finally tried opening his eyes, but it was like trying to lift ten-pound weights with his eyelids. Eventually, he managed, regretting it when the light burned his eyes. He grunted in discomfort but put on a brave smile.

"How are you feeling, Wil?" his mother asked.

"Tired. Sore. Like I got in a fight with a storm and somehow won."

"You did!" Darlene crowed. "Whatever happened, you succeeded! They found you in the center of town up against the fountain, unconscious and cradling something."

"Hmm?" Wil fought to sit and gave up halfway. Darlene handed him a long, thin, silver piece of bone. He jerked away, suddenly wide awake.

"What? What's wrong, Wil?" Sharon asked.

Wil licked his lips and pointed at the bone. It was over a foot long and curved like a saber. "That's…that's a horn," he said. "A nose horn, I believe. From the dragon."

"Dragon?" Darlene's eyes widened. "What dragon?"

Wil collapsed back onto the bed, laughing. "Oh, man. What do people know about last night?"

"Um, the storm was three days ago, hon," Sharon said. "You've been out for this whole time. Doc Hawkins told us you'd be okay, just that you needed rest."

"Gods," Wil groaned. "Okay, so. After I went out to argue with Mayor Sinclair…"

From there he went over everything, from the argument and threats to flying over Harper Valley and Gallard Springs, to where he first saw the dragon in the center of the storm. He told them about the new river, and about expanding the storm until it was too big to hold together. And then about breaking the curse. By the time he finished, Wil was about ready to go back to sleep.

Sharon had collapsed into one of the nearby chairs and listened silently, while Darlene stayed at Wil's side and held his hand tightly. The small hospital room was hushed save for a ceiling fan lazily turning circles above them.

Finally, Darlene said, "Dammit, Wil, you're a hero, you know that?"

"Bah." Wil waved her off half-heartedly. "It's not that big a deal."

"Oh, stop it," Sharon snapped. "You stopped a rampaging dragon and the worst storm in a hundred years. And this entire time, the mayor's been blaming you for the storm itself when you're a damned hero!"

Wil blinked. "Sinclair's doing *what?*"

Darlene winced. She shared a look with Sharon, as if the two were trying to decide how much to tell him. She finally broke, sighing. "He's acting like you're at fault for not handling the storm better. He said you were out of town on personal business to get rich off being a wizard, and then warned about the storm too late to be effective. He's blaming the damage on you."

Wil inhaled and then let out his breath, processing. He was too shocked and disgusted to be properly angry. "How bad's the damage? Was anyone hurt?"

"No, sweetie," Sharon said, putting her hand on his arm. "No one was hurt, but there was damage all around town. Cleanup will begin in earnest once some of the flooding has been taken care of. Some houses have extensive water damage. We're fine, and your house is fine as well. Some broken windows from when the wind picked up, but you should be good to go home soon."

"Assuming cleanup crews don't mysteriously find a reason to not be able to work on my house," Wil muttered. "Wouldn't put it past the bastard."

"I don't think you'll need to worry about that," said Darlene with a smile. "Our Appleton refugees are making themselves real popular. They're just about the only ones without ties, so they don't have anything lost or damaged. A couple of them are good at repairs, and they're offering their services as well as teaching others to help with the efforts. If Mayor Sinclair won't fix up your house, you can bet they will."

That really did help. Wil smiled, and before long, he was falling asleep again.

By the time the next day rolled around, Wil had fallen asleep and woken up again at least six times. Darlene had stayed with him, insisting that his mother go home to get some sleep and do what she could to help others. Bright and early, Wil had his next visitor.

"Hey, there," said Bram, knocking on the door after he'd already opened it. He slunk in and sat on a chair much too small for him, wincing as it creaked.

"So, uh," he started, licking his lips. "Your mom told me what all happened on the mountain."

"Yes?" Wil asked, sitting up.

"Did you really see and touch a dragon?" Bram looked like he was restraining himself from grabbing Wil by the shirt and shaking him, but only just.

Rather than answering, Wil lifted the dragon horn from the windowsill and handed it over to Bram. As soon as Bram touched it, he jerked as well. The horn carried power, and a lot of it. So much that even a non-magic person like Bram couldn't help but feel it.

"Gods," Bram exclaimed, almost dropping it. He quickly gave it back to Wil, who didn't mind the lingering charge of electricity and power in it. It felt a little bit like when he channeled magic, and that would forever be a good sensation.

"I can't believe you defeated a storm dragon."

"I'm not sure 'defeat' is the right word," said Wil dryly. "I think I helped heal it. And kept it from doing more damage, I guess. What've you been up to the past few days?"

Bram laughed, as if Wil had asked him something incredibly funny. "Oh, no big deal, right? Just helped save the town and heal a cursed storm dragon. All in a day's work. C'mon, Wil. I've been doing okay. The brewery is fine. We only got a little bit of the flooding in the fourth field, but no big deal. I've spent the last few days brewing as many potions as possible."

"Really?" Wil was impressed by his initiative.

"Really," Darlene said, putting a tiny hand on Bram's shoulder. "Bram here's been doing everything he can to make sure the doctors have extra supplies, and he's been making a paste to help keep mold away. Recovery's going to be a little slow, but he's been working nonstop."

Bram smiled but looked away as if he were too embarrassed to be proud of himself. Well, Wil wouldn't stand for that.

"I don't even remember teaching you any mold-killing potions."

"You didn't!" Bram exclaimed. "After we found you in the town square and got you situated, I went to your house and made sure all the books were safe and undamaged, and I may have borrowed a few on alchemy to be useful. But I promise I'll give them back as soon as you're good to leave."

Wil shook his head, chuckling. "Bram, I am so incredibly lucky to have you as a friend. No one else would've thought to save my books. You're really liking alchemy, huh?"

Bram cleaned his glasses on his shirt, smiling like a fool. "I do. It's all the best of books and cooking combined. Finding good recipes, and understanding the ingredients and how the preparations change things. It's like brewing beer, only way more complicated and interesting. And I don't even need magic to do it well!"

Not for the stuff he was doing, at least. Wil didn't have the heart to tell him that most advanced potions required a bit of spellwork too. Instead, he just clapped his hand down on Bram's knee a couple of times appreciatively.

"Is there anything we can get you, Wil?" Darlene asked after the conversation fell into a natural lull. "You hungry? Tired? Want to get out of here?"

Wil grunted. "The latter. So much the latter. I've got a lot of work ahead of me and—"

Both Bram and Darlene groaned.

"What?" said Wil.

Darlene reached into her pocket and pulled out a tenner and handed it to Bram. "We made a bet on how soon you'd talk about getting back to work. Bram said the day after you woke up, and I said two days. Thanks a lot, jerk."

"To be fair, you practically poked him into answering that," said Bram.

"I did not," Darlene protested. "I asked if he wanted to get out of here, and he just had to say getting back to work. Look, Wil, there's plenty of work and it will be waiting for you. There's no need for you to push yourself before you're well again. You've done enough."

"More than enough," said Bram.

Wil shook his head. They didn't get it. It wasn't about wanting to contribute more. It was about not wanting to be useless, or to just sit back and let everyone else get their hands dirty. Every day he stayed in the hospital was another day the mayor had to turn people against him. And after Wil had worked so hard to earn their trust.

"I'll rest one more day," he said. "But after that? You'd better break my legs if you want to keep me in bed."

Bram stood, drawing himself up to his impressive height. "That could be arranged," he said gravely. Darlene laughed and shoved him, bouncing back.

Wil grinned and shrugged. "I guess I'll rest a bit longer. Wouldn't want the wrath of the only person in town who's a bigger nerd than me. Literally, even."

What else was there to do but settle back in bed and let himself rest? Idly, Wil picked up the dragon horn again and turned it around. The last thing he remembered before passing out was the dragon speaking to him. Was this horn a gift, or just bad luck on the dragon's part? When he focused on it, he could feel rain at the tip of his senses, just waiting to be called.

But he'd had enough rain for now.

CHAPTER 46

Recovery

When Wil was finally allowed out, he resolved to do as much as he could to help with the cleanup efforts. His loved ones decided otherwise and brought him home to sleep for one more day. His house had already been cleaned up for him by the Appleton crew, who were paid extra for their efforts, at his insistence. Being home did help, and the following day, Wil jumped up, raring to go.

In the hospital, he'd had a lot of time to think about everything. His friends had stayed with him as often as they could, but with as much work everyone had to do, it left Wil with plenty of downtime.

Some of Wil's thoughts were on the mayor and the man's smear campaign against him. As much as Wil wanted to just ignore it and do his job, problems didn't go away if you just ignored them.

He thought about the storm, and relived the fast, draining, chaotic night all over again as he dozed off. From plummeting to the earth and nearly dying to the near hypothermia that came from spending an hour in an inland hurricane at the wrong time of year. Those who knew him called him a hero and brave for facing it all, but mostly...

Mostly, Wil didn't know if he'd be able to do it all over again if the situation came up. It had all been the right thing to do, and he did it instinctively. Now that he knew how hard it could be, would he be able to muster the strength to face with something similar in the future? He hated that he didn't have an answer for that.

And of course at least half his thoughts were of the future and how he could help his community clean up. He had Darlene and Bram bring him news and updates on how everyone's efforts were going, and used that to make a plan.

His initial instincts told him to help the richer farmers, like Mr. Carrey, first. Then he realized that with their money, they already had a leg up on getting back to business earlier than others. But if he didn't show up and help them, chances were that Mayor Sinclair would use it against him. The way Wil saw it, the rich were already on Sinclair's side and he wasn't about to kiss all their asses to *maybe* change that.

That left the poor, the weak, and the old. The people who needed his help the most and would be forgotten if he didn't look out for them.

"Thank you so much for all your help, Mr. Wizard," said old Mr. Maggs. He was a widower in his seventies. Both his kids were in the city, and he was alone in his little house, with a bit of farmland.

"It's my pleasure to help, Mr. Maggs," said Wil, bowing his head respectfully. As tired and battered as he still was, it didn't take much effort to move a bunch of trees and rocks and other debris and get the land back to a workable state. He spent more time carving runes around the house to help with water damage. "If you need anything else, don't hesitate to reach out, okay?"

Mr. Maggs grabbed Wil's hand and shook it enthusiastically. "I will!"

"Well, that was awful sweet of you," said Jeb as they left. "'My pleasure, Mr. Maggs!'" He fluttered his eyelashes dreamily.

"Why did I bring you along again?" Wil grumbled good-naturedly as they went down the lane and off to take a little break. After four hours of having to work slowly to avoid overexerting himself, Wil needed a bite to eat.

Jeb threw his arm around Wil's shoulder and jostled him. "Because no one other than Bram is strong enough to carry your ass off if you suddenly collapse from weakness. And Bram would probably freak out and panic, so you're stuck with me."

"You're in too good a mood," said Wil. "Especially with all this devastation. Why?"

"Sheila's house had a tree crash through the living room during the storm." Jeb's stupid smile only grew.

"And that's a good thing? What's wrong with you?"

Jeb burst out laughing. "It is when it means Sheila is staying with me while her house gets repaired. And guess who gets to help do the repairs? I get to have her close and also get credit for helping her out."

Wil shook his head in disbelief. "Are you seriously using the damage from the storm to profit?"

"Hey, they say every storm cloud's got a silver lining, right?" Jeb winked.

"Turns out it's a silver dragon, actually," said Wil. They headed for the diner. Mack's Shack had been one of the first places to get repaired, and it wasn't hard to see why. With so many on the edges of town taking the brunt of the damage, they needed as many places for food open as possible. There wasn't a line out the door, but plenty of temporary seating had been set up outside. Wil and Jeb walked past that and headed inside.

"I'll be with you in just a—Wil!" Candy looked up and beamed at him. The pretty redhead looked exhausted, but so did everyone else. Only she and a few others were handling food orders for dozens of people. "Let me get some campers to leave and we'll get you a table."

Wil ignored the look Jeb shot him and just shook his head. "That's not necessary, Candy. We can wait, same as anybody else. I got a present, though."

"Oh?" Candy cocked her head.

Wil fished out a sack of bills from his coat pocket and handed it to her. "This is about three thousand zynce. Think this is enough to cover food for everyone stopping by today?"

"Uh, yeah, probably," she said, taking the pouch from him with wide eyes. "Mack wanted to give food out for free anyway, but with all the repairs…"

"Say no more," said Wil with a smile. "I get it. Anything I can do to help, let me know. We gotta stick together during disasters, right?"

"Absolutely." Candy beamed at him. "You're a good man, Wil."

Jeb gagged. "Great, that's going to go straight to his head now. Thanks, Candy!"

They laughed, and soon enough a table opened up. Candy cleaned it off for them and they sat down with glasses of water to start. Wil waited until Candy was gone before saying, "You ever gonna stop giving me crap?"

Jeb pretended to think about it. "Naw. Somebody's gotta keep you honest. Mom and Dad are way too proud of you, Sarah too inconsistent, Bram too much your buddy, and Darlene…well, Darlene's got a good head on her shoulders. She could do better."

Wil shook his head, grinning. "Big talk from the creeper who's celebrating his girlfriend's house being wrecked just so he can get closer to her."

"Yeah, but we both know I ain't a good person," said Jeb. He laughed, but there was an edge there Wil wasn't sure how to address. "Gotta keep you honest so you can stay Mr. Wizard, saving the day and farting rainbows."

"I could do that, you know," said Wil, wiggling his fingers. "A simple illusion and I can blast off seven colors from my ass at any time."

"So," said Jeb, deciding to move on, "you going to just go around paying for things now? You really got that much money already?"

Ah, that. Wil shook his head, shrinking a little. "Not as such. I've got some. I'm doing alright. But that money is from the profits we made going to neighboring towns. I'm doing okay. We'll make it through winter no problem, but a lot of people around here might not. I figured I'd take my cut of the profits and spread them around town for people who need food or repairs. That way it doesn't affect Bram and Darlene."

Jeb stared at him for several seconds before he spoke. "Can I ask you a serious question?"

Wil motioned for him to go ahead.

"Really, why didn't you ever come home when you were at school?"

It was the question Wil expected and dreaded. He'd never lied about it, but maybe it was time to give a more honest answer.

"I told you I had a really tough time at school, right? It was rougher than you think. There were so many times I nearly quit. I spent the first three years wanting to quit so badly because I wasn't sure I could cut it. I missed home so much that I wanted to just…give up. Give up and go home and pretend none of it ever happened. Pretend to be normal.

"But I didn't. I forced myself to stay. I didn't let myself come home even once, because I knew if I did, it'd be impossible to make myself go back. And with everyone counting on me to make them proud, how could I let them down like that? So I kept my head down and worked. And by the time I finished year four, I was finally starting to come into my own. So I kept going to prove to myself that I'm not a quitter.

"I went from struggling to the top of my class. I discovered that I'm bad at highly technical, delicate magic, but I have a great deal of magical muscle and I'm stubborn. It was the hardest thing I've ever had to do, but it let me discover who I am. I won't apologize for that, but I am sorry I didn't do more than write."

Jeb took his time replying. For the first time since Wil had come home, his older brother seemed thoughtful instead of just reactive. "It makes sense," he said finally. "I…*we* missed you so much. It was hard not to be angry at you. I'm not angry anymore. Just please don't disappear again. If you did, I'd probably deserve it, but I want things to be better. And I'm sorry for how I've been."

They sat in silence for a little while as Wil tried to gather his thoughts and figure Jeb out. He decided to go with a cautious, safe approach. "What're your plans going forward?"

"What do you mean?" Jeb asked. "Help with the cleanup because it's the right thing to do, and then just focus on the farm as usual. And Sheila too. I don't really think more than a couple of seasons ahead of time. Kinda gotta know how things go before I can figure out what to do or where to go, you know?"

Wil nodded, trying to think. He had nothing. No matter how hard he tried to come up with things to do for Jeb to help him out or maybe give him something more in life to be proud of, he came up short. He knew it wasn't his responsibility, especially after how things had been that summer, but he loved his big brother. Even if he was a bit of an ass sometimes.

Oh, well. He'd just need to keep an eye out for ways to keep making things good between them. They had peace now, but there was still that edge to Jeb that hadn't been there before Wil went to school.

More than anything, he just wanted peace for both of them. Maybe he could do something about it, maybe he couldn't. He'd never stop trying.

"So who do you think we should help next?" Wil asked. "Tons of work to go around, and if you're gonna be babysitting me while I recover from my heroics, you might as well get a say in where we go."

Jeb's eyes lit up. "Well, damn, Mr. Maggs was a good choice. Let's go around and find everyone who doesn't have someone looking out for them, and start there. Old folks, single moms. Maybe make sure the few people without homes got places to stay. We could build some temporary shelters and..."

There it was. Edge or not, Jeb was a good man. One of the people in Wil's life who'd taught him right from wrong and to always help people. No matter how angry you were, or how much of a grudge you carried, if people needed help, you helped them.

Wil listened carefully, glad to have a chance to rest and serve his community.

CHAPTER 47

A New Harper Valley

After a few days of hard work helping the town, Wil took a much-needed day to himself. Not for rest or relaxation, but to go back to the top of the mountain and see if he could find any hard evidence the dragon was there. Because no one wanted to leave him alone after the storm, his father went with him for company and support.

The first thing Wil did was go to the river he made, even now still flowing down to the canyon, which remained half full. It was so strange, walking through the forest and then suddenly seeing a huge, curved swathe of land winding its way down the mountain and depositing water into what was now a lake.

"You did this?" Bob asked, after they'd stood there for a couple of minutes. His father gaped at the sight.

"Sort of," said Wil, shrinking. "It was all I could think of to do at the time. There was a lot of water pouring down Skalet Peak and I didn't know how long it would take me to stop the dragon. Or if I even could. But I think this is another thing Sinclair is holding against me. He's got an expert coming in to see how badly this is going to affect the ecosystem of the basin."

Bob shook his head vehemently. "Chances are you've saved a lot of lives. Don't even give that windbag another thought. We'll deal with it in time. No one will believe his crap—enough people know how hard you're helping rebuild and that you're a good man."

Wil wanted to believe him. Try as he might, the worry never went away. The only thing to do was change the subject.

"Hey, let me know if you see my rug out here," said Wil. "I lost it when I fell unconscious. Maybe it's down there." He pointed to the new, unnamed lake. Dragon Tear Lake, maybe.

Bob came up beside him and gave the lake a good look. "Huh. Maybe. You'd be pretty screwed if it did end up down there. How long will it take you to make another?"

Wil groaned. "That depends on how long it takes to get everything back to normal. Winter comes with its own set of duties, and it took me a few months last time. But I want to make a few. One for me, Bram, and Darlene. It could be our signature transportation."

"It could be at that. You'd be the envy of the whole town. Might be another thing to do on the side. Make you some money, get you some goodwill, and make Harper Valley stand out against our neighbors. I bet we could be a great example of what a good town could be and grow into." Bob had a thoughtful look on his face.

It wasn't like Wil hadn't thought of it before. If things went sour with the mayor enough that he lost his job, there would be no end to things he could choose to do. He'd lose his house and ridiculous salary, but Wil was a master wizard. He could do anything. Just a reminder of that helped improve his mood.

"C'mon," said Wil. "We got a long way to go to the top."

Every fallen tree and bit of clutter on the path was another thing Wil couldn't help but feel guilty for. The dragon may not have been his fault, but what Wil had done to try to fix things was his responsibility alone. Bob seemed to know what was on Wil's mind because he kept pointing out everything he saw as if it were a good thing.

"I've never seen so many animals out and about!" Bob exclaimed as a doe ran by, barely taking any notice of them. It moved so easily, leaping over logs and even other animals, off to a destination known only to her.

"That's because half the forest was torn apart, either from the dragon or when I made the storm bigger and more powerful." Wil paused. He grimaced, looking around at a particularly bad bit of devastation. "I kind of wrecked a lot of homes, I think."

"Ahh," said Bob, nodding and continuing to walk down what was left of the path. Wil followed along. "It's not the forest you're worried about. If it's about the houses that got blown down, they weren't your fault, Wil."

Wil didn't say anything at first. They walked up the mountain parallel to the river. The rush of its waters served as a constant reminder. It was strange, to be proud of what he'd managed to do but still feel endless guilt over not being able to do it better or with less collateral damage.

"I mean it," Bob added after a couple of minutes of walking in silence. "I know it's been hitting you hard, being out there every day and seeing all the damage. But I got some news that might put things into perspective for ya."

"What's that?" asked Wil.

They continued their climb a little longer before Bob took a moment to sit on a log and grab a canteen from his pack. He took a drink and offered it to Wil. Wil was surprised to find it was whiskey and not water.

"Is that why you've got two canteens for this hike?" Wil demanded, laughing in disbelief.

"You can either give me crap for it or share with me—not both."

"Cheers," said Wil, tilting his head back and taking a swig. The burn brought tears to his eyes, and he welcomed the light pain.

Bob took back the canteen and had another swig before putting it away. "The thing about that dragon and the storms is, we weren't the only town hit."

Wil froze. "We weren't?"

"Nope. Turns out, it's been making its way westward over the past month. Four towns between here and Cloverton were wiped off the map. Two of them flooded out, and another burned down from all the lightning."

All of a sudden his legs turned to rubber. Wil collapsed onto the log as well. He stared off into the distance. Bob took that as a sign to continue. "They said it'd fly for a few days at a time and then land and sleep. And when it slept, the storm would continue on and then…" He didn't need to continue.

"So I really did save Harper Valley." Wil released a breath he didn't know he'd been holding. "If I hadn't acted, then the town really might've been destroyed."

"Right," said Bob, slapping Wil's knee. "So a few battered houses are nothing compared to how bad it could've been. You could keep beating yourself up if you want. Won't do any good, but I won't stop you. Or you could think about all the lives you saved and how much work you're still doing and let yourself feel good for a change.

"I get it, son. I do." Bob's tone softened. "You got the weight of the world on your shoulders, and more power than most people will ever dream of, let alone have to handle. And I appreciate you're using that power for good, and you're trying your absolute damnedest to not abuse it, and to do the right thing. But at a certain point, you gotta just accept that you're trying and move forward, no matter how that responsibility scares you.

"You think this is bad? Just wait until you're a parent. Then you'll know real fear and responsibility." Bob unscrewed the canteen, then thought better of it and put it back. He stood up and offered his hand to Wil. Wil took it and they continued to the peak.

Skalet Peak was worse off than the rest of the mountain. Not a single tree remained upright, nor did the cabin up there. As far as repairs went, it was a low priority to begin with, let alone now with people afraid of the dragon coming back. Those who believed.

"Damn," Bob exclaimed, looking around. "And you survived all of this and fixed it? You're lucky you just needed rest. Looks like a damned war happened up here."

On the upside, it made it easier to look out onto Harper Valley, or even to the other side of the mountain. If Wil squinted, he could pretend he could see Manifee City to the southwest. There was a sort of beauty to the destruction, maybe. Wil pointed to just behind the ruins of the cabin.

"There. That's where the dragon was. He curled up around the cabin and a chunk of the lake. He was so big."

Bob said nothing as they worked, looking closely for any sign of the dragon, proof it had been there. They walked around a deep indent in the mud that time, rain, and other animals had rendered completely useless. Wil groaned after sifting through the mud for what he thought was a piece of a claw but turned out to just be an interestingly shaped rock. He threw the rock to the side and plopped down in the mud, arms crossed over his chest.

"What's wrong? You still got that piece of horn, right?" Bob asked.

Wil shrugged. "Yeah. And it's clearly magical in nature. But there's no proof it's from a dragon, despite my word. And it'll be my word against Sinclair's."

"And the news reports coming in from back east," Bob reminded him. "Other towns were hit. There's no hiding this or pretending it didn't happen."

Wil laughed bitterly. "Hasn't stopped him from trying."

Bob took a long, deep breath. "I wasn't gonna tell you this yet, but I've been giving it some thought and…I think Sinclair's been mayor long enough, don't you?"

Wil blinked.

"What I mean is, it would help everyone out if he wasn't mayor anymore." Bob couldn't fight the growing smile on his face. "He's a greedy old leech, and I'm sick of his crap. I think maybe it's time for someone to unseat him and take over running this town."

Wil put two and two together. "And you think that someone should be you?"

His father just shrugged. "Why not? Can't be any worse than Sinclair, can I?"

"No, it's a good choice. You're a good choice, I mean," said Wil. He stood up, mind racing with the possibilities. "You're kind, well-liked and respected, everyone knows you, and you're honest. Maybe too honest to be a politician."

"Maybe," Bob allowed, "but the election's coming up. Maybe I'll enter and take the job out from under him and focus on pushing for a better town. A new Harper Valley."

Together they headed back to the entrance of the clearing.

"But that'd make you my boss," Wil realized, "and I'm not sure how I feel about that. Though it sure beats my current one. I think I like the idea. What about the farm?"

"Well, I'm getting a bit too old and tired to wanna keep running the place.

I think it's maybe time for Jeb to take over the business for good. But only if I win."

They stopped at the lip, looking at the town.

"*When* you win," said Wil. "And I'll be there every step of the way to help make it happen. Even if Sinclair beats you and fires me, I'm going to continue to make all of you proud."

Bob put his hand on Wil's shoulder. They enjoyed the view for a few more minutes in companionable silence. Maybe he'd never see the dragon again, but at least he had saved the day and gained a memento. It would have to be enough for now. Wil started back down the mountain, Bob just a few seconds behind him.

It had been an incredible few months. From coming back home for the first time in six years to fighting against nature and man to find his place in all of it.

Now, after having wrestled a storm into submission, Wil began to believe for the very first time that maybe he was capable of filling the role of resident wizard. Smiling, he set off for home, his father at his side.

The Piper

Pearl Patterson, eight years old, loved the fall. There was nothing like running around and jumping into piles of leaves, laughing as they flew everywhere. Apple and pumpkin pie, cool evenings, and the last surge of chores before winter became a time of relaxing and family and snowball fights. Well, the chores were done, it was still a little bit before dark, and she had nothing but free time to run around the farm.

Sometimes it got tiresome, being older than her three-year-old brother. He was too young to really play with, the way she liked, and he certainly was too small to climb on the stone wall separating their farm from the Manfreds', and dive into a pile of leaves. Pearl stood atop the three-foot-high wall and prepared herself. She took a deep breath and jumped, swinging her legs out in front of her so she would land sitting.

The leaves caught her and cushioned the fall. The landing stung, but in that harmless way that just exhilarated her and made her want to do it all over again. She got up, laughing and brushing herself off. After scooping the leaves back into one big pile, she froze.

At the edges of her hearing, the sharp, lilting tones of a flute played a little tune. Pearl looked up and around, searching it out. Hearing music wasn't so unusual on its own, but the Manfreds were a stuffy, stuck-up bunch who didn't like music, and the Pattersons didn't know how to play.

But the music came from the direction of her family's farm, on the west side of the valley, close to the forest. Pearl drifted that way slowly to hear better. And with every step she took, it got louder and louder. Before she knew it, she had walked to the edge of her family's property. She stood at the fence.

The music sounded happy and inviting. Just the playful high notes of a flute, rapidly alternating between high and low, as if the hidden player was just experimenting with sounds and having the time of their life.

"Hello?" Pearl called out. "Is somebody there?"

In response, the music changed, a playful flurry of notes like a bird singing. Pearl leaned over the fence, jaw slack as she looked around. A strong gust of wind made her blond hair flutter behind her. "Hello?"

The music stopped. From behind a tree came a little man. He was only maybe three and a half feet tall, not much shorter than she was. He wore funny, bright green clothes that looked like something out of a storybook, and he had a huge, warty nose. His skin was the same brown as the bark of the trees around him, and his vivid green eyes almost glowed.

"Hello, there!" He called out in a squeaky voice, doffing the green cap on his head and bowing low and respectfully to her. "Do you like music?"

He looked and sounded funny, different, but Pearl wasn't scared. He seemed harmless. She just smiled and nodded. "Yeah, I love music! Do you like playing music?"

The brown and green man danced a little jig in place. "I *love* music!" He put his flute parallel to his mouth and blew, fingers dancing over the holes. It sounded like musical laughter, and Pearl found herself laughing along with it.

"What about you, little girl? Do you like dancing? Do you want to dance to my music?"

Only then did Pearl realize how odd the situation was, and how her parents didn't know she was out on this side of the farm. Or that she didn't know who this strange man was, or even *what* he was. She bit her lip, then shook her head.

"I should probably go back inside." She looked back at the house.

"Nonsense!" the strange man squeaked. "You're already here, so why not have a bit of fun with me?"

"Mama said not to talk to strangers," she said, feeling lame for the excuse but also protected by it.

"Ahh, a wise woman," the stranger said, nodding. His big, bulbous nose bounced with the motion. "But consider this." He blew out another song, a fast trill of sounds that mellowed out into something soothing and low.

Pearl looked back at him. A smile spread across her face as the pleasant song lifted her mood and drew her in. It wasn't unlike a lullaby, soft and sweet and reassuring.

Thoughts of her mother, of uneasiness, of everything but the music melted into the background. They weren't gone so much as far away and unimportant. Nothing mattered compared to the sweet song of the squat brown man in his funny green outfit. Pearl found herself slipping through the bars of the fence, taking step after uneasy step in his direction.

The stranger bowed at her, never stopping his song. He motioned with his head for her to follow him and Pearl did, moving in an uneven, jerky manner. She was like a marionette being compelled to dance and move to the music. He ducked into the tree line, and Pearl went after him, caught up in a trance.

Normally, Pearl was kind of scared of the forest. Her parents had told her in no uncertain terms that the forest was off-limits unless she was with them. She could go into it a little, but she had to be able to see home from where she was. If she couldn't see home, then she was too far in and had to go back. Those were the rules. Now that the trees slipped on by her, some part of her that remained in control looked backward.

The house was a rapidly shrinking little box on the horizon. The song never stopped and her feet took her forward until the house slipped behind a thicket of saplings and disappeared from view entirely. Pearl turned back around, uncertainty gone. All that remained was her desire to follow the music wherever it took her.

Into the forest and up the mountain they went together. Animals froze in place, and Pearl was delighted to see a family of deer not far off their path. Their little hooves moved to the music, even if they stayed in place. The green man, as she came to think of him, took them around the deer, moving in circles. Pearl laughed in delight as she danced with the doe, who lowered her head and stomped her hooves to the melody.

And then they were off again, back on a trail only the green man knew.

Up, up, up the mountain they went, Pearl no longer jerky in her movements but smooth and flowing, completely caught up in the music. The green man hopped and skipped along, twirling in place as he played, never once making a mistake. The music curled around Pearl and drew her in deeper and deeper.

They finally stopped in a clearing about fifteen feet across, with no trees and relatively even ground. Clear, except for the ring of mushrooms in the center, about eight feet across. A small opening in the ring beckoned. The green man stood by it, blowing into his flute. He bowed his head and played.

Through the fog in her mind, Pearl felt a sudden spike of fear. Like something bad would happen if she went into the mushroom ring. Panic welled up inside her as her feet dragged her close and closer. She wanted to stop, but her body wouldn't cooperate. She just danced and swayed to the music.

The green man met her eyes. They were filled with wicked glee, mischief, and even loathing. Pearl didn't know why, but the green man hated her. Too late, she knew it was a trap. Tears rolled down her smiling face as she took one last step.

And disappeared entirely.

The green man stopped playing his music. He threw his head back, cap flopping with the motion, and let out a high-pitched, manic giggle. "One human child, delivered as promised."

He blasted one last trill of notes on his flute before he hopped into the ring and disappeared as well. The forest, still and silent, came back to life soon after.

An hour later, Pearl's mother went searching for her, growing increasingly terrified that something had happened to her child.

Pearl was just the first.

CHAPTER 48

First Snow

Wil always appreciated the way the world turned startlingly silent when it snowed. It seemed like as soon as the powder started coming down, the world went quiet and held its breath, waiting. He'd stayed up late the night it snowed, just enjoying watching through the window of his third-story bedroom. After the couple of weeks spent repairing the homes of Harper Valley, it felt like his first proper moment of peace.

Down it came, ponderously slow but relentless, blanketing the entire basin in white. Even now, well past his bedtime, he knew that tomorrow would be the first day of winter, when the residents of the valley took a break and enjoyed themselves. They'd have to make sure their animals were secure, and clean up the roads, but for the most part, it would be a day of rest.

For most of them, at least. The first snow of the season meant Wil had some very important tasks to finish, but that didn't necessarily make it work. He went to bed content, and slept until well past noon, enjoying the cozy warmth of his house keeping the biting cold at bay. When he woke the next day, nearly a foot of snow had piled up.

Wil started the day by getting up and parting the snow in front of his house with a wave of his hand. He got dressed and went out for breakfast, clearing the road as he went. Others could deal with the piles of show he shunted to the sides. The way he saw it, he was helping save them time and providing a path for others.

Once fed, he went home and spent most of the day in his lab, finishing up the prototypes of his latest project. Ones he had no intention of keeping if things went well. He had just finished up both of them when Darlene came down to the lab.

"A beautiful day like this and you're going to spend it in your lab? C'mon, Wil." Darlene was bundled up for the cold, looking cute and fashionable in a velvety red overcoat and black boots. A fuzzy white hat kept her head and ears warm and looked just the right amount of goofy.

Wil looked up from the two sleds he'd been working on. Neither of them looked like anything special, save for the markings he'd carved into them, odd characters that made perfect sense to him but would probably seem like gibberish to anyone else. "I'll have you know I was just about to go play in the snow. Care to join me?"

"Sledding, huh?" Darlene cocked her head to the side. "Is this what you've been hiding for the past couple of weeks? Making special sleds for us?"

"For the town, actually." Wil stood, picking up one sled and handing it to Darlene. It was about six feet long and looked far flimsier than it was. He took the other one and motioned for her to go. He followed.

"I've been thinking about how useful the carpet was," he said as they stepped out into the large yard behind the house. "Useful, but a bit dangerous. I thought with winter coming and how cold and snowy it can get, it might be good to have these in case people get lost or snowed in."

Darlene set hers on the ground and sat down. There were two little grooves for seats, one in front and behind. The front of the sled curled up and around, but there were two handholds built in beneath the lip. "So, how does it work? I'm assuming these aren't just normal sleds."

"You assume correctly." Wil set his down and climbed in. He put his hands on the two bars. "I layered a number of small enchantments onto these that, when used together, make the sled react to water or snow, propelling it forward when wet and—"

"Keep it simple for me," Darlene interrupted.

"Bram would want to hear how it works." Wil pouted.

"So explain it to Bram. Just tell me what to do!" Darlene said with a laugh.

"Fine, fine." Wil shook his head, chuckling. "Grab onto the handholds." When she did, he continued, "If you twist them both, the sled will move forward. If you twist only one, it will turn. It'll take some time getting used to it, but you make it go by twisting back and forth to control it. Like this."

Wil twisted the handles and the sled shot forward, gliding over the fresh snow and carving out a small path behind him. He shifted his grip and the sled turned to the left, skating dangerously close to the small drop at the end of his property onto the road, and going around back to where he started. He released the handles and the sled slid to a stop.

Darlene looked impressed, and a bit nervous. She never did get a chance to fly the carpet on her own. She twisted the handles and almost immediately let go, making the sled fly forward and stop just as suddenly. She let out a laugh as she nearly tumbled over the front.

"Think I should include some kind of harness or tie?" Wil asked.

"Shut up," Darlene said, twisting again and shooting forward. This time she was prepared for it and did a similar loop around the yard. But she didn't turn in time, and went over the side. She let out a startled yelp before she crashed.

Wil shot forward, stomach twisting as his sled shot over the edge too. He sailed over Darlene and landed surprisingly softly, sliding a bit before he saw she was fine and her sled was still moving. Together, their sleds powered down the snowed-in road.

"I'm okay, I'm okay," said Darlene, laughing again. "This is incredible! So much better than trying to trudge along in the snow or wait for the roads to be shoveled."

"Right?" Wil laughed and leaned forward, willing his sled to go faster. Maybe it was just his imagination, but he seemed to buy another few inches on Darlene as they headed toward downtown.

Wil always loved the sight of Harper Valley, but it was a special place when fall started becoming winter. Few of the trees had leaves left and were covered in snow, like the fields, farms, and houses. As they sped through, taking the long way around, Wil let his sled slow down just long enough to wave to children making a snowman. They watched with dropped jaws and widened eyes.

There were a few people in the town square, as there always were, and Darlene made a game of sledding by them close enough to startle them and spray a bit of snow on them. She laughed with delight as her father fell flat on his ass and got a faceful of snow as she passed. Jonjon cursed at them as they continued on.

"Was that really necessary?" Wil called out to her.

"Yes," said Darlene. Well, he couldn't argue with that.

They went alongside the river, not yet frozen over, though its edges were lined with chunks of ice. They went all the way to the north end of the valley, before it sloped down the mountain all the way to Orangeville. Darlene stopped first. Wil did a loop around her and stopped beside her.

"So, what do you think?" Wil asked.

Darlene rolled her eyes. "As if you need to be told they're amazing. It's funny, it's handy, and it'll be really useful. This will be a perfect thing to sell for the winter, if you can make them fast enough. Everyone and their kid will want one."

Wil's smile fell. "Ah, right. About that…"

Darlene sighed. "You plan on giving them away. For free."

"More or less," he said. "I was thinking about emergencies, and how much more ready everyone in the valley could stand to be, right? After the Nullbear and the dragon, I want to be sure that if something happens to me or if I'm elsewhere, people are going to be okay."

Her expression softened. "You did enough, Wil, seriously. You didn't fail anyone." It wasn't the first time they'd had this conversation.

"I know, I know." Wil took a deep breath and forced a smile on his face. She didn't get the responsibility he had, and maybe never would. That was probably for the best. "Just the same, I want to work harder to make sure nothing bad happens, if we can avoid it, right? Ever since I stopped the storm, I've just had this feeling that it's not over. That something's about to happen."

"Like your weird gut feelings about danger?" Darlene asked, turning in her sled and leaning on the curved lip at the front.

"Not quite." Wil paused, grinding his teeth together a bit in frustration. Truth was, he had no clue how to explain it. More than a hunch, less than his gut warning him. Just this sense of something coming.

"Maybe it's just paranoia. Maybe it's that surviving the storm changed me. Either way, I want to make a bunch of these sleds and give them to the city to use as they need. Just in case."

Darlene nodded. "I think it's not the worst idea. You figure we'll give some to the city and then you can sell others for personal use? It'd be perfect to add to all the medicine, beer, and other things you two have been making."

"I might make a lot for the city," said Wil. "Like, enough to give most major households one to use in case of emergency. Or maybe mostly the people living on the fringes, who would be most in danger if they got too snowed in to be able to get into town. I feel like throwing a few at Sinclair and selling the rest just helps his case."

There it was, the elephant in the room. Darlene leaned forward and took Wil's hand in her own. "I can't believe he's still hounding you over the storm, and trying to start things. You'd think he'd use it as a chance to build himself up as some big hero for your actions. Idiot. What are you going to do about him?"

The very question he'd been dreading. "I'm not sure there's anything for me *to* do," said Wil. "He may be a bastard, but he's a safe and well-connected bastard. The way I see it, the best thing is to just do my job well and try to stay on the people's good side while my dad gets ready to run against him."

Elections in Harper Valley took place over the winter. A single season of rest and conserving energy, a season dedicated to thinking about and discussing the year to come. They weren't quite there yet, and the announcement hadn't yet been made public, but in a month or so they would make it. As far as Wil knew, his dad was still talking to some key people about the race.

"So you're just going to hand these over and hope he does the right thing with them?" Darlene wasn't impressed.

"For now," said Wil. "I don't intend on taking his crap or being subservient to him anymore, but I'm not going to make things ugly unless he pushes me. If we're going to get rid of him, we do it the right way. The civilized way."

His girlfriend grimaced. "You do realize he won't be playing by the same rules, right?"

"I know."

Neither of them said anything for a while. Wil knew she wanted to go into a lecture about being less patient and instead being more aggressive. Well, she'd say 'passive,' but Wil fully believed it was patience. There was little point in accelerating things when there was still the chance of fixing things up or finding the perfect opportunity to make a move. It was as close as they got to fighting about anything.

"It's your choice," she said finally, looking away. "I'm not going to give you crap about it, but I do ask that you just keep in mind how much damage he can do if you let him."

"I'll keep it in mind," Wil promised. "I'm hoping these sleds might go toward making some kind of peace. Maybe I'll give him credit if he agrees to leave me alone and play nice."

"Hm. Let's get back," said Darlene. Without waiting, she twisted and the sled did a tight circle in the snow, heading back to town.

Wil followed after her, unable to resist smiling as the sleek sled moved over the snow. They were the perfect speed, without being too dangerous. At least around here. Kids were going to love these, but maybe Wil needed to make them a bit slower. That'd be easy enough next time if—

Darlene slowed to a stop. Wil stopped just after her. There in the road was Sheriff Frederick, bundled up as well but with the silver star of his office on his chest. One hand rested on the revolver at his side. Wil didn't need to be a wizard to have his gut warn him of danger here.

"Mr. McKenzie," the sheriff called out. "Been looking for you."

"How can I help you, Sheriff?"

Frederick's watery, suspicious eyes bore holes into him. "There's a problem," he said. "And we need your help."

CHAPTER 49

The Missing

W ell, that's rich, given the way Sinclair's been acting the past few weeks!"
Darlene wasted no time in laying into the sheriff. "Three weeks of
accusing him for not doing enough to divert a magical storm and now you're
gonna come crawling and—"

"You're not a part of this, miss," Sheriff Frederick said in his slow, thick
drawl. "This is between city hall and the resident wizard."

Darlene looked ready to throw a punch, but Wil stepped in between them.
"She is my business partner and assists me with my tasks. Anything you have to
say in front of me can be said in front of her." He turned and shot Darlene a look
that was equal parts warning and gratitude. "What's going on, Sheriff?"

Sheriff Frederick sniffed, making his droopy mustache bounce. "We've got
five missing people, and the mayor believes it's finally time to call you in on it."

Gods, five missing people and they intentionally waited to talk to him about
it until they had to? Wil didn't care about the distrust or the snub. He expected
those. But keeping it up while lives were potentially at risk crossed a line. It
crossed several lines, as far as he was concerned. Wil willed himself to calm down,
unballing his fists.

"We're on our way. Thank you for the message, Sheriff." Wil kept his voice
even and polite. He and the sheriff didn't get along, but that didn't mean there
was any reason to antagonize the man. Wil tugged on Darlene's hand and returned
to his sled. He flipped the direction and Darlene did the same.

A few seconds later they sped past the sheriff, going over the same trail they'd
made to get there. Darlene waited until the sheriff was out of sight before saying,

"Can you believe these people? They want to bully you into obedience and try to punish you when you say no, going so far as to deny other people help just to make you look bad!"

"He's a bastard," Wil agreed. "But until he's out of office, I need to work with him. I'm pretty angry at him too, but right now I'm more concerned about those missing people. Shouldn't be too hard to find them, so the fact that they chose not to tell me is…" Wil trailed off, shaking his head. "I'll handle this."

"Okay. I've got your back, of course," Darlene said.

Wil smiled at her before taking a sharp turn and spraying her with snow. Darlene cried out in surprise before laughing and going after him. They zigged and zagged around each other in the snow for the five minutes it took to get to city hall.

"Good morning, Ms. Stamos," said Wil to the receptionist.

The receptionist pursed her lips and pointed to the door. Wil inclined his head politely and tugged on Darlene's hand before she could try to defend him. Some people weren't worth trying to change, and Mary Stamos seemed to be the mayor's creature through and through.

Mayor Sinclair faced the window behind his desk. Wil and Darlene stepped up and waited. And waited. Wil sighed, wondering if he should say something about the intimidation attempt being childish when Darlene made the decision for him.

"Are you seriously going to try to posture when you've got missing people and need his help? Because we can go and come back later, when you're willing to act like an adult." Darlene bared her teeth in a fierce smile.

The mayor sighed and swiveled in his chair, turning to face them. His lean, middle-aged face looked droopy and tired. His cold eyes looked annoyed and resentful, as if Wil were a bug he was considering swatting. Mayor Sinclair steepled his hands together.

"I'm not posturing, I'm thinking," said the mayor, sounding much less jovial and a lot more calculating than Wil had ever seen him. "A gentle reminder that you don't need to be here, Ms. Johnson. I'm sure your new business has you wildly busy. Why don't you see to it, and let us do the talking?"

"Are you really suggesting I back off so the men can talk?" Darlene demanded.

Wil took her hand and squeezed it. "She stays. Mr. Mayor, I'm surprised that you didn't call on me earlier. Whatever differences we have, aren't the people of Harper Valley more important than that?"

Mayor Sinclair scowled. "I didn't reach out to you first because I needed to be sure that your new friends weren't the cause of the disappearances. After you brought nearly two dozen bandits into my town to be re-homed and find jobs, the sheriff and I have been waiting to see what kind of problems they bring with them. Transients like them are bad news."

There it was. "My friends from Appleton have been on their best behavior and have, in fact, been a tremendous benefit to this town. Unless you somehow missed the part where they spent the last few weeks rebuilding homes for the community."

"Your *friends* have been paid for their services," Mayor Sinclair sneered. "They were paid a fair wage for their work, and now that the work's dried up, I wouldn't put it past them to start taking from honest citizens of the valley. Their kind is never satisfied."

"Their kind?" Darlene scoffed. "They're from Appleton. They're our neighbors. They've fallen onto hard times, but that doesn't make them any different from us."

The mayor took a deep breath. By the second, he looked more and more ready to throw Darlene out. Wil would've loved to see him try. Instead, Sinclair just stood and went to the cabinet next to the window. He pulled out a decanter of amber liquid and poured himself a couple of fingers' worth. He sat back down with his drink, sipping on it.

"The thing that's really annoying about you and your friends," he started, wincing at the alcoholic burn, "is how soft-hearted you all are. You're still dumb kids, thinking the world's a whole lot better than it is. You don't know how things work. You'll buy a debt for a friend. You gotta give out products for damned near free. The bandits you stopped are actually good people. Bah."

As much as Wil knew he'd never seen the real Mayor Sinclair, the person in front of him now was a complete stranger. There was none of his affable bluster or smarmy positivity. He was older, tired, and bitter. Being the cause of that felt like something of a victory for Wil. He smiled.

"If my friends are behind it, it will be pretty easy for me to tell. I can just locate the missing people and ask them. Or, barring that, go to the places where people disappeared and do a bit of divination and find out exactly what happened. What details can you give me, Mr. Mayor?"

Mayor Sinclair downed the rest of his drink and all but slammed it on his desk. "Five missing people. Two adults, three children. All of them on the outskirts of town, along the forest and mountains to the west and north of town. They were all taken over the last three days."

Darlene made a distressed sound. "Three days? They've been gone for *three* days and you didn't call on him before now? How in the hell did you get terrified parents not to get big search parties going for their children? Especially after Wil already rescued the Lane kids from that Nullbear!"

The mayor's expression darkened. "That's what I've been trying to tell you, you stupid girl. If I let this news spread throughout town, I don't care how helpful they've been, those bandits would've been the first to be blamed. One of those scared, angry parents just has to level one accusation before it turns into blood. You want that on your hands? I sure don't.

"So I waited a bit, and got more information. Because I don't have the same childish faith in bad people you do. I was doing you all a favor, and maybe you should keep that in mind if you wanna keep pushing back against me."

Wil kept his breathing even, forcing his simmering temper to hold just a bit longer. It would be too easy to yell in the mayor's face or threaten him more or just make an ultimatum that may or may not accomplish something. None of that was important now. He and Darlene could be mad later.

"Who all has disappeared?" Wil asked.

"Old Gilbert Sully, both the Benton kids, Pearl Patterson, and Joey Jackson. Not that anyone's really worried about him," Sinclair said with a chuckle.

"What, just because he's homeless, no one cares about him?" Darlene looked ready to jump over the desk and strangle the man, and Wil probably would have let her.

"That's right. He was a somebody once, and now he's just a bum. He isn't much use to anyone, but he still disappeared. For all we know, he just froze to death from last night's snow."

"Thank you, I'll get right on investigating," Wil said, stopping another outburst from Darlene before it began. She shot him a betrayed look but understood. "Is there any other information that might be relevant?"

The mayor shook his head.

"Right. We'll be off, then." Wil and Darlene both stood. Mayor Sinclair didn't bother. Wil made to turn around but stopped partway through, as if remembering something. "There's something else I wanted to discuss with you. I've got a gift for the city. And I do mean the city as an entity, and not you."

Sinclair scoffed but motioned with his hand for Wil to continue.

"Magic self-propelling sleds," said Wil. "With winter at hand, I thought the city could use an easier way of getting around in case of emergencies. For the sheriff and rescue parties or checking on some of the older residents who live alone."

That changed Sinclair's expression instantly, back to one of interest and even greed. "Self-propelling sleds? That *will* be handy. How many do you have for me?"

"We have two, but I can make more before too long." Wil smiled. "Ideally I'd give these away to people in need, but if I don't have your cooperation in distributing them and keeping track of who has them, then I might need to sell them myself."

"Your point is made," Sinclair said with a sigh. "Leave them with Ms. Stamos, and I'll check them out in a bit. The city would be…most grateful for your contributions."

Darlene chimed in, "Just so long as they know those contributions are from Wil and his stupid, childish good heart."

They left together, stopping only to bring the sleds in and stack them next to a confused Ms. Stamos's desk before they walked back out, heading for the Stevenson farm.

"I can't believe you let him talk to you like that," Darlene said. "You deserve better. And you said you wanted to fight back, so why just take it?"

Wil shrugged, stepping carefully to avoid a patch of ice on the ground. Their sledding had helped make a path through the road before crews could shovel it, but it still wasn't completely safe.

"The way I see it, he expects me to be a pushover and not fight back unless I have to. Let him whine and gripe and make threats. We'll knock him off his perch, and then we'll have the last laugh. No use getting too mad about it now, right?"

Darlene thought about it. "That's true. And unexpectedly wise of you. That's my job! So, five missing people. How do you plan on finding them?"

"First, we get Bram. Then I make some wands and go around and collect blood samples to help us find them. We'll go to where they disappeared and work from there. With the three of us, should be plenty safe. With any luck, we'll have at least one of them back by nightfall, if not all of them."

Darlene sighed. "Here's hoping."

CHAPTER 50

Lost in the Woods

After taking a few hours to prepare and talk to scared families, Wil, Bram, and Darlene assembled at the east edge of Harper Forest. It was just before two o'clock and they had at least four hours of daylight left. Wil had quickly crafted some basic wands to use as a focus while Darlene collected blood samples and clothing for him. This time, they got full cooperation.

Bram came packed with the latest fruits of his labor: some basic healing potions, bandages, a suture kit, and water and food, just in case. It all fit in a pack nearly as enormous as he was, but he didn't complain one bit as they stopped just before the tree line.

Wil brought out a wand, carved with minuscule runes to help guide the spell. Tracking wasn't hard, but the focus made it so much easier. Darlene pulled out a sock with a tiny bit of blood on it. She gingerly handed it over to Wil, who tied it to the wand. It looked stupid, but it would work.

"Alright. This shouldn't take too long," said Wil, closing his eyes and channeling just a little bit of his magic into the wood. He felt for the power in the blood and tied it into the simple searching spell. The wand rolled around in his hand before it pointed southeast, where they'd gotten the blood sample.

"Uh. Does that mean the Benton kids aren't actually kidnapped?" Bram asked, adjusting his glasses as the three of them looked down at the wand.

"That doesn't seem right," said Darlene. "They wouldn't lie about this. And even if they were lying, that's three other people missing."

Wil frowned. He twisted the wand back toward the forest, but in seconds it spun around in his palm and pointed southeast. "It's not reading the children's blood at all. That's weird." He set the wand down in the carpet bag he'd brought with them, bringing out another.

Darlene grabbed another bloody piece of clothing, this time the torn off arm of a little girl's dress, stained brownish red with blood. She handed it over to Wil, who ran the dried blood along the wand before tying it on, just to be certain.

The wand spun north, and then east. Away from the forest and back to the Patterson house. Wil dropped it to the ground in frustration. "This shouldn't be happening. Even if they were…were dead, it should lead me to their bodies, at least. I don't understand what's going on."

"I've got a bad feeling about this," said Bram, eyeballing the trees. "Is it just me or does the forest look different today?"

Wil was about to tease him for always being nervous when he looked up and frowned. There was nothing explicitly wrong with Harper Forest. It was the same spread of trees and rocks leading upward into the mountain as it always was, but something did feel different. Off. It was the smell, maybe. When Wil breathed in the air, it didn't fill him with the usual comfort of pine scent and earth. There was something cloying, something heavy that made even Wil hesitate.

"That's weird," said Darlene, taking a step forward. "I've never been scared to go into the forest before. And I'm not scared now," she added hastily. "It's just… nervousness? It doesn't make sense."

"Do you think we should go and get more people first?" Bram asked.

Wil shook his head. "No. The five of them disappeared in the woods, and it's my responsibility to find them, or else our Appleton friends are going to get blamed for the disappearances. You can go home if you want to—I won't hold it against you."

Bram snorted. "You might not, but I would. I'm going in. You can protect us from anything in there, right?"

"Yeah, probably. Just stay behind me, I guess, and we'll see what's going on."

It may have been hesitantly, even begrudgingly, but the three of them entered the forest.

For a while, none of them spoke. The only sound was the snow crunching under their boots, and the occasional rustle of the wind in the trees. In the spring and summer, you couldn't see very far into the forest for all the greenery and life. Now, in the last days of autumn, the trees were all bare, and it seemed an endless white expanse.

They kept their eyes peeled, but there wasn't much to look at, except the occasional small animal, ducking out of sight almost as soon as they were spotted. That more than anything bothered Wil. Though the birds weren't as active this time of year, there should've at least been some birdsong, or even just the cawing of crows.

They took a step past one particularly large tree, and suddenly, the snow ended. Wil stopped abruptly, and Bram almost crashed into him.

"What the hell?" Darlene asked, stepping forward and craning her head in all directions. It was like they'd been transported into a pocket of spring. The trees were all in full bloom and there was no snow anywhere, not even behind them.

"This can't be happening, right?" Bram asked, not moving from behind Wil. "Where did the snow go? What's going on, Wil?"

"I don't know," said the wizard, just as confused and impressed as his friends. He pulled away from Bram and took another few steps forward. Now there were sounds, off in the distance. Footsteps, the crack of twigs being stepped on. More than anything, a feeling that they weren't alone. The trees loomed ominously around them, watching their every move.

"I think we might be in over our heads now," said Wil. He racked his brain trying to think of what could've caused such a shift in the environment, but only a few answers came to mind. None of them good. "How about we go back the way we came and come back with more people after all?"

"Yeah," said Darlene, "sounds good to me. I don't like this. This feels wrong. Like this isn't Harper Forest anymore."

The weirdest part of all was how cold it still felt. The chill in the air was worse partially up the mountain. Wil nodded and motioned for them all to go back the way they had come. Part of him expected that as soon as they went far enough, the snow would return and things would feel more normal again.

But that didn't happen. This frigid dream of spring continued, and the forest only got weirder. Strange, bright pink flowers grew on the side of a tree, shaped like stars with odd dips in the petals. Mushrooms big enough for them to use as chairs grouped up around some of the trees. And directly where they'd entered the woods was a wall of thorny briars, choking the forest and blocking their way out.

"Wil? Please tell me you've got *some* idea of what's happening," Bram all but whimpered.

A dozen possible scenarios flashed through Wil's mind, all of them as possible as they were illogical. "Well, I'm not ruling out the possibility of a bad dream," he joked.

Darlene reached over and pinched his arm.

"Ow!"

"Not a dream, then," she said, a forced smile finding its way on her face. Her eyes darted around wildly, like she expected something to jump out at them. "What else you got?"

"Accidentally walked into a different world," said Wil, rubbing where she pinched him. "We could have been mesmerized or enchanted. Or, worst of all, there's another magic user in the forest and they're messing with us and trying to get us scared and confused. Let's keep moving for now."

They traveled south along the seemingly endless thicket of briars. Twenty minutes later, they were still at it with no signs of an end.

"This can't be real," said Bram after a while. "Could we have actually walked into another world? Is that a thing that happens?"

"Not as much anymore, but when we first settled Calipan, it happened a lot. Before we tamed the continent, there was a lot of magical wildlife here," said Wil, stopping and reaching for the water Bram had brought. He took a few sips and passed the bottle over to Darlene. "Plenty of pocket worlds intersecting with this one before they just sort of collapsed when we kept expanding. But I don't think this is a pocket world."

No one said anything at first. No one wanted to be the first to admit they were scared after spending nearly an hour out there, half of it now in a weird, wrong version of their forest. They just stood there sharing water, until Darlene risked reaching out to poke a thorn on the briars.

Her hand went right through it. "Huh," she said, pulling her hand back. "That's weird."

"Weird? Of course! How could I have been so stupid?" Wil wanted to slap his forehead. He reached out a hand toward the briars, and, as he suspected, nothing was actually there. Nothing would be there. "Okay, get ready for this, everyone. Someone beat me at my own game."

"Ohhh," said Bram in understanding. "Illusion?"

"Illusion!" said Darlene.

"Illusion," Wil confirmed. He ran a hand over the briars and focused. Breaking illusions and enchantments was different from breaking other spells. Illusions like this were often simple but sturdy, blanketed over a large region with just a couple of senses to fool, and usually a skilled illusionist could take shortcuts to make the subjects do the work for them.

Illusions were often discounted or scoffed at by other wizards because of how easy they were to handle once you knew you were dealing with them, but people underestimated the power of a good illusion. Just as they tended to underestimate illusionists. Once Wil felt for the subtle changes in the world brought on by the illusion, it just took magical muscle to disrupt it.

All at once, the trees were bare and they were knee deep in snow, down near the canyon Wil had turned into a lake. If they'd kept going in that direction for much longer, they might have fallen a hundred feet down into the lake. Wil tried not to let that get to him.

"Wow, we really went far, didn't we?" Darlene gaped, looking around to get her bearings.

"But what does this mean?" Bram demanded. "Who did this, and why?"

"I don't know," said Wil, "but whoever did it is very skilled with magic. Probably more skilled than me, possibly stronger. The amount of power it would take to blanket an entire forest in a stable illusion like that...I suppose I could do it if I tapped into the leyline up top. But that might mean whatever, whoever, is out there is using it. And frankly, I don't feel safe barging up there without knowing what we're getting into."

"Another magic user," Darlene repeated, looking up toward the peak of the mountain. "And whoever is responsible for the illusion is likely responsible for the missing people as well."

Again, silence. Missing people were already a big problem, but this...this complicated things. Wil couldn't just go off half-cocked and expect things to go well. He'd been lucky with the dragon, but this new problem—he'd be ready for it.

"C'mon," said Wil. "Let's go to my parents' house. We might be able to get the Appleton crew to help us look, if it means making sure they're not blamed for it."

"Jerry and Danielle still staying with your parents?" Bram asked.

Wil chuckled. "Yeah, they get along really well. We'll grab a bite to eat, talk it over. I'm sure we'll figure something out."

Darlene took Wil's hand and led the way. She gripped it tight enough that Wil knew her to be worried. He was too. Bram tromped behind them, shifting the pack on his back. They headed off for the McKenzie farm.

CHAPTER 51

Magical Threats

All three of them returned, slightly shaken—Wil because he didn't have any answers, only more questions, and Darlene and Bram because Wil was. They were all in a funk by the time they arrived at the McKenzie farm. And by the time they got to the porch, Bob and Jerry knew something was wrong.

"What's eatin' you three?" Bob called out before lighting his pipe and puffing away. He passed it over to Jerry. The two were fast friends and nearly inseparable now. Danielle and Sharon were likely inside.

"There are missing people; the mayor waited to tell me; he plans on blaming it on Jerry and his people if we don't find out what happened; and I found some magic and signs of someone messing around in the forest," Wil listed off on his fingers. "So, all in all, today's been a bit rough. You sharing?"

"Of course," said Bob, and Jerry handed over the pipe. Wil brought it to his lips and puffed, then inhaled deeply. One hit wasn't going to do much, but after the last couple of hours, just the act of smoking helped calm him a little.

Bram sniffed the air. "Your mom is cooking, and she could probably use some help, no?" He unshouldered his pack, set it by the front door, and headed inside.

Wil and Darlene grabbed chairs and dragged them to form a little circle. "He eats when he's nervous," Darlene said, motioning with her head indoors.

"I've got worse habits than that," Jerry said with a belly-jiggling chuckle. "Now what's this about missing people?"

Wil told them about the sleds, which he couldn't resist bragging about, the meeting with the mayor, and then their tense trip through the forest. Darlene chipped in occasionally, adding a detail he forgot or her own thoughts.

"So this is good, right?" Jerry asked after another puff. "It's not like any of my people can do magic or nothing. You're the only one around these parts who can, right? That's why you're the big shot wizard?"

Darlene made a face. "It might clear you and your people, or it might not. Sinclair's going to want to blame this on someone, and I don't think he cares who. If it's not your people, it might be Wil, since magic's involved."

Wil jerked upright in his seat. The thought hadn't occurred to him. At this point, he was still reeling from the fact that he had another wizard to deal with. Or someone else capable of that kind of complex illusion. "Even he wouldn't go that far," said Wil of the mayor.

"Don't be too sure of that," Bob said darkly. "Never underestimate a pissed-off politician. A man like Sinclair, he's built his entire life out of being on top and having people bow down to him. You're refusing, and there's a problem in the town, and if he can kill two birds with one stone...well, you either gotta put an end to this or fly away."

Jerry coughed to get attention and asked, "So, uh, what do you think it could possibly be?"

Wil didn't answer at first. He took another hit off the pipe and rocked in his chair, thinking. "It could be another wizard," said Wil. "That's the easiest answer, but I don't know who it could be. The thing about going to Saint Balthazar's is, it let me network and learn a lot about most of the famous wizards operating today, on top of getting to know the other up-and-coming wizards.

"I can't think of any of them who might do something like this. Mostly because we're all busy. Between the edges of territory where there's still the wild and danger and the war down south with Ilianto, there's a lot of demand for wizards to protect and serve communities. I actually had to fight to get put back here in Harper Valley. There were about half a dozen different places that wanted me."

"Yeah, yeah, brag later," Darlene teased him. He smiled at her, shaking his head and continuing.

"Point is, wizards are stretched thin, and it's not like there's anyone else who wants Harper Valley. If there is a rogue magic user, it might not be a wizard. It could be a witch or warlock."

"Of course," said Bob. "But for those of us not in the know, what does that mean?"

Wil chuckled. "They've got access to magic as well, but it's not a part of them, like it is with me. Witches gain their power from nature and rituals. They're often fiercely independent and not very friendly. Territorial, usually. And warlocks gain their powers by trafficking with other powers. They form contracts with devils, demons, and the fae for a taste of power."

"Are either of those two dangerous to a master wizard?" Jerry asked, uncertain.

"I don't know my ass from a hole in the ground on the subject, but you seem pretty strong."

Wil just shrugged, not sure how to answer that without scoffing at the idea of being powerful. "Any magic user is a potential danger. Witches are tenacious survivors and if one got into the forest and decided it was theirs, it could get ugly. As for warlocks, it depends on how favored they are with their dark patron. I just don't see the motivation for doing this.

"Honestly, I think it might have something to do with that dragon I stopped. Or saved. Whatever." Wil shifted in his seat, leaning forward and speaking more animatedly. "It's been bothering me ever since I woke up after that. What was a dragon doing here, and what cursed it? It called the basin home, but I've seen neither hide nor hair of it since. No one has."

The four sitting there thought about it. Bob packed another bowl for them all, and Wil welcomed the chance to destress and let his mind wander. The best solutions were ones that came to you when you finally let go. The more he thought about it, the more he was convinced the missing people and illusion in the forest did have to do with the dragon somehow, but then Darlene burst his bubble.

"But motivation, right?" she asked, taking the pipe for herself. "What motivation would that dragon have for stealing people and casting an illusion on the forest? You said it looked and sounded sick and out of it. Why would it linger and hurt people?"

Wil didn't have an answer to that. His gut told him he was right, but the answer wasn't complete. Not yet. There were still pieces missing, and it felt like they were right in front of his face. Between the missing children and the illusions, something did come to mind. Especially with the odd plants they'd seen in the illusion, that taste of a different land's spring.

The sun hung halfway over the mountains. Wil stared at it while brooding over the pipe, wishing that inspiration would strike. He got his wish before too long.

"What's that?" Jerry asked, pointing off in the distance. The other three followed his gaze to the next field over, belonging to their neighbors. A bright orange light danced in the air, bouncing back and forth.

Wil's blood ran cold. That wasn't natural—at least, it hadn't been for probably a hundred years. The light flew through the air to a rhythm only it could hear, swooping over the fields as it approached. "That's a wisp," he blurted.

"A wisp?" Bob grunted. "Like, from the stories of the old frontier?"

Wil didn't have time to answer. The wisp flew around in a spiral, climbing higher in the sky until it shone like a little star. The ground rumbled. Wil got up from his chair and stepped off the porch. In the distance, near the barn, all of their cows, sheep, goats, and chickens poured out of their barns and coops.

As did Jeb, who had been taking them in for the night before the wisp appeared. The wisp hung there for a second as all the animals circled around it, constantly moving and following its motion with their heads. Wil had a bad feeling in his gut, just a normal one and not a special one, before the wisp moved again. It took off in their direction, a light tinkling sound in the air as it got close.

The herd chased after the wisp, picking up speed and making a racket as their hooves cleaved through snow and cleared a path right for the house. Jeb ran after them awkwardly, stepping from one gap in the snow to the next until he ended up in the groove the cows had left behind.

Wil ran up to meet the animals, concentrating on the first spell that came to mind. When he spoke, it came out as a long, groaning moo sound as he addressed the cows. "Go back inside, this thing's dangerous! Turn back now!" Cows were pretty easy to bully into behaving, normally. Not these ones.

"Shiny!" one of them groaned.

"Shiny, shiny, shiny!" another cried. The cows got closer and Wil tried to remember how wisps worked. It wasn't an illusion, it was something more dangerous. Mesmer magic.

"Wil, get out of there!" Darlene yelled from behind him as the cows in front came dangerously close to just plowing through them.

"I got this," he mooed back before he remembered to cancel the spell.

The wisp came closer, and Wil swore he heard it laughing in its weird sound, like delicate crystals shattering. It went right past him, the herd picking up speed behind it. Wil had to think fast. He held up his hand and formed a ball of glowing light. He pulsed it rapidly, bright-dim-bright, bright-dim-bright, faster and faster.

It caught the herd's attention and they turned from the wisp to him. Wil froze as they poured in around him, turning in tight circles, their bodies pressing against him on all sides. All the animals, big and small, looked at Wil and the wisp, attention split.

Wil poured a bit of extra magic into the light. Nothing major or huge— just a little suggestion, flashing when the light did. Peace. Calm. Rest. Home. Repeating again and again as he waved the ball of light back and forth and a few dozen heads followed it with interest. Their agitation died down. The wisp sparkled brightly, turning from orange to bright red, and then sped off into the night. The animals didn't follow.

With it gone, Wil released the light and sighed, resting up against their cow Gianna and patting her on the side. "You weren't really going to stampede me," he muttered. "I know you better than that." Gianna just mooed and stomped in place.

"What the hell was that?" Jeb demanded as he finally caught up with the animals. "One second I'm making sure they're secure, the next all the doors fly open and that weird light goes by and all these bastards go running!"

Everyone else came out of the house to see the commotion. They crowded around Wil.

"Well," said Wil, "I've got some good news and bad news. The good news is that I know what's behind the disappearances and this."

"Okay, great," said Bram. "What's the bad news?"

Wil sighed. "It seems we've attracted the attention of the fae."

CHAPTER 52

Under Attack

Fae? Like faeries and stuff?" Sarah wasn't impressed.

Wil sighed. "Yeah, like faeries and stuff. Only, the real thing, not whatever stories you remember. The real thing is a lot more dangerous. More because of what we don't know than what we *do*. And as far as I know, fae haven't been seen in these parts in nearly a hundred years, when they left Harper Valley entirely."

"What do we know about them?" Bram asked, wringing his hands together. At least he looked appropriately nervous, although unless Bram was hyperfixated on something that excited him, he always seemed a little nervous.

Wil's family and friends surrounded him, looking for answers. He took a deep breath and tried to think where to start. "So, they were the original inhabitants of Calipan when we first got to the continent and started spreading. Humans have magic, but the fae live and breathe magic. They look and sometimes sound similar to us, but they're not like us. They're tied to nature and are older than we are by far.

"They're not just one people but a collection of many different peoples. The only things that unite them are that they're proud and easily insulted, they don't tell direct lies, and they have a lot of reasons to hate us."

"What do you mean, 'don't tell direct lies'?" Sharon asked, incredulous. "You saying they're all honest?"

Wil shook his head. "No, as far as I know, they love to deceive people, but they're largely indirect and tricky."

"As far as you know?" Jeb asked, looking back in the direction the wisp had flown. "How much experience you got dealing with them? And why would they hate us?"

"I... None, really," Wil admitted. "They're reclusive and they avoid humans these days. They hate us because we drove them off and took their land, for the most part." That was a somewhat controversial stance at the academy, but as far as Wil was concerned, it was true. "When we made our westward push across the continent, they had to retreat.

"For the most part, we don't mix well, and we came in overwhelming numbers and kept spreading. They're more dangerous than us if we don't see it coming, but we grow up faster and have more kids and our weapons are good at driving them away. If there are still fae around and we managed to piss them off, this could be bad."

That much seemed obvious, but someone needed to say it so they'd understand how bad things could get. Maybe it didn't have to be bad, maybe there was still a way to salvage things. Wil honestly didn't know. Much like staring the storm straight in the eye, it was a problem a lot larger than him. Unlike the storm, it wasn't one he could fight with brute force. Probably.

"So these fae are behind the kidnapped children?" Jerry asked, his arm around his wife. "The ones we're about to be blamed for if things don't get taken care of?"

"Don't worry about that," Darlene said, standing beside Wil. "We're not going to let that happen. We've all seen this and we know what the problem is. Now we just need to take it to the mayor and figure out what to do about it. Right?" She turned to Wil.

He nodded, biting his lip. As he opened his mouth to say something hopefully reassuring, his stomach twisted. He groaned and looked around. The sun had already set and the moon was still rising in the sky, giving him just enough light to see by. He wasn't the only one. Bob pointed at their neighbors' farm.

"Is the Hagger house on fire?"

Gods, it was. "I'll handle this," said Wil, and he took off. He went down the drive, which at the very least had gotten shoveled by his father and Jeb earlier that day. It took him on a roundabout path to the fire, but on the way, it gave him a better look at what was going on. Not only was one side of the enormous house on fire, but there were half a dozen little men dancing in front of it, hollering and whooping at the sight.

When Wil got close enough to see clearer, he stopped before they noticed him. The little sharp-featured men had bright-red eyes that almost glowed, and skin in various shades of brown and green. Funny little hats topped their heads. They looked sinister, but their high-pitched giggles took away some of the effect.

One of them opened his hand and a swirling fireball formed there. He lobbed it at the house in a high, lazy arc that came down on the roof and knocked tiles down, spreading more fire. As one, they howled with laughter, sounding something like "heehee, hoohoo."

The front doors of the house opened and the Hagger family poured out into the snow. They'd been having dinner and their toddler still had a messy bib on and food all over his face. The four of them got away from the house and looked up at the fire, then down at the little goblins, as Wil now identified them. Their ten-year-old daughter let out a scream.

The goblins screamed right back, running around in circles in a panic at being discovered, before one of them had the bright idea of hurling a fireball at the family.

Wil gasped and reflexively threw up his best shield in front of them. A silvery disc of light appeared right before the ball would've beaned Mr. Hagger in the head, and the fireball detonated harmlessly against his magic. The entire family flinched and ducked, but they were safe.

As one, the goblins faced Wil, now unsure of themselves and their situation. Well, they weren't alone. Wil would have preferred they talk it out, but was there any talking to a group of gleeful arsonists? No, he knew what he had to do. Wil spread his legs and dug himself in, feeling for the chill in the air.

As he gathered power from himself and his surroundings, the biggest, wartiest goblin of them all pointed at Wil and said, "Get the wizard!" All the goblins in his gang conjured up little fireballs. That was fine. They were too late.

Cold in the air, cold in the ground, cold in his bones. Wil drew on it and blew out his breath, fogging in the evening air. The snow in front of him twisted and rose, spinning and picking up speed as he swirled the air in a rising tornado. It would've been easier with a breeze, but he had more than enough power to move air around, and with air, so much snow.

The first volley of fireballs flew into his tornado and were promptly flung right back at the goblins, who ducked for cover. Their fireballs hit the ground around them, detonations sending snow flying everywhere. That snow got caught up by Wil's tornado as the flurry grew. Wil sent it up and across the Haggers' roof. Tiles and loose bits of wood went flying but the snow covered and smothered the fire, and Wil released it, letting out a held breath.

The goblins scrambled to their feet. Wil pointed a finger at them and enhanced his voice. "WHY ARE YOU DOING THIS? WHAT HAVE YOU DONE WITH OUR CHILDREN!?"

Wil wasn't sure if he expected a real answer or if he just needed to say it. He certainly didn't expect seven goblins and four humans to start talking all at once.

"You humans have it co—"

"What are those things? Julie, get behind—"

"I'm here, Wil, I got this!" Bram, of all people, came running up, distracting Wil. He jerked around, and the goblins took their opportunity to start running.

"Hey, get back here!" Wil called out, but Bram was one step ahead of him. He grabbed a vial from his belt and hurled it with surprising accuracy. It hit the back of a goblin's head and shattered. The goblin and her nearest buddy fell to the ground, limbs splayed out but not moving. The rest kept on running and disappeared into the night.

"What the hell was that?" Wil asked, impressed.

Bram grinned and pulled another vial from his belt. "A paralysis potion! When we went to the forest, I brought a few different things I've been working on, just in case of trouble."

"Not a bad idea!" Wil said, reaching up to clasp Bram's shoulder.

"What's going on here? What were those things?" Mr. Hagger demanded, reminding Wil he still had a job to do.

"Okay, so," he said, turning to his neighbor. "It's like this…"

All things considered, it wasn't too difficult to explain what had happened. The fact that they had two prisoners who were clearly not human helped. Bram and the others caught up before too long and they tied up the goblins, who couldn't move but were aware enough to follow them with their glowing red eyes. It was more than a little disconcerting, but they were at the bottom of Wil's growing list of problems.

The McKenzie and the Hagger farms weren't the only ones hit that night. Several families had been attacked or pranked or generally annoyed by the fae. Wil found this out when Sheriff Frederick came for him half an hour later with a dead elf in tow.

"What's this thing?" the sheriff asked, letting the sled with the dead elf drop behind him.

Wil looked behind him and winced. The elf was a young-looking female, maybe four feet tall, with golden skin and hair. She had a bullet hole in her chest, and a look of surprise stuck on her face.

"You killed her?" Wil demanded.

Sheriff Frederick shrugged. "She was trying to get the mayor. Found his front door open and a few girls like this surrounding him. Thought they were gonna hurt him, so I fired a warning shot. Two of them ran off, and this one stayed, so the next shot went in her chest. What is it?"

"One of the fae," said Wil, strength leaving him. He leaned against a fence for support, closing his eyes and trying to get the horrible image out of his head. Her blank, staring face was seared into his brain. They were under attack by the fae, and now there was a body count.

"How many others?" Wil heard himself ask. "How many dead bodies do we have?"

The sheriff grunted and said, "Three. One human, two of these fae, I guess. The entire town was hit. The mayor wants to see you."

Wil rubbed his temples. "I'm sure he does. Tell him I need to clean up a few things here and then I'll talk to him. But the main point is, we need a town hall meeting. Tomorrow. This is top priority."

Sheriff Frederick stared him down.

Wil frowned. "Are you going to give me trouble or are you going to cooperate so I can help protect this town? Get moving, Sheriff!"

That may have been the wrong move to make, judging by the way the suspicious old man's hand went for his gun. But in the end, Frederick nodded and walked off, dragging the elf and two tied up goblins with him. Wil walked back to his friends.

"How bad is it?" Darlene asked, face paler than usual.

"Pretty bad," said Wil. "I think this may be the start of a possible war."

CHAPTER 53

Town Hall

Wil couldn't recall the last time he'd been in a town hall meeting, but he didn't remember it being this full. The hall was packed to capacity and then some, with a few people standing in the back and outside the doors. So many people helped negate the growing chill in the air. Or maybe it was just Wil, hot under the collar.

At least one member from every household had shown up. They were ten minutes past noon and still Mayor Sinclair sat in his seat next to Sheriff Frederick, waiting. Wil tried to catch his eye a few times, but the mayor did everything in his power to not look his way. He'd taken the information Wil had given relatively well, and then went back to treating him like a foe.

Wil didn't understand it. He didn't much care for Sinclair either, but you didn't see him deliberately not communicating when a crisis came to town. It was childish and insecure, and it wasn't helping.

Sinclair stood up and walked to the podium. Wil straightened in his chair, looking around the room. It seemed so much bigger from this angle, with floodlights bearing down on him.

The mayor started simply, bowing his head in sorrow. "Thank you for coming here to discuss this current crisis. I understand that many of us have suffered losses and damage from this unprecedented attack. Harper Valley stands as one, and together we will deal with this problem and punish those responsible for the acts of vandalism, arson, and violence against our community.

"You may have heard the rumors, but now I must unfortunately confirm them to be true: a few of our citizens are missing, presumably taken by this new threat. However, Sheriff Frederick has a few prisoners of his own, and with the help of our resident wizard, Wilbur McKenzie, we have every confidence that we'll be able to get everyone back and resolve this. If you have any questions, please direct them to Mr. McKenzie."

Sinclair inclined his head to the town and ducked away from the podium. He shot Wil an inscrutable look, motioning for him to get up. Wil stood and took his place. The town hall was one of the few places truly wired up with electricity and the latest technology, and with the microphone, he didn't even need to enhance his voice. He just had to address fifteen hundred or more people who were scared and upset.

"Hello," he started. "I'm sure you all have plenty of questions, and—"

"You're damned right we got questions! Where's our children!?" A man with a large blond mustache in the front stood up, glaring at Wil as if he were personally responsible for the attacks.

"Mr. Patterson," Wil addressed him, "I'm working on that. My initial search didn't turn up your Pearl or any of the other missing people, but we discovered a disturbance in Harper Forest, and—"

"If they're in the forest, why don't we just all go up in there and find them?" a woman a few rows back called out.

"Did the attackers from last night come from the forest?" another person asked.

"What the hell were those things?"

On and on the questions came. Wil briefly glanced over at the mayor, who looked mildly pleased by his discomfort. Sighing, Wil took a deep breath and raised a hand. All sound cut out as his silence spell blanketed the hall. Although a sort of oppressive heaviness fell over the audience, a weight lifted from Wil.

"Those creatures last night were various members of the fae," Wil spoke clearly into the microphone. "Elves, goblins, hobs, faeries, a wisp…They're all different species but collectively belong to the indigenous population of Calipan. The ones we pushed out hundreds of years ago and who were in hiding. Until now."

Tentatively, Wil released the silence spell. Someone coughed, but other than that, they waited on his word. Wil took a deep breath and continued. "We don't know how or why the fae are suddenly here and causing trouble, but I'm working on it to figure things out. But before I do, we need to focus on the safety of our community. And to that end, there are a few things you should know.

"The fae are highly magical and are not to be underestimated. Even the tiniest of them can cast spells as easily as you or I breathe, and they can be subtle. They're masters of illusions and compulsions. In the past, they've used this for hit-and-run tactics, and, well, they like to cause mischief. As I'm sure some of you have noticed by now."

One hand went up. Wil pointed at Mr. Hagger, who stood. "You were there last night. A bunch of those fae things were at my house and they set it on fire. Is that your idea of mischief?" A few murmurs agreed with him.

"No," said Wil, "not my idea of mischief at all. But it might be *theirs*. In a lot of ways, they look like us, but they are not us. And it's those differences that might save us. Despite their advantage with magic, they are generally a lot weaker than us, and are particularly susceptible to our weapons. They're allergic to iron, which causes them extreme pain and can interfere with their illusions and enchantments."

Most of it was true, though Wil didn't think the residents of Harper Valley cared for the finer details about different kinds of fae. There hadn't been any sightings of ogres or anything truly dangerous. The details Wil had gotten from the mayor, the sheriff, and the people who'd rushed to spill their problems before the meeting made it clear the attack was carried out by the smallest and least harmful fae. He didn't know if that meant something, but he wasn't ruling it out.

"Some things you should know about the fae. They're intelligent, and they're proud. They do not take well to being insulted and it's possible they have perceived something we've done as an insult."

And just like that, the entire hall erupted with protests and angry farmers misunderstanding him. Wil sighed, mentally counted to five, and then silenced the hall again.

"I am not saying they're right to attack us, just that there has to be a motive, and we need to consider every possibility." He released the spell and a hand shot up. Reluctantly, Wil called on the woman.

"What do we do if there's another attack?" Mrs. Lane asked, clutching her son Ralph's hand. "What if they come for us again?"

It was exactly what Wil needed. "I'm glad you asked that, Mrs. Lane. An iron horseshoe above your front door is said to keep them from entering. Additionally, a ring of salt around yourself or your children will keep them from directly harming or bewitching you. It will not, however, stop them from acting against you. There were a few instances of burning houses last night. If you're going to use a ring of salt, you should probably do it outdoors."

Another hand went up. Wil braced himself. "Kenny. Yes, what's your question?"

Kenny Landrome was a few years older than Wil, and the kind of man with only one thing on his mind. "What if we had a good experience with the fae? Does that mean they're not all bad?" He had a sheepish grin on his face.

Wil rubbed his temples. "What happened?"

"Well, there was this really cute girl with pointy ears and leaves in her hair—"

"Did she try to get you to come with her to the woods?"

Kenny paused. "Yeah, she and a few of her friends wanted to party with a real human, and her friends had—"

"Kenny, half a dozen people have disappeared due to the fae taking them. That's what was going to happen to you." Wil grabbed a glass of water on the podium and took a drink.

"So there wasn't a party?"

"This is a good learning experience, actually," said Wil, moving on. "Fae mischief. They're the best liars in the world and it's because they always tell the truth. No fae will ever tell you a direct lie, but they will mislead you as best as they can. For instance, if the elf girl luring Kenny had promised him she wouldn't hurt him, she would technically be keeping that promise when her friends murdered him instead. You understand? And whatever you do, do *not* make a deal with them. You will get the bad end of it."

Another hand went up. "If they're so dangerous, is there really anything we can do to protect ourselves if they decide to invade?"

Wil chuckled. "We tend to be physically stronger, have greater numbers, greater technology, and iron on our side. But with any luck, there won't be more conflict. First, we need to find out where they're coming from. The city's foresters are teaming up with the sheriff's department to lead search parties up into the mountain. We'll be taking volunteers for that, and for the possible forming of a temporary militia for the defense of the town.

"Sheriff Frederick will take over from here and handle recruitment. Support and logistics will be handled by Mayor Sinclair after, for those of you who wish to help contribute resources or time to helping us get these searches started. If you'll excuse me, I have preparations of my own to make."

He moved away from the podium amid scattered, confused applause. No doubt he was leaving them fearful. Maybe more than he should have, considering they didn't know why the fae had attacked. But it was better they be prepared and know what they were up against. Sheriff Frederick stepped up to the microphone, but Wil slipped out a side door.

They all had a lot to do, but him more so than anybody. He was the closest thing they had to an expert on the subject, and it was on him to learn as much as possible and protect the town and investigate, and there was never enough time for it all. Not while wondering whether or not another incident would happen.

"Hey, there you are. How'd they take it?" Darlene asked. She and Bram had waited outside for him, knowing how much work there was to be done.

"As well as can be expected, I guess," said Wil with a shrug. "I told them all the most pertinent info. Now I just really hope we're able to find the source, and find our lost people and return theirs, and figure things out. Maybe come to an agreement. The last thing we want is a possible war. If the fae invade Harper Valley, the military will come and take over until the conflict is dealt with."

That was a sobering thought. Darlene took his arm in hers. "Then we'll make sure that doesn't happen. We'll talk our way out of this."

"In the meantime," said Bram, "I was reading up on some charms that might be helpful, so I took the initiative and started carving them up on hunks of wood. I've gotten pretty good at them, and—"

"Wait, what charms?"

Bram adjusted his glasses. "Nothing impressive or complex. Just something to warn the wearer that someone is trying to mess with their head. It won't stop the attacker but it might give people a warning if one of the fae tries to mesmerize them or use an illusion on them."

Wil nodded, impressed. "That's a fantastic idea, Bram. You get me a stack of carved charms and I'll enchant them later. Darlene, can you get some basic spectacles and bring them to me? I've got something to work out."

Darlene nodded enthusiastically. "You got it."

Although there was a lot of work ahead of them, Wil allowed himself some hope. So long as the three of them were together, nothing could stop them.

CHAPTER 54

Faerie Circles

To the entire town's relief, there were no more attacks for the rest of the day. After the town hall meeting, Harper Valley split into a few groups. Those who would go searching, those who would help organize and manage the people, and those who would go home and take care of their households and make sure no home was left completely undefended.

For all of its flaws, this was the Harper Valley Wil believed in. One that would come together when faced with a problem, where everyone would shoulder their share and work together to fix it. It helped having a common enemy to worry about, but it had been much like this after the storm too. It brought neighbors together in a way few things could.

Wil spent that day in his basement with Bram. Darlene took a prototype sled and ran errands around town for them. True to his word, Bram already had a pile of carved wooden charms waiting for Wil to enchant. He spent a good chunk of his time pouring power into the runes etched in the wood, and then making his own etchings in a handful of spectacles Darlene managed to get at a discount.

The best thing a wizard could be was prepared. All the magic in the world wouldn't do him or the town any good if he didn't put thought and effort behind it. The three of them worked quietly, occasionally sharing a passage in a book about the fae and discussing what they'd need.

In the end, it'd be simple. Bram managed to carve a few dozen charms to alert the wearer if someone was trying to mess with their heads. Wil had the prototype of something he *thought* would work, but it was hard to tell.

"Okay, I'm wearing them," said Darlene, standing on the far side of his well-lit basement. She adjusted the glasses, making a face. "This really isn't the most pleasant way of experiencing the world. The colors are all wonky, and the scratches in the lens are distracting."

"Good," said Wil, "that means it's working. The wonky colors, I mean. There's a lot of magic here from my constant activities and it's saturating the air. My *hope* is, it means it's working. But watch this." Wil held up a hand and a small man in green started dancing on his palm.

Darlene jerked. "Oh, wow, it's glowing. I can see the little guy like he's there, but there's a weird glow around the edges." She took a few steps closer, then stopped, frowning. "Up closer the glow isn't as pronounced. I can barely see it."

"Excellent," said Wil, dispelling the illusion. "We'll be able to see things coming from afar, and we'll have warning when we're close."

They'd already tested the charms on Bram with a simple sleep spell. He had about five seconds of warning before he collapsed to the ground, snoring. Good enough.

They paired those charms with simple wands built with one spell inside of them, ready to be released. When they found something or had an emergency, a wielder could grab it and say the power word and a ball of light would shoot into the air and explode in a burst of sound and color.

The next day, they met up with the townspeople at the Lane farm, the location of which put them in the perfect place for a base of operations yet again. The search for the missing would officially start at noon, but that hadn't stopped a few groups from scouting out the edges of Harper Forest. They returned with little news other than that they'd seen many tiny footprints.

Wil, Darlene, and Bram had brought a cart full of supplies with them and parked it next to the people coordinating things. Wil had taken the time to write out a brief list of instructions for the charms, wands, and glasses and magically copied it a few times to hand out. There were enough charms to equip almost everyone, and one person per search party could wear a pair of enchanted spectacles. Most people carried an iron rod for defense.

Wil carried nothing, figuring his magic and senses would be all he needed. Bram had his pack of various potions, and Darlene wore the spectacles for their group. Most groups comprised five or six people, and nobody had argued when the three of them decided to go it alone. Jeb and Bob were in another search party with the Haggers, while Sharon helped with food and water for the volunteers.

"Now, we already got eyes along the northern slopes leading up to Orangeville, and some people are down by the new lake," Sheriff Frederick explained to the three of them before they set out. "I don't know much about these fae, Mr. McKenzie, but I got a bad feeling about the peak."

Wil nodded. "We'll head up there and poke our heads around," he said, to Bram's chagrin. His friend just sighed and shifted his pack to the other shoulder.

"If we encounter anything, I'll send up a light show. And if possible, let's try to avoid a fight."

The sheriff's mustache wobbled ominously, but he grunted in the affirmative and moved on to the next search party.

"That guy gives me the creeps," Bram said once he was safely out of earshot.

"You? You're, like, twice his size," Darlene scoffed.

"I'm scared of him too," said Wil, starting off toward the forest. His friends followed, naturally falling into step on either side of him as they made their way through the melting snow. "He's close with the mayor and neither of them like how I do things. If things get worse, he's capable of making things really difficult."

"That gives you another good reason to figure things out and fix them," said Darlene, craning her head around and looking at the edges of the forest for any obvious magic. "If you can solve this and keep the public on your side, there's not much he can do to you. And it'll look better for your dad when he runs."

"Good point," said Wil.

"See anything yet?" Bram asked.

Darlene shook her head. They pressed on, conversation dropping as they kept their eyes and ears peeled.

Again, the forest felt different. Wil didn't know if it was just his imagination or if Darlene and Bram felt it too. Anything obvious and Darlene would definitely see it from afar. Bram looked ready to throw the vial he was holding at a moment's notice. Far off in the distance, other groups of townspeople searched too, spread out for the best coverage.

Harper Forest held the same late autumn chill and stillness, though the higher up they went, the thinner the snow was. That struck Wil as strange and backward, but it wasn't enough to say anything. Halfway up the mountain, Bram found something worth remarking on.

"Does that deer look funny to you two?" Bram asked, pointing off in the distance.

Wil followed his finger and did a double take. The deer was pure white, save for the black of its hooves and the bright blue of its antlers. Blue eyes glowed even from afar.

"Yeah," said Darlene, gaping through the spectacles. "That thing's radiating colors. That means it's magic, right? Fae?"

Wil pursed his lips. "Sort of? Under the same umbrella, but it mostly refers to intelligent beings, not magical beasts."

"Is it dangerous?" Bram asked.

Wil shrugged. "I'd hope that if we don't bother it, it won't bother us. Because those antlers look like they would really, really hurt, and it wouldn't surprise me if it could do magic. Let's just head in that direction, but not *at* it."

"Sure, makes perfect sense," Bram muttered, but they headed in the direction of the white hart.

Before long, the hart looked up and directly at them. The three of them froze. Then it took off, heading up the mountain. By unspoken agreement, they followed, watching it disappear behind a maze of trees, some of which had bright, pastel leaves. The trees grew thicker the higher they went, until they reached what Wil recognized as a clearing after the storm had ripped trees from the ground.

"This isn't right," he said, stopping them. There were no fallen trees. Instead, there was a ring of trees with pink and blue leaves, with a gap leading inward. "Those trees aren't right."

"That's so weird," said Bram, stepping forward. He went closer to the gap. Wil came to his senses and tugged on his arm.

"Don't," he said. "We don't know what's in the center there, and I've got a bad feeling about this." Either Wil's imagination was working overtime, or someone was watching them. He looked around, focusing his senses and reaching out with his magic. There was nothing except the ring of trees around them, but there was something beckoning them in.

Just then, a loud, distant pop caught their attention. And then another. Darlene made to move forward but stopped to check with Wil. Her question was clear: Should they go help?

Wil shook his head. "We need to get up higher and check there. If those were the wands, someone else will get them."

"If you're sure," she said. They continued up the mountain.

That sensation of being watched didn't leave; instead, it intensified. All three of them felt it as the mountain changed more and more the farther up they went. The old walkways were different, shifted to the side or steeper than they had been. More blue- and pink-leaved trees littered the land, and the snow was almost completely gone now, despite the chill in the air.

"What does this mean?" Bram asked, as a brightly colored bird watched them from a tree. Every second, its long, curling tail feathers seemed to be a different color. Looking at it filled Wil with awe and a mild headache.

"The weird creatures?"

"The creatures, the trees, the land being different. What does this mean?" Bram turned to them, looking more nervous than ever. "Are they real?"

"They're real," Darlene confirmed. "There's a bit of a glow around them, but it's different from when Wil cast magic, or when that weird deer ran off and glowed extra bright. They're here. In our forest. What's going on, Wil?"

"I don't know," he admitted. "But nothing's attacked us yet."

Another explosion in the air, bright colors flashing for a few seconds before fading out.

"You'd think they'd go for us," said Bram, "considering there's only three of us. Maybe they're scared of you, Wil."

Still they climbed, until they arrived at what should've been Skalet Peak. It had the same basic shape and layout, but now there was a massive tree behind the lake that somehow hadn't been visible from town. In front of the lake lay a ring of enormous mushrooms, each at least three or four feet tall and in all colors and shapes. As with the ring of trees, a gap beckoned them in.

"If I had to guess, I'd say the fae are probably coming from here," said Wil, looking around. It was oddly terrifying, seeing a comforting, familiar place so changed like this. Made to look like somewhere else, for an alien culture's tastes. They weren't alone, and the place was overflowing with magic coursing through the air and into the earth, like rapids, flooding the area.

"You're not kidding," Darlene gasped, looking at the center of the lake, where the feeling was strongest. "That's the most incredible thing I've ever seen!"

Wil held out his hand and Darlene gave him the spectacles. They fit awkwardly but didn't need to be comfortable for him to see the kaleidoscope of colors raining from the lake into itself like some kind of magical fountain.

"Whoa, that's warm," Bram muttered behind them.

"Really?" Wil said. "It doesn't feel warm to me. More like…bright."

"Bright's a good word for it," Darlene agreed.

"You gotta take a look at this, Bram. I know it might be awkward over your glasses, but—" Wil turned around in time to see his friend stumble forward as if he were being played like a puppet. "Bram, no!"

A second later, Bram reached the ring of mushrooms and lurched forward, disappearing from sight entirely.

CHAPTER 55

Rips and Tears

Both of them stared at the mushroom ring, too stunned to move.

"We should go after him!" Darlene cried, rushing forward.

Wil caught her by the arm and stopped her. "We can't," he said, his heart picking up speed and on its way to hammering. "We have no idea what's on the other side!"

Darlene fought him, trying to get at the ring. "He's our friend. We can't just do nothing!"

"You should listen to the wizard, missy," said a soft, lilting tone. A squat man with a magnificent white beard stepped through the faerie circle. He looked ancient and leathery, though his hair, beard, and eyebrows were all a vivid, glowing white that contrasted with his emerald-green eyes. He carried a gnarled staff.

"Who are you?" Wil asked, successfully pulling Darlene back to him. She put her hand on the iron bar at her side but didn't draw it. The short man kept his eye on her.

"Call me Declan," the man said. "A humble gnome, at your service. Of course, we know all about you, wizard. You're quite the topic of discussion lately, I don't mind telling you. I'm glad it was me who got to speak to you and not one of the others."

"Where's Bram?" Darlene demanded.

"Safe," said Declan. "For now. He ended up right in our capital, amid a lot of surprised faces. We thought the compulsions and illusions would help keep people away, but you're a crafty one." He let out a jolly laugh, slapping his knee.

"Give us back Bram, right now," said Wil. Though his curiosity screamed at him to learn as much from this gnome as possible, he couldn't forget his friend. "And the other people you've stolen."

Declan took a deep breath. "Ahhh…no." He turned around to the mushroom ring and waved his hand and the staff. One by one, the mushrooms began wilting, shriveling, and turning a brownish, blackish color before they fell to pieces among the deadening grass. "There we go, no following now."

"You bastard!" Darlene yelled. She drew the iron bar and charged the gnome. Wil didn't stop her, instead gathering his power and deciding on a spell to use. Just as Darlene lifted her rod high, Declan slammed his staff on the ground. The grass around Darlene came to life, growing up and around her arms and legs and tightening, holding her in place.

Wil saw red. "Release her," he heard himself say. "I'll hurt you if I have to."

Declan held his hands in the air. "I'll release her, don't you worry none. I just want to make sure our conversation is peaceable. Besides, I'm here to surrender myself to your custody."

Wil paused. "You are?"

The gnome dropped his staff to the ground, and slowly the overgrown grass receded and withered away. He sat down in front of where the mushrooms had been, letting out an old-man groan as he lowered himself. "Don't get old, kids. Live a short, exciting life, and don't get old." He chuckled, shaking his head and making his beard wobble.

After picking up her fallen iron rod, Darlene looked at Wil. He shrugged, just as confused. Nothing was going how he'd expected, and now a gnome was claiming to surrender. But the fae couldn't tell a direct lie. Wil's gut told him to relax and lean into it.

"Why are you turning yourself in to us?"

"Diplomacy, my dear boy. We have a few of your people, you have a few of ours—all normal when dealing with a hostile foreign nation you were formally at war with, yes? I'm to turn myself in to you for two reasons. The first is a promise: you'll get your people back, and if you're dealing with us in good faith, you'll return ours."

"And the second reason?" Darlene asked, still on edge.

"A message!" The gnome laughed again, as if delighted. "To our very own master wizard here. Truth be told, I have two messages, and although only one is for you specifically, might as well give you the other. Let's start with that, shall we?"

The gnome had a deep, surprisingly pleasant voice that Wil had to remind himself not to get swept up in. He kept his senses sharp and probed for any sign of enchantment or mesmer magic. Nothing. Declan sat there unconcerned, acting as if he was having a lovely chat with an old friend.

"We, the Fair Folk who have the original claim on this land, come to treat with a representative of Harper Valley. Due to circumstances outside our control, we find ourselves face-to-face once more, and due to a history of wanton bloodshed and broken treaties"—here, Wil couldn't help but wince—"we want to tread carefully. We invite you to send an envoy to our capital to meet with the council and decide this region's fate."

Wil blinked. He didn't know where to start unpacking all of that. He worked his mouth but no sounds came out. Thoughts tripped over one another, but luckily Darlene kept a cooler head. "What do you mean 'face-to-face once more'?"

Declan swept his arm out. "You weren't the first people to live here, missy. When you humans came by the hundreds and thousands and settled our lands, you pushed us out and into hiding. Rather than leave, we've retreated into our own slice of paradise, parallel to here."

"The land of Faerie," Wil said, remembering a snippet of the lore. "But I thought that just referred to all of Calipan."

The gnome scowled, looking upset for the first time. "Calipan. Bah. We never needed a name for the land. It was simply the land, a place of plenty and wonder for all. Wild and free we lived, until you humans spread. So we took pieces of the land and ran away with them, living side by side, our worlds just barely touching."

"Until recently," Darlene said, swallowing. "What happened recently?"

Declan smiled again, but it was sadly. "Ask your friend there. He's caused quite the mess. Tore a hole wide open, and now parts of Faerie are bleeding over."

Wil's blood ran cold. "What are you talking about?"

"Surely a wizard like you knows all about how powerful the leylines around here are, eh?" Declan prodded.

All of Wil's work over the past couple of seasons would've been insurmountable if it hadn't been for the easy access to leylines. Hell, he wouldn't have been able to stop the storm if he hadn't—

"Oh, shit," said Wil.

"That about sums it up!" said Declan cheerfully.

Wil opened himself up, reaching out to touch the leyline at the top of Skalet Peak. He recoiled. All that rampant magic flooding the area came from the warped leyline. It felt wrong, constantly spilling and saturating the region until it made Wil's teeth want to buzz. He withdrew his senses and folded in half, hands on his knees, holding himself up.

"I did this."

"What?" Darlene looked between the two of them, not understanding.

"When the dragon was up here, the rain was flooding down the mountain." Wil realized. "I drew on the power of the leyline and I—"

"You changed the layout of the earth and drew too hard on the leyline itself,"

Declan interjected, "cutting off our access and making a huge mess of our two worlds! Congratulations, wizard. We didn't even know leylines could be torn open like this. You're making history!"

Darlene didn't know magic, but she was sharp and took the situation better than Wil did. "So you're saying that by saving the village, Wil ripped open a hole between worlds, and that's why your people have been coming around Harper Valley? And that's why you've kidnapped people?" She crossed her arms over her chest.

Declan sighed. "It wasn't my idea to kidnap them kids. Some of us are itching for a fight. Others want to talk it out and see if, after all these years, we might be able to put aside our differences. That's why it's requested that you send a representative. Someone to speak for the town and make some big decisions. Doubtless, that'd be you, given that you're responsible and all."

Too much. All of this was too much. Wil breathed in and out, trying to fight the surge of panic. Declan was right. If this was his fault, he had to do what he could to make it right. And given that he was the only one in town who had experience with magic and a role in the town government, albeit one not in charge of others...The hard part would be convincing Sinclair that he'd be the one making huge decisions in the name of the town.

"Are you okay?" Darlene leaned over, gently resting her hand on the small of his back and rubbing.

"No," he said, straightening up. "I am not okay. I might've just been responsible for the biggest possible threat to peace in our country."

"But we're not at peace," said Darlene.

"We are compared to what happens if things go wrong with the fae," said Wil, laughing bitterly.

"You're in a tricky situation, wizard. I don't envy you." Declan chuckled, taking out a pipe from somewhere and bringing it to his lips. He conjured a tiny fire and puffed away. After a second, he offered it to Wil, who waved him off.

"This is bigger than Harper Valley," said Wil. "This is something I'll need to inform Cloverton about. Because it deals with the fae, they might want a different wizard to handle this."

"We don't want a different wizard," said Declan, puffing away without a care in the world. "We want you. Send someone else if you're too scared to face up to what you did, but be honest about it."

"Don't call him scared," Darlene snapped.

"No," said Wil, "he's right. I'm terrified. This is huge. But yes, I have to deal with this. This is my problem, my specialty, and my responsibility."

He stared out into the cascading lights and colors playing from the ripped leyline at the lake. For better or worse, because of him, they were making history. A rip between worlds, and the first fae seen in a hundred years, and his own little problem. Whatever happened now would be because he panicked and apparently broke something unbreakable.

Wil would never forget that night, nor the way it had felt when he had embraced so much power and flew his carpet down the mountain. Through all the fear and exhaustion, there had been euphoria too. A sense of the whole mountain at the tips of his fingers, and he had reshaped it so hard, the world itself had changed. Now, he'd make things right.

"Okay," said Wil. "I'm okay. It's going to be okay."

Darlene looked skeptical but she accepted it for the moment. "Then I guess we should get this 'prisoner' down to the sheriff and company."

Declan stowed his pipe away and climbed to his feet, groaning like he was being murdered. "I'll come along peacefully if you give me your word that in surrendering myself as a willing hostage, I'm to be treated like a guest and subject to all laws of hospitality and honor."

Wil considered him. "I'll give you my word if you give yours that you will not harm anyone in Harper Valley unless you're defending your life, and you will do as I say for the duration of this diplomatic mission."

"Hrm." Declan ran a hand through his magnificent beard. "You're asking me to put a lot of trust in you, wizard."

"You're asking him to put a lot of trust in *you*," said Darlene.

"Your people have abducted our children. They set fire to homes, and tried to stampede cattle into my house." Wil's voice held no heat. "If you want me to go on a diplomatic mission to the land of Faerie and risk my life there, then you're going to put your life on the line and trust that I'm going to do right by everyone."

Declan grunted again. "Fine. Agreed. Now, shall we go back and get us some supper? It's been an awful long time since I've had your people's cooking."

Darlene caught Wil's eye. They looked at Declan and then back at each other, carrying on a silent conversation. "And you promise our friend Bram will be okay?" she asked.

"Aye. The captured humans will be questioned to get a better impression of you people nowadays, and then they'll be kept comfortable." Declan smiled, big and honest. "We fae are big on hospitality and keeping to our agreements. So long as your friend doesn't try to hurt any innocents, he's protected."

That was good enough for Wil. "Alright. Let's get moving. Be warned: the people aren't going to be very happy to see you."

Declan shrugged. "Wouldn't be a very good hostage if I didn't accept the risks." He picked up his staff and moved ahead of them, taking the lead through the altered forest. As they descended the mountain, Wil took one last moment to feel the leyline. Its power dwarfed him, yet it was his power that had made it this strong.

Wil shivered and tried to put it out of his mind.

CHAPTER 56

The Human Ambassador

N o. Absolutely not."

Mayor Sinclair hadn't been happy to hear about any of it, but especially not the idea that Wil go as a representative from the town to deal with the fae and make executive decisions.

"It's not up to you," said Declan, tearing into a meat pie enthusiastically.

Wil, Sinclair, Frederick, and Darlene were in the jail, where the fae were behind iron bars, unable to escape even if they wanted to. The goblins looked out at them with murderous eyes. What Wil thought might be a nymph was kept in the far cell, away from everyone else. Declan, on the other hand, didn't look the least bit concerned that he was trapped. All he cared about was the food Wil had made sure he'd gotten after the brief interrogation.

"Like hell it isn't," Sinclair seethed. He turned to Wil, scowling as if he blamed the wizard for the mess. Which, Wil admitted, was fair. "I'm the representative of this town, and I make all the major decisions. It's not for some unelected boy who won't be a team player."

"You don't want Wil to represent the town because he won't bribe you? Gods, you're pathetic," said Darlene. Declan giggled loudly behind the bars.

"Miss," said Sheriff Frederick. "Another outburst like that and I'm removing you."

"Try it and see what happens," said Wil, with a threatening wiggle of his fingers. After the major revelation he'd just experienced, his patience for Sinclair's and Frederick's bullying bluster was at an all-time low. "She was there for the conversation and she is one of my assistants. When I go to get Bram and the others back, she's coming."

The past month or so hadn't been great for Sinclair. After Wil had refused his demands to bribe him, the mayor had gone all out trying to assert whatever control he could over Wil. And a few months ago, it might've worked. When Wil first got back to Harper Valley, he wanted nothing more than to be a good servant to the town, and to respect every position and person around him. He might still have wanted that if Sinclair hadn't insisted on treating him like *his* servant.

"Fine," said Sinclair, "she stays for now. But you are still not going to this other world to represent Harper Valley. This is bigger than both of us, and we need to send word to Cloverton. They'll be the ones to decide this."

"And while we wait, our people are prisoners," Wil shot back. "If we want to get an early start on handling this, we need to act now. For some reason, the fabric between our worlds has weakened, and now there's a bunch of doors open. This isn't going to go away, and this can't wait."

After careful discussion, Wil and Darlene (with Declan's agreement, though he'd be the first to admit he didn't have a vote) had decided to leave Wil's responsibility out of it. It was the final thing Sinclair would need to use against Wil, maybe even get him in real trouble with the Department of Magic or Department of War. The storm dragon's presence and breaking the curse had weakened the leyline, and that was their official story until questioned by someone more important.

"He's right you know, Mr. Mayor," said Declan, pausing to take a slug of barley wine. He made an appreciative noise and silently toasted Wil for it. "My people are quite insistent about speaking with the wizard. He's your best bet for peace. Unless you're the typical human who doesn't want peace. Is that you, Mr. Mayor? You some kind of warmonger, out to poke a sleeping bear?"

Sheriff Frederick drew out his baton and slammed it against the bars. Declan didn't budge, stuffing his face as if nothing had happened at all. "You'll be quiet in there or I'll make you be quiet."

"I wouldn't do that," said Wil. "I promised him safe conduct as long as he doesn't physically or magically harm anyone. You break that agreement, it leaves the entire town open to backlash. And I guarantee you that he's stronger than you are, Sheriff."

"Maybe," said Frederick. "Is he stronger than a bullet?"

All of them started talking all at once, which set off the goblins in cell four to screaming and pounding on the cages, and the nymph on her own to sob uncontrollably. All of them continued on, louder and louder, except for Declan, who ate his pie while humming, unconcerned with the chaos around him.

So Wil did what he'd done at the town hall—he blanketed the jail in silence. He was gratified to see Sinclair, in particular, enraged by being silenced. The mayor jabbed a finger in his direction and screamed silently in his face, going off on a tear only he could hear. The only one not silenced was Wil. He'd apologize to Darlene later.

"Forgive me for the quiet, but I feel like I'm not being heard," said Wil. "I'm going to represent this town. If you don't like it, complain about me to Cloverton. Maybe they'll even do something about it and you'll get your wish of being king of the town. But you'll also be the person who lost Harper Valley their wizard in the middle of a crisis.

"You," Wil continued, turning to Sheriff Frederick, "will treat our captives as if they are human prisoners." He paused. "Maybe better than you normally treat prisoners. You're going to do this because we want our people back unharmed, and while you may not believe the fae when they say they're fine, I do. And I'm the expert here. I will get our people home safely."

He smiled at Darlene. "I appreciate you coming with me. I won't turn you down, but it's going to be dangerous."

He released the spell.

Darlene spoke, and thankfully everyone else remained quiet for a while. "It'll be dangerous, but you can handle that. You need me, or at least someone else, to help keep an eye out for you. I can see the mayor or sheriff wanting to send security with you, or some handler." Darlene shot the two a dark look. "I know how Wil works, what his weaknesses are, and how to work with him. I see and think of things he doesn't."

"Your big contribution is common sense?" Sinclair asked, all but sneering.

"Declan," said Darlene, ignoring the mayor, "when we get to Faerie, how long will we be traveling to the capital?"

Declan paused, wiping his mouth with his beard. Somehow, the hair looked clean within seconds. "Oh, that depends on which entrance you take. I think after today, and with me successfully making contact with Master Wilbur, most of them might've been closed or temporarily blocked off. We've been having a devil of a time keeping them—"

"Declan," said Wil.

"Right! A few days' travel, probably, if you take one of the lower doors to Faerie. It should spit you out in the countryside. Luckily, all roads lead to Oakheart Spiral. Shouldn't take you more than a week or so to get there."

"A *week*?" Sinclair's eyes nearly bugged out of his head. "You want us to trust Wilbur with our peoples' lives while we wait for a minimum of two weeks for him and the others to get back?"

"Not at all," said Declan. "Time goes by much faster in Faerie. For every day spent out here, it's a week in there. He'll be back in three days, tops. Probably."

"Are you trying to tell me that some of our people have been locked away in your damned faerie world for over a month now?" Sheriff Frederick's face turned an awful shade of red.

"And treated well," Declan added. "I don't know if you're much of a student of history, dear sheriff, but traditionally speaking, your side has been quite awful to ours. We strive to be better, and to do things the right way when it comes to handling prisoners and intelligence."

"Like hell," Frederick growled.

"All of our captives are still alive." Declan's voice lost all humor. "Can you say the same, Sheriff?"

"So, a week," Darlene said, interrupting the next blow up. "What kind of reception can we expect? How likely are we to be in danger and need of defending ourselves?"

The gnome considered it. "Just the two of you in this scenario? Mild danger, but not from any of my people. We've had a lot more time to think things through and come up with how we want to do things," he said. "And by now, instructions will have been sent all around to expect a human wizard and a possible companion or two. Send any more than that, and my people might be inclined to fearful responses."

"That sounds an awful lot like a threat to me," said Sinclair. "Either do as we say, how we say it, or you'll regret it."

"You would know all about that, wouldn't you?" Darlene shot at him.

Wil preemptively silenced the room again. "It makes sense. And once again, Mr. Mayor, I'm not asking. Darlene and I will go, we'll represent the town, and we'll seek peace. I will not make any promises I am not capable of keeping, and I fully intend on making sure there's peace and open communications. Send your message to Cloverton if you need to, but we'll be gone before they can do anything.

"Look, Bart," Wil continued, feeling wrong for using the mayor's first name. "I'm not only your best bet, but you can think of it this way: If it goes well, you can take credit for sending the best man for the job. If it goes poorly, then I overpowered you and went on my own. It's a win-win for you. Let me bring our people home."

"Oh, am I allowed to talk now?" the mayor asked after a few seconds. "You raise a point. If things go poorly, your death or disappearance means all my problems disappear, and I can get in a new wizard who will work with me."

Oh, that silly bastard thought all wizards would play nice. Wil almost wished Sinclair could have what he wanted—then the mayor would experience how much quicker to anger Wil's peers were. If they went a week without cursing Sinclair or giving him chronic nightmares or even reducing him to a pile of ashes, Wil would be surprised. But for now, his proposal worked.

"Fine. Then we're agreed. We'll take a few days to prepare and then set off for Faerie." Wil let out his breath. Such a headache for what should've been a clear, simple discussion. He motioned with his head, and he and Darlene made for the door.

Wil paused. "One more thing. My mother is going to come in and feed the prisoners from now on. I don't trust either of you to treat them well. Once again, I am not asking."

When they left the jail, Darlene let out an exaggerated shiver. "I'm not asking, huh? You're really growing, aren't you? Just a couple months ago, they would've walked all over you."

"A couple months ago I wasn't completely fed up with his crap," Wil returned, almost smiling. "Now? He'd better stay out of my way. Let's go see my parents. Tell them what's happening, and that we'll be gone for a bit."

"I can pack us some clothes and basic food to take with us," said Darlene. "I assume you'll be able to lighten the loads. Aside from supplies, what are we going to need?"

Wil thought about the dragon horn on his bedroom desk. "More power. Just in case of trouble."

CHAPTER 57

Off to Faerie

It took a few days to get ready, and Wil felt terrible for the delay. Every day he spent working on his project was another week with Bram and the others trapped in Faerie. Even if they were being treated well, it was an awful amount of time for children to be separated from their parents in an unknown, unfamiliar world. With that in mind, Wil went as fast as he dared go. This was not a project he could rush.

The staff rested on his worktable, five feet long from the base to the flared opening at the top, where the wood swirled in a spiral. All along the shaft Wil had carved out runes and designs meant to flow together when he channeled his magic, picking up power and momentum to produce a spell far greater than anything he could do on his own.

Every wizard eventually made a staff, but Wil figured few would have one as excellent as his had turned out. At least, in theory. There was still one last touch—one tricky final step that would make or break his efforts. But fail or succeed, they couldn't afford to wait another day.

Wil turned to the dragon horn. It sat a foot away from the staff, not close enough to really interact with it or connect, but he still thought he could feel the buzz from both. Hopeful thinking, maybe. Wil picked it up and turned it around slowly. Such a small thing, just over a foot long and battered-looking, but it held more power than all of him.

It had been nerve-racking to carve the horn. One wrong move and it would've snapped or otherwise been rendered useless. Somehow, through all the pressure and urgency, Wil's hands had remained steady. It was time.

He slotted the dragon's horn into the top of the staff, through the grasping wooden fingers. The horn's power flowed downward, filling every mark and notch he'd painstakingly made in the staff.

Wil held on tight, pouring his own power into the already overwhelming mix. Everyone's magic was different, and personal. When he reached into the staff with his magic, he felt the power and potential fury of the dragon the horn had belonged to. It wasn't hot-headed or vicious, nor was it vengeful. There was purpose to it, a calm determination that spoke to Wil. It had the potential for the bright, clear skies that nurtured the earth, but also the fury of the heavens.

Wil had never been one to give in to fury, but maybe he needed to sometimes. More than anything, he wanted this mission to truly be about diplomacy and building bridges, but there was too much history between their peoples to count on it. He'd need to defend himself and Darlene, and possibly also the abducted people of Harper Valley.

The storm beckoned, and Wil answered the call. The staff came to life. Wil stood and left the basement, stepping out into the bright late morning. Above him, dark clouds swirled together, blotting out the sun. Rain fell then, fast and heavy as if it had been raining for a while. The clouds lit up. He welcomed it, holding up the staff.

Wil gathered his magic and let it flow in the air around him. The horn glowed a brilliant purplish white. A heaviness filled the air, pressing down on him, gathering. For a split second, Wil pictured this all going wrong and him stupidly dying an hour before he was supposed to head out.

He had just enough time to laugh before lightning crashed down to meet him. Power swept over him and threatened to bowl him over, but he stood his ground. The lightning met the storm dragon's horn and lost. The staff absorbed the bolt. And the next one. And the next one, until it was all Wil could do not to scream with agony and ecstasy.

Then all at once, it was done.

Wil's knees buckled and he let himself fall into the snow, clinging to his staff. The staff glowed that same white purple of the horn, lighting up every rune and marking. In his hands was a portion of the power of the dragon, enough to dwarf him. Or make him a giant, if he were to use it. He got back up.

He felt good. Strong. Ready.

Darlene and his family were waiting for him on the porch at the McKenzie farm. Darlene and Sharon had packed everything they'd need, from camping supplies to rations to clothes and anything and everything for their trip that Wil could shrink down and lighten up.

"Well, now, look at you," said Jeb from the porch. He stood, looking Wil up and down. "Hell, I can feel that thing from here. That's what you were working on?"

"Sure was," said Wil, pounding the staff against the ground. The miniature thunderclap was probably showing off, but he couldn't help it. It channeled his magic like an extension of him. "Just in case we need to defend ourselves."

Jeb whistled. "You know, I was going to offer to come along as muscle if you needed it. I'm startin' to think you might not need me."

Oh gods, that's exactly what they needed, Jeb on a diplomatic mission.

"We're going to keep it calm and cool-headed," said Wil. "The gnome said our people are okay, and the fae can't tell a direct lie. So we're going to operate under the assumption that they're dealing in good faith. However, I'm not stupid. It's bound to be dangerous there in the same ways that one of them being here is dangerous. I can keep us safe without being aggressive about it."

Jeb nodded appreciatively. "Good. Then you get those kids and Bram back, and me and the others will keep a watch out in case they come back on their own."

Privately, Wil didn't think they would return before the mission was over, but it didn't hurt to stay vigilant.

Darlene shouldered her pack and picked his up, eyes drawn to his new staff. "Look at you, a real wizard now," she said. "Did it go like you planned?"

"Better."

"Does this mean you're about ready, then?" Bob asked.

Wil nodded. "We can go at any time. I'm ready if you are, Darlene."

"I'm ready." She looked nervous, but she meant it.

Sharon threw her arms around Wil. Wil hugged her back, squeezing tightly. As confident as he was, there was always a chance things went wrong. It was probably all Sharon could think about.

"Be safe in there," she said. "Don't start trouble, but don't take any crap either. You've got a pretty good head on your shoulders, but for goodness' sake, don't trust too easily when you're there."

"I won't, Ma," said Wil, releasing her. She hugged Darlene next, whispering something Wil didn't quite catch.

Bob pulled Wil into a big hug, slapping his back heartily. "You're more than capable, Wil. You'll do this right and get those people back, and then when the time comes, we'll take on Sinclair and knock him off his post."

"I'm looking forward to it," Wil said.

Sarah rolled her eyes but came up to him and hugged him anyway. Rather than what he expected, it was a real one and not a dead hug. "Don't do anything stupid, and come home safe." And then she pulled back.

Wil smiled and took it all in one last time before he left. The house, his family, the land in winter. There was no telling what awaited them, no telling how different it would be. So Wil drank it in, and then he and Darlene left.

They headed to the forest. They walked in silence, the thoughtful kind. Wil spent that time going over everything he knew about the fae in his head and worrying about every last thing that could go wrong. His thoughts ran away from him until they reached the tree line, when he finally quashed them down and embraced the unknown.

"So how are we supposed to cross over?" asked Darlene, when they made it past their forest and into the first signs of the faerie invasion. A mushroom as tall as a tree pushed its way past two birches. A bird with four wings sat on top of it, watching them.

"I'm not sure," said Wil. "I figure if we keep going, eventually we'll find another—oh!"

A bouncing ball of light bombarded them flashes, coming from around the mushroom. They covered their eyes, and Wil prepared himself to defend against an attack on his mind, but it never came.

"Is that another wisp?" Darlene asked, ducking out of the way as it came within inches of her head.

"Looks like. Following them is usually a bad idea, but maybe it's a guide sent to help us." Wil shrugged, tightening his grip on his staff.

The wisp flew up and down quickly.

"A guide, then. After you, Sir Wisp," Wil said, gesturing magnanimously.

Darlene rolled her eyes but chuckled, and together they followed the wisp through the forest. It stuck to the established path, more or less, except for patches of forest that were no longer familiar. It didn't take long to reach their destination, only twenty minutes or so. There was an air of finality when the wisp stopped in front of a ring of mushrooms. It flew all around it and then inside, where it disappeared.

"I guess this is it," said Wil. "You doing okay, Darlene? You can still turn back if—"

"Finish that sentence, Wil, I dare you." Darlene bared her teeth in a fierce grin. "They have Bram, and even if they're treating him well, they took him and the others and are holding them as a threat. Someone needs to come along and make sure you don't get too soft-hearted around the fae. From what you said, that would be a mistake."

"It would," said Wil. "So I'll be glad to have you around. You've got your spectacles and iron bar?"

Darlene pulled the spectacles out of her pocket and put them on. She patted the iron bar at her side. "You've got your staff, we're packed up, and we're not afraid. Right?"

Wil shook his head. "I'm terrified. This is bigger than anything I've ever done, but there's no one else who can do it. So I will."

"Shall we?" Darlene held out her hand.

Wil shifted his staff to the other hand and took hers. Grinning through their fear, they walked through the gap in the ring.

About the Author

SmilingSatyr is a millennial bookworm and the author of the Friendly Neighborhood Wizard series, originally released on Royal Road. He writes stories because he's not really equipped to do anything else—them's the breaks!

DISCOVER
STORIES UNBOUND

PodiumAudio.com